The Five Unnecessaries

by Laura J Campbell

Copyright 2022

All rights reserved. No part of this book may be reproduced or used in any manner without the prior written permission of the copyright owner, except for the use of brief quotations in a book review.

The Five Unnecessaries: Book One of the 27th Protector Series (3rd Edition)

Originally published 2018 by Laura Campbell, all rights reserved

To my husband, who never gave up on me.

– Spring –

CHAPTER 1

Grey shouldn't be a color. It's a void.

A grey sky hides the sun. The low clouds threaten storms, without the promise of rain or sun. There is no hope to weary leaves or thirsty grass. It is not darkness or light.

I shook my head, as if to release my restless thoughts. Grey couldn't be that bad. I pulled my dresser drawer open and saw the grey pants and shirt I would wear: the same outfit everyone would wear today. I stared at the grey cloth through the dust floating in the lamplight.

No. It was a void.

I heard footsteps running across the floor right outside. The sound of a little hand knocked on the door. My brother's laughing made me smile, helping my mind wander out of the grey and into childlike wonder.

They would not wear grey today. We wore this color to symbolize sorrow and hope; the light is never able to burn the darkness out. The Territory had found a way to save a few lives, stealing them from the death sentence of being labeled an Unnecessary. But the little boys who ran down the stairs didn't know how powerful the darkness was and didn't know that thousands still died. The boys would wear white, like the other seven-year-olds; oblivious to the fact that despite all our bravery, we were losing a war.

I changed quickly and sat at my desk, squeezed my pencil between my fingers and scratched out a few sentences. I wanted the thoughts to leave me and stay on the paper, not haunt me. I also wrote a few sentences about the growing flowers, how the sunbeam had traveled across my wall at dawn, and the jealousy of innocence. But then I kept thinking about the ceremony. I sketched a picture of the Arches on the next page.

In just a few hours, the leader of the Territory would announce the twenty-six girls who had trained for five years so that they could have a different name: a name that would define them forever.

Protector.

Someone who was brave enough to fight a losing war to save one person.

We marked this significant event with both somber ceremony and elaborate celebration, a mixture of pride, mourning, and hope. For decades, the Territory had gathered all its members to honor the Protectors chosen each year and remember our history. But over the years, our scars had healed, so instead, it had become more like a party. The festivals and feasts marked the joy we felt in the only hope we had.

But today, all I felt was the scar. No one thinks about their scars or usually looks at them with more than a glance. But when they focus on it and remember the moment of injury and the pain, when they trace the scar with their fingers and remember the blood and fear, they feel queasy as if it were a fresh wound.

That's how I felt today.

The feet ran by my door again, followed by the louder feet of their older sister. They would be wearing white. I would be wearing grey. Megan would be wearing black.

"Enough," I said, almost startled by the sound of my voice.

But then, I whispered to myself, "This was always going to happen." I realized that talking to myself out loud was strange, even for me, and tried to calm myself calm by listing everything that would remain the same. The ceremony would be the same twenty minutes: someone would share our nation's history with cheap and fast words and then summarize the reason for the Protectors. Then the Head Trainer would name the Protectors of the 188th generation. The festival would begin after the feast, and I would feel sad because we'd miss most of it. We could never afford the individual shuttle tickets to and from our local transport station and the festival lasted too late to make that trek at nighttime.

When I was younger, I had begged and pleaded and promised I would run home after the festival and wouldn't whine about being tired. I still had crystal-clear memories of the one night I finally convinced my parents to stay until the fireworks. My father had laughed at each of my over-excited reactions. I recalled the strange details that only a child would, like how many lights were on each carousel or the name of the doll I won at the prize table. As promised, I had walked the entire five miles home without complaining. My muscles ached the next day, but I did all my chores and extra washing just to ensure our trip to the festival the following year.

But the next year, Olivia came.

By the time she was old enough to walk the five miles after the long day, Dylan came. And he came with Richard. In five years, we had become a family of six— a miracle, as some people proclaimed. Even with the Shield Vaccine, twins were so rare that people doubted they existed. Sometimes people looked at my brothers as if they were fairies or talking animals: a myth from before the Republic ever put the Serum in our water. When the Council had learned that my mother was pregnant with twins, they paid a specialist to come out every week until she delivered. It made our family famous in the Territory.

Today's events would have the same effect. Strangers would whisper about us, but for very different reasons. This year, the Outskirts had someone who attended and ranked in the Academy, of which only prospective Protectors and trainers were allowed to attend. The Council would choose from them today. While they could pick anyone from the Territory, almost every Protector for the last century had trained in espionage, combat, medicine, and history at the Academy, starting from age twelve. There were about thirty girls accepted into a class each year.

But my mind was only on one member of this year's class: Megan. Although she'd been a classmate at grammar school for a long time, she rarely talked to me. I tried to justify it. She lived far away from me. She liked different things. She was athletic, and I was one of the few into the arts and writing. She barely talked to anyone, there was no real reason for it to offend me – except one.

She was my cousin.

Megan's name would be spoken after dinner sometimes, while dishes were being scrubbed. My little sister, Olivia, would ask my mother questions about my mother's childhood: when she had lost her first tooth, if she ever fell out of a tree, or if she had any sisters. That last question created joy mixed with pain- a smile with eyes glossed but never crying. My mother had one sister: Megan's mother, who'd held Megan for only four minutes before she left this world. It had crushed my mother, but she'd moved past her grief to care for me and to help Henry, Megan's father, with a new baby.

My mother helped caring for Megan for weeks. But then, simple acts of love became complicated, eroded away by jealousy. Henry asked his own mother to move in and care for the baby as well. His mother resented my mother for living through childbirth. After Olivia and the twins, his mother retreated even more from our family. What should have been an opportunity to become a stronger family turned into scenes with awkward strangers with shared grief.

So, Megan and I were just that: awkward friends. There were a few times a year I remembered we were family. On Rosemary Day, when we would all give a flower or herb to someone who has lost a loved one, I would pay half my allowance for the perfect flower for Megan: a pink rose for someone who had lost their mother. Megan always picked a dozen violets for me, because I had lost my aunt, and she always wrapped the lavender in lace for my mother, who had lost her sister. She gave it to me at school, where her grandma couldn't see her. I would spend the rest of Rosemary Day searching for more lavender for my mother.

The lavender from Rosemary Day still laid in a tiny jar from last year, dried up on a windowsill. My mother would stare at it while doing dishes. The unspoken grief haunted us all, for a person I never met but never stopped missing.

After her grandmother passed away, Megan was alone most of the time. Her strength, solitude, and determination ensured her spot in the Academy by age eleven. It tore Henry apart. She had ruined his only goal, to keep her safe, with her willingness to be a warrior. But at some point, he changed his narrative. It was unhealthy, even. He would joke about her taking down Sentries and officers and saving hundreds of pregnant women and Unnecessaries: an over-exaggeration to keep his worst fears at bay. Now, nothing could hold back the fear that Megan wouldn't survive, and we'd get more flowers every Rosemary Day.

There was a rhythmic knock at the door. It was Olivia's way of playing a game to tell me breakfast was ready. Her knock always sounded like a song, and I had to guess what it was and sing it as I went downstairs.

As I descended, I sang, "Row, row, row your boat."

Giggles. Eggs. And...

"Is that bacon?" I asked in shock. Mom smiled in response.

"Aislyn, your father is usually not one to surprise me or spoil me, that's for sure," she sighed, taking a bite of the waffle with bacon on top, "But when he does, he has good timing."

I took a bite and sank down into my seat, my own worry evaporating for a moment.

"Speaking of timing…" my mother continued.

"Not this again," I sighed. "I told you, I'm not ready to make a decision."

"Every test and every teacher says you are, and there might only be an opening at the University for a month. It's a miracle there's any at all," she answered in a rehearsed tone. "What are you afraid of? Failure? Embarrassment? Being challenged?"

"Not in that order—" I said, without much emotion, but also not arguing.

"But you said you wanted to be a writer," Olivia interrupted. "What's wrong?"

I looked back at my mother. "Don't look at me, Aislyn," she said. "If a ten-year-old can realize you're scared, you're in trouble."

"There's a lot of public speaking and I'd have to enroll in a sport and there's a ton of things I would never want to do—"

"To become who you are?" my mom cut me off. "You can't run away from who you're supposed to be. It's scary, and it's a lot of work, but if you don't do it, I fear you'll regret it."

"That sounds poetic."

"Because your father said it first," she said, winking. "Heaven help me, I could never say anything like that, but he has better timing and far more—"

Almost on cue, my dad burst into the room and set off the usual hugs and kisses and screams that daddy was home. As they mobbed him, I turned to my breakfast, focused on the bacon in front of me and thankful that my mother's lecturing would end for the day. I froze when I heard Richard yell out a question.

"What are those tickets for?"

Both my mom and I spun around so quickly it must have seemed comical.

My dad grinned, getting the reaction he wanted from the six shuttle tickets in his hand.

They were orange.

That meant round-trip.

"We can go to the festival?" I blurted, making Olivia scream in shock.

"How in the world...?" Mom started.

"Sweetie, you wouldn't believe it!" he started, ignoring Dylan who was straining to see the tickets. "Last night, the prep team from the Council came by the shop to get food for the feast tonight. They wanted venison because they wanted food unique to each region this year as part of the feast. They bought ten bucks and two does!"

Mom's eyes widened, both surprised and suspicious. We always had enough money, but only just enough. I always imagined that she had a storm of worries raging, with rain made of grocery and clothes lists and claps of thunder that cried, *"We should have saved it."*

Dad knew the whirlwind had started, too, because he got back on his knees and said, "It's not just what they bought, sweetie. Instead of paying me the price on the tags, they gave me the two thousand they had budgeted."

Mom let out the smallest laugh before she put her hand up to her mouth, forgetting she had no real reason to stop it. Olivia hugged my dad and tackled him to the floor. The younger ones squealed like crazy as he tickled them, even though they had no clue that in a single day, we had gotten about twice as much money as Dad usually made in a month. I forgot my age and jumped on the pile. He kissed me on the cheek amid the chaos.

Our home was always generally happy, but this was different. This was the bliss that made mom ignore us running in the house and left me too excited to finish breakfast. This happiness left books dropped, hands unwashed, chores undone, and me running upstairs chewing on the last piece of bacon. This wasn't just home; it was bliss.

I could hear more talking downstairs, but I didn't care. I quickly got my phone out and messaged my friends that I would be on the shuttle. I got my pack, journal, and pencils, then turned to the last page I had written on and realized I only had about ten pages left. A thought fluttered, and I silenced it out of habit. I only got a journal for my birthday and wrote in every inch. Each year, I ran out of space earlier despite writing smaller, but today was different. Maybe today I would get a different response. I ran downstairs and put on the most charming voice I could manage.

"Daddy, you know I noticed my journal- is really, really full, which is good because I've been writing so much lately.

But there are only ten pages left, and since we're headed to town..."

He laughed, then taking a sip of his coffee. Mom shook her head.

I stood still, already scared that my request would go nowhere.

"Well," Mom said, "at least you waited five minutes."

"What?" I asked.

Dad said, "Your brothers and sister had much less self-control and asked for every toy under the sun about three minutes ago. We said everyone can get one thing. And I already knew what you would pick. Aislyn, whether you want to finish in University or not, you'll always be a writer. And we'll always love you for it."

His brown eyes were warm, in the way I knew he was always proud of me, and even my mom's usually critical and challenging tone was soft when she spoke, "Still, timing. You only have a week."

My dad winked and whispered, "She had to sneak that in."

I whispered back, "I know."

"Just don't stop because you're afraid," my dad whispered. "Always take the step that makes you scared."

I nodded, hearing the running of everyone coming back downstairs, with water bottles, bags, and coats. Those restless legs, now full of anticipation, ran to the shuttle station and jumped on the shuttle platform, not even still when they were only standing. Many people were coming to look at the twins, to say how cute they were, and to marvel at Olivia's curls and her cute smile. Even at ten, her features were angelic.

I was invisible, as usual. There was a time when I would have felt jealous, upset just to be the wallflower. Over time, I realized I enjoyed being unnoticed. I saw the tiny details that my obscurity afforded me. I saw so much beauty in writing it down: An old woman twirling her wrinkled finger through Olivia's curls, my mom's smile at the boys' excitement, Richard quickly eating the pieces of breakfast he had hidden in his pocket, a handshake between friends, a whisper that made my mom fight back tears. I only heard one sentence. "Your sister would be proud."

I turned away for a moment, long enough to notice an indistinguishable expression of one man feeling too many emotions at once.

Fear, worry, pride, joy, loss, fatigue.

He was waiting on the other side of the platform, gazing at us from a distance.

Henry.

I ran to him without hesitation, not thinking of what I would say. I would regret saying the wrong thing, but I'd regret silence more. What would I say?

Congratulations? No, it wasn't an accomplishment. Megan was being chosen to throw herself into life-threatening situations.

Sorry? But no one should ever apologize for her bravery.

He saw me coming as I called, "Uncle Henry!"

and to my surprise, he opened his arms and I crashed into them. Decades of awkwardness faded in moments.

As he hugged me, I felt his muscles shake even under the tight grip. He was grasping for something I could never give: anything that would make the next year bearable.

He released, and I couldn't stop myself from asking the question, though I could see that his usually friendly features were tired, and his blue eyes were bloodshot.

"So, all the rumors are true? Is it a sure thing?"

Even though he seemed nervous, some pride leaked from his voice. "Well, Megan ranked twelfth out of the thirty this year. And they are sending a private shuttle for me, so..."

"Yeah, that sounds about right," I said as casually as I could. But my stomach swirled, even though it was my heart that ached.

Casual wasn't working, so I chose the most obvious truth. "Well, a private shuttle is nice. I guess you won't have to deal with a bunch of people saying awkward things."

"Yeah, I think that's the idea. Some people found a chance already. They want her to succeed or be safe. To save lives in the Republic but not leave the Territory. But she can't do both." He looked off into the distance and nodded, deciding to change the subject. "How long has it been since you've seen her, Aislyn? Has it been since she left for the Academy?"

"Yeah, must be," I said. "Four years."

He was beaming as he said, "You should see how much you two look alike now. So much alike."

There was a noise behind us; his shuttle had arrived. It was a small hovercraft, but it didn't need rails like the transports we were taking. It was the specific shuttle Central Command used on missions. I had never seen one so close, and it made everything feel more urgent and real. A young man popped out of the shuttle.

"I'm Parker, sir," he said, then looked curiously at me.

"See?" Henry reached out to push my shoulder playfully. "I told you that you look alike. She's my niece," Henry said, pointing to me, out of an unfamiliar gesture of introducing me. The co-pilot nodded to me, then looked behind me.

Henry had now seen my parents from a distance. My mom blew a kiss and waved along with the twins, Olivia yelled out a good luck, and my father held his hand up without moving, almost like a gesture of faith.

"I'm sorry, sir," Parker said, genuinely. "But we're on a schedule."

Henry nodded and grabbed a small bag, heading to the shuttle.

I realized I was the last – maybe the only one – to talk to my uncle before he would sit under the Arches today to hear his daughter's name called out. As he slid the door to the hovercraft closed, I yelled out the only thing I could think to say over the engines.

"I think she's brave."

He turned around slowly as I continued, trying to keep my voice from cracking so he could still hear me. The co-pilot froze, not sure if he should continue or let me speak.

"She's really brave. Much braver than me, brave enough to go anywhere her heart leads her. And I think that means she's exactly where she needs to be. Her bravery won't fail her. It won't fail you."

The hovercraft charged up and revved louder, Parker hit the button to close the door. As it began to close, I saw Henry look at me through teary eyes, creased from the smile on his face.

Parker nodded to me, and then warned, "You should back up a bit, miss." The door sealed. The co-pilot checked the front corner of the shuttle, sealed his door, and Parker strapped in within a few seconds in one fluid motion he had practiced a hundred times. I felt a warm rush of air, and then the shuttle blew past me. Henry had been crying and smiling, which oddly enough, made me sure I had said the right thing.

A much larger engine rumbled lower and lower, and I turned to see our transport arriving at the platform. I clumsily snagged my bag, journal, and pen. My mom was waving me on as I sprinted to her. But I slowed down and turned back to where Henry had just departed.

My daydreaming mind wandered to thoughts of the Academy, of running, breathing, and living for a purpose beyond this small community, hoping for a chance to go to the festival, or wondering how many more years to stay in school. My excitement from this morning seemed shallow now. But I dragged myself back to reality, where these simple amusements would always be the highlight of my year.

Being a Protector was out of my scope; it always had been. I was never good enough— not brave enough, fast enough, strong enough, smart enough to be a Protector. They never picked girls like me. I had never cared, except for this one moment.

I knew it wouldn't last long; I would push it away.

But I couldn't. The anger stayed. It froze me in time, ignoring the urgency of my mother's voice calling me. I remained unmoved, surrounded by the grey steam from the shuttle whipping around me.

And I was angry that I wasn't brave enough to be chosen. I was angry they never gave me a second thought. I was angry that Megan could go save the world and I couldn't.

And I didn't know why.

CHAPTER 2

The shuttle shifted to top speed before we found our seats. While the boys ran to the window, I noticed that Olivia didn't dare complain about not getting to sit there. She held the edge, her fingers sinking into each line of the corduroy fabric beneath her. I smiled, thinking that she must be clinging to every memory of today as tightly as she did that seat.

I saw several friends from my school, including Amy, whose mouth gaped open when she saw me in the aisle. She asked if she could find me later and then hinted that Daniel was coming with their group. She giggled and ran down the aisle, my dad rolled his eyes and gave me a warning look.

"So, what do we do when we get there?" Olivia asked for the tenth time.

Mom gave her an understanding smile. "It's the same as last year, sweetie. You'll be in with the other kids your age and those who have volunteered to watch you. The fun happens after the ceremony."

"When do I get to go to the Arches? Is it interesting? I wish I could see Megan. Could they let me in?"

Mom shook her head. "No one ten or under. Rules are rules."

Being with the children's room at Olivia's age meant helping to watch the younger children and toddlers, an exhausting task. When I was her age, it felt even more tedious because I had finally learned the complete history of the Territory, our rebellion against the Republic, and the first and only time the Society Party ever retaliated.

"Daddy," she asked, "is that the river from the story?"

I looked out to the water glistening in the sun, away from the sister who still had the innocence to call it a story— this horror the Society Party would place in our hearts. Our teachers would constantly remind us to say the Republic was not the enemy; the Society Party was the true villain. The Republic was full of victims, just like us.

"Yes, that's the river," my dad said into the silence. "And do you see the filter down there? The grey structure that looks like a dam with yellow stripes?"

Olivia leaned over to see the filter, the only reason we hadn't died.

Or rather, the only reason any of us were alive to begin with.

Two centuries ago, the Society Party had all but brainwashed the people of the Republic. The Republic's citizens gave over their freedom, their right to religion, and their right to have children of their own in exchange for the promise of a life of perfection. The illusion of their enlightenment and advanced philosophy allowed the Society to create any rule to bring happiness to its people by relieving them of the "responsibility of choice." The Society Party considered themselves more humane than any other civilization in history because they allowed only the most potentially successful and perfected people to live. They believed any child who was flawed in any way, physical or mental, should not be allowed to steal the joy and peace of anyone else. Such a specimen should be labeled as such: Unnecessary.

Any baby in a lab that didn't meet with standards, any child who began to show flaws as a young student, or any woman who would hide her imperfect baby… they were all enemies of the state.

"But not everyone agreed with the Society," my father continued where my inner thoughts had stopped. "The Society had made enemies, and many people will never equate genocide with mercy. They're smart and kind and knew love. But with many forfeiting their children to the Society Party schools by age three, those who did not comply with the mandates began to stand out. They had pushed humanity to new limits— except some people felt the new limits were not human at all. However, everyone who opposed the Society was labeled 'intolerant,' and the intolerant were not to be tolerated."

"Is that how the Territory started?" Olivia asked.

"That was the beginning of the idea of it. They realized that they didn't have a choice but to escape the Republic. The Society Party was spreading the lie that anyone who disagreed was dispensable because they disturbed peace and happiness."

My father stopped explaining there, most likely because the twins were listening now. And how could he explain to them that, according to the Society, we weren't alive? If someone could not experience everything in life because their morals or physical or mental defects prevented it, they were not worthy of life. The Society Party continued to use media, advertising, and propaganda to continue asking the question, "What else is unnecessary and holds back humanity back from the happiest experiences?"

The Society Party answers this question each Jubilee Day. Every seven years, the Society Party declares a new rule "ensuring freedom" and then focuses on enforcing that law, as well as all the previous Jubilee laws, for the next seven years. This was the refusal of religion, the burning of history books, the dissemination of traditional schools, and finally, the rule that all children would be quality controlled. They mandated that all babies must be engineered in laboratories, ensuring more conformity and quality. This policy also saved women from the pressures of pregnancy— losing time, physical confidence, and emotional attachment. They declared "Vessels" criminals for harboring an Unnecessary.

It was on the seventh Jubilee Day, two hundred years ago, that the rebels escaped and established the Territory.

The Territory's founders had given up on protests or legislation. The Republic prepared for resistance as the fourth Jubilee Day approached. They were nullified by their compliance. Our ancestors used the celebrations and parties in as a cover for their escape. Twenty-four thousand souls crammed into hundreds of small shuttles and traveled through paths in the forest until they reached a clearing more than a hundred miles away. The Society Party was naïve enough to believe in their victory, so they never saw the escape coming. They threatened to destroy the Territory at first, but then didn't bomb us or send troops.

Dylan hesitated, then asked, "Why didn't they bomb us?"

"They would've lost their authority, built on an idea that they really wanted peace and happiness and transcendence. If they had killed us, even as Unnecessaries, it would have revealed their barbaric nature. Even now, the Society still can't justify killing all of us, which is the only reason we're all breathing."

Olivia looked out the window at the massive water filter as our shuttle rushed by it. The dam measured eighty feet long, and the twins gazed at the men standing on it, their little voices commenting on what the workers were doing.

"Where did they put the Serum in, Daddy?"

"Well," Dad sighed, "we don't know, sweetie. We think it might have been somewhere up here."

The Serum: a silent weapon for a quiet but violent war. They couldn't bomb us or send in troops, so they did something sadistically brilliant. They killed our future.

By the time the first doctors of the Territory discovered the Serum in the water, there had been four miscarriages. In the months that followed, not one woman became pregnant. There were only three healthy babies born in the very first months of the Territory; their mothers had all been late-term when they'd escaped the Republic. By that time, scientists had determined that the Territory had been poisoned. Every woman's fertility was weakened or destroyed. If they continued to drink the water unfiltered, no girl would grow up able to bear a child. Those three little souls that survived the escape from the Republic were the last babies anyone would see for nine years.

My father glossed over that in a few sentences. "A decade later, the famous Dr. Long developed the cure: the Shield Vaccine. You and Aislyn both have it because you got tested."

"And you have to get tested," Olivia said, trying to emphasize what she had learned. "Or you could die."

Being experimental, a handful of subjects had died in the first year of the vaccine. Doctors tested each girl for the possible fatal reaction. If so, the vaccine was not administered to that child. It was rare, but I remember my Mom comforting her friend a few years ago. Her friend had come home from the Med offices crying, as she held her one-year-old girl after her second failed vaccine test. Every other mother would try to comfort her, a mother who would have to one day tell her daughter that the Society Party had killed her chance to carry a child.

"When did they make the law to kill all their babies?" Olivia asked.

"Two hundred years ago and try to keep it down," my mom sighed, worried about what the boys would overhear. She touched her daughter's curls, clinging to what innocence was left.

The boys wore white. Olivia wore white, yet today I realized how old she was— and how much she was beginning to see the darkness in this world. Thousands of lives lost because only perfection mattered. No one was safe because they might not be "alive enough" to live. If it didn't hurt your brain that someone could have such a twisted logic, it tore your heart.

"I can't remember what they call them: the mothers who still get pregnant and want to keep their baby," Olivia said, her face scrunched.

"A Vessel," I reminded her. "A Vessel is an enemy of the state because she's harboring an Unnecessary. The children, all the Unnecessaries, get named when the Protectors rescue them, with or without their mother."

"And then they go to the shelters?"

"Yes. And most are adopted right away, like your friend McKayla. She can't remember being in the Republic, though."

"How do the Protectors save them?" Olivia continued with anticipation and a twinkle in her eye.

"Well, you know, Protectors are amazing," Dad started in a dramatic tone, making Richard stop chewing whatever he was eating. Dylan leaned in closer, listening intently. "And their trainers, some of the smartest and strongest men and women in the Territory, teaches them how to look, talk, and blend into the Republic so they can infiltrate it, find Vessels and Unnecessaries, and get them out. They can live out in the wilderness for a week before and after they sneak into the Republic. They can even help a Vessel by delivering her baby in the forest, carry a baby in their pack, and use technology to outwit the thirty Sentries and the army of police. They can also spy on some important people in the Republic, and find answers to questions. They can communicate with the Territory in a way the Republic can't track."

"How do they do that?" Olivia asked.

"No one knows," Dad said, in his best story-telling mysterious tone. "It's a secret."

He talked about more legends and more famous stories of Protectors as the shuttle drove by the Training Circles. Each Protector was trained in Central Command, next to the Arches. Over Central Command was their Training Circle: stone cylinders, fifty-feet tall and covered with glass domes, though some opened to let in sun and fresh air. Each Protector had the five-hundred-foot circular space to prepare for missions. They were the only ones allowed inside of their Circle or Central Command. Their glass rooves made them look like diamonds in the late morning light.

"Megan will be one of them?" Richard asked, almost dazed.

My mom touched his head. "Looks like it, my dear."

"The only thing I don't get is why," Olivia said as she looked out onto the Training Circles that awaited their Protectors.

"Why Megan would want to do it?" I asked.

"No," she answered. "Why can't they just let everyone live?"

I looked at Olivia's eyes, but I couldn't keep her gaze.

How do you explain it to a child— man's corrupt desire to control the masses? How do you explain that people gave up life's beautiful mess for fake perfection, pleasure, and comfort? How do you tell her that they tried to kill God so no one would ask if they had a soul that could be damaged? How do you tell her that she doesn't know the worst of it yet? I probably didn't either.

How do you explain to a ten-year-old girl that hell can exist on Earth if you don't fight to keep it at bay?

You don't. You do what my mother did.

You put your arm around that child, pull them close, and whisper truth into their ear.

"Because that means they lose something they aren't willing to: their power. Everyone protects what they aren't willing to lose."

As I looked out at the horizon and the Circles, I realized how true it was. We weren't willing to lose the lives the Republic stole.

The Protectors risked their lives for the chance to steal them back.

CHAPTER 3

The stone Arches towered above me, so beautiful that my eyes stayed on them despite bumping into people next to me. Each Arch grew higher and wider, awakening a feeling of vastness I never knew in any other place in the Territory. The stone and marble pillars stretched across the arena below, with ten feet of clear, blue sky between each arch. Even though the Arches were spread apart, the carvings on them formed a single mural across the sky, with the clouds moving through it like waves.

The wind pushed at my back, propelling me forward. The room always felt natural and open, so unlike the government buildings in the Republic. I remembered Megan would walk through one of the stoic, white buildings holding her breath that she would live. I became queasy with fear again.

I thought of leaving, but I wanted to support Megan. Besides, I wasn't allowed to leave, by order of the Council. The Council never wanted to appear overbearing. They were fair and just, although never perfect. Some citizens of the Territory still felt ignored, timely laws were not passed fast enough, and fathers grumbled about politics while chopping wood or doing dishes. But for the most part, our people adored the Council and the High Counselor, Richard Eldridge.

Eldridge rarely spoke, but when he did, it mattered. He left the squabbling among lower-ranking members of the Council.

He focused solely on the Protectors' training and development. Some called him obsessed for staying in his office instead of holding press conferences, meditating in prayer instead of attending meetings, and disregarding some of the most luxurious attributes of being High Counselor. He would give up his spacious rooms to sleep on the floor in Central until he knew Protectors were safely home. His critics would accuse him of incompetence, but his supporters would label it passion.

I kept moving walking under the Arches. I recognized my friend's mother, who gave up her seats when they saw us coming up the aisle. My mom thanked her, and we squeezed into the last few seats. I was on the end and as people passed, I soaked in their expressions and words. Some were reverent, others passionate, others impatient for the evening's events. I hoped to write them down in words later, the bits and pieces of truth hidden in this canvas; the tear creased in a wrinkle under the one woman's eye, the stage engineers moving the microphone and quickly taking it away again, who was pulled into her seat by a scolding mother after she was caught flirting with a boy, a couple rushing to their seats, a pregnant woman surrounded by admirers. All of them would put their lives on hold for a few minutes to hear Eldridge summarize our two-hundred-year history, sounding like my father on the train. Then Head Trainer Hannah McKinney would name twenty-six Protectors.

Someone came across the stage and welcomed us all to the commissioning of the 188th generation. I recognized him but couldn't remember his name. As people settled into their seats ready to listen, he left the microphone and walked back behind the stage.

I turned to look at my father, only to see his confusion. A few whispers rose above the silence until it grew to a buzzing murmur. People continued their conjecture as a stranger came across the stage. I hadn't seen him before, but he was not wearing a grey linen suit like all of those before him. He wore white, like the Protectors and trainers. He took a breath and spoke with an authority I hadn't expected from his nervous demeanor.

"My name is Commander Luke Patterson, and I am, as of a few days ago, the new Head Trainer and director of the 188th Generation."

I strained my memory. Had we pushed the usual history lesson aside for a speech from the new Head Trainer? I realized that I had no memory of anyone other than Hannah McKinney being the Head Trainer. I listened to Patterson run through some of his credentials, which sounded impressive. He joked that he once got outwitted by Bridgett, a very famous Protector from a few years ago, and that comment eased some of the concern with laughter. His expression would shift from focused to playful, as if trying to cut the tension that began with this announcement.

"No doubt…" he sighed, "That you are wondering why the order of this ceremony is different. We will not be reviewing or revering our history today. I would like only to tell you one story, but that will have to wait. We will now name the twenty-six Protectors of this generation and acknowledge their efforts, their passion, and their destiny. Thank you."

The whispers echoed again. Patterson waited for the noise to subside, shifting cards in his hand and taking a deep breath before continuing.

"The First Protector is, and was always meant to be, Brianna Coulson, who has chosen to serve for a third year."

My father whispered, "What?" under his breath. Most Protectors served for only a year, with only some serving for two years. Most Protectors considered it dangerous, whether from burnout or fear that the police would connect them to people's disappearances. People stood from their seats as the applause rose like a wave. Brie took her place on stage; strong and silent, as I had seen in broadcasts. Her blue eyes focused on a space above the crowd, and she didn't respond to the applause with any difference in her expression.

"The Second Protector is, and always was, Tessa Franklin, who has also decided to serve for a second year."

The whispers started again, most likely because no one expected two Protectors to repeat service years. It was usually kept to one year, to ensure they weren't captured when someone might recognize that people disappear after meeting them. Tessa had racked up impressive numbers in her first year. She was fast and smart, one of the top trained in athletics and broke records that had stood for decades. She waved to a few people who screamed her name. A few fans in the crowd whistled as she bowed, I turned to my mom and asked, "Why do I feel like this is a popularity contest?"

Mom sighed and said, "Because sometimes it is."

"Why has that never bothered me before?"

She smiled at me and said, "You're old enough to see it now. That's all."

The third Protector was a new name: Lillian Hoover. Patterson continued with the names, but his voice sounded muffled against my raging thoughts. The shallowness of seeking fame might have drawn girls to pursue this path, but it seemed like such a stark contrast to the heart of their mission.

Everyone continued to gossip each time they clapped and cheered, using the crowd's applause to muffle their guesses as to why the ceremony had changed. I rolled my eyes as I heard someone behind me whisper, "There's finally going to be a musical event this year." Then I heard Patterson yell her name: Megan Crawford. She had ranked fourteenth.

Henry was right; Megan and I did look similar, but her hair was more auburn and her eyes were blue like Henry's, instead of my simple brown. She waved and smiled at the crowd, but shyly, even as we stood and cheered for her. She shook hands with Patterson and took her place on the stage behind him, glancing at us for a moment and then her eyes resting on her father in the front row.

Patterson called more names, with everyone thinking that the surprises were finished. But he had one more.

"And the 26th Protector of the 188th Generation is, and always was, Evangeline McKinney."

That name got a lot of shock and awe. Evangeline McKinney was the daughter of Hannah McKinney, the former Head Trainer and legendary Protector. Hannah's sister and aunt had preceded her as Protectors. Her husband had died years earlier on a mission to the Republic, while she had been pregnant with Evangeline, who became a famous child as she excelled and advanced in the Academy. But no one expected Evangeline to serve this year, even as a legacy in the making. Being a Protector was the family business. At fifteen years old, she was the youngest Protector ever.

My mom whispered, "That's why Hannah had to quit."

I nodded. "I get it. Hannah couldn't be the Head Trainer with her daughter in the field. She'd be compromised."

Evangeline took her first steps on stage; intentional about her movements, not waving and smiling like the others. She looked like she couldn't care less what anyone else was doing, but not in an arrogant way. She flashed a quick smile at Eldridge, gave a casual nod and a high-five to Patterson instead of a handshake, and took her place in line. Evangeline seemed like the kind of person I always envied— so sure of herself, right down to her quirky salute to the Academy Principal.

After that, Patterson made some acknowledgments for the staff at the Academy. A teacher had retired, but no one was listening to the accolades.

Their eyes would dart around the stage where the twenty-six girls still stood. The girls left the stage with their Head Trainer, and to the sound of cheers and yells, and I was sure Megan didn't hear me, but we screamed her name anyway.

And finally, Eldridge walked on the stage.

"Well, you all have had ample time to wonder why I neglected to share our usual history lesson. I'm sure you've come up with many theories, most likely, all of them wrong." He got laughs from the crowd. "I will delay you no further from experiencing something that has always been, and always will be, an awe-inspiring, ever-terrifying entity: change."

He paused for a moment, as if to draw in everyone's attention. But he didn't need to stop. Everyone was silent.

"Change is what we cannot predict, but sometimes need, and in the realm of the Protectors, someone knew that. Someone who we still consider the best and bravest of them all. Naomi was twenty years old when she addressed the Council, asking for action against the Republic for their lack of respect or humanity concerning those whom they deemed unnecessary. That Council did not react. They told her that they could not take action. They said it was 'regrettable.' She decided that living with regret was worse than dying; she risked her life to be the first one in fifteen years to enter the Republic and come back. And she returned with a Vessel. And you all know Naomi's story. She recruited helpers. The Council eventually supported her. She started the Academy. But what you may forget is that something happened in the fifteenth year of training Protectors. She never explained it completely, and claimed she never could."

I heard my father sigh. I almost looked to him for a reaction, but I could hear his breath evening out. At least he had guessed what was happening.

Eldridge took a breath before continuing. "Naomi chose twenty-five girls to join her the first years, and then she chose twenty-six girls. But one year, she didn't. She needed change, or so she wrote in her journal. And after naming her Protectors, she surprised everyone, maybe even herself, and she named one more. Just one more."

"It's been more than twenty years," my mother whispered. "I barely remember the last time...tell me he didn't."

My father whispered back. "I think he did."

Eldridge had chosen a 27th Protector.

The 27th Protectors were legends: the ones chosen because they excelled in a specific skill that was desperately needed. They never trained at the Academy, but they were exceptional in their work. The first one, who had been chosen by Naomi, saved more Vessels than anyone else that century. Another 27th Protector had developed the best spy-craft techniques and saved countless lives through medical research. The 27th Protector of the 158th Generation had created the technology that all current Protectors still used to remain under the Republic's radar.

Eldridge continued, "The truth is... there is a 27th Protector for one reason. We need her, and we didn't know it until now. So please, 27, our first words to you are an apology. We forgot to tell you that you are a hero. Hear our apology. We did not value the gifts you had to bring, but we hope you bring them now. You didn't fight, or even ask to be a part of this, but now we have a chance to fix what we couldn't see was wrong. And in that way, 27, you will protect us all. So, protect us."

He stopped suddenly, backing up from the microphone. As Patterson came out, the tension grew. He didn't speak at first. I had a feeling there hadn't been a silence that thick under the Arches in thirty years.

Patterson finally moved, adjusting the microphone. He began to speak a few more words, but I only heard my own voice inside of my head: A voice I instantly tried to silence.

What if... ?

No.

It could be.

No.

But maybe...

No! The Council would never have let him. I'm nothing. I can't.

But that doesn't mean a part of you doesn't want to see...

I finished the voice's sentence— *to see what it would be like.*

I buried the thoughts, shushing them as if Eldridge could overhear the debate screaming in my brain or Patterson would call my name instead of whoever they had chosen.

Eldridge appeared to be waiting, looking out into the crowd, seemingly looking at no one in particular.

Except I could tell he was looking at me.

I slowly shook my head, my eyes still glued to him, but he only responded with a strange expression, a slight smile and sad twinge in his eye, as if to say, *Didn't you know? This was always going to happen.*

Patterson took a deep breath as I held mine, in the very last moment of normal life I would ever know.

"The Twenty-Seventh Protector of the 188th Generation is, and always was, Aislyn Williams."

CHAPTER 4

If there were whispers or screams from the audience, I couldn't hear them. All I heard was my heartbeat, my blood pumping, echoing in my ears. It helped me remember to breathe, keeping rhythm so I didn't pass out. I was trying to find the bravery to stand up. I knew I had to move. I had to move now.

So. I moved, amazed at how obedient my muscles were under the circumstances. They froze, for a moment, and then followed orders again by shuffling out of my seat a few steps.

I stared at Eldridge, ignoring my mom's hand squeezing mine. My dad released a heavy sigh. I risked a glance at them, hoping they weren't crying, but only my mom's eyes shimmered. My father's eyes showed forced pride and courage.

"Don't be scared," he whispered. "Take the next step."

The thick silence continued. I now realized why the candidates from the Academy sat in the front seats. The walk from the middle seats under the Arches seemed to take forever. The slight buzz of conversation made me feel an urgency to get backstage, but my muscles wouldn't go faster.

My father's words echoed. I took a step. I remembered how Evangeline walked up, with confidence. But I didn't have that, and I couldn't pretend now. I looked at Patterson, as Eldridge was no longer on the stage. Had I missed that? Where had he gone?

Patterson maintained focus, but his brown eyes seemed sympathetic. The Academy students glared as I walked past them, furious at being snubbed for a person who had never trained one day in their life.

I felt my legs ready to give way right as I got to the stairs, but I pushed forward.

You can do this. You can't do this. You can. You can't.

A song played in my head in time to the slow procession of my march to the stage, a horrible rhythm of doubt and courage fighting a battle neither of them could win. Because the one thing Eldridge had failed to mention was the 27th Protectors' survival rate. Being a great leader in the business of Protecting led to martyrdom. Only three out of the eight 27th Protectors had survived their year in service. I tried not to think about that as someone snapped a picture.

Patterson took my hand, his expression unreadable. He smiled a little and shook it, taking my forearm to hold on to me for a second and pat my back like he had the other Protectors.

"Eldridge is waiting for you," Patterson whispered. "Behind the curtain. You're doing great. Give one small wave to them, then you can go."

I barely put up my hand, but I nodded to the audience. Some applause rose, along with some cheers and yells. I was about to be more overwhelmed than I already was.

"That's good," he said. "Move now."

I obeyed without thinking. Patterson continued to address the crowd a few seconds later. He was covering for my shock by saying more eloquent things and smiling, both of which I would never have managed to do at that moment. I went through the parting in the curtain in the back of the stage. Eldridge wasn't there. No one was there. No one ordered me to move now.

So, I didn't.

I bent over, my hands and one knee hit the floor. My fingers spread beneath my shaking arms to try to hold my weight.

I must have said it under my breath twenty times. "What were you thinking?" Other 27th Protectors wanted this, desired this, or felt snubbed when rejected by the Academy. They were brilliant. They probably dreamed of being named.

The applause rose again. It was coming from outside the curtain. I stood up, almost ready to run.

"So, you react to simple escape reflexes? That's a good sign."

Eldridge was behind me. My emotions surged, not sure if I should attempt to lunge at him in anger or break down and cry. But I respected him, and his sentence had piqued my interest enough to keep all my emotions concealed.

"Escape reflexes?" I asked. "They're just applauding."

"Yes," Eldridge said as if pondering that, "but applause is threatening because, in its absence, silence would take its place. With no applause, there is a void of disapproval. It's easy to be frightened by applause because you are afraid that it's all that matters and you fear it's end. It's addicting. Let's go, shall we?"

I didn't want to agree. I wanted to refuse. But I walked with him instead, if only because his words seemed true in a way that no one else had been able to express

"So, how are you holding up?" Eldridge asked casually.

I felt grey: the white was confidence and the black was fear. By the time we had walked down another hallway, I still hadn't answered his question.

I had no desire to talk, choke, cough, cry, plead. Nothing.

"That good, huh?"

I almost choked as I spoke. "I feel like I will freak out at any second, and then— I just don't."

"Well, that is interesting." He said it with a look of kindness in his grey eyes. "What is the part of you that is about to panic saying?"

"This is insane. I can't do this," I said, almost too loudly. My anger now threatened to burn through the uncertainty that kept me calm so far.

"I see. You feel underqualified then?"

"Yes! In all respects!" I answered, nearly shouting at his casual tone of surprise. "I hate technology, I can't run, I've never held an MCU, I throw up when I see blood, I can't ever seem to fit in here. I'm not committed! At all!"

"How so?"

I took a breath. "I have loads of questions and doubts about what Protectors do. Why do we place the Unnecessaries in shelters? Why do we have so many rules? Why do Protectors train with a trainer they don't choose? Why don't we declare war and save everyone? Why do we only choose twenty-six if more want to go or less want to go? I have loads of questions with no answers. I have doubts stacked as high as the Arches, and you picked me without asking!" I stopped, realizing I was yelling.

He was calm, almost infuriatingly so, as he said, "My dear, I would never risk the lives we rescue, those Unnecessaries and Vessels, by putting them in the hands of someone I didn't think could handle it. Ever. And I still chose you."

I didn't have a reply, taken aback by his declaration. I choked out, "What makes you think I'm able to handle it?"

I regretted asking the moment it left my mouth, worried he might now reveal something about myself I didn't know.

"Oh, I didn't," he said, but then didn't explain, as if the answer was obvious. I couldn't figure out if I should be concerned about his sanity or draw on the apparent confidence he had in his decision. In the end, I abandoned both to stare at the door sliding open in front of me as we approached.

"To your Circle, 27." He pointed at the door. "Actually, to another hallway with boring, metal walls in Central which leads to a dull room where everyone is waiting to go to their Circles."

I hesitated for a moment, but a slight thrill compelled me to step into the small device that resembled an elevator. The unit began by moving sideways; it lurched to the left and then changed directions to move downward. It made me more keenly aware that I was standing in the center of the most innovative technology in the entire Territory. Unless you were an Academy student or a Protector, no one passed the Arches.

"Considering your fears, 27," Eldridge spoke again, "I should tell you that many opposed this decision for fear of change and what it could mean. Other kind-hearted souls opposed you because they think…" He trailed off, but I finished his sentence.

"I'm going to die." The statement felt heavy as I said it out loud. I was furious that he hadn't said it.

"Well, yes. You will die. I suppose we all will. But unlike them, I have faith you'll live long enough to save lives. And despite what they say, they are not afraid you'll die. They're terrified that I'm right, and that you'll live long enough to do something differently than the status quo. Any changes could force them to rethink things: training, the Academy, missions, and even how we help our victims. People really don't like thinking. It's a nuisance."

"So, are you telling me not to be a nuisance?" I asked, wandering through the words of his cryptic warning.

He smiled. "On the contrary, I'm looking forward to it."

I shook my head, speaking very softly. "If you are looking for someone with passion and strength to bring down a broken system, you didn't pick her. I don't have what you need."

Still staring at the wall, he said, "Not yet. And I'm okay with that. You have one thing, Aislyn, that will ensure you gain that passion and strength you need."

"What's that?" I asked as the elevator door opened.

"Curiosity," he said, now turning to me again. "It got you through the curtain on stage and through the elevator, kept you walking and talking to me, and it will get you to your Circle. It will get you to the Republic. It will lead you to the first person you will save. Your curiosity will keep you going until your scared and you need bravery to survive. Do you see the door down there?" He nodded down the hall, about twenty yards away. "I will let you walk to that door, without me, for three reasons. One, I'm late for a meeting. Very late. Two, because your curiosity will remind you that if you die one day having not walked down this hallway, you will regret it. Not everyone would, but you would."

His words echoed in my head. They bounced, almost as if my mind were the stoic metallic walls surrounding me. All the daydreams I'd ever had about seeing Central, the Circles, and even the Republic came rushing in like a flood.

I wanted to know. A part of me wanted to play the part, fight the war, save a life— to bleed, love, scream, cry, live. I needed to know everything I would miss if he had not called my name.

"Fair enough," I said in surrender. "But sir, what's the third reason?"

"Oh," Eldridge started, changing to a playful tone, "if we were standing outside that door instead of right here, there would be thirteen girls with their ears pressed up against it struggling to summarize our conversation to the other thirteen lovely ladies in the room. We train spies for a living, Aislyn. It's a tricky business."

I closed my eyes and stopped myself from laughing, feeling that at least his last comment made the Protectors a little more human than I'd imagined. But only a little. I kept my eyes focused on the door, not moving as he spoke again.

"People find what they are looking for, Aislyn. See if you find it. See if it makes your heartbeat faster and your soul fight for something. Be curious enough to find a reason to be brave, and bravery will find you."

By the time I turned around, he was walking back down the hall. No word of goodbye or any other gesture. He left me in the hall with his last words echoing louder and louder in my mind. The other twenty-six girls were waiting for me— no, waiting for someone better than me— to open that door.

But he was right. I was curious to a fault: a fault that could kill me, and probably would. But it forced me to take a few steps, and I surprised myself by not even hesitating before I pressed the button and opened the door.

I dreaded the silence that permeated the room.

It confirmed that they had all been either talking about me or trying to listen to Eldridge's last words to me.

Probably both.

It resembled a sitting room at a hospital, with comfortable furniture with plain colors on the walls and fake plants on stoic surfaces. The room had metal wall panels but no screens or any other sign of technology. Many of the Protectors sat rigidly in the metal seats. Some were leaning against the wall, oozing confidence. All of them remained frozen, except for one.

"Here you are," Tessa said, walking to stand only inches away from me. She looked at my eyes, but then proceeded to glance over every part of me.

"Here I am," I searched for Megan, but I couldn't see her. Their silent appraisals could only lead to one question, but none of them asked.

"Chosen to be the 27th Protector. You have to know that we've been wondering why," Tessa said, as if setting me up to explain. But I kept scanning the room for Megan and finally determined she wasn't in the room. After a quick count, I noticed there were only twenty-four girls staring at me.

I risked asking my question first.

"Where is—?"

"Meg's down the hall with Eva. They'll be back in a second. I don't think it's an issue, but they wanted to check."

I realized this was a test; would I understand enough of her vague clues to guess where they had gone? I briefly wondered if I should fake it and say, "*Oh, yeah, that makes sense.*"

But I already guessed I couldn't fake Tessa out.

"Check what?" I asked, officially admitting my ignorance.

I was right; it was a test.

She didn't get a chance to answer my question before three of the girls groaned.

"She doesn't even know basic policy?" someone asked.

"Okay, so you never read Naomi's Manual, or any of the amendments, or any regulations. You probably aren't here for physical abilities— no offense. So, is it Tech? Medicine?"

"What? No!" I said. I was thinking about how I could defend myself or justify my presence with some skill, but bragging about how to rewire or jump-start a generator might sound laughable to them. "I'm not bad, I'm just... not amazing."

"At Tech?"

"At anything," I shouted, my defeat sinking in. "I have no idea why he chose me."

There were several reactions that followed. Eyebrows raised, scoffs escaped, and a head went down into someone's hands with a groan. Someone from the back of the room said, "Well then... she's gonna die."

"Perfect," Tessa said. "Classic crazy Eldridge. Let's pick someone with no qualifications. Maybe she'll even come in and tell us we're too competitive or any of that other crap he's always spouting."

Under her breath, she said another word that I tried to ignore. It sounded as if she cursed, but I had never heard that word before. Maybe it was Republic slang.

"What if that was the reason? Would that worry you?" I didn't want to antagonize her, but I thought back to her waving and smiling at cameras, wondering if she did it just for the "hero-status" and perks. "Would it mess with your numbers or your next press appearance?"

I said it far more confidently than I felt, but any confidence evaporated in the heat of her glare. Everyone else's reactions were more mixed this time. But I heard someone say, "Oh, here we go. At least we get to have fun."

"I do like the numbers. And the attention. And I don't let criticism stop me. I don't care what you think, 27. I have other things to worry about, and if you weren't a newbie, you would know that." Tessa paused, taking a breath only to lower her voice. "What you should worry about is that for every child we save, ten times more people are dying. You don't know about Sophia, who we lost last year. She was betrayed and murdered by a Society Party agent who pretended to be a Vessel— just for the chance to kill one of us. Most little schoolgirls like you don't know that we have more Sentries and technology to beat than ever before, and that we have less of a chance to find someone who wants out of the Republic. Before you think that you can judge us or change anything, maybe you should fall in line and try your best to learn how to save someone. Or don't you know why you are standing here?"

I soaked in her words.. My ignorance unnerved me, but I answered her question.

"I'm only hear because I was chosen, and to see where this goes." I was once again speaking to a silent room. She stared me down, her criticism echoing behind her sharp dark eyes.

"Not good enough. I've done this for a year, and that was long enough to know that you don't belong here."

I hated the silence. I would lose any credibility by saying nothing, but I couldn't argue with her.

Then, the last person I'd expected to argue with Tessa spoke from the back of the room.

"Yeah, well, I've done this for two years, which is long enough to know that you, of all people, shouldn't be the judge of who belongs here."

Brianna shifted from the wall she'd been leaning against. She didn't move as much as glide, like some kind of force propelled her every movement. People moved back, like a sea parting around her. One look at Tessa's face, and I knew what these two Protectors thought about each other, despite polite gestures in public.

Brianna continued to speak in response to Tessa's silence.

"And beating up on the ignorant and incompetent rookie is not going to make her any better. So back off."

I was so happy Brianna was defending me I didn't even care that she had just insulted me.

"This was Eldridge," Tessa said. "It's some political agenda to push the ideology that we shouldn't be soldiers."

Brianna moved to within inches of Tessa. "We are Protectors, not killers. And despite your confusion on that, it doesn't matter. It doesn't matter if it is political or if she ends up surprising us and lives the year. She belongs here for the same reason you do."

"And that is?"

"Eldridge chooses. That is the reason, maybe the only reason, I still try to respect you. He chose you. He chose her. You're here. She's here. Get over it."

Brie pivoted, her blond hair floating behind her as she glided back to the wall. She didn't even look at me. By the time she was there, the door opened to reveal Megan and Evangeline. I desperately wanted to talk to Megan, but instead, Evangeline asked the one question no one could answer.

"Why is she here? What'd I miss? Is it Tech? Med? Some weird mutation? Super strength? What can you do, 27?"

"Apparently nothing," I answered as nonchalantly as I could, which was enough to get a scoff from Tessa again.

"Oh," Evangeline said, sounding surprised, and I braced for an impact. "Well, you haven't passed out since they called you. That's something of a strange miracle, I almost did." There was an even more relaxed tone in her voice when she asked, "Is there food? I'm starving. I didn't eat this morning because unlike all of you, I hurl when I'm nervous."

I almost laughed but stifled it. Everyone either smiled or rolled their eyes at her as she continued to babble, so I assumed it was her natural personality.

"Well, so sorry that we missed Tessa being mad again, but we confirmed what we needed. Megan is clear. There is a by-law! Gotta love by-laws. They let cousins fight in the same generation."

I looked at Megan, but she shrugged. "Two relatives can't be in the same class at the Academy. Clearly, the intent was that no two relatives would ever go to the Republic at the same time, to prevent being compromised or training with a relative."

"But," she jumped in, "they didn't have enough foresight to write a contingency for a 27th being chosen the same year that their relative would graduate from the Academy! Score a point for the incompetence of underdeveloped legislature. Candy?"

I shook my head. She shrugged and moved on with her bag of candy to plop on the couch. Her behavior seemed strangely comfortable. She likely grew up rooms like these while her mother worked long hours.

"Any other news?" someone else asked.

"Why do you assume I know everything, Abby?"

"Because you do."

"True," Evangeline said as she got up to grab more candy.

Megan sighed and stepped into the center of the room.

"They convened the Council. Unscheduled debate session."

"And Tessa," Evangeline added, "don't even start. They're not changing their mind. Aislyn is here to stay. Didn't you hear Eldridge? She's under divine calling to protect us all." She pointed absentmindedly as she sunk in and laid on the sofa.

Tessa's death glare rested on Evangeline, who just winked.

Lillian called out, "Our trainers! Is the official list out?"

Evangeline widened her eyes and half sighed. "It was out, and then some intern grabbed it and said it wasn't ready. That's what the meeting is about."

"So do you remember who was on the list?" Abby asked.

It shocked me that someone thought Evangeline, as unfocused as she seemed, could memorize twenty-seven names.

But her lopsided grin grew into a full smile, and I swallowed my disbelief as she spoke.

"First, Brie, still stuck with George and probably skipping every lesson. Tessa, same thing. You're still with Sir Avery."

I wondered why she called him 'Sir', but quickly assumed that Tessa's trainer might be as arrogant as her.

"Abigail, you got Clara. So sorry. Our hearts are with you." Evangeline patted Abby's head as she sank on the couch with her.

"Emmy, you got Maria. Hope you love sit-ups. Lynn, you have Will, Michael is shadowing this year. You'll hate his running schedule, but he's one of the best at Tech and will let you work on side projects as relentlessly as you want. Send the Council flowers to say thank you."

She continued like this through most of the names. I tried to learn what I could from the list, taking the rare chance to collect information their comradery had already afforded them. I found out Crystal hated running just as much as Cassidy, and they both loved tech classes. Lydia sounded thrilled to have a Trainer who specialized in medicine, as did Ivy. Someone called Evangeline by her name and she stopped dead and said "Eva." I noticed that everyone called her Eva. I also made a note that Abigail went by Abby, Brianna went by Brie, and Lillian went by Lynn.

"Stop! Who got pulled up?" Tessa interrupted. "Patterson had to get replaced because he's Head Trainer, and 27 needs a trainer, not that'll it'll do any good. Was is Dylan or Zoe?"

The Academy chose only thirty girls to train as potential Protectors, but even fewer girls and boys to became trainers. Trainers studied for two years after the Academy, shadowed for three to five years, and served for a decade to mentor Protectors before finding another position in Central or the Academy. It was rare to find someone who was devoted enough to live a life devoid of family and friends for two decades.

Though most of the Protectors held contempt for their trainers, Chloe laughed. "Oh, I hope it's Dylan. He's so hot!"

Eva sighed and conceded, "Dylan, who I will admit is muscular and attractive, will be assigned to Kayla. But she– along with the rest of you – will forget that when you're all climbing up fifty-foot sections of wall! He's a tyrant about the wall! Anyway," Eva continued. "Zoe and Michael are still shadowing, and the other apprentices will serve in Central."

"Wait. Who got promoted?" Brie broke her silence and statue-like posture for the second time, staring at Eva intensely.

"Collin." She gave Brie a knowing look.

Cassidy opened her mouth just to close it again, Tessa looked up in shock, and Lynn stifled a laugh.

"He's only shadowed one year!"

"He's too young, I thought. He's like nineteen, right?"

"That stinks for Zoe who has three years of shadowing."

"What the—?"

"Whoa," Eva shouted holding up her hands. "I'm not Eldridge, who at this moment, is answering all these questions."

"Okay, but at least he's shadowed, and with George and Brie. It's not that big of a deal," Lydia said though she looked panicked. "Unless I'm with him. Am I with him?"

"Nope," Eva said.

Everyone froze. I couldn't wait for someone else to ask.

"Eva," I stuttered, "who did they assign Collin to?"

"Eldridge assigned Collin to train the 27th Protector of the 188th Generation," she said pointing at me, "who is now interesting enough to be the center of attention again. Sorry for that, Aislyn, but I just realized there's food over there. Have fun!"

Everyone else stared at me again, but only one of them spoke their collective thought as my stomach sank.

"She is so going to die."

CHAPTER 5

"There is an incredible spread over here! Why is no one eating this?" Eva said, pointing at the food on the table. "Get carbs while you can!"

"Collin? Really? Can they even do that?" Lynn asked.

I needed answers, so I searched for Brie's eyes, hoping she would break her silence again. I silently begged her for answers.

She sighed, and said, "Collin is competent. He's super focused, especially spiritually. He's a purist. He's an idealist."

Tessa interrupted, "Ugh, Eldridge loves him! I wonder if that will change when she doesn't come back from her first mission."

The only person I trusted so far was Eldridge, so the fact that Eldridge liked Collin and Tessa didn't was slightly encouraging.

But only slightly.

Brie continued, "With this being his first year training, you're both—" someone interrupted with what I guessed was a Republic swear word. Brie ignored them. "At a disadvantage."

I wanted to defend him or ask more questions, but I was struggling to not to throw up, since it was my only virtue so far.

Any hope I had to bridge the gap in training was disappearing, if the person training me was as inexperienced as me. I almost wanted to go downstairs and tell the Council this was a horrible decision and that I wanted Sir Avery instead.

"So," Eva continued, swallowing her food, "Collin is in the hot seat right now, even though he probably isn't being allowed to talk, so we might as well eat this not-so-mediocre food for another thirty minutes until we can go to our Circles."

I felt claustrophobic. I wanted to get out of the room. I'd rather be on a mission in the Republic than stuck here waiting.

"Well," Lydia said loudly, "I wish I knew what was going on down there, don't you?"

The silence continued. Tessa and Brie stared at each other, but it was no longer with contempt. Tessa whispered, "C'mon."

I realized that Lydia's statement was not a vague wish; it was a challenge.

Eva's eyebrows jumped up twice, but she remained frozen, waiting on Brie. The only thing to interrupt the tense silence was the tapping made by Cassidy's foot.

Brie put her hand on her hip. "Don't get caught."

"Don't get caught," nearly every voice in the room echoed.

Eva spoke quickly. "I'll get audio with Cassidy. Visual?"

"Yes!" Cassidy shouted and jumped onto the couch.

They moved fast, pulling out what I assumed were portable comms. They pulled two from the side cabinet and synced them. Eva caught a small speaker someone threw at them. They began opening the back of the speaker, exposing the circuit board and cutting one wire to attach it to another. The one wire on the matching comm was cut and fused with a tiny device that Cassidy took from her pocket. A little smoke rose from the tool.

"Is that a..." I started to ask, but then said, "What is that?"

Eva winked. "Miniature soldering iron. Want one?"

All the technique and skill enthralled me. Their proficiency erased any chances I had of catching up to their level. Meanwhile, Tessa kept reading off what sounded like random numbers to Brie who was typing them in an Mobile Computing Unit, or MCU, which I had never seen except in a textbook.

Megan came up from behind me. Trying to be casual, I asked her, "So, this is what you learned at the Academy?"

[48]

She sighed. "Some of it. I can't do it as well as they do. At the Academy, we didn't need to master all the subjects to succeed. Only Brie and Tessa have mastered it all. A techie might find an opportunity to break in a lab. Another girl's extended medical knowledge might help her spot a Vessel faster. You will rescue who you were meant to save. That's what we're supposed to believe. You should believe it, too. If you do, you'll be fine."

I wasn't sure what to say, but whispered, "Thank you."

Tessa yelled at Cassidy to try another code. Cassidy punched in three more sets of numbers before her hands went up in triumph. Tessa said, "Confirmed."

Brie said, "That means they're done, Eva. And you're not."

Eva answered vacantly, "Thanks for that. It's inspiring me."

I walked up to Eva, who was still working on the comms, and asked, "Are you sure we should be doing this? We're not supposed to be there."

"I hate to break it to you, 27, but in six weeks, we're all going to be in a place where we aren't supposed to be. Get used to it."

She intricately worked her way with the wires on the second comm. Her movements mesmerized me as if they were a thread and needle in my mother's hands.

I wouldn't see my mother stitching clothes tomorrow.

I wouldn't be sewing tomorrow.

I wouldn't be pricking myself with my needle.

I wouldn't be giving up on sewing and joining the twins in running around the house with the leftover shreds of ribbon.

A strange, overwhelming rhythm of panic started beating. Everything I thought I was going to do had changed. And not one moment of my life was guaranteed from now on.

"Megan, you got the wall?" Brie called out.

"Yep, on it," she said, handing Eva back the map. "Brie?"

As I tried to make a mental scan of the map, Megan headed toward the wall. She removed a silver panel that looked like a vent, curled into a ball, and without warning, fell into the black void behind it. The breath in my lungs escaped before I could speak, but Eva threw the comm right through the hole in the wall and I heard Megan say, "Got it!"

"Video?" Eva called out.

"Should be good. Go, Megan," Tessa said.

Within a few moments, a scratchy voice became recognizable through the receiver, but then dropped back into static, silence, then more voices. I realized Megan was picking up voices from different floors as she dropped past them. The fifth floor was all static, and then Patterson's voice cut through.

"— in assigning her to Collin. This wasn't my call, but I stand behind this decision because I believe in his abilities."

Another voice seemed certain as it interrupted.

"We have shared a concern that everyone is ignoring: that considering her lack of training, this is not faithful or brave, but a silly emotional decision. It is just foolish. We risk her death or even more severe consequences, as Zander stated."

"What's up with the video?" Tessa asked. "I want to see if Zander is still there since Avery is quoting her."

"We can't hold video very long. They keep scrambling the feed. It must be something the Council does to keep that room secure."

Lydia sighed. "Their tech is more advanced than at the Academy."

The curls of Cassidy's hair bounced each time she hit several keys, whispering, "Work, work, work!"

"This process has existed for years before the Academy started. We need to trust it," a Council member called out.

Cassidy sighed. Eva must have given up on video because she put her feet up onto Cassidy's lap as they watched the speaker.

I leaned in as well, feeling my body strain from the effort it took to stay still and not shake so I could hear every word.

"Nor do I doubt Collin's effectiveness, but this may end…"

There was some static.

Lydia shouted some instructions I barely heard as the voice continued. "—I am just asking for a simple evaluation of Aislyn's abilities before we assign her a trainer."

"Tech?" another Council member said. "It must be Tech, right? What else could the girl excel at? I've seen her transcript."

Avery continued, "Regardless, this is reckless. You all know what we've been facing of late. Assigning 27 a trainer who doesn't agree with the changing philosophy of our training is ridiculous."

I wanted to ask what he had meant by the "changing philosophy of training," but I wanted to hear his statement more.

"This is another bad choice due to an archaic system. The idea of just one trainer for each apprentice is an ancient and ineffective use of our resources. We need to change or we risk her life! If we had trainers who excelled in each area instead of one—"

The arguments escalated. I was trying to pull a sentence out of the shouts and yells, but all I heard was a few words.

Then something jolted me. The door behind me slid open.

I jumped slightly, turning to see Eldridge in the doorway.

The visual monitor continued to show static, but the voices from the Council echoed throughout the room. No one moved or flinched, except for Eva, who leaned back and smiled.

"Richard, whatever brings you up to our humble waiting room on this fine day?" Eva was so dry and non-reactive it made me want to hit her, but I remained frozen with everyone else.

The High Counselor smiled a wry smile and said, "I told everyone I would come and check on you. But honestly, I left because it seemed they wanted to talk about me behind my back. Are you all having fun yet?"

"Yep, a blast!" Eva said. "Just like they imagine us: bonding and laughing while braiding each other's hair and talking about how much we will enjoy cauterizing bullet wounds and eating meal bars for weeks on end."

"Good! And I'll be happy to report that to the Council. I'll even throw in that one or two of you are a little uneasy with me picking Aislyn, since this is obviously infuriating Tessa."

Tessa opened her mouth, yet despite his playful tone, his sudden stern glare stopped her words and she swallowed instead.

"As they'll probably be talking about how senile I am soon—"

Eerily on cue, there was a sound from the comm of an unknown voice saying, "—if Eldridge hadn't chosen her in the first place! The man is too old and going mad."

"Ah, and there it is," Eldridge said, amid the bellowing accusations that were now defending or attacking him. "Lots of yelling… someone says 'order.' Yes, well, that's enough to be going on with. I'm going back down. Have fun!" There was a thud in the wall. "Oh, and tell Megan I stopped to say hello."

He turned, and the door slid shut behind him with a loud clang. Lydia was the first to say, "Is that normal?"

Everyone looked at Brie who shrugged as Eva said, "Yep."

Over the comm, the conversation moved on to three tedious minutes of a dull voice reading the law as it pertained to Eldridge's right to select a Protector and their trainer. Someone then shouted, "That being said, Patterson, is there anything more?"

Patterson sighed into a microphone and said, "To be honest, sir, I think there's only one person to defer to. Only one."

There was silence. I wondered if there was some movement we couldn't hear.

"And how convenient for me," Eldridge said, now into a microphone, "that I found him pacing in the hall outside. Collin, you have the floor, young man."

I almost took a step back, but I didn't know why. No matter how I felt about Collin being my trainer, I could not have wished upon anyone the torture of being in the Council room at that moment.

But my pity didn't last long. It was burned out by fear.

What if he rejected me? I could only hear his breath, but it sounded sure, focused, and deliberate. I no longer felt nervous that he would be my trainer; I was terrified he wouldn't want to be.

"Council," his voice rang out. "Many of you know my convictions, and why I aspired to do this. I have a great amount of faith in the Council and in Eldridge. And faith, by definition, declares nothing to be impossible."

I noticed that Eva had transformed from playful to focused, with an indistinguishable expression on her face. She closed her eyes as he was speaking. Brie stared at the wall blankly, but she rocked back and forth instead of standing still.

"And if you have declared it impossible, so very impossible that she could even live, let alone succeed, then I have every reason to take on the task of training her, despite every reason not to. I have every reason to try now. While I respect your concerns, I'll take my shot at the impossible. And I will follow Eldridge's order and train the 27th Protector of the 188th Generation."

The breath I let out was too loud for the quiet room, but I didn't care.

Collin believed I could do this. I might end up hating him, becoming his friend, or both. But I wasn't alone.

Eldridge's voice rang out through the room. "Ladies and gentlemen, I believe that is settled—and bravely spoken, I might add. The standings remain unaltered. Dismissed."

There was a loud sound, which I assumed was from a gavel, which called the end of the meeting. Eva went from listening intently with her eyes closed to jumping the sofa, leaping over it and running to the hole in the wall as she shouted out, "Thirty seconds."

"Thirty seconds!" she called.

Everyone moved, as if it were a dance they'd memorized.

"Comm," Eva yelled as she caught the MCU Cassidy threw at her. "Cassidy, Reagan, you're on the wall."

Eva threw the MCU to Brie, who was screwing in the final casing to the comm but caught the MCU with ease. Eva opened opened the wall as Cassidy threw Megan's comm to Tessa. Megan's hands came out of the wall first as she pushed herself out to land softly on one knee, like a cat landing on a perch.

Tessa said, "Everyone act natural; don't mess this up now."

I put on my best deadpan face, but I could still feel the weight of Collin's words, as if they were forcing the blood through my body faster. The door opened. A security officer came through followed by Patterson, who stared at the girls and then at me.

"Are they playing nice?"

"Yeah," I said, more apprehensively than I would have liked.

I was a little shaky. He squinted at me. I realized I could be nervous about a lot of things. A cover story materialized in my mind.

"No really, it's been fine. But no one could answer my question, sir. It's just... they all got to see their parents today. Say goodbye, you know. And I didn't."

"I said maybe she could see them at the feast," Brie blurted.

Tessa said, "I think she should see them in a private area to say her goodbyes, especially with her chances."

Eva and Lynn said their opinions over each other.

Patterson put up one finger, silencing everyone. He turned and said, "Banquet. It won't be private. I'm sorry, 27. You may stay with your family instead of sitting up at the head table." He nodded to his left. "Ladies, you'll be reporting to your Circles before the banquet, as planned. Sorry for the delay."

Nobody did anything at first, and I realized they were all waiting for Brie, who moved intently for the door. Tessa jumped up after Brie, still glaring at me. Everyone else naturally went in the order Patterson had called out their names, with Eva passing me last.

"Nice cover, rookie," she muttered with a wink.

I stood in the empty room. I was never meant to see this room. I was never meant to see a Circle. I felt scared and enthralled all over again, but I knew I might always feel like I did at that moment: alone, confused, and a few steps behind everyone else.

CHAPTER 6

When I caught up with Eva, she turned to face me, and said, "So, any burning questions before you get to your Circle?"

"Um…where are we? Underground? What about Central?"

"There's only one stairway and one elevator that goes up to the Circles from where we are. Central is far larger than most people in the Territory realize. There are five floors underground, wide as all the Circles – even larger if you include some places I can't tell you about. The stairway comes up into the garden in the center of the Circles and that one- and only- stairway also leads straight to the Central Hub if you go one floor down. You'll catch on."

We turned to walk down a wide hall that curved around long sets of doors and offices with open windows.

On the other side were doors with numbers and names that were much larger. At first, I wasn't sure what they could be, but the second door read "*Avery.*"

"Are these the trainers' rooms or their workspaces?" I whispered to Eva.

She looked mildly impressed at my guesswork. As the rest of the Protectors marched forward through the hall, she walked backward, trying to read my reactions as she explained.

"The left side are sleeping quarters. Their offices are embedded in the inner circle on the right."

"So," I asked, staring at the rooms, "their sleeping quarters are right next to their offices? It sounds a little intense. Do they want to make them obsessed with their job?"

"No. And by no, I mean yes. They do the legwork while you're on missions. Trainers run all the EEs and Tech Handlers run station maintenance. Your handler will monitor you in the Republic if they can. You call your handler if you need an EE."

"An EE... that's an emergency evacuation, right?"

"Yes," Eva said matter-of-factly, "and don't think an EE means they get you out of the Republic or even Zone 3. It's just Zone 2 or Zone 1 evac if you have a problem. They sometimes have to tell you to hold tight if there have been drones in the area. They also give you a pep talk now and again."

"Isn't that what your trainer is for?"

"Ha! No, your trainer is there to hate you and make you a better Protector by placing insane amounts of mental and physical pressure on you."

"Why?" I slowed down almost to a stop. She grabbed my arm and pulled me toward her so I would stay close as we walked. She spoke quietly, almost whispering.

"It used to be, when they first built those Circles up there, that Protectors were trained differently, which is what the Council was arguing about. With the Republic's kill order for any suspected Protector, and the public more suspicious than ever, a trainer's only job is keeping you alive. The only thing is—"

She turned around, even as she looked like she was about to continue. I was following so close to Eva that when the line stopped, I almost ran into her. I wondered how much I would stare at her brown, flipped-up hair in the next few weeks.

Patterson explained the procedures to get around Central and our classes, then proceeded to explain the biometric security.

"You will need to place your hand on this pad to go up to your Circles now, but then the hallway cameras will scan and give you priority access to every location. Stare ahead at the camera. The scanners will record everything we need before you go up to your assigned Circle. You will watch the mandatory simulcast when you arrive."

Each girl placed their hand on the pad and stared at the strange robotic arm scanning them as if it were normal. Patterson would say the girl's name and Protector number. When he got to Eva, his smile disappeared. The computer was already responding.

The biometric robot said, "Scan complete. No I.D. needed. This is Evangeline McKinney, juvenile, daughter of Hannah—"

"Stop." Patterson's voice was short, as if his throat was tight. He let out a breath. "I'm still in shock you're here, kid. Just yesterday I was yelling at you for running down the hall, stealing my comm, or climbing the challenge course. You're too—" He paused, looking at the floor. "You're not supposed to be here."

"Don't give me the 'you're too young' speech, Patterson. It won't end well." She smiled, but then looked unfocused and phased. "None of us are supposed to be here."

Patterson looked at her, and in a more official sounding voice, said, "Director override. Change Evangeline's profile name to the 26th Protector of the 188th Generation."

The computer arm blinked green. Eva nodded, then bounded up the stairs two at a time.

He nodded for me to move to the sensor. I stepped onto the blue pad. It responded by lighting up with my every footfall. I could see my breath in the blue light as if it were freezing outside. With one quick laser swipe, the readout displayed all my information, from my blood type to my heart rate to every inch of my body.

"Register Aislyn Williams as the 27th Protector of the 188th Generation," Patterson said while typing something in his MCU.

The computer answered in a digitized, yet polite tone. "No previous information is recorded for this student. Are you certain this is not an error?"

For the first time, I really stared at Patterson. His entire demeanor and physical appearance was athletic and sharp, like a soldier mixed with a scholar. The moment I'd seen with Eva might have been the only time he hesitated to do anything all day. But he was hesitating again. His brown eyes seemed to be evaluating me, looking darker as he squinted.

"This is not an error," he said loudly, almost as if he was trying to convince himself. "Add file. Title, 27th Protector."

He nodded upstairs as the light turned green. I followed without saying a word. We walked up the four stories in silence. He paused and looked at me again at the top. The door opened to a near-blinding light. I looked out at the stone, enough to see the trees and the famous garden on the edge of the Circles.

I could hear my voice ringing inside my head. *This is your chance; tell him you can't do this!*

I wished I were one of those people inspired by courage, passion, or a voice in their head. It would make the moment more meaningful.

There was no voice from the heavens. Only silence.

Then, within seconds, there was a surge through my heart— a burn in my hands that made me close my fists in determination. There was a push on my heel. I heard the echo of Patterson's voice as if was speaking again: *"This is not an error."*

I looked out over the garden. The walkway was lined with vines twenty feet high, climbing what appeared to be air— most likely invisible twine attached to the top of the wooden posts above. There was a small willow tree leaning over a pond. The air smelled of roses and lavender. There was more green than I had seen since summer in every field in just one hundred yards.

"It's beautiful," I breathed out, then realized it was an uncharacteristic thing for a Protector to say. "Sorry."

Patterson said, "Never apologize for seeing beauty in this place. We remember it here. Or we'd lose our minds in sorrow."

I gazed at the rock in one bed of the garden as we walked again. I noticed the names written and etched on them.

"Names of Vessels that died in childbirth," Patterson explained. "There's Protectors' torches over there."

I turned to him and nodded, finding I no longer wanted to look at how many rocks there were.

"There has to be over three-hundred... why are there—?"

"So many?" Patterson said. "Remember that many Vessels can't carry a child to term. The rocks are meant for you to remember them, but also for you to remember your first lesson. You can't always win, and you won't. Don't let failure play games with your head. Your head needs to be clear."

In about half a minute's walk, we stepped out of the garden onto the grey brick patio. The Circles were larger than they seemed to be from a speeding shuttle. I could only see six cylinders from where I stood because they blocked the others, each of them as wide as my house. What I also never saw from my shuttle seat were the vine and floral carvings that went up the fifty feet of the grey stone.

"The outdoor training forests are on the other side of the Courtyard. The Training Circles are all centered on the garden, where we are standing now." He paused. "Which makes this a great time to tell you where we are. Well, where you stand with me," he sighed, moving his fingers against his forehead, then stood unnaturally straight and still, his brown eyes now looking a little kinder than his demeanor. "I realize the disadvantage you have and how much you may have calculated your chances for survival. I don't know your character, your skills, or anything about you. But I trust Eldridge. So, for now, I'll trust you. My gift to you is that you don't have to earn it; it's yours. Figure out a way to do this, Aislyn, and don't break that trust."

"Thank you." I added a quick, "Sir."

"Your Circle is there. I walked you up because you don't know the numbers yet," he said matter-of-factly and pointed to the cylinder to the right, tucked behind the one closest to the garden. "You are the only Protector allowed in your Circle unless you invite another Protector in. You must give them permission, or else they can't enter. You decide if you want the glass roof open or closed. It's your arena, but it has only one rule. You follow your trainer's orders, no matter what, every time. Most of your training will happen in the rooms of your Circle. Your trainer will walk you through the five areas in your Training Circle. These rooms are inside against the wall of your Circle. One is for sleep. Each of the other areas is for teaching specific subjects: medicine, history, tech, and physical endurance. The center is the largest space and for additional training. Oh, and don't listen to anyone say that you're taking up space. We sometimes use the 27th Circle to spar, because it's usually empty." He paused. "Just waiting."

Where's—?" I almost asked about Collin but remembered I wasn't supposed to know his name yet.

"Waiting." Patterson nodded. He looked impatient and very still again. The pep talk was over.

I nodded, as I had seen everyone else done. "Sir."

"27," he said, turning on his heel. I began walking to my Circle, listening to his footsteps run away from me. I heard him speak sternly, I assumed to someone in Central. "Coming down now, you better have audio online in ten minutes, Joel."

My feet slowed as I approached my Circle. I stood as still as the stone in front of me, staring at the open arch with no door. I couldn't resist placing my hand on the curves and bumps of the carvings in the grey rock. I saw the names carved in the leaves.

A breeze crashed against the unmoving stone and brushed my hair against my face. I stood in the archway, gazing into the structure, my brown hair and the sun clashing against the white and grey mats in the middle. I stepped toward the only other figure in the room. He was lingering, staring at the opposite wall and rocking back and forth on his heels, no doubt questioning his own right or ability to be there.

Collin must have heard me because he froze completely with my third step.

"So..." I started a sentence I couldn't finish, not even sure if I was supposed to speak first.

I stood, staring at his dark blond hair, wondering what he must be thinking.

He turned, the anxiety in his eyes disappearing only moments after they met mine. My fear lifted like a fog, disappearing to show the blue calm of a cloudless sky—the same color as his eyes. His face seemed chiseled like the stone surrounding him, but softer somehow. The last part of his hair curled up slightly. His brow rose a little as a slight smile curved his lips. He sighed.

"You don't know what to say. Thank goodness I memorized my speech, or I wouldn't know what to say either."

I breathed out, and my lips smiled before I bit the bottom one. I wasn't expecting for him to be so normal, and yet he was—how did Eva say the trainers looked? —perfectly toned. Collin went to step toward me, hesitating for a second, and then took a few determined strides to reach me. I relaxed enough to let my hands move to my sides from behind my back. He reached out his hand to take mine, and I tried not to shudder from his touch: the first touch my hand had felt since they named me a Protector.

"My name is Collin, and I solemnly swear I will do anything and everything I can to prepare you, to help you protect those who you choose to save, and"— he paused his oath with a shuddered breath— "to help you survive any obstacle that may be in your way so you may return. The world will begin again for you and whoever you rescue. But for now, this is your world."

He awaited a response I feared I couldn't give. Instead of trying to think of an eloquent sentence, I told him the truth.

"I should say something just as beautiful, but I can't shake the thought that—that I'm not going to be able to do this, no matter how hard I try."

"I understand," he said, more sympathetic than I'd expected. His rough hand squeezed mine. "Can you try? Try to make this your world, and see if you can make a new one for someone else?"

"Yes," I said, focusing on his blue eyes again as his creased brow relaxed.

He squeezed again. "That's all I need. You want the tour?"

He released my hand, leaving me with a temporary confusion I pushed to the back of my mind. A part of me knew we had a schedule to keep and I remembered trainers were harsh. I was certain that this was to calm my nerves.

Each room in the Circle was how Patterson had described it. The rooms were shaped like an arc, built to be a seamless part of the Circle's wall so that the middle area remained open. Every door was glass—even the room with the bed, although there was a privacy screen that covered half. The Tech room was full of wires, several tables with open comms, and four computing units.

"Tech is not as complicated as it looks, most of the time. You don't have to rewire comms, boost signals on your mobile computing unit—or MCU—or show off like some other girls can. Your basic training will include recognizing which wires to disconnect should you need to use darkness as a cover, like cutting power to a building, for example. You will learn some basic maintenance for your MCU and how to communicate with us while you are in the Republic. We will focus on essentials, especially using commonplace tech in the Republic. Next."

We entered the next room, which was the physical training space. He placed his hand on the doorway and nodded for me to go into the room first. His tone hardened as we entered, sounding more urgent.

"This is for your lifting. There's a treadmill, though no one uses it much. I will not flinch on your running schedule. I will never budge. You will hate me, and I know it, but these girls can run ten miles in the woods in the morning and run another five later that day. I need you to get up to that level or you won't survive. You also need to work on upper-arm strength so you can climb and walk long distances while helping a Vessel or holding a baby. Most Unnecessaries are children with flaws that have been identified at five years old while in schools. You need to be able to carry them. If you don't train hard in this area, you risk their lives as well as your own."

The room felt colder than the air in the center of the Circle, with several soft blue lights on the equipment. They shifted every so often and faded. I must have let my confusion show, because Collin continued in a conversational tone.

"The lights change to represent different times of the day. We can also alter the temperature and humidity. I can even make it rain in here." He looked at his wrist unit, which I assumed was a small MCU. His voice sounded forced again. "Gotta keep moving. Next room."

The next room only had downloads, books, a monitor, and a couch. "This is the history and culture room, or as everyone calls it, HistCulture. The desk is a workspace for you to plot out scenarios and stories based on what you have learned, which will be a good deal of the homework you will receive. The couch doesn't come standard, just in case you go in another Protector's Circle and wonder why you got special treatment."

"I'll have to spend a lot of time catching up in here, won't I?"

"Yes," he said. "At the Academy, they watch one video lesson a week over an academic year, aside from survival camp months. So, they have watched 150 hours of footage you have not. Obviously, that's a lot to take in. It's my job to prioritize what you watch, read, and are tested on so you have what's most essential. You've still seen some videos from the Republic in school, so it's not like it's foreign to you. There are also listening tapes with language idiosyncrasies and different vocabulary they use. We call it Common Phrases. You must listen to one tape a day, at least, and then repeat it."

"I could always listen to those tapes while I do laps, right?"

"No! Remember the quadrants! That's what every instructor will tell you. Understand?"

I stood still. I remembered that after this tour, I might only see anger for the next six weeks. But I had hoped, however briefly, that maybe Eva and the other girls were wrong.

"Do you understand?" he asked again, not angry, but urgently.

"Yes."

"Good. You can't ignore that rule," he said, looking down at the floor instead of at me. He looked lost in thought, temporarily confused, but maybe I just imagined it. He set his jaw and looked up again. "Since all the other girls have had some time together, I asked if one of them could view the HistCulture videos with you. I have your reports to complete in the evenings, along with mission prep and my training."

He moved us into the last room. This room was white, sterile, and had two computing units (one an MCU) surgical tools poking out of a flap on an open backpack, and 3D models for fetus sizes inside a stomach.

"Medical. This is where you learn everything about pregnancy and birth we can teach you: what stage the mother could be in, any complications that could affect a mother's ability to make the journey, and how to use everything in the pack to deliver a baby. In this area... well, to be honest, I am hoping you will be at an advantage. You've seen three babies born, right?"

"Well, yes, but I got sick at the C-section with the twins."

His voice contained a controlled disappointment. "Okay then."

An alarm beeped on his watch. He hit a button, still looking at me as if waiting for the punchline.

"Is it time?" he asked, lifting the watch up from his wrist.

"Yep," a voice said, "We're all a little stressed, but still running on time despite all the crazy new decisions, including new Head Trainers, new Protectors, and... you know... you."

"Yeah, thanks for that," he said, turning away. "What's up, Sam? Simulcast still on?"

"Yeah, but you have to move rooms," Sam said. "I had to set up that Circle in twelve hours, all secret and silent after Eldridge banged on my door at midnight, dude. I'm not getting a return signal from the Med monitor. Is it on?"

"Yes." Collin sounded irritated as he moved toward it. It was on, but all that appeared were different colors of static.

"Well, I'll send it to the HistCulture room instead, since it's receiving a signal," Sam said. "And no worries. Let's all pretend none of us are messing anything up today, especially you. But *especially* me. And I need that paperwork. It's twenty pages, so drink coffee and get it done. Sam, out."

I was smiling at Sam's last comment, until I noticed that Collin was still staring at his wrist. I thought about my day so far. His day wasn't going much better. Since I couldn't tell him it would be okay (I had to remember to respect him, fear him, or hate him), I decided on a different approach.

"Thank you for explaining everything. And thank Sam for getting the room ready. It couldn't have been easy." I paused before saying, "It couldn't have been easy for... anyone who had to change everything last minute. I'm sorry."

"You don't have to apologize, 27," he said, though I saw his jaw twitch and relax. "But thank you, Aislyn."

He nodded, and we walked to HistCulture. I took a chance to keep the conversation going. "Is Sam Tech? Or is he... my Tech?" I asked, hoping he would understand.

"Sam is Tech, and yes, he is your Handler," he answered. "Any time you call into Central, it will go to Sam or Liam, his assistant, who makes sure Sam sleeps once in a while. You'll get to see them tomorrow."

By the time we entered the room, the monitor was on, displaying the Territory's flag with a timer in the corner counting down from five seconds until Patterson appeared on the screen. "Hello, Protectors, trainers, Council members, Hand, and support team members. Today, we announced the twenty-seven Protectors of the 188th Generation. Now, as many of you know, we expect many more trials this year, as well as the unique trials that come with a Jubilee year."

I shuddered as I remembered detailed stories and horrible news reports reviewed in school history classes. Jubilee Years had horrible new laws and standards from the Republic, especially for Protectors. The statistics Patterson reported in the first few minutes made me feel defeated. More Protectors had been killed. More Vessels hadn't made it home. More Unnecessaries were entrapping Protectors. More death.

Then, Patterson shifted, trying to share more of the success stories. He spoke for ten minutes, with a hundred images of children that had been saved in previous years. But I barely saw the images or heard the words. I felt numb with fear.

Until I saw Olivia in a picture.

She was in her school dress, standing next to her friend McKayla, an Unnecessary who was saved five years ago. He was mentioning the details of her escape, but I ignored him—though not because of fear this time. Because of Olivia. She played with McKayla almost every day, and loved her, even though she was bullied sometimes because of it.

I struggled to see past Olivia's face, but couldn't.

Olivia was already more of a hero than I was, because she had loved someone and would do anything to help her.

The next image was a Vessel holding her baby. And then, all I saw was Olivia, in every other face Patterson placed on a screen in the minutes that followed.

They were all sentenced to death for daring to be alive.

And something else replaced the fear. Anger burned it out.

I regretted ever being afraid of anything and scolded myself for my selfishness and uncertainty.

"You okay?" Collin asked. I saw him smile a little as I whispered my response.

"No. But I don't need to be okay. Not anymore."

Hours later, at the banquet, I was still thinking about my declaration—along with all my regrets.

I regretted not asking who had created the beautiful white dress I wore when I found it hung in my closet. I regretted only getting a wave from Megan instead of a hug as we lined up for the feast. I regretted not having the curiosity or courage to ask my mother if she ever foresaw this fate. I regretted not hearing Eldridge's speech because the twins swapping food under the table had mesmerized me.

But I didn't regret the kisses, or bouncing her on my knee, or hearing the words "don't be afraid" from Olivia, or twirling in my dress a few times. I didn't regret writing my name under the table in ink, wondering if it would be the last time I would ever write it.

From then on, I was 27. Even Collin was calling me that.

The beauty and regret met and danced around my head all night long.

The media stayed away from our table thanks to Patterson, who assured me I would have privacy. All the other Protectors sat at a large table, with thirteen on either side of Eldridge, who sat in the center with Patterson and Hannah beside him. So, most of the attention was diverted to more willing participants, like Tessa and Abby, who did several interviews and posed for pictures more than a dozen times. At one point, Collin walked over to the table and introduced himself. He asked my mother to pack a bag for me with some personal items and said Liam would pick it up in the morning.

Everyone ate the food, applauded the speeches, and left the tables for the festival. The Protectors began to return to their Circles. I choked out a breath thinking the goodbyes would start, then I noticed Eldridge walking closer to our table. He gestured for me to come over to him, which I did.

"You can have an extra few minutes, 27," he said with a smile. "I need to talk to Collin, apparently."

My eyes searched for Collin. When I found him, I could tell something was wrong. His expression was tense as he argued with a very expressive Avery. Hannah interjected, then stopped to glare at Eldridge and me. She didn't need to say a word for me to know that she blamed me for all the words being spoken. Collin's tone sounded defensive, but I couldn't make out any words.

"I'm not supposed to ask what's going on, am I?"

"Well, my dear," Eldridge sighed, "I suppose asking is okay, but expecting an answer would be less likely."

"I thought you wanted me to be curious," I said sarcastically.

"And so I do," Eldridge smiled. "To that end, I have one gift that will make up for tonight's forbidden question and for a year away from your underestimated, beautiful, ordinary life—which was apparently more interesting than my speech."

I swallowed, feeling a little more nervous. "What is that?"

"An answer. An answer to many other questions. To feed your curiosity whenever you may find yourself either bored or in need of life-altering wisdom."

Even as I heard his words, I was still a little unsure of what he was offering.

"So, when I have a question, I can just come to you?"

He laughed, which he stifled as he spoke. "My dear, I am slightly important, I'm told. I'm technically running a country and an undercover operation to steal hundreds of lives from their oppressors. But being in charge also gives one some clout to do things like choosing a 27th Protector and talk to them whenever I want. So yes, I'd pause all of it to answer one question. Your brothers inspired me, I guess, to do as much as I can and get away with it. Maybe they were more inspiring than my speech after all."

With a solemn look that then turned into a playful wink, he left the now-empty room.

Collin and Avery must have taken their argument elsewhere.

I didn't know what to say as I came back to the table. Would there be a teary goodbye, a lot of runny noses, questions I couldn't answer? But there were just giggles to a joke I missed, and a smile from my mother when I told her I had twenty more minutes. Dad resolved my silent debate with a question.

"What if you weren't afraid? What if it was just another twenty minutes?" he asked, but my mother's face looked weary and scared now. The three of us knew that this still might be the last twenty minutes with them I'd ever have.

"But you're not afraid, are you?" Richard said, looking at me like he had all night, as if I were a hero from one of his comic books. He was then hit with another grape Dylan threw from under the table.

"Yes, but someone who is very wise once told me that I should take the next step, even if I'm scared."

My father's lip quivered, but he bit it.

Richard shrugged. "That sounds like a Dad sentence. I thought you said it was someone wise."

Olivia spit out her water she was drinking. I laughed so hard that I missed a few moments of Dad chasing them, tackling and tickling as he ran around the table. I asked Olivia to repeat her lists of jokes from school. We played our game; I sat under the table and Olivia knocked rhythmically on the tabletop instead of my bedroom door. I played hide and seek in a dress made of the white silk, which I dirtied by climbing under the hundreds of tables in the room. More beauty and regret crashed into each other until all I could hear was the echo of laughter that hid the silent tears.

And before I knew it, I was in front of my Circle again.

With every step toward the back of the room, there was an empty echo through the ceilings out into the stars. I could hear the laughter, screams, and excitement from the carnival.

I wasn't going.

I wasn't getting another notebook.

I wouldn't write tomorrow.

I wouldn't be watering my daisy.

I wouldn't be packing up for the spring semester.

I wouldn't taste wood as I chewed my pencil.

"Get some sleep, 27."

While Collin was the only other one allowed in the Circle, his voice still startled me.

I swallowed. "I can't."

"I figured. I have something that might help." His eyes softened as he pulled out a strange, worn book with ink on the edge of the pages. "After the first seventy years of the Protectors' missions, they put together a book of advice. Everyone gets a digital copy, of the Protector's journal on their MCU, but there's one copy—just one—that's still paper and ink."

My fingers grazed the worn leather book—though not very worn for something a hundred years old. I opened it up, and there were words: handwritten, some meticulous, some messy and yet all perfect. I flipped through ivory pages until I got to the first. There was a note written in the margin with a pencil, fading but still readable. I stared in disbelief and noted the signature.

"The first 27th Protector, and the second, and..."

"This journal," he said without moving, "was passed on to every 27th Protector. And it is the only one allowed to be altered, added to, or written in. The rest are all digitized now. Only those named as 27th have ever looked inside. It is your link to them and a part of your legacy now."

He walked away, saying nothing more. I changed out of my outfit into what I was guessing were my night clothes. They were smooth linen and felt amazing on my skin. It was white. As I looked through my whole wardrobe, I noticed all of it was white. No more grey; no more in-between.

I sat on the bed and opened the journal. My head was full of random thoughts—some accusing, some full of fear, some making excuses. I read the words scribbled an age ago by someone like me, chosen instead of resolute. I read the note in the margins again.

You are asked so many times in life to help. Voices whispered or screamed or silent: "Will you help me?" You say, "I would love to," and you move on, leaving an awkward silence. Hope deferred. Today, someone asked me for help. It was more complicated, but not really.

Someone named me the 27th Protector. They asked me to help. And I found myself responding with the words I usually say. "I would love to." There was a reason not to, so I would usually say that. But in the silence, I spoke three more words that changed everything. "I would love to. So, I will."

Those last three words echoed through my exhausted mind. I closed the book and lay down, eager for the bliss of sleep. But those three words escaped from my lips to fill the horrible void she talked about, fighting all my worst fears with hope.
They asked me to help.
I would love to.
"So, I will."

CHAPTER 7

Two days had passed since I had been renamed a number. I'd promised that I would try to save a life. But I didn't know if I could, because my chance to do that was being judged by how effectively I could reach a stupid piece of red tape on the floor.

My knee shook in front of me, crushing under the weight of a one-hundred-pound barbell balancing on my shoulders. If I had enough strength, I'd throw the weight off. Or onto someone. I would have loved to throw the barbell at the person who had been screaming at me for the past two days.

"Move!" Collin yelled, his eyes looking tortured instead of the calm blue I had first seen. He kept repeating it, echoing off the walls in the room, stifling from the high humidity being simulated from the steam walls. I was afraid he would make it rain again.

I felt a burning inside me, motivating me to move forward. But the blaze that propelled me fought against the burning in my muscles, like fire fighting fire. My leg could not pull up from behind me fast enough to do another lunge. The mist forced me to take shorter breaths. I felt as if I was drowning on land, unable to breathe the air.

"You need to go faster!" he shouted again. "It needs to be a fluid motion. If you stop, it only makes it harder!"

My thighs burned, but I used any strength I had in reserve to push up and make another lunge, then another. I stopped again, as the weight felt unbearable, and my knee hit the mat in front of me. The piece of tape was still four feet away, mocking me.

"You are not just doing an exercise." He dropped his face down into his hands. "Remember why."

The barbell on my shoulder burned as if the metal was hot because my anger surged. I knew why I was practicing this. It was because the girl behind a dumpster in the Republic right now or the boy cowering in the sewer might not be able to run or walk at a good pace. They could be a lab defect, a botched job because someone thought they could do better than God at splicing DNA together. That child needed to cling to my back while I ran, or a drone would end both our lives. They would be five years old.

So, I thought of the girl grasping, crying, scared, and lost without me. Collin still had his head turned to the side, revolted by my lack of effort. I wish I could've done the same.

Any trust between us had evaporated in just two days of training. But I tried to hear the girl as if she were real and her voice would burn in my ears and give me the strength I needed. I pushed ahead one more step, but my ankle almost twisted.

"I can't do it!" I meant to scream but almost choked. Collin surprised me by crossing the room in seconds and removing the weight. The pressure and pain evaporated the instant he pulled the weight off seemingly without effort, but an equal amount of shame came crashing down on me.

"One step," Collin sighed. "It wasn't enough. Push yourself more than that for me."

"For the record, I didn't do it for you," I said, infuriated at both Collin and my lack of progress.

"For the record—" he said, then stopped himself. "That's a good thing. You remembered why. Pulse."

I held out my wrist, and he placed his two fingers on the edge and pushed down. I tried to breathe deeply to slow my pulse. He had criticized it too many times, as if my heartbeat had a flaw like everything else about me. Yesterday, he had said a few encouraging things, but shook his head as if he had just made a mistake. All his other words cut deep at any confidence I'd built, but when I would cry or scream, he acted like he would regret it. Briefly. It was like riding a wave; either lifting or crashing.

He spoke, calmer than I expected. "You need to keep up the momentum, so all the weight is moving forward with you, not pulling you down. Train your mind with a simple thought: you stop, and you die."

"So don't stop?" I asked, still out of breath.

"And don't die," a voice called from the archway. I was still looking at Collin, whose irritation was instant. There was a small twitch in his jaw as he turned toward the voice.

"Eva, you aren't supposed to come in here," Collin yelled.

"Doctor's orders. It's his class." She smiled and saluted. "And technically, I'm not 'in' her Training Circle yet."

Collin moved his watch up to his mouth and spoke into it. "Record, file four, physical training. First attempt: six feet, pulse at a hundred after two minutes." He then looked at me, as if calculating my chances of survival. "You're due for your first lesson in Medical, and they've assigned you a travel guide again."

"Yeah, all these exotic places around here can get confusing," Eva said smiling.

"Well, you don't want to be late," Collin said as I grabbed my bag. He paused, changing his tone. "And you're going to do great. I'm sure you will. Focus on what you know, which might be more than the other girls in the room for once." He finished with an encouraging smile as if we could have been friends for years.

"Thank you, I... It means a lot that—"

"Go," he interrupted, the coldness back in his voice, glancing at Eva. "Before you're late. Now!"

"Got it," I said, moving as fast as my sore legs would carry me. They felt like jelly and my knee buckled and then popped a little.

"Ah, lunges," Eva sighed overdramatically. "So, how many times did you make it to the line before wanting to cry?"

"How many times? I didn't even get to the red tape!" I said, then felt my leg buckle again. "How many did you?"

"Oh, I'm sorry," Eva said. "You didn't... you only did one, or half... that's good! Halfway is good, more than halfway, so..."

"Eva," I stopped walking to face her. "How many times?"

She answered, hesitantly, "Almost three, but I stopped short of three. I couldn't feel my ankles anymore. I'm so sorry."

I closed my eyes, and my head fell. She patted me on the back, almost mechanically. We walked through the garden, opening the door to Central.

"You can't keep doing this to yourself, you know," Eva said, taking the stairs down two at a time. "I mean sure, you're hilariously underqualified, but physical training has lots of different aspects. As long as you can run, you'll be okay. You will do a lot of running—from suspicious people, down sewers, trying to find lost kids, and my favorite, away from Sentries who can potentially kill you."

"That's supposed to make me feel better?"

She looked indignant. "Yes! Look, right now, we're in nice, safe training rooms with LED lights and misters. Our trainers are yelling at us, but there's no imminent danger against us or an innocent child. Some people can't find the motivation here. Trust me. You'll run faster when there's a drone, or when the person chasing you has a real gun instead of an MCU and a bad temper."

I wondered if it would be different if there were a child in my arms, depending on me. Would it be better if the flurry of insults from Tessa didn't distract me? I tried to keep my knees under my burning legs as I walked through the second floor of Central.

We began our way around the circular walkway hovering over the workstations. We could see through the grated metal floors and over the railing as we curved around the chasm of Central Command. The five large CUs in the shape of a star lit up with activity. All five of the techs and assistants stood at their stations, likely responding to the flurry of alarms earlier that morning.

Patterson explained that with no Protectors in the field, more Unnecessaries and Vessels were captured than normal. A Vessel had been caught and executed trying to escape this morning on 44th Street. If that wasn't enough to make everyone tense, the Society Party had made another propaganda piece to celebrate Jubilee Day. Collin told me that Central had been targeted three times in the last fifty years, which civilians were kept unaware of, resulting in several deaths and injuries of staff members.

The reports of drones in Zone 2 had everyone on edge. Except for Eva. Her casual nature almost irritated me as she yelled down to the Hand.

"Hey Sam, you working on your hack still?"

Sam looked up, scrunching his blond hair as he worked. "Yes, 26," he yelled back, "thank you for shouting confidential information, that's very helpful." His tone was serious, but he smiled. "It's going about as well as you'd think. I'm two cycles into an algorithm and just hit a wall. Where are you off to?"

The other techs seemed cold and impersonal compared to Sam, who was witty and friendly. When no one was listening, he had told me, "All the people who say you won't live more than two weeks all have a lower clearance level than me. You're going to be fine, 27. Wait and see." It almost made up for him overwhelming me with every function and fact about my MCU.

"It's confidential," Eva yelled back teasingly.

"Oh, well have fun in Medical then," he said, and Eva cursed under her breath. Sam added, "How are you doing, 27?"

"Can't complain," I said, which was true. I didn't think I could.

"Well, have fun bringing life into the world; sounds gross."

Another voice called out, "Shut it, Sam, I'm trying to work!"

"Oh, I'm sorry," he shot back, "you were promised that you would work in a silent and stress-free environment. Oh, wait, no you weren't!"

We veered off another hallway as they continued to argue. The hallways strung out from the Central Hub like a web. We passed several people, including Liam, Sam's assistant, who waved as we passed.

Room 271 is Medical. I tried to burn that into my memory. Eva couldn't be my tour guide forever.

Like all the other classrooms, the long rows of chairs faced the front, each with stands for our Mobile Computing Units to the left of the seat. Eva placed her MCU on one, then slid into her chair and scrunched up, so her legs were under her. Eva was hyper-studious in classes, against her usual playful nature.

I followed suit and placed my MCU on the small stand. I pretended to be busy watching the lesson download, but in reality, I was looking around the room. Megan was talking to Tessa, Chloe, and Lydia. Brie was staring at her laptop and reading notes—though, considering her competence, I couldn't imagine why. She would talk to Ivy once in a while. Most of the conversations were random, but a lot of them centered on morning workouts, how horrible breakfast was, and how frustrating lessons had been yesterday, at which point there were some annoyed glances at me.

Tech had been the worst. Someone asked me to cut a wire on an apparatus, but I chose scissors instead of the isolated wire clippers. Everyone sat through a huge lecture on safety and tool identification. Every other Protector already knew this stuff, so instead of listening to the instructor, they glared at me. I should have been paying more attention, but I couldn't listen to him over the shame of their disapproving stares.

An opening door interrupted my thoughts about the previous day. A man entered through the side door and swiftly crossed to the front of the room. I realized that I recognized him. He was the doctor who had been assigned to my mother and the twins.

"Well, as I have met everyone in the room, we can avoid long introductions. But in case you all have dizzy heads from morning exercises, I'm Dr. Swanson. We will start our lessons every day for the next three weeks with Brie and Tessa sharing some case studies with us. This is not a science class and it is not medical school. You need not memorize the names of every artery and body part. As you know, most of your education will focus on the basics of coaching women through childbirth, midwifery skills, and emergency procedures. A story would be better than you memorizing terms in a book. That being said, Brie, you're up."

Brie moved swiftly. She looked dead ahead, avoiding anyone's gaze. Her blue eyes were not harsh but calculating. She looked less confident than normal as she spoke.

"My first two missions were Unnecessaries, so I was on run three when I was trying to get my first Vessel out. She was twenty-five weeks along, and the baby looked great. I did a quick ultrasound to confirm pregnancy. She seemed genuine. That's all I needed, but I was still cautious."

I couldn't imagine Brie as a beginner, unsure of herself in any way. Seeing her be nervous while speaking to us was weird enough. I made another note about the ultrasound check. The day before, we had all been warned about "false pregnancy traps." Sentries would entrap Protectors using a decoy Vessel. The woman would lead a Protector somewhere "safe," like their house, and the Sentries would kill the Protector. As much as the handheld ultrasound was to check on the health of the baby and the mother, it ensured our safety.

Sam told me we would train daily to detect the signs that someone was lying, including elevated pulse, sweat, dilated pupils, and intuition. It was the only test I wasn't worried about. Having twin brothers would make me an expert.

Brie continued. "While my Vessel cleared the test, I was not very thorough. We got out through Sector 8 and made our way to a safe spot in Zone 3. I wanted to check the baby again. The baby's pulse had dropped a little, enough to worry me. I did a more thorough exam, discovered the issue." Brie paused and looked at Dr. Swanson. He shook his head. She continued. "I called for an EE as soon as we got to Zone 2. Until then, the mother just took frequent breaks lying on her back. The official ultrasound confirmed what I had suspected. Anyway, about seventeen weeks later, a beautiful baby was born. She named him after my father, Lionel."

Her eyes drifted before she went back to looking as firm as usual. She glided back to her seat. Dr. Swanson took her place seconds later.

"I asked Brie to leave out one detail so I could ask you a question: what complication could the Vessel have encountered?"

No one answered at first, but a few hands jumped up, including, to my surprise, my own. Eva and Lynn stared at me, both of whom had been rapidly taking notes until that point. Cassidy was still trying to search on her MCU—unsuccessfully, based on her animated hand gestures.

"13?" Dr. Swanson said.

"One possibility is Placenta Previa, but you would need to confirm that, or you might miss preeclampsia or a wrapped umbilical cord. However, because it only happened after long stints of walking, I would check for Placenta Previa."

Lydia, in the last twenty-four hours, had again demonstrated why the others had nicknamed her "Doctor." The fact that she knew the answer didn't shock me. The only thing that shocked me was that I had the same answer.

"All right, if anyone had their hand up who was going to say Placenta Previa would now raise them again," Dr. Swanson gestured, and my hand went up again without thinking.

Seeing this, Lynn mouthed, "What are you doing?"

"27?" Dr. Swanson called out. "Explain Placenta Previa and its complications."

Lynn and I were still looking at each other when he called my name. She looked shocked, and her eyes widened as she turned to the front so quickly her curls bounced comically. As I looked forward, almost everyone, except Brie, was turned around to see me.

"Yes," I answered, my voice dripping with uncertainty. "Um... the placenta forms not on the side of the"—I wanted to say belly, but remembered the term—"uterine wall, but on the bottom of the uterus. That means that the baby, when reaching a certain weight and mass, presses on the placenta, which is its source of nutrients and air. This causes the baby to suffer from oxygen deprivation and a slow heart rate. In some cases, it can lead to miscarriage or developmental problems. The mother should rest on her back for at least an hour to alleviate the pressure and ensure the baby has unlimited nutrients and oxygen. This would make walking long distances over rough terrain impossible." I took a breath, feeling a little brave for adding the last part. "And this situation would always necessitate an EE out of Zone 1 or 2."

The words felt jumbled coming out of my mouth, like I had gotten them in order only seconds before I spoke them. It surprised me when Swanson said, "Perfect answer! Now, would everyone else please stop staring at 27 and look up at the revised file 54C on the screen?"

Despite his order, almost everyone still looked at me.

"This will inform you how many hours of rest your Vessel needs based on their gestational week. Your Ultrasound App File 10 will set alarms to remind you to stop if you put in the parameters, and... for heaven's sake, can I have your attention?"

I looked up from my MCU to see that there were seven people still gazing at me, including Tessa, who tried to adjust as the doctor scolded the class.

"Okay, well, we might as well clear this up. Aislyn's brothers, Dylan and Richard, both had issues with Previa, and I had to put Mrs. Williams on bed rest. Nothing so complicated. Aislyn's seen more babies be born than any of you, as her mother helped the midwife in that region. Can someone summarize 54C please?"

Sarah explained that Previa always required a C-section. Eva whispered something toward me, but our instructor interrupted.

"26, do you have something to add?"

Eva smirked at me and then composed herself to ask in a serious tone, "I was asking 27 how early her brothers were born, as most Previa cases are not only C-sections but also premature."

Whether the doctor knew that Eva had lied or not, he moved on. "Yes, actually, thank you, and we need to consider the complications of an early birth as well."

The rest of Med wasn't that difficult, but strangely familiar. Leaving more confidently than I had entered, Lynn noticed and asked, "So maybe Medical is your hidden talent?"

This was the game. With every class, people stared, asked, and poked, all trying to discover what Eldridge had seen in me.

"No, and that'll be clear when I puke at the sight of blood," I said, staring straight ahead, trying not to think of blood at all. "The beauty of life is really gross. That fact isn't lost on me."

"Really?" Eva said.

"C-section. Just C-section." I was talking to her as she was walking backward again. "Swanson was right. My mom gets called to every neighbor's house when they're in labor. She's kind of seen as the expert, so she helps the midwife. I tagged along. I could handle the normal blood from birth, all the expected things, and the placenta at the end... But cutting someone open? When Dylan and Richard were born, it was different. I barely watched the beginning of the procedure, and then I couldn't watch at all."

"Because your head was in a toilet?" Eva asked.

"I didn't make it to the toilet." I swung my bag over my shoulder.

"Oh... that's unfortunate," Lynn said. "Where to next?"

They had changed the agenda, moving HistCulture outside to the garden, according to the memo on my MCU. I was looking forward to breathing in some fresh air and being in the sun. I almost smiled as I saw the garden, until I saw who was standing in it. I grimaced, wondering if Collin wanted to insult me one more time this morning. But his eyes weren't harsh. He was looking at a flowering bush around a rock in the memorial garden, his eyes soft and lost in thought.

I heard Eva whisper, "Aislyn, I don't think you're joining us."

"Why?"

I looked at her, then turned back to Collin. His hardened features had already returned.

"You aren't going to HistCulture," he said.

"What? Why not?" I sounded angrier than I felt. I had finally survived a class with at least a little of my pride intact.

He sighed and pushed his hand through his hair as he spoke. "Look, I talked to the instructors after you left for Medical. They said you need to catch up first or you'll be lost in today's lesson."

"I wasn't lost in Medical! You're only afraid I'll mess up and make you look bad and—"

"I knew you'd do great in Med the first class! That's not the problem," he said and looked to his right. "Eva, I think you need to leave."

"Hey," she said, "I was going to tell her you're right, and it's not about her skill or—"

"26, I need you to leave. Now."

"Yes, sir. Leaving." She grabbed her bag and jogged toward the garden.

I turned back to Collin, his eyes straining to understand me.

"Why can't you just listen? No other Protector would even think about doing what you just did. I gave you an order, and you undermined my authority in front of another Protector."

I wanted to yell in response, except it felt like he was the one in pain instead of the one inflicting pain on me.

"I guess I'm not like the other Protectors," I said, but realized that wasn't going to help if he was embarrassed. I almost didn't want to say it, but I started anyway. "I'm sorr—"

"Seven laps," he interrupted. For a second, it looked like he didn't expect me to apologize. But he clenched his jaw, staring at the brick ground instead of me. "No. You're not like the other Protectors. And that's the problem. Seven laps, around Central. That's about four miles, so get going."

My legs shivered as if in fear of not being able to finish, but I locked my knees and moved quickly. I dropped my bag, turned my MCU to monitoring mode, and placed my MCU onto my back pocket, all while trying to stare at him defiantly.

His icy gaze stayed on me as he ordered, "Go. Now."

I ran. My only relief was that at least I'd be running away from him. But I was also running away from the tall flowers blooming in full, beckoning me to come, look, and be still again. Eva's eyes seemed to say, "*Sorry, I just made it worse,*" as I passed her.

Megan nodded, and said, only loud enough, "Don't worry, you did great in Med. Just run and done."

Tessa spoke to Ivy and said, "At least he's trying to whip her into shape."

Brie was the last person I ran past. She repeated Megan. "Run and done, 27. Get it done."

The girls often used that phrase, and it gave me the littlest hope. But my fury kept me moving, especially after seeing Collin as I finished the first lap. But about halfway through the second lap, my legs felt like lead. I regretted embarrassing him, but resented having to run seven laps just because his pride got hurt. I had both the desire to challenge him and to trust him, but the latter was fading more every hour.

I was on lap three, still arguing with myself and him in my head, when I slowed down. And as I slowed, the rhythm began—the rhythm that had started when I knew I wouldn't see home for a year. It grew louder as I remembered I may never see home again.

I'd never run around the house playing hide and seek again.

I'd never hear giggling behind a tree again.

I'd never run just to tag them again.

I'd never run to chase butterflies.

I'd never run with them to see if the moon followed us.

My throat tightened. My lungs screamed as they missed a breath they needed, and there was a burning in the back of my mouth that I hoped was only anguish rising.

I slowed down and turned toward Collin, who hadn't seen me yet. But instead of seeing his hard glare, I saw his head in his hands as he ran his fingers through his hair, pulling and grasping, like he was more sad than angry. Maybe he was plagued with the same anguish I was, wondering if there would ever be a time when I wouldn't fail at this.

CHAPTER 8

I was on my fifth lap when he stopped me. I must have been panting, even as I stood still. He looked up and took a deep breath as he moved toward me.

"You're done for now. Don't do that again, 27," he said. "Please, don't do it again." His tone was softer, as if he meant it.

I knew I had no other choice but to be the good soldier and force myself to say, "I won't."

He studied me, then said, "Okay. Pulse."

I reached out my hand and he placed his fingers on my wrist again. I was so furious—livid, even—but the person I was angry at disappeared again, leaving a nineteen-year-old boy who wanted to hear about Medical, who laughed about what Tessa's reaction must have been when I knew the answers.

"She taps on things when she's jealous, so I think you got her!" he said, smiling, then paused. His tone shifted again. "Look, I shouldn't have to give you an explanation every time I give you an order, but I should've given you one this time. I don't think it's a good idea for you to go with the others to HistCulture. They told me this morning that they weren't reviewing anything they learned at the Academy. They're jumping into new policies, and they want to focus on the recent issues of entrapment."

"Yeah, I've heard," I said and tried to hide my nervous reaction, but it was as fast as a reflex.

"They left it up to me. I'm asking for your trust." He pulled his fingers back, grazing my wrist as he said, "Not bad, but we will walk the next three laps, maybe add a few."

I noticed his hand stretched out to his fingers, as if a spasm went through it before touching his watch.

"But that'll take—" I stopped short of saying it, seeing his face. "Sorry."

"This part isn't a punishment. We're going to break the compartment rule for a bit and mix some physical training with your first HistCulture test. Before I can teach you anything, I need to know what you understand about the Republic. Shall we?"

I started to walk, although his pace seemed a bit fast for talking.

"So, what do you know about our enemy?"

"That question couldn't be vaguer," I said, and he laughed with me, which felt strange. But I caught the trick question he had asked. "However, the motto I remember hearing growing up was that the Republic is not the enemy, the Society Party is."

"Good. We can skip some chapters on that. Why does the Society reject us and think of us as expendable?"

"I remember reading about it in ninth year. They view the value of human life only in terms of 'freedom.' If someone isn't free to experience everything, they aren't fully human. Any genetic imperfection or moral belief can restrain the human experience—creatively, intellectually, or sexually. The body and the mind shouldn't be restrained from achieving happiness and fulfillment. So, it's mercy to kill someone who doesn't agree with them."

"Yes," Collin said. "In simpler terms, there's an analogy they like to use for Unnecessaries. They refer to them, and even us, as moths and prefer to see themselves as butterflies. The moth makes the butterflies' lives less attractive, less appealing. They feel the pursuit of spirituality or any deeper human connection is the only proof that we are deficient because we need to pursue such ridiculous ideas to make our pitiful lives worth living. That's why when a 'moth' is born, discarding it is the humane response. That way, everyone is happy and comfortable. No one questions their happiness and comfort, so the public elects the people that promise them more happiness and comfort. It's a cycle."

I had a thought and a question, but didn't want to be embarrassed by the sometimes-cliché remark we all had in history class. As I looked at Collin, his calm was back, his brow was smooth, and he looked as if he wanted me to ask a question.

"So, my teacher once ranted on and on about the Roman Empire. I bet they don't at the Academy—"

His laugh interrupted me. "Oh, I grew up on rants, Aislyn. But yes, we've all heard the whole 'bread and circuses' Roman Empire concept. And yes, the Society stole their strategy. Comfort sells votes."

"But why attack Vessels?"

"The same reason they attack over-emotive children. You can't feel attached to someone and still be duped by the lie that perfection matters more than souls. If you really love someone, you will fight for them. They only want people fighting for themselves. This way, the Society can be who they love most because it promises them personal success and comfort. The Society found the perfect 'bread and circuses.' A life lived in comfort was the new 'bread' and casual sex was the new 'circus.' Turns out a relaxed, happy person can easily ignore blatant death. *Brave New World* and all that."

"What's that?"

"Oh," he said, looking surprised, "it's a reference to a book called *Brave New World*. It doesn't exist anymore, but we have some records of its summary. I've read it several times."

"Let me guess? It was burned on the second Jubilee Day?" I asked.

He nodded. "Yes. And as much as I hate what they stole from the Roman playbook, I hate the stuff they stole from the Nazi playbook more."

"So, the book summaries. What are they?"

"Small digital files—the memories and synopses of all the books that have been burned. I spent my time growing up reading through them. I loved them, and as a trainer, I had unlimited access. It drove my instructors crazy how many I would ask for. There's one... it reminds me of you being overwhelmed."

I almost missed a step, confused by his words. "How?"

He smiled, looking hesitant now. "The main character had a name like yours. She fell down a rabbit hole to a new world. And then she goes to this tea party and meets this mean queen that would remind you of Tessa. And a crazy guy in a hat that would remind you of Sam. And she can't get out of the place..."

He trailed off. I looked curious, almost smiling at the wonder that had made him seem so childlike.

Collin smiled. "I'm sorry. My mind's been on other things so much... I forgot the name of the place she landed," he said as his smile faded. "Besides, we shouldn't be wasting our time talking about it. Pulse."

We had finished far away from the garden, in the forest training area. I gazed at the wild trees and the fifty-five-foot-tall climbing wall I would have to tackle soon. I felt out of breath from just looking at it. He still had my wrist, grazing it with his fingers when he spoke again.

"I know it seems I can be too hard or even angry, but there's a reason."

"Other than you being my trainer?"

"Yes," he whispered. "And I should tell you." He paused, looking conflicted. He opened his mouth to continue.

He would never get to.

Even if he had spoken, I would have never heard it.

A blaring alarm filled the air, echoing off the stone, screeching from every direction. I covered my ears, staring up at the speaker a few yards away. The tone of the alarm was unmistakable.

"Is that a drone drill?" I screamed.

The alarm then changed to deep tones that only sounded every three seconds.

"No! The drill wasn't until next week," he yelled, as if he were trying to talk himself out of the terror building.

I couldn't talk myself out of my panic because of Collin's words yesterday.

"You are the only target the Republic can justify because you invade their land. They can only kill you. And they will take every chance to kill you."

A voice shot from Collin's watch.

The alarm paused and then began again, every three seconds.

"Aislyn?" Collin said so quickly I barely recognized my own name.

I wasn't looking at him. My eyes were fixed on a flare of light that streamed across the sky miles away.

A voice I didn't recognize shouted from his watch.

"Missile launched!"

The explosion echoed. He cried out my name again and pulled me down. The ground shook, enough to make me reach out for his shoulder.

Collin's comm screeched and Liam's voice shouted, "Drone in Zone 2. Looked like a flyover, but the target was lit, and they hit it. If they get you on infrared and target— Where are you?"

Sirens sounded through the valley from far away.

I imagined my mom, rushing the twins and my sister downstairs for another drill.

But the drone wasn't coming for them. Only me.

Collin squeezed my hand and screamed into my ear. "Follow me. I know the fastest way. Do you understand?"

"Yes," I said, my body shaking my voice. "Don't stop."

He looked back at me, as challenge. "And don't die."

He pulled away and ran, and so did I. My arms pumped, but already ached. My feet hit the ground hard, despite me wanting to go faster. The sirens rang out in a specific rhythm, meant to communicate the location of the drone to other stations.

Within a few seconds, Collin yelled into his watch, "I need something closer than Central. We're by the woods, near the wall."

This time, Sam answered, "You should have enough time to get back here. You can't use second. It's only Tech allowed."

"They have thermal imaging on," Liam added, a little more panicked. "It's confirmed. They still might not get that close, but if—" There was a pause. He never finished the sentence. He just begged, "Just run."

By the time I got to the garden, I had fallen twice. The terror hit my chest every time I hit the ground, but I tried to use it, hoping it would make my legs move faster. As long as my feet kept moving, we would live. That was the truth or lie I told myself to keep me running and not pinned to the ground.

Collin could run faster, but he kept pace with me. We were almost to the door when I saw Patterson open it. I fell again, cursing as I hit stones that cut through my skin. This time, a different siren rang out, in a faster rhythm. The drone was in range. The panic held me down, widening my eyes, trying to remember the stones I would see if I died the next moment.

But then, Collin's hand came in view. I grasped it. He pulled me up and dragged me forward to the door. My lungs were burning, I wasn't getting enough oxygen to register what Patterson yelled as we passed him.

On the first stair, my legs fell beneath me. In one movement, Collin threw my arm around his shoulder, lifted me up, and swung my legs under his other arm.

"Clear!" Patterson yelled. "Close the doors!"

I heard the first clang and Collin whispered, "It's okay."

I looked up to see five steel doors slowly close over the stairs, one after another. Collin pulled me in closer with each loud clang, even though each door would have meant we were safer.

"Why are they in our airspace?" Collin shouted in shuddered breaths.

"I don't know," Patterson answered. "They know we train around this time of year. We do our intel, they do theirs. Some trees fell under that ice storm, many near the T20 substation. They saw it during a flyover and took their shot. It's in flames."

"T is food and supply, right?" I asked, and Patterson nodded.

The second siren ended just as Patterson was about to speak. They were out of our air space, but another alarm was still going off.

"A T-station isn't as much of a liability. But still, this is the closest they have ever gotten to Central in a while," Patterson said. "We need to track them."

Collin carried me down the stairs. My embarrassment overcame the pain in my legs as we approached the Central Hub entrance.

"Collin, I got it. Put me down."

"Not yet, Aislyn. Not yet," he said, his words dripping with worry. Maybe he had guessed I didn't want him to carry me into Central, but his grip felt firmer. And his worry confused me.

Patterson reached for the door handle at the bottom of the stairs.

"Take a minute," he said. "And 27, a two-thirty time for half the yard? Some girls might even be impressed. Keep it up."

He shut the door behind him, leaving me panting in Collin's arms. I felt my legs again, still resting on Collin's bicep. It felt strange being so close to him, yet not uncomfortable.

"You okay?" His jaw shook before he clenched it shut.

"Yeah," I blurted out. He was blinking away the sweat. He looked up the stairs, where the security lights still blinked in patterns. I found it hard to breathe even as I gasped for air.

He whispered, "Maybe one day, it won't bother you that you may die. I'm supposed to be training you to think that. But know that it will always terrify me. Always."

The shock of his words stifled my already struggled breaths. He set me down on the platform, and I slid my arm off his shoulder.

"Jog in place, so you don't pass out."

"Why would I pass out?"

He sighed as if I should know. "You just sprinted. This is why we have cool-down laps. Your heart is still pumping blood to your legs. While you were running, the legs pumped it back. The heart hasn't caught on yet. It's sending the blood down, but unless you're moving, nothing's pushing it back up. You'll pass out because your body doesn't know what it needs to do."

As I jogged in place, I couldn't help but think of his explanation. Maybe that was why I felt like I would pass out emotionally all day. I wondered if my body would ever catch up to my heart enough to do what I needed to do.

CHAPTER 9

Every other Protector was huddled under the second-floor mezzanine, looking down into the center of the Hand. The panicked shouts continued, leaving me to conclude that the drone was still in our airspace. I supposed that Cassidy and Eva had been recruited to help with satellite surveillance, because they were at CU stations on the main floor. Collin went with a few other trainers, but almost instantly, I could sense it was combative.

Before she was out of earshot, I overheard Emily say, "You were supposed to be in your Circle. You risked everything for this stupid ideology and you keep breaking the..."

I didn't know what to make of her accusation and decided that there was a more viable threat to worry about. I felt nervous and bold at the same time. I didn't join the other Protectors and instead walked to Eva on the CU. I watched her work silently. Then, she stopped typing, not even turning around to talk to me.

"Hey, 27. Way to skip HistCulture and almost die. Classy."

"Yeah," I said, matching her nonchalant tone. "It was so much fun. You should try it sometime. Did the drone... ?"

"Leave yet? Yes. Did it mean to fly in our airspace? In my opinion, no, which I'm writing up in this report that will most likely be ignored. It did mean to blow that station, though. It locked on pretty early and was able to hack the order that was confirmed by the Sentry who authorized it. But once it scanned and didn't find any power source, they could tell they hadn't hit the intel jackpot they were hoping for. Did you actually run half the yard in two minutes and thirty seconds?"

"Apparently. What do you think they wanted to hit?"

"Probably a Q-station that has the works—basement, intel, functioning command area, and a whole Med outfit. Home away from home, full bath and two bedrooms. R-stations are only communication and camo tents. And two-thirty? Dang! See, I told you all you needed was some mortal danger for motivation."

I caught sight of Eldridge, who came over to Eva's station, nodding to me first, but then focusing on Eva.

"All clear? Joel says we are, but he wants your opinion."

"That's more respect than I deserve, but yes," Eva sighed. "In fact, it looks like the last command code is to return to base."

Eldridge looked at me expectedly. "You survived."

I sighed. "Barely. I didn't expect that to be my first encounter with the enemy."

"That's not the enemy," Eldridge said, staring at one of the display screens. "No, that was a bully. A bully tells you that you're worthless, but in your heart, you know better. The real enemy is attacking the people you will save, telling them the same lie. But they don't know it's a lie. You'll tell them. You'll fight for them. Worry about the true enemy, Aislyn. Leave the bullies to us."

He walked away, leaving me with Eva still typing, only stopping to nod. Collin walked up to us.

"We can go back up. You've got work to do after lunch."

The edge had returned to his voice. He didn't even make eye contact, and the calm blue eyes and almost-ethereal features had all faded again. He was standing right next to me but felt miles away. Avery and Clara walked past us, looking at me as if evaluating me. I turned to follow Collin up the stairs.

He started, "I'm going back to the Circle to prep for this afternoon. We'll have one more round of physical, then

Medical, then I'll choose one Common Phraseology lesson that you haven't reviewed yet before HistCulture tonight. Get something to eat. Two proteins, only one carb. I'll allow two fruits today, to get your blood sugar back up. Understood?"

"Yeah," I said.

The second bell rang. Joel's voice came over the speakers. "Skies are clear."

Collin looked like he wanted to say something, but then turned and darted down toward a hallway.

I dragged my feet through the cafeteria line and to a table. Eva caught up with me. Tessa glanced at me and shushed Lynn.

"Lynn," she said, "Aislyn's not ready for that information, or her trainer would have allowed her to come to class, you know that. Responsibility for intel makes you a great leader."

"You know," Eva started, "this isn't about—"

"At least one thing Collin is getting right," Tessa interrupted Eva, ignoring her, "is not trusting her with everything at once. I'm so glad your trainer trusts you. You deserve it, Lynn."

I stared at my food, trying to ignore her passive-aggressive trap. I noticed she only praised other Protectors when I was around and she wanted to point out I was failing.

"Could you grace another table with your 'responsible' presence, Tessa?" Eva asked.

"I don't remember asking you for your opinion—"

"Leave the table," Brie said as she sat down and dropped a tray in front of her. "Now."

Tessa said, "Aislyn can't become stronger if she is allowed to fail with no consequences. Admitting her weakness is healthy."

"So is leaving the table," Brie said with a look on her face that almost made me want to run again despite my exhausted legs.

Tessa picked up her tray and left. Brie didn't look at me, but ate her eggs, which she had with every meal.

"Thanks," I said and stared at my food, not even sure I should thank her. None of them looked at me.

My lack of ability probably still embarrassed or worried them. I wondered if they all thought what Tessa said was true, even if they had the decency to not to say it out loud.

"HistCulture videos tonight?" Eva asked. "You said that Collin might let someone come and watch with you, right?"

"Thanks, but I couldn't keep you from advanced Tech lab."

"Oh, I finished Tech. I passed the final exam before breakfast this morning." Eva smiled at my shocked face. "So, after today, I just have to show up when I feel like it."

Lynn dropped her fork on her tray. "Are you kidding?" she said, almost yelling. "I passed already, but my trainer is still making me go!"

"Lydia? Chloe?" Eva asked.

"I could only pass one final," Lydia said, "and that would be Medical. But I don't mind going to class."

Chloe said, "Passed. And I got cleared to skip."

"I hate my trainer!" Lynn said.

"Well, that makes all of us," Cassidy said, before she slammed her tray on the table.

"See, now we're bonding through whining, like real women. What's wrong with yours?" Eva asked.

"I'm guessing diet restrictions because you didn't pass your five-mile test," I stated confidently. Everyone looked at me, and then at Cassidy's tray.

Eva started laughing and stopped herself with a forced cough. "Sorry," she said. "Carbs much?"

Cassidy had almost nothing but bread or breaded items on her plate. She was skinny, so it wasn't surprising.

Cassidy stabbed a roll with a fork and twirled it. "I can do a mile in under seven minutes, but I can't break five miles in under forty. I just run out of energy, so it's carb-loading for me."

Eva wasn't laughing anymore but staring at me curiously.

"What is it?" I said.

"Nothing."

But she kept looking at me, like she was expecting something to happen. She was evaluating me, but unlike when Avery, Hannah or Collin stared at me, I found it reassuring instead of uncomfortable.

"Wait until next week, right?" Cassidy said, glaring at the roll she'd impaled.

"What happens next week?"

"ISO week, meaning isolation," Lynn answered. "This week, we have classes, we see each other, and we get a break from our trainers. On Saturday, we start one week of personalized teaching meant to target our weaknesses and strengths. Just us and our trainers, kicking our"—Brie gave her a jab and Lynn rolled her eyes—"*butts* the whole time for not being perfect little saviors who can rescue fifty Vessels and still eat enough carbs."

Cassidy finally dropped the roll after taking a bite. "I'm going to be sick! I hate everything on my plate!"

"Hence your skinny little body," Eva said. "Eat."

"Running will be the theme of my ISO week if that's how punishments are doled out," I said between bites of chicken.

"At least you haven't had to run around with no shoes yet," Megan said as she sat down at the table.

"Why wouldn't I be wearing shoes?" I asked.

"The shame run," Eva said. "Megan never disobeyed any instructor, hence no shame run on her record. She's usually the one looking at us running with no shoes while she is excelling at everything else. But she always winks at us, so we like her."

Megan laughed. "If I don't improve my Medical score, I might have my first shame run and lose some points. But points don't matter unless you want to make it to the broadcast, and I hate public speaking."

At the end of training, there would be a simulcast sent to the public. Those who ranked highest would share updates to the Territory. Tessa was on last year and would undoubtedly be on again. I imagined Brie and Lynn would interview again as well.

"Doesn't it hurt, though?" I asked. "The shame run?"

"Oh, no," Eva said. "They have you run along the grass border around the whole complex. It hurts nothing but pride."

I felt a jolt of anger I tried to control, but sometimes training left me as disgusted as Cassidy staring at her bread she'd just folded into a cube.

Before I knew it, I was heading to Tech.

Room 110.

The Tech room was simple in structure, just like a lot of the other ones. It had plenty of wires, different MCU's, and other gadgets along the wall, many of which I figured I would never know how to use. But most of the wall was taken up by a map with dots all over Zone 2 and Zone 1, along with a list of times.

Within seconds of taking our seats, Patterson and Carlson came in. They were talking feverishly, but low enough that I couldn't hear what they were saying over our chatter. A few people nodded discreetly toward them. Brie, without turning toward us, gave a wave with one finger, put her hand in her hair, and then put up four fingers. It confused me, but precisely four seconds later, the chatter died off, just enough to hear Carlson say ". . . why T-stations need basic camo, and budget restrictions—"

Carlson stopped talking as he turned toward us suspiciously.

With a sigh, Patterson said, "All right, ladies."

The only four people who were still talking fell silent and turned to face him.

Tessa said, "What budget restrictions?"

Brie shot Patterson a question. "Is this because we lost the station on 29th Street?"

Patterson rolled his eyes. "Well, Eric in Intel will be thrilled with you. Nice job."

Lynn smiled as she let out a quiet sigh of accomplishment. "You, too! You're raising spies. Irony is awesome."

Patterson gave a stern look to all of us as he left out the front door, leaving us staring down at our Tech instructor once again.

"Okay, so, considering the events of the morning, this lesson couldn't be timelier for you twenty-six ladies... Oh, sorry, Aislyn, it's just a habit. Twenty-seven ladies. You are about to get a rundown of communication procedures, including EEs."

First, he reviewed the stations and what made them different, then explained that we confused the enemy by only entering certain stations at certain times.

"When we pick you up in the field, we plan to make it appear random. With this pattern, you see, there is no reason the Republic would check the same station more than once a day because only certain Protectors can go to a specific station each day. That means if you need an EE, you will have to check your MCU for what station you need to reach and at what time. You may be closer to another station, but if your target station listed is ten miles away, you need to reach that one. Too many of you at a single location risks exposure.

"Now, what will you do if you are here"—he pointed at the map—"and your station for the day is up here, fifteen miles away, but your station for the next day is two miles away?"

Carlson continued scenarios for nearly an hour until each one of us had answered. He explained that the simplest of T-stations were nothing more than abandoned fiber-optic cables underground. We hooked our MCU's onto that cable and communicated with Central, which we would practice doing for the remaining classes that week.

"These stations are ideal for simple status updates. We need to know your mission status and that you and your Vessel or Unnecessary are safe. We need an ETA. Even if you are not asking for an EE, we want communication from an R-station a week after extraction."

He paused, but the room got a little quieter as he said, "To let us know you are safe while you are still in the Republic. Well, that's the big secret, isn't it?"

I was already looking at the instructor, but in seconds, everyone else's eyes were glued to him as well. It was silent. This one piece of intel was always excluded from any information ever given to the Territory on broadcasts or to us as students, but I now realized that those in the Academy must have never known either. Only Tessa and Brie sat back into their chairs while everyone inched up to the edge of their seats.

"Yes, we can communicate with you within the Republic. This is most likely the biggest secret you will ever know, and we guard it closely. You will tell no one after you leave here. The first thing you should know is that we time all communication. We check on all Protectors simultaneously by hacking the Republic for only three minutes at different times each day. That's it. One five-minute hack is all it takes for us to see you are alive."

"But we can't send a message to the Territory?" Megan asked.

"You don't message us at all. You never communicate, 'I'm okay' or 'Vessel suspected' or 'Unnecessary.' There's no phone."

Cassidy raised her hand to answer one riddle. "We buy our phones there, in the Republic."

Carlson smiled and nodded. "Good start. Keep going."

"We use coded messages," Megan added.

Carlson said, "But not encoded. 3, go ahead."

Lynn looked half amazed at the logic of what she was about to say. "We message someone who lives in the Republic."

He smiled. "Go on, 3"

"We have... an assigned phone number. You give us a number before we leave, a person you've chosen with high message volume, so they ignore many of their messages. They don't recognize us, and they'll most likely just discard our messages. But you will know it's us..."

She had hit the part she was unsure of, but Eva knew the answer.

"Time! We all message at the same time of day, on the minute. Maybe it's a different time each day, but we all message at that time, to our assigned numbers. Then it looks like a simple hack of several random phones!" Eva sat back in her chair and swore using a word from Common Phrases. "That is so brilliant!"

"Yes, 26, thank you for that, but please watch your language. But yes, as far as it concerns the Republic, you are messaging like the masses. They won't know to track a phone you bought from their markets, like thousands of others, and they will not be able to decipher anything strange in your messages because the phrases you'll use are so common. When we see the message sent at the right time— say 3:24— to the receiver assigned to you—let's say Bob Smith who lives on Ninth Street—with the message 'Hey you,' we know that you're safe and about to start a mission. We record the number from the phone. We can track you. We can contact you if a security breach occurs to tell you someone has compromised you, after which you will ditch your phone and run for the border. Those procedures are in section nineteen."

"What if someone messages the same message to the same number at the same designated time as us?" Lydia asked. "How would you know which number is ours?"

"It has happened, actually, but not two days in a row. If we watch close enough, we know it's you. Now, if you all will open your MCUs, under file four-three-four, you will find the message schedule and a coded index with the translations of your messages' contents. As I said, 'Hey you' will inform us you are on a mission. 'Some party' will tell us you have a Vessel but feel like a Sentry might be on your tail. Please memorize all the terms, all examples of verbiage you will hear every day in the Republic. You should memorize the schedule in three-week intervals, but it's something to do when bored in the woods on your way to the Republic," he added. "While this is the most effective and discreet way to communicate, the person who receives your message may respond to you. This is rare, with most people receiving over a thousand messages and ads a day, but it can be awkward. Make an excuse and then switch right away to the secondary number we give you."

Eva once again swore under her breath and said, "Brilliant."

It was. Our most vital communication was undetectable to the Society. We would use what I hated most about them as one of our weapons: their lack of emotional connection. They had hundreds of friends, friends with benefits and lovers, but they didn't grow attached enough to feel anything.

Their enemy sent them a message every day.

And they never knew.

CHAPTER 10

A warm day in spring always made me homesick for summer. I wanted to be laying in the sun, basking in it, rolling in the grass with the boys, or writing under a tree.

But I wasn't.

I could barely breathe at all, staring not at the sky but at a mat getting closer, then pulling away, getting closer, then pulling away. While my arms burned and pushed, the mat got closer, pulled away, closer, then my head fell into it.

Get up! the voice in my head screamed over and over, but it had gotten a lot less desperate. Now, it screamed harder and louder. And then, the voice screaming at me was no longer mine.

"Get up!" Collin yelled, almost right over my face. I pushed my arms up to brace myself, but I couldn't do another push-up. My stomach screamed when I pulled it in to straighten my back.

"You will fall at twenty feet again if you can't do this!"

Bringing up the first day of ISO week and the disaster on the climbing wall only pinned me harder to the mat. I had miscalculated and failed to call for tension in my rope until it was too late. I tried to make it up a few more stones when my arm cramped. I missed the hold. I had fallen ten feet before tension hit.

Collin kept bringing it up at every opportunity, especially because there were four other Protectors and trainers there.

Including Avery, who screamed up at Tessa the entire sixty feet, which she had scaled in record time.

I'd already imagined the conversations that had happened behind doors. I didn't know if Collin hated me. At first, he thought I had broken my wrist and looked concerned. But since the incident, he had been overly critical, terrified that my skills (or lack thereof) would embarrass him again.

"I'm done. I can't. I'm sorry." My voice cracked as I got to my feet.

He stared at me with disgust. "You have to—"

"Forget it!" I snapped. "Just... I'm done."

"Fine. You'll do a run after Medical. Let's go."

He didn't assign me a punishment right away, which was surprising after a tense few days. Only a few things kept me going, like watching videos with Brie. My disgust at the Republic had only grown, learning how they prevented empathy and only encouraged self-promotion in schools. They had nearly everyone brainwashed before age ten, which is why there was an age limit for Unnecessaries. Most flaws were found between ages four and seven, but it still made me sick to think that we had to limit how many people we could save. But then I thought it would be a miracle if I could save anyone. I dreaded every step as I walked to Medical.

But despite the pain, my eyes widened in shock at seeing what was on the table. My disgust evaporated. I turned to Collin, every hard edge removed from his face to reveal his own sense of wonder. He was even smiling.

"That's... Is that my... ?"

"It's your pack. One of them, anyway, but it is yours. Some of them are designed to be more fashionable, but they all have the same supplies. Initials are on the bottom and the back of the shoulder straps, in case you get it confused, but it's in the same thread as the bag so it's not easily seen. It's complete with everything you'll ever need for any mission, any pregnancy, any Unnecessary. Your job is to become familiar with it. Where to find everything, how to retrieve the first tool for identifying a

Vessel and be prepared to use it. But first things first. Put it on, 27."

My hand grazed over my initials and along the strap. I went to lift it, expecting it to be heavy, but it was super light. He laughed at my shock.

"Well, you may have to walk a hundred miles with it on your back. We're not sadists."

That was debatable.

I opened it to reveal rolls of canvas filled with instruments, tools, scalpels, pre-filled syringes, and other medical supplies stashed in each rolled-up piece. I could also see the meal bars and medicine. In the front pouch, the most accessible pocket, was the MCU. Unlike the bulky MCU I had for training, this one was small and sleek.

"Your best friend," he said as I reached for it. "Notice what else is accessible? The only thing in your front pouch?"

I kept eye contact with his softened face, his blue eyes almost mesmerizing me with the wonder behind them. I moved slowly, intent on making this moment last as long as it could and pulled the other item from the pouch.

"Ultrasound attachment, right?"

He nodded as I attached the mechanism, and luckily, got to the right screen with a few remembered strokes. By the time I looked up, Collin nodded in rare approval. He pointed to a prosthetic on the table.

"Seriously? You want me to try this out on the weird belly thing?" I asked. "I used this on my mom. Do I actually have to pretend the plastic belly person is real?"

One look from him told me I did. It took me one minute to check everything in the prosthetic mother-to-be.

"Heart rate of the baby, normal. Mother's heart rate, normal. Baby is at eighteen weeks. No Previa. Baby's features look good. No complications foreseen. Time to trudge through crazy wilderness, as long as she's not made of plastic."

He raised his eyebrows, but a look of nervousness returned as he said, "Your goal is to find what you need in one minute, for any situation you might face. So, you will start by unpacking it and repacking it. The goal is to do it twice in five minutes. Go."

There were some duplicates, but each rolled-up canvas pocket held sufficient tools for most foreseen complications and some unforeseen ones. The birth-kit canvas had everything for a normal birth, with some suturing tools. The C-section kit had almost every surgical tool, including a local anesthetic needle, four scalpels, and strange forceps. Then there was a stitches kit, a wound kit, a poison kit, and a kit that included survival tools and allergy medicines, bug spray, and simple antibiotics. The mesh and two foldable poles for my small camo tent were so compactly folded, I wasn't sure I could duplicate it. There were excellent pain killers and very expensive and rare body glue that would heal almost any deep wound. And of course, sanitation powder bombs. I had used one in the group Med class last week. One pinch of the capsule, and sani-powder was released in a five-foot radius.

"And don't forget your oxygen concentrator. This device will compress the air into a higher concentration of oxygen, if you have a preemie younger than thirty-four weeks. You hook that up to this hose, it'll go in the baby's nasal passages. It also includes your thermal blanket. If you empty your pack, you can pull out the safety supports that are sewn into your bag and carry the infant in there, with the oxygen mask. It's like a cradling blanket. You just can't run, or you'll risk injury from shaking. Now for the real test. It's all packed up, and you have a thirty-five-week C-section. Go."

I opened the pack, but as I grabbed at a kit, he said, "Stop, wrong one."

I fumbled out the right pack... three minutes later.

"Okay, just—" Collin was interrupted by a message on his watch. As he read through it, his face fell. I was about to ask what was wrong when he said, "Don't worry about it. A small cyst, early contractions, second trimester. Go."

As I tried and failed again, his motions became more forced, and the edge returned to his voice. Scenario after scenario, I was clumsy, horrified of getting something wrong, and ended up dropping my scalpel on the floor, choosing the wrong kit twice, cursing, and pulling out almost every wrong tool for my wound kit. By the end, his eyes were closed in quiet anger, his broad shoulders hunched over the table. His watch continued to receive messages that only made the tension worse.

"All right. Well, you got four kits right, but your time is horrible. I guess our goal will be two more right a day until we get to all twelve. We'll work on speed. And not dropping things."

I packed it up again, as ordered. He said I had to take my HistCulture test before watching more videos that night.

"Fine," I said and zipped up the pack.

He put out his hand on the bag.

"You don't care, do you? About any of this?"

I stared at him, glaring through the anger that created the strange haze that separated us.

"Just because I can't do it—"

"You can do it. I wouldn't have agreed to train you if I thought you didn't care if they died. I expected you to react when you saw what you were up against, or when I challenged you. Do you not see that? Do you not see the hell they live in, being killed for existing or loving? Or do you seriously not care?"

It had been three days of ISO, and I knew we were both wearing thin, but his accusation cut deep like a weapon. And I reacted with the only weapon I had: my screaming voice.

"Do you not see me? There isn't a single muscle in my body that isn't screaming with pain! My brain is pounding, I am starving, and I am exhausted!"

"See, that's the attitude. Everyone else has those same problems, but they're dealing with them. You, though? You don't seem to want to connect with any bigger picture other than yourself. Someone chose you to do this!"

"Yes," I yelled, "And I don't know what he was thinking! You meditate enough; you figure it out! It's not for me, that's for sure."

"Is that why every time you meditate or pray, you fall asleep?"

"First of all, I haven't slept through the night since I got here! And second, I'm not like you, okay? When I meditate, I don't hear from the heavens or get a reason to do this. I hear silence."

"That's because you don't believe in this, and you don't—!"

"Don't say it again! I care!"

"But not enough!" he screamed back. Then, his voice changed to something that was much quieter, more concluding, more condemning, and more disgusted. "Not enough."

His glare was harsh. Once again, his emotional whiplash had overwhelmed me more than any drill or exercise.

He was already holding out his hand. This was the third time in three days. He didn't need to say anything. I had raised my voice, lost focus, and shouted at him. I untied my shoes, handed them over, and ran out the door.

I was two footsteps onto the hard stone when I told myself to get all my yelling and crying out of the way. I was already on a shame run. But I couldn't let his words go. I had to defend myself.

I turned around to go back into my Circle, another accusation ready to throw at him, but shock caught the words in the back of my throat. I retreated out of the doorway, so he didn't see me, peering around the side of my door enough to see him.

The scene wasn't what I had imagined. He wasn't walking around angrily or calling Patterson to complain. He was on one knee, bent down on the mat, hands intertwined around the back of his neck, his elbows closing off the rest of the world. His knuckles were white.

I moved my head back into the archway, feeling a little strange to by spying on my own Circle. His shoulders shook as if his breaths were shuddering and painful. His arms fell, he picked up the shoes, threw them back down, then headed back to the Med room with the pack clutched in his arms. I heard him repeat under his breath, "God, please let her be okay. Just let her be okay. I don't want to do this to her, please..."

I backed away before he could see me and ran for the tree line. I had never been so confused by Collin than today. I thought I had imagined the mood swings and the inconsistency.

I was oblivious to anything else as I ran past, but then Tessa said loudly enough for the few people around her to hear, "Look who's still running with no shoes." I ran faster to escape it. To escape everything. I decided to cut through the garden.

The pain from my feet hitting the stone were nothing compared to the pain of not knowing whether I could do this. No one thought I could do this.

Except one man: the one who chose me.

And that man was standing right in front of me.

I had to stop hard in the garden, where I remembered I shouldn't have been running. Eldridge stood among his group of assistants. He opened his mouth to speak but closed it when he saw my feet. He turned to his assistants and spoke with the authority that came from a direct order.

"Everyone, head down to prep for the meeting, and then we'll move out. I'll be there in ten minutes." All of them obeyed silently, some without looking up from their MCUs.

"Hi," I said, curling my exposed toes.

"Oh, don't be embarrassed about that. We are looking for a tinge of rebellion in you. In all of you, come to think of it."

"It's, like, my third run this week." I wanted him to understand that I was failing everything, and he was as much to blame as anyone.

"Hmm... well, that was unforeseen, but hardly your fault. Why don't you walk with me?"

I nodded, thankful that this chat with Eldridge would get me out of the rest of my shame run. Then, I stared at him, wondering why he had bent over, before I realized he was unlacing his shoes.

"Sir?" I said, my voice shivering a little.

"Oh, it's a wonderful day, you know. Warm. Sunny. That day that spring steals from the winter cold. And who wants to have shoes on after all?"

He began to walk, and I felt an outpouring of respect and compassion at seeing his bare feet.

"So," Eldridge said, "I do have to insist on something, because I believe in impeccable timing."

"Okay," I answered, a bit worried.

"What were you thinking about right before you stopped?"

"Well, to be honest, why you chose me."

"I told you already, I didn't," he said. At seeing my strained reaction, he added, "I have to admit, I never would have thought that the answer would come in prayer one day, but it did."

I suppressed rolling my eyes. "Well, if God is real, and listening, why doesn't he just end this? I don't get the point of telling him anything if he isn't going to save their lives."

"Well, God is giving people the gifts and abilities and the courage to save their lives. That, by definition, is something."

"So, where does that leave me?"

"I would think in a pretty significant position," he said, trying to be playful.

My anger burned. "If you're going to say that God chose me, then I'm proof He doesn't know what He's doing because I couldn't be less qualified to do this!"

"My dear, my decision to name you the 27th Protector doesn't waiver just because you can't do twenty push-ups or lunges. You're saying you've failed at something you've never tried to do. You have more faith in your failure than I have faith that you will succeed. Stop doubting yourself so much. It sounds exhausting."

I pondered his words, not quite digesting his belief in my abilities; I couldn't stomach that kind of hope right now. But he was right. I hadn't even tried this yet. The truth was, every time I imagined saving someone, talking to an Unnecessary, or delivering the baby of a Vessel, I had a rush of adrenaline, and my mind went wild with anticipation. But when I trained, I felt the failure already. I risked asking him another question.

"Sir, why is there this crazy disparity in training? One second, it's all, 'go meditate and pray for bravery and selflessness,' and the next, it's yelling and screaming, 'Go faster! Push harder!' and the next, we're cramming too much data into our heads for it to stay there and learning how to treat PTSD. It's confusing."

Eldridge seemed to ponder for a moment.

"What is your job, 27th Protector?"

I couldn't think of a response that would sound appropriate. He knew what my job was.

"Aislyn, don't you think there is an enormous amount of disparity in what you will do? You will cheat death against impossible odds. You'll fight an officer or a Sentry. You'll be striving to elude an enemy, for the chance to do what? See an infant in its first moment of life? Comfort a crying newborn? Sing an abandoned child to sleep? Is this not a horrible disparity?"

I took in a breath but held it for a moment, lost in the story he had painted. If that was the story I was going to live, I would do anything to prepare for it.

"It's hard," Eldridge said, "I am a little surprised to hear that you and Collin are struggling, but everything happens eventually."

Confused by his last words, we walked silently back to my Circle. I wondered what Eldridge knew about Collin that I didn't. As we turned the corner, I turned to face him, only to see his assistants hovering about two yards away.

"I'm guessing you have somewhere else to be," I said.

"Yes. We are talking to the new recruits who will start in the fall at the Academy. Someone wrote me a speech. How very convenient to borrow their words and not use mine."

"What do you wish you could say, Sir?"

He smiled. "What I told you only a minute ago. That they must discover how to survive in a world where sorrow and joy and pain are as sharp as knives. The disparity, as you call it. If they can survive it, they can help someone else survive. And I wish I could tell them success doesn't depend on climbing up walls or how many lunges they can do or how much data they can stuff in their head. I wish they'd believe me. I don't know if they would."

I exhaled loudly, reprimanding myself a little for my childish whining and realizing he was still talking to me.

"Yes, they would believe you," I said, but shook my head. "Even if my training gets better or I start to wrap my head around this, I may not be the 27th Protector that everyone's expecting."

"Oh, but didn't I tell you?" he asked, the playfulness in his voice returning. "I'm looking forward to it."

Eldridge turned and entered the Circle with me, bare feet hitting the mats as we entered. Collin was bent over papers again, rubbing his head through his hair as he spoke into his watch.

"Sam, tell Hannah I'm ignoring the diet suggestions for Aislyn. She needs all the energy she can get, and it's not my fault half of the Republic has an eating disorder. I'm not putting her on restrictive diets until the last two weeks. That's the minimum."

"She's not going to like—"

"Deal with it. I'm reading over the last of the reports now."

His lower lip moved as he read. So focused. So driven. Of course Eldridge would get to see this side of Collin. All I ever saw was the angry, riled mess, who acted like he hated himself and me.

Collin finally heard us and looked up.

"Aislyn, where have you been—whoa!"

A jolt ran through Collin's body. A small smile escaped me.

"Sir?" he said, sliding off the table and standing at attention.

"Collin. You were awake until midnight with all of this, as far as I could tell. Remember to get some sleep, boy, before you die."

"Sorry, I'm getting ready for the meeting with Patterson."

"Try to think about what we discussed the other day. If anything, try to remember that she wasn't the only one I chose."

Eldridge left quickly. I went over to the table where Collin was staring at his MCU. His brow creased in concentration, and bit his lower lip as his fingers raced and pounded against the screen of his larger CU screen.

"So, you're meeting with Patterson?"

"Yep, and Avery, Hannah, Emily, and Clara. And I'm going to get ripped to shreds," he said matter-of-factly, but I could see his one arm shake a little. For one moment, I wished I was doing better for his sake, but maybe I'd be doing better if he didn't turn into such a tyrant during physical training. The anger that had led to my shame run returned.

"Is that why you said that I didn't care? So you can tell them that's why I'm not doing better?"

The stack of papers crashed onto the desk as he threw them down.

I had done it again. I took the jab.

"Sorry," I quickly muttered. "I don't know why I said that."

He lowered his chin and pushed a slow breath out through his lips. But it wasn't anger in his eyes; it was something else.

"I do. You hate me right now. I'm trying to follow a plan and a method of training I don't even—" he cut himself off. "And that plan is for you to be working so hard that you hate me, only I didn't—" He stopped again, only not because he was angry.

It was almost as if he was in pain.

"So, what? You have to plan to be a sadist?"

"Maybe. But not tonight. I called in a favor. And as much as you hate me, Aislyn, I'd like to think I pay attention. You need a friend. And since it can't be me..."

He smiled again and nodded his head. I turned around to the most beautiful sight I had seen in three days.

"Eva?"

"Happy Iso-Week-Mid-Break-History-Video-Watching Day!" she said. "Say that stupid phrase so I can walk through the door, Aislyn. And Collin... five videos? Seriously?"

I offered Collin a little smile and mouthed, "Thank you."

"You're welcome," he answered, but his joy faded an instant later. He clenched his jaw and threw three bags full of evaluations over his shoulders. It represented a burden much heavier than the papers those bags carried. "Don't forget about the test! I need the numbers before I start in ten minutes. Try your best. Please."

I turned to Eva. "I, Aislyn, the 27th Protector, give Evangeline McKinney, the 26th Protector of the 188th Generation, permission to enter my Circle on the 8th day of training."

It sounded official, but left me feeling vulnerable, like somehow I was faking it. She came up to me, and for some strange reason, I hugged her. I wasn't a "huggy" type of girl. But I was so desperate to talk to anyone who couldn't send me on laps, make me read four-hundred-page Med manuals, drill me, or yell at me.

"I know, 27," she said, hugging back. "It's all so horrible. The good news is that in about five weeks, you'll be in a completely different place... where everyone will want to kill you."

I broke away to see the expected smirk. She nodded to where Collin was sitting.

"I couldn't help but overhear... test first?"

"Yeah," I answered. "The final on the Republic class system."

"Oh, have fun!" She rolled her eyes. "I'll be over here choosing what horrible crimes against humanity to study tonight."

I turned the CU on, put the earphones over my head, turned the mic on, and began the first question. A computer-generated voice spoke.

"Name the six classes of the Republic, in descending order."

"Elite, Citizen, Libertas, Terra, Sub-Terra, and Unnecessary." The corner of the screen flashed green, confirming my answer was correct.

"Explain the non-working classes and how they maintain the Society's power."

"The non-working classes, or people who do not have to maintain employment—Terras, Libertas, and Citizens—make up a little more than half of the population. This ensures that the Society can maintain control through democracy, as these groups almost always vote for the party because they receive an allowance that drives the economy. The Libertas can work to earn a Citizen commission of two million dollars, guaranteeing that their family will be Citizens who receive an allowance four times larger than Terras. Citizens rarely work, but are paid more and strive for Elite status: a five-million-dollar commission. Elites also control most of the Sub-Terras."

"Explain the role of the Sub-Terras."

I caught my breath, sickened by the computer's emotional indifference. I swallowed just to make sure I didn't get sick.

"A Sub-Terra is a child of a Terra or a Libertas who is created should they reach their debt limit to the Society Party. The Society can force the debt onto the Sub-Terra—or indentured servant. The parents aren't emotionally attached enough to the child to care, and many view Sub-Terras as Unnecessaries. Even as the debt reduces, most Terras will keep spending money while their child works to pay it off. Since Sub-Terras cannot vote while paying off debt, the Republic does not see them as a threat. The Sub-Terra doesn't protest, because they hope to gain a higher status one day. Once they pay off their debt, they often forget their past, seeing it as a rite of passage to their allowance."

"Explain the vulnerability and psychology in a Sub-Terra's worldview that could affect the outcome of a mission."

"After years of not being in control of their own lives, they think nothing they do affects any outcome. They are brainwashed to follow the Republic's rules for survival, so sometimes they can change their mind about escaping to the Territory mid-mission. A Protector also might need to convince a Sub-Terra that our services are not for free. They don't trust that anyone will ever love them or want to save them without using them for something later. Children have PTSD and detachment disorders."

"Finally, what is the most significant thing to know about the class system?"

"The farther up you go, the less likely it is to find a Vessel or Unnecessary who is wants to escape. Citizens and Elites are loyal without question. With every level, dependence on the Society Party heightens because the Society Party gives them more. And with every level, they become more and more selfish, uncaring, and more of an..."

I ended my sentence with a word I hoped the computer could register. I didn't know if they allowed curse words on exams. I felt like someone had to say it, instead of it being so mechanical.

"Good for you! Get it all out!" Eva yelled in the background, and I smiled.

As I joined her, taking a seat on a large cushion, a score of 95 percent flashed across my MCU. About two seconds later, the MCU beeped again.

I glanced at Collin's message: *"Great job. We needed that score. I can throw it in Avery's face."*

But I was already distracted. "So, when was your shame run?" I asked Eva.

"About four o'clock. Why? Did I miss you?"

Collin messaged me again: *"You can do this. I'm sorry."*

"Yeah," I said offhandedly, "by an hour."

She looked at me curiously, then at her feet. "You noticed the grass stains, didn't you?"

"Yeah," I said, finding my thoughts wandering back to Collin's message until I noticed Eva was staring at me again. "Why does Collin have to meet with the other trainers?"

"Reasons, but mostly so Avery and a few others can tell him you're going to die."

"Oh," I said with little emotion. I didn't want to be overdramatic, but I wanted to know. "Do you think I'm going to die?"

"Nope."

"Why not?"

"Aislyn, I've seen Protectors for a long time. And despite how overwhelmed you feel right now, you will eventually see your gift. I've already seen it. I hope I'm there the day you figure it out."

She stretched out on the couch and continued. "As I'll be obligated to be a classroom with you that day, most likely, I won't miss it. I'll be the one saluting you, watching Tessa turn purple. That'll be the icing on the... ooh... cake."

I let her have her food envy moment, grabbed the remote, and pressed play.

Five hours later, Eva said goodbye. She left me alone in the room. It took four echoing steps through the Circle for me to feel the depth of how empty it was. Every muscle argued with even the smallest steps. They throbbed, leaving me with the pain of knowing they still weren't strong enough to fight, run, escape, or live.

I told myself to look up; the moonlight was filling the room. The moon must have looked beautiful. But I couldn't look at it. I felt the guilt of Collin's words crush me, Eldridge's words confuse me, and my own thoughts criticize me. I didn't want to give myself the pleasure in seeing even the simplest beauty.

The weight of my shame pulled my head down. I lost track of time for minutes, maybe an hour, feeling as cold as the stone on which I stood. It felt for a moment like I might never move or see beauty again.

And I fell asleep, with the moon left unseen; possibly as lonely as me.

CHAPTER 11

Ten days later, I sat up in bed to write in my journal.

"The air is still, and beautiful, and cold, and clear. Why is it so hard to breathe?"

I stood to see if that would help. My legs protested, stiff and aching. Today had been a nightmare, starting with mock C-sections. I had thrown up, as predicted. We had become familiar with PTSD therapy techniques. We also practiced using phrases to give in response to common questions that Vessels and Unnecessaries asked on the journey back to the Territory. They also trained us in techniques to soothe a child's night terrors, making us watch hours of children who suffered them.

It made my heart feel tired, but my body was sore because I had climbed the wall three times. I don't know what hurt more, that I only made it to twenty-eight feet the third time or that I had to endure more passive-aggressive torture from Tessa. Tessa, in the past week, had praised the bravery of every Protector who she thought would succeed, then just glared in disgust at the rest of us.

There would be silence when I came down the rope and jumped off the wall, barely landing on my jelly legs. Brie and Megan told me I did okay, but my twenty-eight feet did little to impress Collin.

Collin. Hours earlier, he'd wanted me to try to climb the wall one more time before ISO week. I'd refused, and his reaction didn't surprise me at all.

"Take a lap, Aislyn. Whole complex."

"I can't! I won't! Tessa will be there and make sure I don't—"

"Shoes off! Now!"

He looked more scared than angry, like always. I ripped off the velcro of my shoe, stifling a laugh.

"What's so funny?" he asked.

"I just thought about how happy you'll be when I die. Maybe I'll finally make my trainer proud. You care more about being right than you do about teaching me what I need to know."

I threw my shoes on the ground and headed out the door. Within seconds, I could hear him beating the crud out of the punching bag. I ran past the threshold when I heard him yell in frustration.

For all my claims of being emotionally spent, tears had still come to my eyes. It was my fault, too. I didn't want to see Tessa's reaction if I failed again. I should have tried again and ignored Tessa, but I couldn't.

I wanted to hate Collin, but I still didn't. I couldn't hate anyone so devoted to anything like he was. He had this dual of anger and regret that danced around each other. In all my effort to uncover why, all I could see were flashes of pain. I just didn't know why that pain could make him so guilty.

When I got back, I felt the same whiplash that Collin always gave me. Only it was more acute.

Eldridge was right: a Protector felt sorrow, pain, and beauty, all as sharp as knives. But the beauty cut the deepest.

Collin had been in the Circle running around with a five-year-old girl, playing tag. I remembered that we were supposed to talk to an Unnecessary child about their experiences and recovery, but I had forgotten it was on the schedule. Her story was as heart-breaking as I would expect. Her mom had abandoned her at age two because she looked unpromising in emotional stability and early IQ tests. She'd dropped the girl off at the usual children's center, and a Sub-Terra that was installing some hardware had overheard her talking to the instructor. The Sub-Terra knew what would happen, so she hid the child in her work bag, took her to the shuttle, and kept her safe for a few days. But she ran into a street where a Sentry was on duty—and Brie, hiding from the same Sentry, chose her van to take cover inside. She drove them both to the border and to freedom.

Little Allison's face lit up as she told me she wanted to be a veterinarian. I decided not to tell her my father was a hunter who killed animals and talked about my sister instead, to which Collin winked, whispering, "Good call!"

Collin had then proceeded to ask her questions, letting me listen to the answers, which were to show how the PTSD therapy had helped. He had played tag, hide and seek, and must have spun her in circles a hundred times.

Collin was hypnotic when he smiled and laughed with her. He'd told more silly jokes than I thought one person could memorize. His eyes had been the calm blue I rarely saw now, under a brow that didn't seem worried or exhausted. He'd left with her on his shoulders, looking as if he wished it would last.

The weight of a million lost chances to be friends with him crushed me. I felt pinned down. Stuck. Trapped.

Now, the clock read 11:45 p.m. And since I would lose all my freedom in twelve hours, when ISO week began at noon the next day, I claimed what freedom I could. They had never told me I wasn't allowed to leave my Circle after dark, but as I took my first step outside, I wondered if an alarm would sound. I took a few more steps out, but only silence answered my straining ears. For a few moments, I stood frozen, waiting for anything to move.

But nothing did. A slight breeze blew my hair. It seemed so long. I would have cut it last month if I had been in school.

I probably wouldn't be cutting my hair again.

I wouldn't be cutting the flowers when they bloomed soon.

I wouldn't be ripping up homework and running through hallways again.

I wouldn't be...

"Stop." My voice—even my breath—was ear-splitting in the silence that the dark had made into a vacuum. The moon was not out tonight, so I walked to the other side of the garden, past the Circles and the torches of fallen Protectors.

The door to Central opened. I ducked, but stopped when I saw who it was.

"Sam?"

"Whoa!" He almost dropped his MCU, catching it after the fourth clumsy attempt, only inches before it hit the stone.

"Sorry," I whispered.

"Aislyn? What are you doing?"

"Walking. Can't sleep, so..." I answered carefully. "Where are you going?"

"Oh, server room."

"Oh, that's interesting. I could... that's... um..."

He laughed. "You don't remember what a server is, do you?"

"It has something to do with computers, right?"

"Well, you're not wrong," he sighed. "Come with me."

Minutes later, we walked along the border near the forest, a few hundred yards from the wall. It loomed over me, but my attention was drawn to the square metal door I had passed a hundred times. Sam hit five buttons, and it slid open. A steel grate slid to the side and revealed a lit spiral staircase. As we descended, circular walkways led down to five computers.

"It's like another Central! It's a replica, right down to the staircase and the Hand... Why are there two command centers?"

"Well, it's far enough away that if the other one is bombed or infiltrated, this one will be safe. Especially since we encased this one in a lot more steel. You just saw two of the doors open on top, but there are ten that automatically seal this thing off when I close it up. Everything we need is in here. Most of the software and hardware in Central doesn't store all the pertinent information. We pull it from here."

We stepped down, and I took everything in.

"So, does the... fiber-optic cable come in here too?"

"Yeah, right over there. These are the servers—which, by the way, are the systems that manage access to our data. Everything needed to hack the satellite for your phone information every day. That server contains all the pertinent video files. That computer over there calculates probabilities."

"Like our chances of survival?" I asked, wondering if I even wanted to check my stats.

"No, it's got a bigger job. It's trying to track patterns, rumors, and other factors to predict the new laws of Jubilee Day. It also searches chatter and messages from polices and Sentries. If there's a breach, and they find out our message pattern, we know it."

"Is that what happened, three years ago?"

"Yep," he said. "Five Protectors died in one night."

He plugged in his MCU and typed. There was a gentle white noise from the fans, some beeps, and the whir of information. This must have been Sam's paradise. I felt strange for interrupting.

"So, when was I supposed to see this?" I asked, curious again.

"Never." He answered quickly, still focused on his work. "The Protectors don't normally talk to us, unless they're on a mission, so we don't show them this stuff. It's not for you."

"Oh," I said, suddenly self-conscious to be somewhere I wasn't supposed to be. "Have I offended you? I can go."

"No," he said, looking up. "I mean, you can stay. It's just... you Protectors don't bother to talk to us much, Aislyn. The trainers barely talk to us, unless they're on an EE. We don't really matter as much."

I took a sharp breath, wondering who thought they had the right to tell him that. But no one told him. I had perceived the same thing, in a thousand non-verbal cues that Tessa and the other Protectors had given to all the support staff and their Handlers, in the way Avery walked by Liam like he was a nuisance. They were undervalued and overlooked constantly.

Without over-emotionalizing or thinking, I cursed.

"What did you just say?" he said, looking confused.

"I mean it! It's bull. You can't say things like that. Sam, you're one of the most committed people I've ever known, and if you ever even think that you're not a hero again, I'll punch you. I can actually do that now. You matter, Sam."

He stifled a laugh, said a quick thank-you, and with a deep breath, kept working. I returned to staring at the consoles, at the long abyss and the blinking lights. They were mesmerizing, like stars dancing. My eyes felt heavy. Within minutes, he had shut a tray, slid it back into a tower, and pulled out his MCU.

Out of some protective feeling or because he perceived my tired loneliness, he walked me back to my Circle. I hit the pillow and replayed the lights in my head. For some reason, they comforted me. They were proof of hundreds of people who worked themselves weary to be a part of this.

My next thought was at 6:00 a.m. the following morning. We were going to be in the second ISO week after only one class today, and I could barely get through morning push-ups.

"This is, again, why you can't do the wall," Collin yelled.

I kept doing the push-ups, trying to push away the failure, push away the doubt, push away the fear.

You could've done it...

Push.

You didn't have to worry about what Tessa thought...

Push. Collin was yelling again.

You can save her...

Push. Push. Push.

You can't...

I watched the teardrop fall from my eye and hit the mat below my shaking body.

The girl. She would die. Some idiot will leave her little beautiful soul alone to die. I was going to kill her, too. Because I couldn't get her out with my weak arms; arms that now convulsed under me.

"You need to be able to do—" Collin stopped mid-yell. Before I knew it, he was pulling me up.

"Are you okay?"

He was back—the boy with the calm blue eyes, his voice dripping with concern.

"I just... Allison... she..." I couldn't control the tears. "I'm not going to save her or any..."

"Take a walk, 27." It wasn't cruel, but it felt urgent. His jaw seemed to shake before setting. "Clear your head and go to Tech."

"All right." I left, wondering why he let me off the hook.

Before long, I was in the garden, sitting and waiting for something that wouldn't come: a clear head. I could hear Cassidy's voice approach.

"It's encoded, so you have to hack it, but you have to keep putting in codes every minute, or there's an alarm that— Aislyn!"

"Hey. Are you all headed to—?"

"Tech is canceled," Lynn said. "Some emergency meeting downstairs. Rumor is that it's a Jubilee Day clue. They told us to go back to our Circles, but it is right before an ISO week so... we're walking really, *really* slowly."

No explanation was needed.

I had wanted to ask them, and now seemed like a good time.

"Why do you still respect your trainers? I mean, really, why do any of them even sign up for it if they don't like us?"

Lydia sighed. "It takes a special person to teach twenty-six girls how to cheat death. And you should know we'd given our other instructors a lot of grief at the Academy by the time we got here. We have it coming."

"That, and for the past decade, they've been looking for ways to make it more of a military operation," Cassidy said, "or at least some people are. Our trainer is just part of that process."

I had realized that, thinking Eva would know more and have more commentary, but Eva was uncharacteristically quiet.

I sighed "Well, he's committed. He's there all the time, he never leaves. He goes from nice to cruel, and then looks wrecked by it. It's just hard—" Their shocked faces stopped me. "What?"

"I see my trainer for three hours a day," Lynn said, confused, "even in ISO."

"Maybe that's because I'm a 27th, but that still doesn't explain why he's nice, and then—like he's catching himself doing something wrong—he's angry again. But he acts so stinking concerned other times... I don't know."

Lynn opened her mouth to say something, but Cassidy cut her off.

"Aislyn, trainers only have one mode. Anger. I mean, I guess he's pushing you, but that's the normal part."

Lynn turned slowly, looking curious, but not at me.

"Wait a second... Eva, you aren't talking."

Everyone pivoted to look at Eva. I finally saw something I had only heard about: her panic face. She had frozen, except for her eyes, which darted, avoiding any eye contact.

"There are only three times in history when she didn't jump in a conversation like this," Lydia said, "and all three times, she knew everything that was going on and refused to tell us." She blinked and hesitated for a second, looking like some pain had sprouted up. "Second year in the Academy, she came back to her room. We were all talking about the alarms going off at Central. She didn't say anything."

"Was that the night that five people died?" Cassidy asked.

"Yeah..." Lynn intoned, maybe regretting that Lydia had used that example. "Eva, spill."

The silence dripped with a tension that made any breath seem to take too long. She seemed detached, even while staring at me. Azaria and Megan walked across our path behind us.

"Eva's panic face. Didn't expect that," Azaria said.

Megan looked at me curiously. "Who died?"

Eva's eyes were now dashing from side to side again. She seemed suddenly small compared to the rest of us. But I wanted to know what she was hiding too badly to feel very sorry for her.

"You're not going to tell us, are you?" Lynn said, defeated.

"No," Eva said, barely moving.

Lynn took a step forward. "You should at least tell 27."

Eva looked at her, blinked, and nodded for them to leave. Lynn backed up and walked away. Cassidy all but ran. Azaria and Lydia peeled off with Megan, who gave me a shy wave and wished me good luck. We were alone for thirty seconds before Eva spoke.

"Too bad an evaluator for intel didn't see that. It was a perfect scatter pattern."

"Eva, what's going on?"

"Like they said. Someone died. Or something. An idea. Collin's idea." She looked like she was a million miles away. After a pause, she found my eyes and started again. "It's not the big deal they are making it, really. Trainers are like us, whether they're girls or guys. And... it might have come up with the other trainers, several times—or many times—that unless he trained you with the planned curriculum, he'd fail, and it would define him."

"What would he do that was different?" I asked.

"He's..." She hesitated, then seemed to start over. "Sorry, I can't tell you everything. I promised I wouldn't. So, I'll tell you a little. I remember when Collin came to tour the place when he was shadowing with Stephanie for a week. He talked to Eldridge and my mom about ways to change training, even at age fourteen. He wanted to make training pure again, like what it was decades ago. A trainer used to be a guide, a friend, a confidant, not a drill sergeant. Collin wanted to destroy the idea of the quadrants being segregated. The quadrant concept is only utilized so we can streamline training to be more militant because some Council members want us killing Sentries. Patterson isn't on board with that, and he was eager to give Collin wiggle room with different methods, different techniques, and help him break down the quadrants. He was going to defy my mom, Zander, and so many others and prove that we don't need to be soldiers. But then..."

"He got assigned to me?" I whispered.

"Yeah. That night, Avery and my mom ordered him to do it by the book. To be harsh. To train you the way that they would train you, no matter what he thought of it."

That was why he could be so normal and friendly, only with the hard edge that turned on and off. He forced himself to push me, tortured along with me.

Eva stopped for a second and sighed. "I overheard them talking last night. Patterson told Collin he still had the freedom to do this differently. But he—"

"Collin said no, didn't he?" I asked. I wasn't sure if this was the part Eva couldn't share.

"He said... he didn't know what to do anymore, along with some other things I won't repeat."

"Eva?" I said again, as threatening as I could sound.

But a different look was on her face when she looked up. "No, Aislyn. That's all I can tell you." She looked sympathetic. "But that doesn't change your pain. And I'm sorry. I don't know what he's going to do today. I don't know what this week will be like for you. But I think it's up to…"

I interrupted her by getting up and leaving.

I hoped I wasn't hurting her feelings by leaving her mid-sentence.

But seconds later, she jokingly yelled, "First one is free, by the way. Next time, I'm bribing you. With cake."

I kept walking. With every step, I willed myself to keep going so I didn't lose the nerve to start a conversation I didn't know I could finish. I resolved to give him one chance; I would ask him, not accuse him.

As I entered the Training Circle, I saw him standing with his back to me, almost like the first time I had ever seen him.

"Why?" I shouted, wishing that hadn't been my first word and hoping anger wouldn't cloud my brain. "Why in the world does this need to be like this when you don't want it to be?"

He turned, his eyes confused and apprehensive, looking tired and haggard—the opposite of the day we first met.

My voice rose this time. "This isn't what you want to do. This isn't who you want to be. I know that now. You never wanted to train anyone like this, but you do it anyway. Why?"

He shook his head, catching up quickly. He stood up, walking towards me, yet still defensive. "I don't want to hurt you, but I need to push you. It's about legacy and your missions succeeding and you…" His voice rose to match mine, emotions weaving through it. Urgency. Need. Fear.

"You take Avery's advice, then? So your career can survive?"

He took a breath to try to calm himself. "It's not them, and it's not the career. I'm worried... I'm worried that they're right."

"That you'll never get to be a trainer again if you don't fall in line and do it their way? That you'll miss your gold star on your endless papers?"

"I'm worried if they are right and if I train you the way I had planned, that you will d—!" He stopped short, choking on the last word. The breath fell out of him, his eyes squinted under his crushed brow. "If I defy the other trainers' methods, and you died, how could I forgive myself? How? What if I tried to win a point and I lost you?"

He stared at me with compassion that I could never mistake for a lie. The tears in my eyes stung. His breath shuddered until he clenched his jaw.

"Aislyn, the instant I was assigned to you, I was terrified. I shouldn't tell you that, but it's the truth. Yes, I wanted to change things. I wanted to change physical training, give you a chance to recover and use different muscles every day. I wanted you to read Protector profiles instead of just hours of HistCulture lessons. I wanted to encourage you and give you positive feedback rather than bullying you. I was so empowered because

Eldridge chose me, but then... they got to me. Avery got to me. And I read your file. The file of a smart, funny, beautiful student and friend and sister and daughter who I was going to kill if I messed this up. I thought that if I forced myself to be stern and follow the plan, I could keep you alive."

I closed my eyes for a second, breathing in what he had said. But in his declaration was the hope I needed him to see again.

"Collin, what if you were right? You believe in destiny. I doubt mine sometimes, all the time, actually... but that doesn't matter. Collin, you... you believe it. You actually believe in so much more than me, and I can tell. What if that's why Eldridge chose you? What if you train me, and that's how I don't die?"

He stared ahead, taking steps forward, and seemed torn between saying something or remaining silent.

"Collin, what if the Council didn't ask you? What if Patterson didn't ask you? What if I asked you?"

"Would you ask me, 27?" he said, now sure of his words. "If it means you might not get more Vessels than Tessa? If it meant that we were outcasts? If it means I can never push you enough to get up the wall faster than Lydia? If it means you would fail tests and never get to prove to Tessa that you were good enough? If it meant being different from everyone else?"

I stopped short. He had found my weakness. I wanted all the trainers to change, not only him. I hesitated to answer, feeling guilty for being swept up in their game just as much as he was. A part of me knew I shouldn't care whether I was ever as good as Tessa in anything, but I realized that I already did.

Collin's eyes didn't break from mine. "And would you even ask me: the rookie, the loser, the idealist, the dreamer? The person who still has to keep things from you and can't even tell you..." He paused, but returned his gaze, more intense.

"Would your risk your life, 27, after I've already failed you, and still ask me?"

The words I spoke next were strong enough to push out any fear I had left, but they still came out as a whisper.

"Yes. Collin, will you train me?"

He kept his gaze on mine, searching for the friendship we had denied each other for the sake of playing the part they had forced us to play. And one word escaped from him; from the fear that had pinned him down.

"Yes."

It felt like breathing after being underwater too long. I hoped he didn't see it as childish, but I held out my hand like I had the first night I met him. He reached out to grab it, and whether because I had been vulnerable or I had chosen a new path, my fingers burned as they met his palm and curled around it.

"Let's try this again," he said, "If you can forgive me."

I nodded, as he squeezed my hand harder. I smiled subtly, keeping my eyes on his face, which was changing to look more curious that solemn.

"Aislyn, can I ask you a question?"

He had said my name, not my number.

"That's usually my line," I said. "But sure."

"I talked to Patterson last night, but who told you—oh, never mind." He rolled his eyes. "Eva."

I couldn't help smiling, and it diffused the serious atmosphere as he shook his head in laughter.

"I might get her cake! On second thought, I don't want to encourage her that much."

"She did say I had to bribe her for the next one."

"How much did she tell you?" he said, looking nervous.

"Nothing else," I said quickly, remembering Eva's words.

He looked relieved, but closed his eyes, as if in pain. He shook his head, then looked distracted. "And why aren't you in Tech?" He at his watch. "They canceled Tech. I missed that."

"Why would all the Tech people be in a Council meeting?"

"Don't worry. It's probably about some intel chatter."

"Like that server crunching numbers for the Jubilee Day law in Secondary Central?"

He looked shocked. I bit my lip. I had just earned his trust.

"Aislyn, how do you know about that?"

"Um... I was talking to Sam randomly one day, and he..."

"I've been trained since I was thirteen to tell when people are lying. You haven't yet, but you're about to. Don't try it."

I felt nervous to break his trust, but I said, "He showed me the alternate Central and the server room when I couldn't sleep."

"He worked the graveyard shift last night. What were you doing wandering around at midnight?" Collin shouted.

"I'll never do it again, I swear..." I told him.

"No... You're fine, actually, I don't think there is a rule against that. But why aren't you sleeping? I thought it would be two days of homesickness, but you should be fine by now."

I shook my head. "I only get about four hours a night."

He put his head in his hands. For a second, the torture was back, but then it faded. "I'm sorry, Aislyn. I should've asked."

I sighed. "Well, I should've told you," I admitted.

"Okay, we're running, not lifting. You can't do muscle development on such little sleep. We'll go for two miles."

"What do you mean? Together?" I asked.

"That's the plan. We run together. And that'll give us time to review all the words for Common Phrases 1, and I'll tell you how to shut off the power to a server," he paused, seeing my reaction. "Afraid I'm going to cramp on your style?"

I stifled a laugh. "No, I just got used to being alone."

"No one should get used to being alone, Aislyn. But it's your choice, if you're still mad or you need time to forgive—"

I interrupted. "Don't apologize again. I forgave you. It's worse if you keep saying it, as if you don't believe me."

"I'm sorry. I mean—"

He tried to keep in his laughter, but mine burst out. He smiled, almost apologizing again as we laced up our shoes and started. The first few steps felt strange, as if filled with a hope I hadn't felt since my name was called. We ran past the garden and past Eldridge sitting by the rocks. He spoke, just loud enough for us to hear, as we ran past him.

"It's about time."

CHAPTER 12

"Okay, so, who is Hanover?"

Collin sat cross-legged on my feet, putting pressure on them so I wouldn't lift them up off the ground as I did my crunches. This was the tenth HistCulture question he had asked during exercises that morning.

I answered Collin's question with only one word that would have left no doubt in anyone's mind what I thought of Hanover.

"Well, he certainly is that and worse," Collin said matter-of-factly. "But just in case the computer doesn't count Republic expletives as answers, could you answer a little more thoroughly?"

I crunched up and wrapped my arms around my knees. "He's a current Elite representative. He is responsible for creating thousands of advertisements that brilliantly lock people into more debt so that Sub-Terras work their whole lives for the sake of their 'parent' buying more things they don't need."

"Good answer," he stared at the paper. "Keep your stomach tucked in more as you come up. Protect your back. Tell me what to do if a Sub-Terra has a panic attack when they get to the forest?"

I answered in fragments, every time my chin was near my knees. "Tell them... specifically... what they can earn. If you tell them... they can have it for free... or we will give them a real life or even they can keep their baby... they act suspicious..." I stopped and laid on the ground, trying to focus as my stomach burned.

"That's a good answer," he said reassuringly. "And it's enough crunches, too."

The last week of ISO had been tough, but not in the way I expected. Collin had transformed my entire daily routine. I could now pass the most rigorous of Common Phrases tests, complete two sets of lunges with the weight bar on my back and climb to the forty feet mark on the wall in under a minute. He had explained muscle confusion, and how it would work to my advantage. My legs and arms were sore, but today would be crunches and miles.

I dreaded going back to group classes. I finally felt safe with just Collin and me, training in our Circle. Tessa's words and glares replayed in my mind, no matter how many days we'd been apart.

"Okay," he said as he popped up and reached a handout to me. "So now you've done your crunches and told me all about your first year in middle school, breakfast."

I felt embarrassed for a moment. "Sorry, I rambled."

"No, really. It was fascinating. I loved hearing you talk about it. I never got to experience that much awkwardness. I'd rather have run ten miles a day!"

"Some days I would've, too," I said, shaking my head.

"Oh, good because we're doing six today, but..." he was leading into it.

I groaned but stopped when I saw my breakfast.

"What is this?"

"It's... is it not bacon?" Collin asked.

"I know what bacon is," I snapped back.

"Well, you didn't know what a transponder jammer was yesterday. Just making sure," he said playfully.

I glared.

He looked offended. "Oh, that's a Brie-strength glare, you can't give me that. I just gave you bacon."

I laughed, then stared at the bacon. "We only had bacon on special occasions, like Christmas and Rosemary Day and the last day of the school year and the morning of the cerem—"

I bit my lip, wishing I hadn't thought about that morning.

But Collin must have figured it out. He looked nervous.

"Hey, Aislyn, if you don't want it, I can take it back down."

I snapped out of my memory. I took a bite.

"It's bacon, Collin. Of course I want it."

He laughed, but still looked a little concerned, taking a seat, but leaning in to hear me. "Aislyn, what was it like?"

"What?"

"Christmas. Rosemary Day. The last day of … I think I never had a last day of school."

"Don't they have summer at the Academy?"

"No," he said, shrugging, looking at the wall. "I mean, obviously it's summer, but we still have classes and drills. I had an extra flex class. That's when I would read the summaries of the stories I was telling you about. But I never had… summer."

I paused. If these words would be the only way Collin would understand summer, I wanted to use the right ones.

"It's like sunlight became a solid thing, instead of just light. It could fuel you, with warmth and just the feeling that anything was possible. We'd tear up all the papers and run through the halls, like they were huge snowflakes in the wind and fury of us running, and the teachers would swap out their chairs, as some part of a competition to see who would get the best one. And there was music, from some random band member, and some prank—"

I stopped, before the rhythm began, and ended with, "And there was bacon."

I didn't want to continue. It hurt to remember what I might be giving up, but then I saw his reaction.

"Keep going," he said, now leaning his head on the wall.

And I talked, for maybe thirty minutes, about all the beauty he had never known. About the twins getting their bikes on Christmas morning. About the year I got the lavender for my mom in the special jar that kept it fresh longer. About the year the dandelions came early. About the Christmas I got my paint set.

Every time I would feel I wanted to stop, I'd just look at his eyes, with wonder at my silly, everyday joys and the words I used to describe them. With every moment I paused, he took a breath, as if otherwise he was holding it.

His watch beeped, drawing him out of his trance.

"Sorry, that was just…" he shook his head. "I could listen longer, I promise, but we really can't."

"I know," I said, almost relieved that we could stop, but then terrified of what he had said earlier. "How many miles today?"

His one eyebrow raised, and he smiled back. "I need you to try for six today. You can get to eight next week."

"Right," I said, tightening my laces.

"Aislyn, you can do this."

"Yeah, if I can get over my second mile hurdle," I responded. "I can't seem to recover from... never mind. I'll get it, it's okay."

"Well, let me go with you again," he offered.

I wanted to protest, but I didn't have the energy. When we had run together the night before, it was only one mile around the compound. But a long run always ended with my rhythm of panic. I would be on the ground, covered in sweat and fear, with every future moment I would ever miss weighing on me.

"Are you sure? You have a meeting, I thought."

"No, I don't. All the other trainers are prepping to repair the station hit by the drone and camp out in Zone 2 a bit."

"That sounds important. Why aren't you going?" I asked.

He didn't answer. He looked in the middle distance while tightening the laces on his shoes.

"Collin?" I asked, feeling guilty. "I'm sorry, if—"

He cut me off. "No. You don't get to apologize. Let's go."

He stood up, and despite his short sentences, he seemed calm. We started, stopping only a few minutes in to get some water. I tried to recall the map again, or other HistCulture facts.

We passed some trainers on their way back to their Central, who glared at him. Collin ignored them. He didn't miss a stride. He kept talking, continuing to explain the colors that were fashion trends for Citizens this year.

"Collin, thank you," I panted.

"For what? The green is hideous, way too bright. You shouldn't be thanking me—"

"No, I mean... you won't let me apologize." I caught a breath before continuing. "I can tell no one approves of how you're training me, and I don't want you to have to regret—"

"Don't worry about them," he said, though he sounded like he was almost trying to convince himself. "I don't regret anything. You, on the other hand, will regret the color green ever existed."

I stopped quickly to focus on keeping my breathing at an even pace. Jealous of his ability to talk and run, I listened to him continue to talk about the latest trends for upper classes. He noticed I was panting.

"Are we going too fast? Do you need to slow down a little?"

"Yeah, a little."

We continued on the path leading to the center of the forest. My white shoes like a strange contrast to the green, the brown, the natural colors on the path. The smell of life was permeating everything. Reminding me of home and every story I had just told him this morning.

It began. I tried to control it, tried to listen to Collin chat about working with Sam. But it was right before the start of the third mile when the pace dropped, and the rhythm began, because I saw a berry bush.

I would never pick the berries again.

I would never throw them at my brothers again.

I would never be scolded by my mother again.

I would never pull them out of Olivia's hair again.
I would never braid her hair afterward.
I would never sing to her again.
I would never be... I would never be...
My breath shortened. My eyes blinked back tears.
"Aislyn?" Collin stopped telling whatever story he was telling. "Aislyn, talk to me."

I didn't answer him at first. My legs were lead. Fear had paralyzed every muscle. I collapsed, just able to get my hands and knee under me before I hit the ground. I kept saying, "I'm fine."

Collin ignored my words. His hands grabbed my head and cradled it closer to his until my eyes were only inches away from him. He was looking for any sign of dilation, most likely. His fingers took my pulse. His hands felt warm, which meant my skin was clammy.

"Collin, it's nothing. I'm sorry. When I'm alone, I think... that I'll never be... I'll never see... What if I don't make it—"

There was a choking sound from the back of my throat that made him look even more concerned.

I would miss it. Everything I had been before or dreamed I would be. My fears spilled out in words he had never heard, speaking them out loud for the first time: never singing, never sewing, never braiding Olivia's hair. For two minutes, I poured out everything that had echoed in my mind for weeks. I tried to hold back the tears, wiping off my eyes and nose in one swipe. But it threatened to come back. I didn't want him to think any less of me than he already did. I half expected him to be disgusted and leave me there.

But he didn't.

He leaned my head up again, the fingers that had been taking my pulse moving back behind my neck, grasping it with the intensity he wanted me to have when listening to his words.

"Aislyn, you will always carry this fear. But for everything you can never be, you will be so much more. You are called to something better than fear. So am I. So are the Vessels and the Unnecessaries waiting for you. Don't give up. It's just a year."

"Not if I don't come back. Not if I—"

He pulled me in before I could say anything and gripped me in the strangest, most unexpected hug, my hands still keeping my balance on the ground, my head tucked into his shoulder, breathing choppy breaths, heaving out worry, and trying to contain sobs. I thought he might say something else, but I was glad he didn't. It might make it way too personal, and I wouldn't know how to react.

But he said the one thing I didn't expect.

"Don't give up on you, Aislyn. I never will. I never will."

I buried my head in his shoulder, wishing my tears would end, but he pulled me back so I could see his eyes.

His hand remained firm. He leaned his head on the other side of mine, whispering words I could barely understand that helped fight the fear away and prayers he must have prayed as a child. He repeated, "Don't give up on you" over and over again. After a few minutes, my breaths deepened and slowed. Collin pulled away; his eyes burned into mine. His brow creased with worry, and his mouth opened as if he had something to say, but no words came.

I nodded.

Without saying a word, I stood up, my knees only shaking. He didn't catch me or move to help, maybe because he knew the value of me coming up for air on my own.

I looked down at my watch and said, "Two-point-seven miles. Three-point-three to go."

I ran at the same pace before we'd stopped and crashed for my emotional breakdown. I felt petrified that he had lost respect for me. I wanted to apologize, but that would mean I'd be fishing for his opinion; I hated when people tried to do that.

He spoke a few minutes later, when we had established our pace again.

"There was this Protector in... the 144th Generation. She saved one of the first babies from the lab. She rode on top of this train to get in the facility and found this perfect little soul who was going to the furnace because he had a genetic mutation where one eye color differed from the other: heterochromia. She was the first ever to break into a lab, disguised as a nurse. It was ironic. She had always wanted to be a nurse."

He paused. "Maybe instead of thinking about the things you'll never get to do again, you can think of all the things you will get to do that are still… you. That are still a part of you. They can still be your dreams. You just have to dream all over again."

I kept running, remembering the last thought in my rhythm.
I would never sing again.
But I would. I would sing again.
I would sing to a baby two minutes after it was born.
I would sing to a little girl who'd never heard a song.
I would sing to a boy lost in the woods.
I would sing again.

At the end of the six miles, I finished stronger than I ever had. We stopped right in front of the Circle, feeling my heart race, but my last steps were solid instead of weak.

Without thinking, I put out my hand. His hand hovered over it for just a second, enough for me to see a tiny shake, and then rested his fingers on my palm. He waited, counting, closing his eyes. His touch felt warm. As he pulled his hand back, the warmth didn't fade as fast as I thought it would.

"Your rate is good for that kind of run."

"You mean the run where you emotionally throw up all over your trainer?" I was trying to be light, but I felt awkward.

"Yeah, that kind," he said with a skewed smile. "Take a walk to cool down. Garden. Ten minutes, then we're hitting Medical."

I stepped out, thankful for a little break. I turned back to look at him, but he wasn't watching me. I felt a pang of guilt as I saw his weary chiseled face. I thought about that tired face all the way out to the garden and the story he told. I recalled all the stories I had heard, so lost in their details that I didn't notice who was in the garden.

"Find anything lately, curious girl?"

Eldridge was sitting on the stones again. At first, there weren't any assistants immediately in sight. Then I looked around and saw a group of them all looking very exasperated.

"Sir, I'm sure they get annoyed waiting for you."

"Oh, yes, but why be a politician if you can't annoy your staff once in a while? Besides, I told them they need to calm down and see the garden, too." He looked around me, eyeing up his agitated workers and sighing. "Not that they're listening. I guess people still don't know the difference between what they need and want. What about you, 27? What do you want?"

I sat down across from him. "The more I train, and the more I feel like I could do this, and the more I wonder why any of us are doing this. Why don't we end this war? Why play the game of saving one by one? Why not free them all?"

"Oh, well, I wasn't expecting a question that silly for a while."

"I'm serious," I said angrily.

"So am I. I would have thought you could find this answer. We do what we do for a reason: war is a game no less costly than this." He stared at me, sighing. He was already old, but not nearly as old as he looked right now. "Real war asks for dying rather than living. That is the nature of war: kill for power. This way, we stay safe and save who we can. The Republic is bound by their own declaration of mercy and enlightened thinking. They can't kill innocent people in the Territory. Just us. And because we have no weapon that can erase the kind of brainwashing the Society has imposed upon their people, if we fought a war, we would fight it against the victims, not the enemy. That enemy would kill us without remorse. This way, you erase the death. One at a time."

"It feels so... status quo?" I said. "Just go, save one, come back, repeat. And it's like... that's how people treat it. Like a job. And they're the trophies we win rather than people we free."

"I know. But if it helps, think of it as a war. I believe you have observed by now that you twenty-seven girls are not the only soldiers. You see how Sam and Liam fight. Most people don't, but you do. But take a chance and see everyone, Aislyn. Our soldiers in this war also adopt children, sing to them when they wake screaming at night, work at the Academy serving future heroes by getting them food and cleaning their laundry, and counsel the Vessels who can't even process their emotions. Would you rather be part of any other tedious status quo?"

I looked at him, his words stinging after my recent revelation. Maybe I would've answered differently two weeks ago, before I saw the people who believed in this and their odd mixture of hope and worry, grasping for a chance to save a life.

"No, I wouldn't."

"Then you've said enough goodbyes to your old life, or are tears during runs normal now?"

I closed my eyes, now knowing that it wasn't a coincidence that he was in the garden after my last run. I wondered if he had security cameras. But he winked.

"You were always going to be scared. I called it, remember? Just keep being curious, and you'll find what you need."

His short silver hair shone in the sun as he stood up and meandered back into the darkness, where more worries waited.

I walked back to the Circle, telling Collin my cool-down was fine. I thought Collin would react, but he stared at a book. He opened his mouth as if to ask me a question but stopped.

"Collin, what is it?" I asked, nervous.

He sighed. "Let me get your pulse and your blood sugar."

I reached out my hand for him to take my pulse, cringing only slightly at the prick of the needle on my finger.

I felt vulnerable enough to ask, "You can tell me. Really. After all, I think I've told you enough about me. Probably too much."

"No, not too much. If I had to lose anything so beautiful, I'd probably be freaking out, too."

I wasn't sure what to say. His hands still laid heavy on my wrist, holding it, but his demeanor had shifted.

"Something is off, with your numbers. I missed it, and it's been throwing your whole training off." He leaned in, pulling a strand of hair away from my eyes. "Aislyn, you're lying. I can tell you're still not sleeping. And I need you to tell me why."

I didn't answer. I couldn't tell him.

"Is it like the forest? Like an anxiety attack?"

"No," I said quickly. "And I'm not just saying that."

He nodded. "Maybe..." He moved his hand to my fingers as his other hand laid on my wrist. "The Republic is horrid. It's like watching a nightmare. Maybe if your HistCulture videos were earlier in the day—"

"The Republic will bother me when I'm in Zone 2 with a child they tried to murder or a baby they tried to burn alive," I answered. "You and I are fine now since you're not sending me on shame runs. The truth is... oh, you'll think I'm childish..."

"Aislyn, it's fine. Just tell me."

I held my breath, then let it out in a slow stream. "It's just that I always used to talk to Olivia when I went to bed. She would lie down, and I would tell stories or tales I made up. You know, what battles the fairies would win or how many stars it took to create a flower or what Jack once did with a few magic beans."

"That sounds beautiful," he said. "Again, all the reasons to be afraid. Things I'll never know."

I paused, trying to tell him without my emotion taking over.

"I'd write after the stories," I continued. "She'd fall asleep as my brain started imagining, and I'd write in my journal. I feel like I've broken a pattern." I stared at the ground. The rhythm began.

I wouldn't be reading.
I wouldn't be writing.
I wouldn't be—

But I would be.

I'd be writing debriefs.

I'd be telling fairy stories to Unnecessaries, hiding in a Q-station.

I'd be writing down mission plans.

I looked up at Collin, trying to change the subject. "Didn't you listen to stories as a kid?"

"I can't remember," Collin said, staring at the ground. "For the last ten years, I've fallen asleep in my barracks, a small room with one glass window and a glass door. Seen but never heard. I don't think my dad ever read me stories, now that I remember."

"What about your mom?" I asked.

I instantly wished I hadn't. His eyes got distant, his mouth opened, but his voice caught in the back of his throat.

"Did she... like Megan's mom?"

"Yeah. But not like Megan's mom. Not in childbirth. I was two years when she... You know what? This isn't about me. We don't have to talk about it if you don't want to."

He diverted quickly. I debated arguing, but I decided there were too many other things I wanted to understand about him. I didn't need to ask him about the thing that would cause him pain.

"I'm sorry I asked," I said, feeling like it wasn't enough.

He smiled, with a quiet thank-you that I wasn't expecting. I wanted to ask him more, but bit my tongue so hard I winced from the pain. He sighed, as if unsure of what he was about to share.

"When I grew up, I would talk to God as I fell asleep. And yes, it's why prayer is vital to me. It's like breathing in something when oxygen isn't good enough anymore. It defined me as I got older because I loved it. I could either be devoted to it—believe that God was there—or I'd have to admit I was crazy for my whole childhood. But I didn't feel crazy. Not at all. It was like talking to a friend. And maybe it's all in my head, but the whole time I was training you like Avery, I could hear a voice telling me to do what I knew was right. Again, like a friend."

He stopped and asked intently, "I don't suppose you'd want to try that?"

I felt jealous. I had never even heard of prayer defined that way. I was beginning to believe his definition of God was more genuine than the one I had formed from stuffy old ladies shushing me in church or gossiping about who wasn't following the rules. But I wasn't ready to let God in my head.

"Not yet."

He nodded, his hands pulling through his hair once more and his eyes finally meeting mine.

"Well, I'm not an eight-year-old girl and you can't braid my hair," he said, making me laugh. He sounded unsure but sincere, "but if you need someone to talk to or tell stories to… I'd stay out of the room…but you could talk to me until you fall asleep."

I stared at him, my trainer who was choosing to give up more of his time, risk more vulnerability, and show more compassion. My brain screamed, *"This is not a good idea. You should say no."*

But instead, I said, "Okay."

A few hours later, after mind-numbing HistCulture lessons and another failed C-section attempt, he came back into the Circle with a bottle of water. I had already gotten dressed and was in bed, with my usual headache and soul-ache returning.

He sat down in the threshold, his back against the door frame. There must have been a rule that he couldn't cross into my space, which I think I remember reading from a random manual.

"So," he said, "what was the first thing you talked about with Olivia?"

I smiled at the irony of that moment. "What I did that day."

"Hmm. So, what did you do today?"

I laughed, despite my headache. "Well, I had a better day than the last few weeks. My trainer isn't a jerk anymore."

"Yeah, he was acting like a real jerk for a while."

I smiled at his ironic tone, but then I almost choked up. "My friend told me his mother died. I never knew. I hope when I told him I was sorry, he believed me. Because I'm so—" I paused for a moment until his eyes moved from the floor back to mine. "I'm so sorry."

He nodded, looking solemn again. "I'm sure he believed you."

I took a breath and continued. "And I ran six miles without dying. I finished my lessons. I threw up when I tried to do a C-Section again. And yet, I feel okay. How was your day?"

A boyish smirk crossed his face. "You know, a friend of mine mentioned stories today, and I think one of them sounded familiar. She said there were magic beans. I remember there was a beanstalk, and a giant, and some... cows? Or was it sheep? And a goose and golden eggs. But I don't remember what happened. I don't know how the story ends."

"Well then..."

He listened with the intensity of a child, smiling at the pure wonder of the beanstalk, the giant, the goose, and the eggs. At the end of the story, my eyelids were falling, despite not wanting to miss the strange wonder in his face. Collin sighed, looking at the door frame instead of me now.

"It's a good story," he said, as if to himself. "I like Jack."

"Why?"

"Get the eggs out. Save the goose. Sneak them away from the giant. It's like what we do."

"Well... I guess so. It is what we do." I sank into his words. The last thing I heard was my own voice, a thought that escaped my mind, spoken right before sleep overtook me.

"But it's such a strange way to fight a war."

CHAPTER 13

The sweat ran down my forehead, burning my eyes. They remained open, glued to the climbing wall towering above me, until I looked down at the beads of sweat on my wrist. Collin's fingers swept off my arm to grasp my hand.

"Okay, are you ready?" he said, looking at his watch.

"I just ran two miles. No."

Collin's eyes were blue and convincing. "Say yes."

"Yes," I said, certain I had lied to myself.

"Okay, your time was thirteen minutes thirty, which is awesome. Your pulse is fine. You got this, Aislyn. Go."

I ran the last few steps to the wall, where twenty people waited—probably for me to fail. No one cheered. No one cheers if they think they will end up being embarrassed for believing in you. Tessa made sure that if anyone cheered for me, they would lose their credibility.

This time, I reached twenty-five feet at a steady pace, but at thirty feet, I slowed down, unable to find a good hold. I didn't want to look down. Collin shouted at me to look up. I was running out of time.

"Just because you failed yesterday doesn't mean you can't still do—," Tessa yelled up. Patterson had probably told her to shut up. That encouraged me to reach for the next stone grip.

But the lowering of expectations made my heart sink in dread. I hated how Tessa's words echoed louder after she said them.

I heard Megan's voice scream up, "You're already most of the way there! Go for fifty, c'mon!"

I reached up, but my hand cramped, and I quickly reacted again, my fingers burning. I had a blister from the previous day, and I was pretty sure it had popped. I was only at forty-two. I ignored the pain and looked up again, unsure which rock to reach for. I reached, then lunged out to get to the stone farthest away. It was riskier, but it was the only way to reach fifty in time. Three more pushes, one near slip, and one more stone.

Fifty. I'd made it to fifty. Under a minute.

There were some claps and whoops from Megan and Collin. Tessa was predictably silent.

"Oi!" Patterson called. "You're bleeding. Come down."

I looked at my blister. For a small wound, there was a lot of blood. My heart was racing as I came down. Patterson nodded, but then turned to Avery. Tessa complained that it was unsanitary for her to go up the wall now.

"Good, I'll go," Megan said, pulling the carabiner out of Tessa's hands. "We've got the same blood, so I don't care."

Her eyes met mine with pride. She winked, but then Patterson ordered me to get a bandage before I could thank her.

"Good luck!" I shouted as Collin pulled me away, talking to me all the way back to the Circle. He wrapped a bandage around my finger, apologizing every time I winced.

"It's okay," I said, trying to keep my breath steady. He checked my pulse again. "But you could have told me it hurts to land like that with almost no tension from seven feet. Why did you do that?"

"Well, most times, when you jump in the Republic, it's almost a ten-foot drop from a fire escape. You need to get used to it. We're practicing rolling when you fall next week."

I looked up at the cloudy sky, desperate to find something other than his hand touching mine to think about.

"So, I have a question about HistCulture."

He looked at me curiously. "Yeah, anything. What is it?"

"This morning, I was watching a video. With only Sub-Terras working because everyone else is granted allowance, where does the Republic's food come from? I understand the Republic claims it all comes from farming machines, but I just can't wrap my head around it. Do they really get it for free?"

"They have food production units like we have, but much more advanced. It only takes two people to grow food on, like, two thousand acres or something, from seed to harvest. It's crazy. Our smartest scientists still haven't figured out how it works—not even with blueprints that we've hacked a few times. It's an energy source issue. We can't replicate it, or we may not even have discovered whatever energy source they use. Lynn's a bit obsessed with it. She calls it her problem."

"Still," I said, "it's sad they miss out on it."

"On what? The joys of weeding and thorns?"

"Yes," I answered, ready to argue, but he continued.

"I know what you mean," he said. "They never get to see something come out of nothing, or the shine on the first leaf that comes out, or the feel of the briars and how it feels to save the roots of the plant from the weeds. You're right. They miss all the joy because they want none of the pain and waiting."

Every time he shared how he saw the world, I would lose myself in his words and my heart would race. His hand was still on my wrist. I hoped he wouldn't wonder why it was beginning to race while I was standing still.

I wanted to divert, hoping he wouldn't mind that I pulled my hand away a little sooner than normal. "So, what's the agenda for the rest of the day?"

"Well, you've got more speed drills with your pack, a test on Common Phrases, and we're going over cultural details not in videos." He held out a small energy bar and a drink.

"What kind of stuff?" I asked before taking a few bites and taking a sip. I instantly wished I hadn't.

"Ugh!" I reacted.

"Like drinking coffee without gagging. Sorry, you've got to master this. They drink this every day in the Republic."

"Then it proves that they make bad choices in every area of life," I reacted again. "The coffee the other day wasn't this bad."

"I added sugar and cream. You've got to drink it both ways."

"Why?" I said, but it was muted because I had taken another sip and was wrenching at the taste.

"They don't want to gain a lot of weight so they avoid sugar. It's an acquired taste, and you'll get used to it," he said. "And that's enough. That stuff dehydrates you."

I thanked him, rinsing my mouth out with water as he continued.

"But this proves my point, Aislyn. It's all… small things. For example, when you walk, you act like you have a place to be or a reason to get there. In the Republic, they don't do that. They kind of wander, meander. Try to walk like that. Go ahead."

"Sorry, I need to learn how to walk?"

I was disheartened to have to re-learn something I had been doing for almost sixteen years. But I tried. He corrected me several times. He said my feet were going too high. He kept repeating, "Keep your feet low," until I glared at him for the fifth time.

"Try this," he said. "You told me that you walked in that meadow, then you were ten. No plan, no agenda. Walk like that."

I was shocked he had remembered that story, but I tried to remember how it felt. My feet walked, just above the ground.

"That's perfect. Daydreaming for hours made you great at this, didn't it?" He answered my angry glare with a playful grin that made my irritation melt away. "Now, try some Common Phrases for shopping. Say a few of them while walking... shops above Fourth Street. Remember, keep your feet low and light."

After I had completed the next task, he added, "And their eyes linger, they don't stay focused easily. Yes, that's it!" He paused, and I tried a few more phrases, drinking the coffee again. "Remember, your hands and feet shouldn't have any momentum. They do tend to move a bit more to music if they hear it."

"How?" I asked. "You sing to music. Or dance a reel to it."

"Their music is different from ours. Vastly. It has much more of a rhythm, very technical sounding. But either way, most dances end with someone hooking up with one or more partners off the dance floor. So, most of the lyrics..."

"Early teenage hormones wrapped in one-night stands?"

"Yes, and that's more polite than I would have said it," he said with disgust. "The other prevalent style of dance in the Republic is more traditional, for the balls that Elites and Citizens attend. Very orchestral, with slow, formal dance moves."

"When are we going over dance?" I asked, a little excited.

"We don't. Brie had some basic lessons, and they were torture for her. We rarely send a Protector into a club or a party. The parties in the center city are very exclusive, and the style of dance is drastically different, with songs hundreds of years old and even more difficult."

"Like..." I wanted to scratch an itch I just realized I had.

He sighed. "I should've known better. Hang on," he said, then held up his finger as he walked over to HistCulture, only to come out with what looked like a small MCU the size of a key.

"Play Dance 1, lower-level basic street music... track six."

Collin spoke into the device, but it was the walls that came to life. Suddenly, the entire Circle emitted a low bass sound in a quick rhythm, mixed with an angelic voice among the grungy, electronic beat.

"It's... It's just so..." I looked at him, biting my tongue.

He whispered. "You can say it. I know what you're thinking."

"It's beautiful," I said, still guilty for saying it aloud. "So, you just kind of..." I bounced while walking, pulled my arms up, and spun around twice before I noticed his stunned face.

"What? Did I do something wrong?" My hands were still up, and I felt frozen in his shocked gaze.

He continued to stare at me. "No, that's actually... Can you do that again?"

I did it again. He said to copy him for a few more moves. I copied, perfecting them after the second time he showed me. Compared to combat moves, climbing a wall, or doing crunches, these moves seemed simple, even if it made my muscles ache.

Ten minutes and a few moves later, I asked, "So, can we try Dance 1?"

He looked at me, his eyebrows raised. "We just finished it, Aislyn."

"That was... what? That's it?"

"No, seriously. It usually takes girls months to perfect what you did in twelve minutes. We haven't been able to train anyone to dance like this in years! You... can do... this is fantastic! Do you know what this means?"

A relieved sigh escaped me. I knew what it meant. I was going to not fail at something. On the other hand, I was still suspicious of my own ability.

"But, Collin, aren't the seasonal balls harder to get into?"

"Yes, but it's a lot easier to teach you the classical and Latin songs, even though you'd need a dress to get into a Citizen or Libertas party. But if you got in, there'd be Sub-Terras serving everywhere below floors." He paused nervously. "Do you mind if we try that?"

"No, go ahead."

"Play Dance 2, classic music, for Aestas ball."

Within seconds, a very different music filled the room. It was slow; it sounded ethereal, soft, and flighty, with violins and cellos.

"This is a preview of Dance 3. The Libertas, Citizens, and Elites tend to have more of a diverse taste in music, like I said."

"Okay, how do you even dance to this?"

He sighed. "I hope I remember this song. Well, here we go." He reached out his hand, looking at me tentatively before breathing with the hint of fear I had seen earlier, "Oh, um... you don't dance alone to this one."

"Oh," I said. I paused for a moment, not wanting to make it more awkward. I moved forward, feeling exceptionally unprepared to be so close to him.

"So, um," he continued, "it's mostly a lazy waltz... but you don't know what that means. Think in three counts, down, down, up. Your partner would put one hand out, and you rest one hand with theirs. Like that. Um... and I just wrap my fingers lightly around, and you put your other hand on—yeah, my shoulder."

I did, and he gave me a shy glance. He reached behind me, and before I could ask what he was doing, his hand was on the small of my back.

"Sorry, I'm just going to... Just trust me."

He pulled me closer, until I was only inches away. I was glad he was not taking my pulse right now.

"You okay?" he asked.

I nodded, not answering so I didn't lie. "Now what?" I asked.

I didn't want him knowing that I was nervous, and hoped he couldn't see the tension in my eyes as they scanned the small pieces of stubble on his otherwise flawless face.

"If it's this tempo, step out, then two small steps, but very smoothly, and think down two, up one. Yes, that's it. Follow my lead. Keep your back straight, arms up, but shoulders down."

I moved out with him, from side to side. As I sank into the beat and the movement, I dared to look at his eyes.

"You're doing great," he said, smiling, "which is so weird. Brie really struggled with this last year."

Anger simmered inside me, and I told myself it wasn't jealousy at the thought of Brie dancing with him. I almost shook my head, reminding myself that I was in training. This was nothing more than crunches, wall climbing, or running. It wasn't personal. But that truth both relieved and stung.

"Bet you still would've rather had them as Protectors some days," I said offhandedly. "It would have been easier."

To my surprise, he stopped mid-step, pushing against the small of my back so I wouldn't step out from where he now held me.

"Look, I know I said I was sorry, but it'll never be enough. I can't believe the way I acted those first weeks. But you called me out. The real me. You made me care about all this all over again. You made me care about things I had never even known about. Aislyn, you should never think I'd want anything other than this."

He must have known I couldn't breathe, that his next words would ruin me.

"You should never think I'd want anything other than you."

He stared at me in a way that made me think he could read every thought I was thinking. Only I wasn't scared. I wish I could just tell him, but I didn't even know what I felt.

"You need to be just a little closer," he added.

I stepped closer, feeling his breath on my cheek as we continued. I silenced the voice in my head that was asking me what he meant by that. This was probably the most important friendship of my life, and it had to keep me alive. I focused and started practicing Common Phrases again.

We perfected several movements of the dance while laughing and forgetting all the surrounding stress. Dance 4 was even easier, because I just had to take cues from Collin. I forgot to breathe a few times but convinced myself it was ridiculous to think about him that way. We only stopped to eat meal bars, which seemed extra tasteless today.

"I'm going to call Faith at the Academy and ask her for Dance 10. I'm too far behind on updates to teach you. Faith hasn't personally tutored someone for years. She'll be thrilled," he said, looking at his desk.

"What's this?" he asked, holding up my MCU.

"I was listening to the field studies," I said quickly. "I was just writing down notes. I liked the one quote. *'All of this begins and ends with you finding something worth dying for, then living for it.'* It helped me get through the last day and I just—"

He stared at the paper, with a strained reaction. I couldn't read it, but it looked like pain.

"She was the 167th Generation, right?" I said, still drinking my coffee without reacting.

His eyes finally looked up, his expression unreadable. "165th," he said, trying to shake off his tone. "It's a good quote. You should remember it. Ignore all that, I don't know what got into me."

I wasn't sure if he had snapped out of it or if he was playing a part, but I didn't have a chance to ask him.

"Happy not-ISO-week video party!"

Perhaps thankful for the distraction, he turned to Eva and smiled. "She just finished!"

"Ugh, tell me that isn't coffee?" Eva asked, then winked. "I thought Collin was done torturing you."

"She doesn't have to finish it," Collin said. "Seriously, water for the rest of the night." He threw me the water bottle.

Eva said, "I might even need some coffee. I'm exhausted. I have to pretend to be pregnant in a forest again tomorrow."

Eventually, we all had to run at least one field test at 90 percent. Someone had to pretend to be pregnant, wearing a synthetic belly that could simulate an entire birth process.

"When's your test?" I asked.

"Oh, I passed already. Yesterday, with Brie. It's why I'm not at the shelter with everyone else. Why aren't you at the shelter?"

The other Protectors had all gone to the shelter to meet former Unnecessaries who had been rescued, but I was too far behind. I didn't feel like Collin apologizing again, so I owned it.

"Catching up," I said. "I've got a lot to learn. But while I was learning how to walk… I think I missed my run."

Collin paused, and looked at his watch.

"Yeah, you take a lap," Collin said. "We'll be here."

I nodded to Eva and left, still looking at Collin, staring at the paper on the table. I was glad to leave the Circle for a second. It had been an oddly intense day, but as I left, all that ran through my head was the music. I was humming when I passed the garden, unexpectedly hearing Eldridge say, "Nice tune."

"I didn't expect to see you here," I said, jumping slightly.

"Oh, I certainly hope not. Everyone needs to be surprised." Eldridge smiled, almost as mischievous as my brothers' grins.

I may never see my brothers smile again.

Quickly, I killed the budding rhythm and replaced it with a new one.

I'd see a Vessel's peaceful smile as she rubs her belly.
I'd see a baby smile at leaves.

"Any questions today?"

I shook my head. "Just a few. Sir, why don't we have music like the Republic's? Like anything like the Republic does?"

"Many people are very wise, Aislyn," he sighed, "and I hope that gives you hope. But, I'm afraid, many are foolish. When we broke off from the Republic, it was for exceedingly good reasons, as I'm sure you are well aware."

"Yeah, I've seen enough videos to know that. But the music, the dancing, their paintings... are they so wrong that we have to banish their creations and ideas? All of them?"

"Of course not," Eldridge said, and his lack of defensiveness surprised me. "But fear lends itself to avoidance. And so, the Territory avoided all association with anything in the Republic. A quiet tragedy to not see beauty where it is—which, oddly enough, we accuse them of regularly. It's music, it's not a life."

"But what if music was supposed to be someone's life?"

"Touché. Your question requires an answer I don't have, Aislyn. I honestly don't know how to convince the people of the Territory that the Republic can create anything good. If you find that answer, 27, let me know."

An assistant rushed to us and said, "Sir? It's urgent. You're needed in Central right away."

I must have looked worried, because Eldridge turned to me and said, "Oh, Aislyn, don't worry. It's not your turn to worry. Out of the million problems a day, I can't ask for your help to solve them. Not yet."

I gave Eldridge a thankful smile as he got up and moved quicker than I thought he could go to the door.

By the time I returned to my Circle, Collin was gone.

"Where'd Collin go?"

"Got called. Ran downstairs. Why?" Eva said, sorting files.

"Oh no." I said it mechanically, starting to wonder if I should be worried. I looked back up at Eva, only to see her panic face.

"What happened?"

"I was talking to Eldridge," I said, pointing behind me. "And someone pulled him downstairs, said it was urgent. In Central."

"That's not good."

I heard footsteps running behind me and turned to see Collin in the doorway, panting.

"That's worse," Eva added.

He shook his head. "Downstairs. Both of you. Now."

We ran to the door, took the steps down two at a time. When we reached the Central Hub floor, Patterson's voice became clearer.

"... confirmed. They were ten miles out when the signal died."

I turned to Eva who whispered, "Brie and Lynn. They were on a field test. That must be them."

"Something went wrong," Collin whispered. "Lynn was messing around with an EMP design. She succeeded. The Electro Magnetic Pulse went out and fried everything. That means that their camo tent won't work. Their MCU's are out. It's just supposed to be the monthly, off-season flyover, but most of the trainers are still checking on stations." There was fear in his eyes.

Someone yelled that the scheduled departure time for the drone hadn't changed. I looked up on the screen with a countdown. Fifty-seven minutes. I quickly put the pieces together as the voices became muffled around me. The countdown seemed to surge through my body, matching my heartbeat as it got faster.

Brie and Lynn needed an EE, but nearly every trainer was at the station. The Protectors were at the shelter.

"We're still only staffed for one recovery shuttle and we don't even have their exact location," Sam yelled,

"No," Eldridge said, walking to where Collin, Eva, and I stood. "We've got enough for at least one more."

Everyone turned to us, but Patterson looked directly at me. While others turned back to their screens, his eyes stayed locked on mine, as if waiting for confirmation. I nodded, feeling braver than I felt. He opened his mouth, hesitated, and then turned around, pointing to Sam while yelling out orders.

"Three shuttles. One with the trainer apprentices and Zoe is on point, one with George, Eva, and Michael. One with Collin, Liam, and Aislyn. Make it happen."

Someone pulled Collin away, speaking quickly to him. Eva ran over to where George was waving for her. Eldridge stayed, staring at me, as someone jabbed a comm in my ear.

"Well, Aislyn, it looks like I won't be waiting long to ask for your help after all."

Ten minutes later, my fingers pulled down the straps of my pack to secure it to my back. Most of the medical canvas rolls had been taken out. I pulled at my standard black camo suit. I had waited weeks to put it on, wondering how I would look in it. Now I didn't care.

The hurried energy of people prepping our shuttle made me cling to the straps of my pack again, so none of them would notice my hands were shaking. Collin kept giving me directions, which I followed without asking questions. We ran the half-mile to the shuttle yards. I couldn't speak at the pace we were running, but Collin might not have answered me anyway. He was too busy listening to Sam to give him coordinates.

When we arrived, one shuttle was already taking off. I waved at Eva getting in the second shuttle. Collin turned to me.

"Stay with me. Just keep up, do what I do."

I nodded, copying Collin's movements closely. I stepped into the shuttle, threw my bag in the space under the seat, and strapped into the restraints. Patterson must have been behind us. He ducked his head in the open door just as Liam started the engine.

"Four miles, directly east. Start there, where Sam said to check." The other shuttle took off as he spoke. "They have south and north. You have coordinates of the last comm check?"

"Yes," Collin yelled over the engines. "I'll signal with four-thirty-three or eight-twenty-two once we have confirmation. I've got this, sir. I'm ready."

Patterson looked at him for a moment, then at me.

He didn't have to say it. And I couldn't fake brave now, with the shuttle engine rumbling beneath me. Instead, I asked with a shaking voice, "And I'm not. But it doesn't matter, does it, sir?"

Collin looked from Patterson to me, even while putting his MCU in the shuttle's computing unit.

"Sir," Liam turned around and shouted, "we're cleared. Waiting for confirmation code from you."

"You knew I wouldn't be ready," I choked out, but my voice was stronger as I continued. "You still called my name. You said you'd trust me. You promised me."

Patterson stared at me, even as I swallowed the rising fear. I didn't want him to see it.

He nodded, shouted, "Launch code four-ninety, YTPQ. Hit it!" and he closed the door.

I shivered as the shuttle took off, leaving the spinning lights of the shuttle yard behind. I'd never moved so fast in my life.

"Info in the SCU?" Liam called back.

"Yes," Collin said. He finished typing on the shuttle computing unit, closing his eyes as he folded the screen down. His mouth moved slowly, as if reciting something in his mind. I stared at the shuttle station until the lights were gone and then gazed forward. I kept listening to my breath, expecting it to stop from the fear of dying by a drone strike.

But it didn't. It kept going faster. I found myself taking in all the details around me. I started looking out the window.

"Remember, we need to slow down at three miles out. We don't want to miss them," Collin said to Liam.

"You thinking intervals every minute?" Liam shouted.

"Yes. Sidelights on. Aislyn," he turned to me and grabbed my arm, which was starting to shake, despite my best efforts to keep it still. But instead of telling me to calm down, he kept talking.

"Because of the range of the lights, they will see us before we see them. They've fried everything electrical, but Brie is old-school. And she's good. She'll probably have a small fire signal or something to get our attention. Every minute, we'll also stop, cut engines, and listen for anyone calling out to us. First stop is now."

I nodded. My focus drove out my fear. He released my hand. It was now perfectly still as the engines died. I stared out into the night, careful to not focus on the area that was lit, and looked for a spark. Nothing. We sped for a mile. Stopped.

Nothing.

We made our next three stops. Liam said that they hadn't reported in at the station, two miles away, so they were most likely still headed back to Central. No other shuttles had responses.

"Thirty minutes," he called back. We stopped again and cut the engines. We listened to the sounds of the forest and strained to hear a voice. Collin moved to my side of the shuttle.

"Anything?" he asked, his breath making clouds on the windows.

"No," I whispered, terrified I'd miss their footsteps or voices as I spoke. Liam started the shuttle again. Collin strapped in next to me this time. His shoulder pressed against mine. I kept my voice low. "Are you going to be this worried? When Protectors are out on missions?"

He breathed out a single laugh. "Probably. I'm already as worried as I'll ever be."

"Because you're out here?"

"No. Because you are."

I turned to him. My hand moved too quickly, but then I pulled back just enough to have it rest by his, until only the edge of my finger grazed his. I was worried he would move his hand away, but instead, he grasped mine, holding it tightly.

I told myself to focus on the mission, thinking I'd have to repeat that to myself to remain on point. I opened my eyes again as Liam yelled he wanted to go another mile.

But I saw something.

"Stop!" I shouted. "Stop now!"

Liam hit the brakes so hard, I nearly fell to the floor. Collin caught me, steadying my shoulders. I reached for the handle and pulled myself up as Collin punched in the code to open the door.

"What did you see, 27?" Liam called.

"Blue. I saw light reflecting off of something that was blue. A blue square. About the size of an unrolled canvas."

"Brie?" Collin yelled, his voice echoing in the valley of trees. It was only a second before broken twigs indicated movement. "Brie, answer me!"

"Collin?"

"Yes!" he called out, cupping his mouth with his hands. "Can you see the shuttle?"

"Yes! What's going on?" Lynn shouted. "I know I messed up with the EMP, but..." She fell, cutting her sentence short.

I ran to her, now more certain of their location.

"There's a drone, first class," Collin explained. "It's scheduled to launch in—"

"Nineteen minutes!" Liam finished.

The twigs broke faster now. By the time they reached me, Lynn's arms and legs were scratched and bleeding.

Brie wasn't even out of breath. I grabbed Lynn's bag for her and headed to the shuttle. Brie took a seat as I pulled Lynn up into the shuttle cabin. Collin sat next to the SCU and picked up the headset while holding on to Lynn's arm as she strapped in.

"Patterson, do you read me? Eight-twenty-Return in progress. The team is intact. Do you copy?"

Patterson's voice filled the shuttle cabin. "Collin, please confirm. All of you?"

Collin looked at Brie, who was now rubbing Lynn's back as she leaned over. He smiled at her.

"Confirmed. All of us."

Yells and whoops echoed with static from Collin's earpiece as I pulled mine from my ear, wincing but smiling. I breathed deep, feeling a rush of adrenaline as the shuttle took off.

"Hey, Collin," Brie said, "tell Patterson I might endorse your plan to do field tests in the forest by the wall from now on."

"I hear you, Brie," Patterson yelled over the earpiece. "And tell Lynn that we should keep amateur EMP building techniques out of field tests."

"I'm so sorry," Lynn looked up, her face still white. "You had to come get us, and... how many shuttles are out? Why are you and Aislyn out?"

"Everyone else is at the shelter or still checking on stations," Collin said. "There are three shuttles. They're all headed back."

"You mean..." she stopped, putting her head in her hands, "I just risked the lives of everyone who had to come out here?"

I couldn't imagine her guilt, but I wasn't going to allow her to feel it.

"Yeah," I said with sarcasm, "because we're all training to do this so we can be safe and cozy in our beds now, right?"

Brie laughed, which I had never heard before. It gave me a chance to catch my breath, shallow even after the short rush to get in the shuttle. Then she looked at me, as if she had seen something she wasn't expecting.

Collin smiled, holding Lynn's hand, mouthing, "It's okay."

"Think about it this way," Brie said as the shouts in the speaker continued. "We're all still in mortal danger. And this is as safe as we'll ever be."

A few hours later, I sat on the edge of my bed, watching Collin lean back in the threshold. When we'd returned, Lynn and Brie had been taken in a room to debrief. I had gotten a quick smile from Patterson and a wink from Eldridge. We were all in Central by the time the drone took off from the Republic.

After heading back to my Circle, I had tried to distract myself. I spent the next twenty minutes telling Collin Olivia's favorite story.

"Well, at least our shuttle didn't turn into a pumpkin when we were almost too late back to Central," he said.

I laughed. "I wondered if they danced the way the Elites do. I was confused by those scenes as a child, when the girl met the prince at the ball. I wonder if someone in the Republic would know it."

"You mean a story where the prince finds the servant girl from the basement and they dance together and live happily ever after?" Collin said. "They'd both be disappeared in no time."

"And disappeared means dead," I said with a hollow voice.

"Not now, Aislyn, or you'll never sleep," he said. "Sometimes, you can't afford to think about it."

"I can't think about that, a C-section, or being out there on a shuttle in the woods tonight. Or how Brie can be so calm when talking about dying. There are lots of things I can't afford to think about. Aren't there?"

I wanted to wait for a response, but his eyes were closing, before he forced them open. Collin warned me this would happen when the adrenaline rush died off, but I felt sorry for him. So I pretended to nod off. I didn't want him to wait up just because I couldn't stop thinking.

"Aislyn, you awake?" he asked to the darkness. I realized that he probably said it every night, after fairy tales and recaps from the day. Every night that I left the conscious world behind for dreams, he was here, asking if I had gone. I kept my head still, my eyes focused in just one direction and my breathing steady. I was satisfied with my performance when he began to leave... until the footsteps stopped. Then got louder. He was returning.

The doorway creaked a bit, probably as he leaned on it, before I heard his voice.

"You're not the only one who has thoughts they can't afford to think. I need to tell you the one thing that I can't. And I can't." He sighed, making me almost open my eyes. I kept them still and shut, desperate to stay hidden in plain sight as he continued.

"You made me... feel too much. And every day, I tell you every reason you should care about the Unnecessaries so you can save them. But by teaching you that, I started to care about you in ways I never should have. And I'm afraid I'll never be able to tell you how much. I almost became something I wasn't... just to save you. But it's almost as dishonest, really, that I could feel this way about you and not let you know. But you've forgiven me before, Aislyn. So maybe one day, if I confess everything I'm hiding now, you'll forgive me again. Not for hating you. This time, you'll have to forgive me for... all the things I can't say."

As he left, I continued to feign sleep. I strained every part of my body to keep it still while a part of me wanted to run away and another part of me wanted to run after him.

Because I felt everything he did, even if I didn't understand it yet. It felt like it did two weeks ago.

I didn't know anything all over again.

CHAPTER 14

A few days later, I went for a run even before Collin came into my Circle. I messaged him as the sun was rising, telling him where I was so he wouldn't worry. A pang hit my heart; soon, he wouldn't know where I was for days, maybe weeks on end.

I pushed it out of my mind, along with the fear of failure since, for the first time since I'd arrived, I felt like I might succeed at something. I still struggled to understand Tech, but Collin kept re-wording things until they made sense and taking me to Secondary Central with Sam to try some new techniques. I had completed the last of my Common Phrases lessons while running, doing push-ups, and during lie detection testing yesterday—which made it extra difficult, but invigorating at the same time.

Before putting the MCU down, I realized how comfortably it rested in my hand. How familiar it was to go for a run outside of my Circle. How much I now knew the person I'd just messaged. My arm twinged, letting me remember how sore my muscles were. Despite my proficiency, Dance 5 had proven to be more challenging than I imagined. I didn't even know I had muscles in places that were hurting. I wrote that in my journal quickly while lacing up my shoes, hoping it would make another 27th Protector laugh someday.

My private lessons were taught by Faith Bakerson, one of the few HistCulture instructors I got to meet in person. The last of the HistCulture videos were due this week, which I was dreading. I had mentioned I might go crazy with my overloaded schedule, and Faith asked Collin if I needed a break.

"Depends. What did you have in mind?" he had responded.

"Well, tomorrow we are going out with Brie to interview some saved Unnecessaries. I realized you've never been to the shelter. You missed the last trip, which was good because you rescued Brie and Lynn," Faith said. "You could come."

I gave Collin a "please, please" look, and he said it would be more beneficial than more push-ups. So, he had changed our itinerary, moving my run to dawn.

By ten o'clock, we were strapping into the private shuttle headed to the shelter. Brie was there to visit one of her rescued children, who she had missed on the field test with Lynn. She shared some stories on the way.

"So, why are kids born from Vessels integrated into our society, but most Unnecessaries are sent out here?" I asked.

"The main reason is that they've received enough rejection from society, so even the normal peer rejection of childhood would be too painful," Brie said, looking out the window. It was difficult to read her emotions, but from her tone, I didn't think she agreed.

"It seems harsh," Collin added, "but they need to build up their self-worth and learn some cultural customs, so they're more likely to succeed in the Territory. They need mental health tools to help them cope with what they've been through."

"But it's almost like we're ashamed of them, too," I said. "Like we don't want the responsibility of compassion for them."

"I realize that," Collin sighed. "But these aren't resilient kids, Aislyn. They have patterns of thinking that are harmful to themselves or others."

The driver announced we were almost there. I stared out the window. I realized how quickly it was coming, and for some reason, being on a shuttle again reminded me that in four or five weeks, I might be on a shuttle home with a Vessel.

When we arrived and opened the door, there were screams, hugs, and flowers in a flurry of arms I didn't expect. Kids surrounded us. One asked me for my photo, another for my autograph, and another asked what kind of shampoo I use.

"Whatever is in the bottle," I said. I kept walking quickly as Collin laughed, pulling me through the mob.

We spent the rest of the afternoon in the sun, in the glow that shimmered off dandelion fuzzies as they swam by in the wind, being carried to infest their garden. It was a stark contrast to the grey stone that had surrounded me for the last few weeks.

There were more children at the shelter than I realized. Collin had said the caretakers were the unsung heroes of this strange war, and their compassion convinced me he was right. They showed extreme patience, led each child with songs and positive language, and displayed grace and love to each child who asked a question. I also witnessed what Collin spoke about on the shuttle: the trauma these children had experienced had left them scarred. One girl kept asking me if she was still doing well enough, more than twenty times in one hour. Another sang to herself as if in a trance. A young boy had an anxiety attack after lunch. He screamed and thrashed on the floor for five minutes. They sedated him and sent him to Medical. His house mother cried with a counselor, explaining, "It's been four months, I thought he was over the worst of it."

Brie spent most of her time with her Unnecessary, who was about to be adopted. The girl made Brie smile in a way I'd never imagined. She also spent a lot of time with a two year old that looked up to her like an older sister. The older boys found tackling Collin to be more exciting than group therapy. I laughed as they wrestled him, climbed on him, and ran with him. He begged me to tell them a story, which I did, and then Brie chased them all down, playing hide and seek— and not letting them win even one game. I tried not to get lost in the horrible rhythm of not playing with the twins again, and got lost instead in watching Brie, shocked by her joy.

We sat on a bench, looking at the trees while Collin took his turn teaching the kids how Protectors are trained. It was part of the children's history lesson for the day. Brie liked silence, but it was a little too awkward for me, so I started talking to fill the void.

"Hey, you were really good today. With the kids." Even as I spoke, expecting her nonresponse somehow made my sentences always come out in broken phrases. "I didn't know that you were so good at that. I hadn't imagined you with babies, which is silly."

Brie spoke, but as if she were speaking to herself. "I love kids. I could be surrounded all day, like this. The first time I held a baby was one of the best days of my life. My cousin. But my mom never got me dolls. I would go over and play with my friend's dolls. I always thought it was because of money. So did my friend. So, she let me borrow on the last day of school. She said I could have it all summer. Wednesday. I remember it was a Wednesday."

I listened intently. Not only was this the most words Brie had ever spoken at once to me, but her words were haunted. My throat began to tighten at seeing someone so brave look defeated.

"I didn't get it," she continued. "My mom came in and saw me just playing with it, cradling it. I remember being so proud, so happy, showing her my baby doll and wondering why she was crying. And she wouldn't stop."

I started to envision the scene: her mother, despairing as she saw what could never be—Brie as a mother. Little girl Brie helplessly wondering what was wrong. Her little voice saying, "Why are you crying, mommy?" The conversation that followed.

"She told me several times before I understood. The test showed that the Shield Vaccine side effects would have been deadly for me. The results stated I was highly susceptible, so my mom decided not to take the risk. I didn't get the vaccine. My

Serum test was positive by the time I had started school, even with my mom trying to filter the water."

"I'm sorry," I choked out. She'd probably think I was an emotional weakling. "There's nothing... there's only pain, and no words can do anything to it. I'm sorry."

"I can tell," she said, turning to look at me finally, and I thought the awkward silence would follow, but instead, she kept talking.

"My mom came in the next day. It was a Thursday. I remember it was a Thursday. She saw me playing with the doll again. She was probably worried I was in denial, but I wasn't. I had stayed up all night and made a fake outpost station out of blankets and chairs. I had the doll in my backpack from school, and told her that if I couldn't be a mommy, I would be a Protector. And that was that."

She stood up, eager to evade any other questions. I realized the passion that fueled her, that had wielded and molded her into the perfect tool to defeat the Society. And while she might have wanted to escape it, I had to ask one thing from her.

"Does that make you hate them more?"

She turned around and considered that for a second. The moment lingered long enough for her blond hair to move in the breeze, making her stillness seem unnatural and strong.

"It used to. But then, I went to the Academy. I went on missions. Held a mother as she died. Saw a baby dead in the street. Heard a gunshot kill a friend. And then I see them walk by—unscathed, handing over their loyalty just to avoid anything real, gritty, or hard, even love..." She sighed. "After seeing that, nothing could possibly make me hate them more."

She turned and walked away, taking a place near Collin to answer the kid's questions. Collin looked over a few times. I tried to wipe the tears away quickly, but he came over to sit with me.

"You okay?" he asked.

I shuffled my feet in the dirt.

"You know, I was just thinking of the way the people walk in the Republic," I said, looking at my footprint fading as the sand sank in over its edges. "Do they ever realize that walking so lightly and smoothly means they never make an impression or leave a footprint?"

He nodded. "Their steps are busy, but never meaningful. Patterson said that once. Speaking of Patterson..."

"He won't be happy if we take too much longer on a field trip, will he?"

Collin smiled. "No."

In a few minutes, we were leaning back in the shuttle seats. I studied the dust dancing in the changing streaks of light from the setting sun. Collin had ignored four signals from his MCU, throwing it to the side and looking back out to the shelter. We were going so fast, but for some reason, the world seemed to stand still. I felt like staying on the shuttle, never getting off, forgetting our mission to just keep driving with Collin and Brie in our memories of both pain and joy, fear and happiness. The disparity screamed. Everything Eldridge had ever said to me seemed clearer.

I went back to my Circle and changed for my run, which I wanted to take for a change. I needed to go to the forest to cry about Brie where no one would see me, especially her. The miles seemed eerie in the leftover light from the sun, deserted and quiet. But I didn't cry. When I returned, the center room in my Circle looked ominous in the dusk.

I went to the video part of the library only to see a note.

"Hey, I have a meeting tonight. It's long, sorry. I'll be back by eight. Eva should be over soon."

Below it was another note.

*"Hey, I have to run scenarios with Cassidy tonight. Watch whatever, just **not** what we were supposed to watch tonight. I'll help you out later or Collin can help."*

And another note scribbled on the side.

"From Lynn: Sorry I'm stealing her. From Eva: Oops, didn't realize Collin was in a meeting. Skip it. Don't watch it alone."

I reached out to touch the corner note. I felt cherished and loved in a way that only scribbled writings can express.

Several videos were cued up for this week, so despite the warning, I chose the video according to the schedule. And within five minutes of viewing, I realized I had chosen the wrong one. I had put on a propaganda film for recruiting Medical staff in the Republic to test the babies for deficiencies.

It wasn't only that the doctors looked perfect, but their logical, grounded voice describing the necessity of destroying 'specimens' made my throat burn. They described every part of the process in a three-month-old's evaluation, with as much passion as I had seen in Brie today. They sounded excited and logical, making jokes and explaining the process like any other doctor I had met. Another doctor calmly described the list of ten imperfect traits to avoid, along with genetic anomalies, ranging from genome syndromes to missing limbs to two different eye colors.

Termination at age six was considered merciful. No drugs were needed to dull their pain of the incendiary pillars. That would be a waste of resources to dispose of an Unnecessary.

I watched, even though I wanted to look away. Today, I had seen their Unnecessaries. I had held them, hugged them, laughed with them. I stood up, not able to watch any longer, filled with too much anger, nausea, and disgust.

As I stepped out of the room, my breathing became uneven and shallow. The video continued playing in the background, and I thought about the little boy having the anxiety attack at the shelter. I thought about Brie holding another small toddler whose mother had died to bring into this world. I thought about all the lives they killed without calling it murder.

And I hated myself for everything I couldn't do.

I hated the fact that I wasn't stronger, faster, smarter. I wanted to be Brie. I could fight them that way, just brute force, wit, and strength that would evade them.

I had replaced my horrible rhythm with hope, but the hope evaporated – and it left me feeling desperate with anger.

With each step, I neared the punching bag. I let loose a few punches. A fury entered me, and I punched it harder than I ever had before. It felt satisfying to hit it, to beat something, to have my hands burn from the slight tug from the plastic on my hands. My fingers clenched so hard my knuckles were white, then red. It didn't matter. I didn't want gloves. My hands began to bleed. I should have stopped, but I couldn't. The phrase Collin had once said echoed in my head, a dreadful pattern.

You care.

But you don't care enough.

Not enough.

I hated myself much more than I hated them.

I failed to hear the footsteps running in. Collin's hand grabbed the bag.

"Aislyn? Aislyn, please, talk to me. What happened? Was it Tessa? Did you think of home? Are you afraid again? You can tell me."

That's what he thought would be bothering me. Drama. Or homesickness. I hadn't cared about the children who were always homeless. I punched harder and faster, as if beating all of the selfishness out of me.

He asked me again, repeating my name. I finally stopped, leaned against the bag. I wanted to talk, but some horrible choke in my throat made it impossible to do anything but cry. I looked up and saw him staring at the monitor. I glanced at it. It was an incinerator and seeing a glimpse of it almost made me vomit.

"Aislyn, you weren't supposed to—"

I crashed under the emotional weight, as if each stone of my Circle were stacked on top of me. He moved to catch me as I collapsed, sliding off the bag into his arms.

"It's okay, it's okay..." He stopped, sounding like he was choking. "You know what? It's not okay. I've lived with it so long, I forget. It's not okay. But you will change it. I promise. I am doing everything I can so that you'll have a chance to change it."

I was angry with him for having the audacity to hope. My head shook, his words echoing again.

"I don't care enough. I'm not good enough. Not enough."

He sighed and shifted to cradle my head in his arm.

"Aislyn, you're enough," he said with a calm authority. "I should have never said that. You are more ready than you know. You saw them today, and I could tell it changed you in a way you wouldn't have let it change you a few weeks ago. It gave you a flame, but that flame must give you light, so you can keep shining. Not a fire. A fire will consume you in anger or despair."

I steadied my breathing, trying to remember Brie's story and not get as angry as she must feel all the time. I shuddered a few breaths, easing into deeper ones. It was enough to silence the horrible voices in my head.

"Aislyn, can I pick you up?"

I hesitated, but then nodded. He lifted me and carried me to the bed in Medical, where he gently lay me down and got a cloth for my hands. He patted the antibacterial cream onto each finger. I sank into the blanket, feeling drained.

"Do you want to tell me a story?" he said as he wrapped the gauze over my knuckles.

I swallowed. "I don't have one."

"I've got to remember... How about another giant story? There was a boy, a giant, and a stone. The boy didn't have a chance. He was the smallest. He was the least of all the soldiers, but he took the stone... and the giant fell. The giant fell."

But that night, I had a horrible dream. The giant destroyed some eggs before I could rescue them. The boy ran out of stones to throw. Except it ended the same way.

The giant died.

The boy freed the rest of the eggs.

He had placed himself in the sling instead of the rock and died to kill the giant.

Then, he came back to life and said my name.

I woke up terrified. Collin was sitting in the threshold, wrapped up in the spare blanket and sleeping. I pulled the sheet back over my sweat-drenched body and tried to forget it.

One thing had changed.

Now, if I had to die to save the golden eggs, I would. I didn't care. And I wondered if that meant that I was ready.

I think that was exactly what it meant.

CHAPTER 15

I blinked to make sure I had read the message correctly, but I had; the first mission was only two weeks away.

Collin sat on my feet as I did crunches. He continued to poke fun at the story I had told the previous night about a princess who spoke to trees. He interrupted the morning silence by pointing out the most obvious plot holes, like the squirrels living in the trees becoming homeless if the trees were following the princess.

"Dead, homeless squirrels," he said, as I pulled up to my knees and glared at him. "I'm just saying. Itinerary is on your MCU. Five more!" he added when he heard me sigh in pain.

I continued to crunch up, hating the sight of my knees.

He continued, "After Intel—two more, Aislyn, push through—we'll have Faith come up and try Dance 7. Now, in a Sixteenth Street café, would you order coffee or tea?"

"Tea, if dressed as a Terra. Coffee with honey if any higher rank," I answered as I finished the last crunch.

He smiled, then stared back at his MCU. I took a moment to catch my breath, my chin leaning on my knees.

"Two more weeks," he said. He hadn't moved his hands, now nearly touching mine. We stayed there, inches apart. I breathed in as he exhaled, feeling nothing I never had before while terrified I was feeling it.

He leaned in slightly, but jolted up from where he sat. "Room Three-Forty-Three. Don't be late."

"I won't." I got up from the mat and moved for the door.

"And Aislyn, do me a favor."

"What?"

"Don't hold back. Speak up," he said, winking.

I ran under my archway and through the garden, wondering what he had meant. I stepped across the garden, taking a moment to touch the leaves of the vines that had stretched themselves across the arbor. I left all the beauty behind and went down the cool, echoing cylinder of Central's stairs, resenting that it kept me away from the growing leaves and sun.

I found the room, but stopped short when I walked in. The hologram platform up front displayed a street and people walking, fifty feet deep by thirty feet wide. All our seats, which had full-size CU platforms, appeared to have holographic pads on the side. Now I knew what everyone meant when they said it was "the cool room," and I had to agree.

"Told you so," Cassidy turned around to say, as Eva giggled, and Lynn stared at the room in awe.

"We saw this on the tour we took when we were thirteen. I thought maybe I had just blown the awesomeness out of proportion. You know, like when you're a kid and it's amazing, and you go back five years later, and you think it's lame." She sighed in contentment. "This is so not one of those times."

It wasn't until the instructor walked in that I noticed Tessa and Brie weren't there.

"Plug in your CUs so we can get started," the instructor said. "My name, as many of you know, is Eric Mallard. If I do my job, all of you can fake their way of life... and come back alive." He moved across the platform intently as holograms appeared on either side of him.

"Many people think of what you do, Protectors, as a rescue operation, and so you think regarding ops, protocols, and techniques. Next week, we will focus on lie detection and your combat lessons, with as much 'real life' as we can simulate. But this week, we are focusing on the basics of blending in, finding a target, and creating a story. Because as spies, that's what you are: storytellers."

I looked up for a second, intrigued by the words he had used, but also by the holograms all showing thousands of interactions with people. Eva moved her hand, hovering over the notes in the room's front. She swiped toward the hologram beside her, and the notes appeared on her display.

"I know, right?" she said, smiling at me.

I reached out my hand, impressed and eager to try it myself, except I froze as I heard the instructor call my name.

"Aislyn, on the day your names were announced, your fellow Protectors bugged the Council room, which Patterson and I monitored—with quite a sense of pride, ladies. There's something we could never figure out, however. When Patterson came in, he asked Aislyn a question that was answered with a perfect cover story. Who gave it to you?"

"Oh, here we go!" Eva whispered playfully, but I felt embarrassed, despite not needing to be.

I didn't answer, so Eric continued.

"The cover story was perfect: that you wanted to see your parents. Your execution was excellent, Aislyn. This is a perfect example of how any mission could fall apart without a realistic cover story, I'd like to give the stage to the person who created it."

Everyone paused. Eva, Lydia, Cassidy, and a few others pointed at me. The instructor looked shocked and then looked at Megan.

"I was in the wall," she shrugged.

He seemed to ponder that, but then turned to Megan and gave her a thumbs up. "Nice work," he said, then turned to me like he didn't expect to see me sitting there.

I took a breath and answered, "I sounded nervous, so I had to think of something to be nervous about."

Eric tilted his head to the side. He hesitated, but then pointed behind him. "Aislyn. Platform. Now."

I stared at him as he moved back down the slanted floor and to the platform. I walked onto the platform, almost worried I might break it, so I stepped very carefully. Several 3D figures appeared, in perfect proportion to where I was standing and their distance from me. There were structures and people surrounding them, even traffic, but they projected further than the classroom. I couldn't see anyone in the classroom anymore.

I heard Eva say something from the back of the room, for which Eric scolded her.

"Really, Eva? Language!" He turned back to me. "Look for anything suspicious or out of the ordinary. And try to ignore all the visual effects that seem fake. You're trying to answer one question: Vessel or Unnecessary?"

"Unnecessary."

I answered so quickly that I almost shocked myself.

"Food vendor," I continued, seeing the stand a few yards away. "It seems like it would be hard for an Unnecessary to gain food without money, and the obvious answer would be that they steal food when it's available. There are three men over there, in a conversation with the owner, so it's a perfect time to take something." I circled the figures as I spoke. "So, my goal would be to get within sight of possible entry points and the store window would make sense, because the view of the alley is perfect, even though it's on the corner of the opposite street."

Eric pushed a button. There was a sound, a strange buzz, as I walked to the store window. A hologram figure, a young female that looked like a Citizen or Elite class, spoke.

"Which is your favorite?"

With a glance at the nearest calendar in the window and the street name, I fell into character.

"Well, I'm not sure because I'm thinking pink. But it's perfect for a party I'm going to tomorrow."

"You are so right. I have a party on Second Street though..."

It was a test, but I had the answer.

"Too bad it's not in red and a bit longer cut," I said, catching a movement in the alley out of the corner of my eye.

I turned and made my way casually across the street, making sure to keep my feet low. I made my way to the stand, and glanced at the menu and looked disinterested. The hologram turned, so I didn't run out of space to walk. I continued to seem disinterested in the menu from behind the cart, imagining how foolish I might look from off the platform. Behind the dumpster, I saw a little girl. I squatted down, almost losing my balance having to remember there was no real wall behind me. But at that moment, the hologram disappeared.

And revealed an astonished class and instructor.

"Comments?" Eric said.

No one spoke. No one moved. Eric looked at his MCU.

"So, this is how we score. Forty percent is on your strategy, looking for the correct target in the correct area. Movement, conversation, and effective location without detection in the simulation is the other sixty percent. Like this." There was a score on the screen, showing everything he was saying again, with a scoreboard that showed *80 percent*.

"So, what was my score?" I asked. He stared at me, and I cleared my throat. "I mean, that wasn't my score, right?"

He lifted one eyebrow. "Of course not."

The score changed to *92 percent*.

I scoffed in disbelief and looked out to the class, who I thought would be as shocked as I was. But not everyone was surprised. Lynn, Cassidy, and Megan were smiling. Eva shifted in her seat, smirked, and gave me an exaggerated casual salute.

"I told you so," she called.

"As a spy, ladies," Eric said, eyes on me, "you write yourself into the story happening around you. It requires skill, but also imagination, intuition, and observation skills. Aislyn, again."

He pulled up three more scenarios. But no matter what character or new elements were added to the hologram floor, I could see my mission. A woman grazing her belly seconds after seeing a Sentry, a child avoiding eye contact even though he was well dressed, and a girl with sunglasses on a partly cloudy day. A Vessel. An excellent pickpocket. A girl with heterochromia.

Each scenario ended the same way: find, meet, and as I was about to make contact, the scene would disappear. After the third scenario, the three scores appeared: *96 percent, 92 percent, and 97 percent.*

"And with that," Eric announced and sighed, "the three highest scores ever on a final exam."

"This isn't the final exam," I said.

"Well, it was supposed to be!" Eric said with frustration. "I'll have to write a new one. And I hope everyone was taking notes."

Everyone had been typing on their MCU's, except for Eva, who was still beaming at me.

"Com, call Collin." Eric's voice was deadpan. I didn't realize what was happening until I heard Collin's voice answer.

"Collin here."

He put down his water bottle loudly. "It's Eric."

I heard a stifled laugh.

"She beat the test, didn't she?"

"And my final. I'm kicking her out until next week. And I don't want to hear an 'I told you so.' You need her?"

"No offense implied to 27, but yes, there's a lot we could work on up here. I'll tell Sam to change her itinerary."

Eric pointed to the door, and I was free.

I resisted the urge to celebrate. When I got to the garden, I allowed myself a single skip, a turn on my heel, and another dance move before reaching out to touch the green leaves. No one would see me.

Eldridge wasn't there, which made me a little sad. I would have loved to let him know that he hadn't picked a defective 27th Protector.

As I walked through the doorway of my Circle, Collin was in the center, leaning against the table from Medical, grinning. His eyes lit up when he saw me.

"I knew it. I knew you had it in you."

"How did you know?" I asked as he gave me a quick hug.

"Story!" he beamed. "Even though we train Protectors to notice details in individual segments, they can't always creatively put it all together. You notice everything, I can tell you talk. Of course, it's a lot easier to put all the pieces of the puzzle together if you don't train in segments, so..."

I smiled. "You just got proven right, didn't you?"

"A little." He pulled back to reveal the table behind him.

"Collin, I'm going to take a wild guess that the Med table isn't in the center of my Circle because it's being cleaned."

"Nope, and it's in the center because I want you to place it in the center of your mind right now. We need to move past every distraction at this point. You now have the confidence you need to do this. We have to conquer the one thing you lack the confidence to do. Figured since you are on an emotional high, maybe we can use it."

He pulled the sheet off the table to reveal what I guessed was underneath: the prosthetic used for a C-section.

"I can't make someone bleed. I can't cut into..." I stopped talking before I said much more. He leaned toward me as he spoke.

"Do you know why we end up doing most emergency C-sections?"

"Brie told us some stories in Medical. The two C-sections she's had to do were because the mothers died. They don't genetically engineer women to carry children. Brie said the one mother was just too weak, and the other just had her heart broken by being pushed away by someone she had gone to for help. Her vitals were slow, her BP was low, and she just flat-lined during an early contraction."

I was getting lost in the story, my blood boiling, and he came up to my side with my pack. He spoke inches away from my ear.

"Brie had about sixty seconds to start the C-section before the baby died. You're Brie. The Vessel is dead. The baby is going to die. What are you going to do next?"

I closed my eyes for a second and tried to imagine what it would be like, in a forest, watching someone so brave die in my arms because I couldn't save her. There was a baby still kicking, moving inside, about to suffocate to death—not because his mother wasn't brave, but because I wasn't. My breath quickened. I felt his arm next to mine.

"There you go. Now it's your story. Every breath is treason. Every moment is fear. But every life you save is hope. You've got fifty seconds. Go."

Within two seconds after opening my eyes, I was working. Within twenty seconds, I had made the first incision and clamped the faux-uterine wall so I could make another, which I did much more precisely. I pulled out the prosthetic baby within fifty-five, struggling to keep a hold on to the synthetic head, covered in the red fluid they used to simulate blood. The baby had blue feet. I had the suction tube within a few more seconds and removed the excess from the doll's mouth, who was letting out a strange mechanical cry. I clamped on the cord quickly and wrapped the baby up.

Collin said, "You did it, but you missed—"

"Cutting the cord in a second," I said quickly, then turned away and vomited.

When I stopped, he said, "Just cut the cord, give me the rest to clean up, including the synth baby, then go take a shower. I'll get someone to clean up. It's all good. Really. You did it!"

I felt weak, but his joy helped me stand up straight and jokingly say, "You can cut the cord and name her, if you'd like."

He laughed, nodding to the door. I was nearly to the shower when I saw Liam.

"Hey, where are you going?" I asked.

"Apparently to pick up a bodily fluid spill," he said with a smile.

I blushed. "What? You're Tech! That's not what you're supposed to... you're too qualified... no!"

"They have no one to send up but me. Besides, I feel bad for you. I know you've been stressing, and to puke and not finish..."

"I finished, Liam. I did it... then I was sick." It sounded better in my head, but he just smiled and shocked me with a quick hug.

"I just was sick, Liam," I said as he pulled away.

"Yeah, and I'm going to go clean it up. It doesn't matter."

"Touché," I laughed and continued toward the showers.

I was drying off when I opened the locker to choose another outfit out of the usual selection of white. The field clothes, black outfits, and Republic clothes were now hanging inside. I reached out to touch them, but then pulled the door across to slam it shut.

Every time I felt ready, I wasn't.

I ran upstairs, past the garden, when I realized that everyone was there, probably taking a small break from class. I thought I'd walk over and chat with Eva when I heard Tessa's voice.

"Another shower visit? I guess someone vomited again."

I almost kept walking. But today? I had finally had enough confidence to face her.

"Yeah, I just performed a synth emergency C-section, with a score of ninety-five percent, and it was a little messy."

"Why was Liam called up? Did you puke all over the baby? Poor thing. I feel pity for anyone you convince you can save. You'll kill them before either of you make it out."

At this point, I realized only six people were talking, but I couldn't make out a single sentence. Just a string of indistinguishable words.

"You don't have to pretend," I yelled, still staring at Tessa. "I know you're all listening."

They all stopped to face me, including Eva, who winked. But as I finally had all their attention, I decided I was going to make it count.

"I know I didn't always want to do this, but I do now. And I am not as useless or scared as you think I am. And I have found what you, for all your skills, have forgotten."

"What would that be?" Tessa replied.

"I want to save one life, not as many as I can. Not to get friends, or to become famous, or to fashion yourself a hero, or even to make yourself feel better. I didn't do the C-section because I had to do it for training. I did it for the one child I can save."

"Only you're not going to save them until you fall in line instead of trying your soft training where you throw away quadrants and need someone to run with you everywhere, holding your hand. Weak trainers make weak Protectors. They should have never let Collin anywhere near here."

She had done it. My respect for Collin was the only thing keeping me composed in this argument, but now I was desperate to defend him. I know I should have walked away. Instead, I said, "So, I should've become a passive-aggressive monster like you, treating no one with respect unless they worship you?"

"Maybe if you cared more, you'd understand why I fight so hard, and why I won't let up on you. Do you even know what Hannah and Avery say—"

I cut her off. "What makes you think that I need or want your opinion or that it matters? I don't give a—"

I was about to curse, I was about to scream, I was about to make combat training from two weeks ago look like child's play, but a hand grabbed my arm and pulled me back, unyielding, pulling me five steps away from her instantly.

"Stop," Collin's voice whispered. "Stop right now. You're just giving her ammo." He kept pushing me away, toward my Circle.

"You stop!" I turned to face him, trying to pull my arm free. "I was about to... Collin, this is embarrassing."

"Well, don't worry. She's not allowed to fight with you either, and"—he turned to look behind him, then back to me—"Yeah, Sir Avery is not too happy."

I turned to see Avery towering over her, angrily moving his arms around as he pulled her from the group.

I faced front again and said, "I'm okay," and he let go of my arm. "Collin, I'm sorry. She gets to me. I don't know why, and—"

"I know why," he sighed. "No one can remember a time when she wanted to do this for a good reason. And that is why I don't want you watching the Territory broadcast tonight."

"She's on the broadcast tonight?"

"Yes, she is. And you can't watch it."

"Why?" I asked, feeling more jealous than I wanted to admit.

"Don't watch it. It's an order."

"Okay. Sorry."

I debated telling him what she'd said about him, but I figured it would only stress him out more. Instead, I managed a smile and remembered that I had just mastered a major hurdle.

We went to the forest, going over possible scenarios for that night's field test, setting up camp, and the simplest survival skills for if I lost my pack. These lessons included a warning to never start a fire or else drones would find us. After hours of drills, high jumps, and techniques running through the brush faster, I went back to my Circle. Collin went to his weekly meeting, leaving me to think, meditate, or read. But a part of me stared at the screen that wasn't on in the HistCulture room.

I wanted to know what she was saying. I tried to push the temptation out, but after looking at the clock, and knowing Collin wouldn't be back for another hour, I couldn't resist. As I turned on the monitor, Tessa was already on stage, talking into the mic as Avery stood behind her, cameras flashing at every angle.

"—the priorities are different this year. We're all ready for the kind of training changes we need to keep us alive. Everyone has been on the same page with more militaristic training and it's been perceived so well by all of us."

I stared at her image again, already burning with anger. She answered a question about the friendship and comradery of the Protectors this year. "Honestly, I've tried very hard to cheer other Protectors on, more than I have in the past. It's been refreshing, because there's been a lot of perfectionism and competition. But after last year, I wanted to be a mentor more than a competitor."

I heard it but could barely believe it. She was twisting the truth so much it was almost a lie, yet it wasn't. This was the reality she'd created. She cheered on certain people, using silence as her exclusion and her silent judgment, making everyone else feel small.

Someone asked her about the more dangerous conditions. She answered, "I want everyone to succeed. There's only a few trainers using the old methods, and I think we'll prove by the end of the year that it's not effective. We'll have to see what happens, I guess."

"Aislyn?"

I froze, hearing the anger in Collin's voice as I turned around.

But he didn't look angry; instead of rage in his eyes, there was only confusion and betrayal.

"Did you hear her?!" I exclaimed. "She's twisting everything, she just insulted you and basically said she hopes I die to prove you wrong? And she—"

"Doesn't matter!" he yelled. "You promised me. You promised me we would do this differently, when you asked me to train you. You said you wouldn't care what anyone else thought!"

The weight of his words crushed me. My betrayal was much worse than Tessa's. One look in his eyes told me that, although his image was blurring in my tears.

He sighed. "I didn't want you to watch it because I didn't want it to distract you. You'll replay her words in your mind, and it will tear you down! You didn't trust..."

His brow creased, and he held a fist over his mouth.

"You're right," I said. "I said I didn't care what she thought."

It had been weeks, but I remembered the punishment for breaking a promise to a trainer—and I had broken more than a promise. I took off my shoes, feeling the cold floor beneath me.

"What are you doing?"

"What does it look like?" I asked, my tears fading under my determination.

"Yes, but I wouldn't make you... I didn't tell you..."

"You don't have to. It's not a punishment. It's a way I can tell you that I'm sorry." I handed him my shoes.

"Everyone will know," he said, almost exasperated. "They'll see you running barefoot. They'll guess I told you not to watch it, especially after today's fight, and they'll know you did and—"

"I don't care! Being obsessed with what they think made me break a promise to you, one of the few people in this whole place I—" I stopped myself before I said something neither of us was ready for. ". . . That I care about."

He held his breath, in the silence before my last words. His breath shuddered as he let it go. I didn't wait for a response before running out of my Circle. I couldn't say anything else I might regret.

"Just two laps," he called after me.

The cobblestones were hard beneath my feet, but once I got to the grass, they felt fine. My heart ached more than my feet ever could. Collin and I had finally become friends, and despite my self-inflicted punishment, I worried it wouldn't be enough to fix it, to fix us.

"Don't," I said out loud to myself as I ran past the first corner of grass.

I had struggled to admit how I was feeling. I had rejected it only because I had feared it. Even if he did love me, he couldn't afford to speak the truth. And neither could I.

To my horror, I passed a group that included Tessa. Her reaction was predictable, but I looked ahead. I did hear Megan, who smiled, jokingly saying, "We saw that coming."

"What'd you do, 27?" Eva asked, breaking from the group to run backward beside me.

"Not now, Eva."

"Fair enough. Tessa always lies in broadcasts. Don't let it get to you," she said, winking. "Are we still on for tonight?"

"Check in with me in ten," I said, a little out of breath now.

"Will do. You got this. Keep those feet moving."

She peeled off, and I kept running.

Tessa said something, but I ignored it. I didn't even hear the words. I only heard Collin, begging me to trust him.

I headed back into my Circle. Collin sat next to my shoes in the center of the white mat, his head down. I sat across from him.

"Did anyone see you?"

I nodded. "Yeah, even Tessa. Don't care."

He looked at me curiously, and then his tone became more serious. "I said I would never send you out without shoes again."

He took a second to grab my shoes in his left hand and held them out to me. As I reached for them, he moved his right hand to touch mine, and I grasped it.

"Really, Collin, don't worry. It was oddly therapeutic. No more drama over Tessa. Promise."

His broad shoulders straightened, almost looking surprised.

"Am I still...?" I started.

"On for the field test with Eva? Yes. You up for that?"

"Yeah," I said. My hand squeezed his as he pulled me up. My body ached but letting go of his hand felt worse.

Collin grabbed his MCU and opened the files we needed. He asked if an EE would be allowed in the first day of Zone 2 for a Previa at twelve weeks. I answered, "Yes."

The review questions pushed my feelings to the back of my mind. I wondered if I would ever get a grip on what was going on in my heart or control what I was beginning to feel for Collin.

"Would you order an EE for a Three-Twenty-Seven-DC situation?"

The answers to both questions scared me.

"No."

CHAPTER 16

"You know, this is the life. The great outdoors, the sounds of the forest, the beauty of nature with no one around... except the four cameras representing the horribly critical teachers and Head Trainers waiting for you to mess up."

"Eva?" I said. I had to listen to every word from Eva, which was starting to annoy me, despite my laughter. Eva was playing my Vessel for the field test. She rubbed her enlarged belly but seemed disinterested. It was a synthetic birth kit set at twenty-five weeks, simulating a baby's vitals. True to the name, it would eventually simulate a birth as well.

"You're supposed to be making this a little more realistic," I stated. Since the beginning of the test five hours ago, we'd made past the "Zone 2" border, according to the simulation map on my MCU. Being one mile from an EE zone pickup spot for the next day, we could stop where we were instead of having to travel closer. So, we made camp. I used the small knife in my pack to hunt a rabbit. Eva realistically reacted to having to eat the animal in a way someone in the Republic would.

"How could you kill an innocent, living creature?" she cried dramatically.

To calm her down, I explained that it was the only way we could survive, and used some other phrases I had memorized. It wasn't until ten minutes later that I told Eva how I'd actually love to answer the question.

"You live in a culture that abducts children, burns babies, and kills pregnant women. This is a rabbit. Eat it."

Eva cracked up laughing, but said she was glad that was not my official response, as it would have meant a repeat field test and she was tired of being pregnant.

The Society Party's new campaign for a vegetarian diet meant that when we ordered food in the Republic, we'd often be ordering only vegetables. When I asked Liam about it, he'd said that there had been recent shortages in the meat market. Because they wanted to make sure that no one felt deprived or unhappy, they had just reinvented "happy" again.

When I asked Sam which theory he thought was correct, he had said, "Efficiency in all things. The Society probably did it to solve two problems we know about and three we don't."

"Oh!" Eva interrupted my thoughts with emotionless acting. "I feel the baby kick. How amazing." She checked her clock and took another bite while rubbing her belly again.

"What do you think we will talk about?" I asked. "With them? Even with Unnecessaries? I know we have to say things from our script and from our therapy book, but..."

Eva must have already pondered this, because she had an answer ready. "I want to tell them they're brave. Brave enough to walk away from everything they've ever known because they want to do the right thing—in a world that doesn't even teach them that there is a right thing. I couldn't imagine that."

Eva shook her head, not giving me time to respond before jumping back into character. "Will I get to keep my baby when we get there?"

"Yes," I answered, getting back into character myself. "There are homes already provided for you, and you will have a year to get settled. Some retired Protectors will check in on you daily, to help you assimilate to our culture. You will love it. Really. Everyone there believes in this mission." I could hear my great tone change to uncertainty at the end.

"Well, that almost convinced me," Eva said. "What happened at the end?"

I had still been thinking about my conversation with Liam and Sam. They had told me that no Protector had ever defected.

"I guess I'm always afraid. Afraid that one day, a Protector won't buy the truth and trade it back for the lie. That a Protector will, or already has, bought that lie. That one day, we will be betrayed because we had the audacity to think all Protectors were guiltless." There was a pause. To lighten the mood, I added, "Too bad no one ever rebels in the Republic."

"Of course they do," Eva said. "They come with us."

She looked at her watch, and her eyes widened.

"What is it?" I asked.

"Oh, a great question, Aislyn! Perfect lead-in. Um... there's a huge puddle under me," she said mechanically.

"Your water broke!" I yelled. "First, sit down. Oh, right, you are sitting down. Good."

I went through the list. She needed to stay seated. There was no reason for me to call for an EE until I could give them a scenario. I got out the ultrasound and hooked up the monitor as Eva tapped her hands on rocks next to her.

I took a few minutes and ran through my script for the quick summary of childbirth, explaining contractions and medications.

"You will always be okay," I added. "From now on, you're okay. You have no contractions yet, according to the monitor." I felt the synth birth belly, and it was soft.

Eva looked at me, surprised. "Good, I feel reassured and all, but... um... hang on, Aislyn." She touched her earpiece. "This isn't the scenario they told me we were doing, and I don't think the suit's working, Patterson."

Suddenly, there was a beeping sound on my MCU. The belly under my fingers stretched and became hard. Contraction. From the smirk on Eva's face, it seemed I wasn't getting off easy. I didn't get to my painkiller canvas roll fast enough, and Eva let out an ear-splitting scream, which only ended after I got the appropriate dosage in the needle.

"There is no way a pregnant woman would scream that loud on a first contraction."

"You never know," she said. "They might. What are you injecting me with?"

"Painkiller and Terbutaline," I said as I flicked her artery one more time and jabbed her with the faux-pain meds, which were actually saline. "If you get the chills, it's the side effect of the meds."

I ran through the list in my head, brought her "vitals" up on my MCU, explained that I was getting us an EE, pulled out a heating blanket, and ran full speed for the comm station. After a mile or so, I saw the small camo flag in the ground, opened it, and clipped on the MCU within seconds.

"27 to base. Come in, base. In need of an EE. Have a premature birth, only thirty weeks. Water broke already."

I waited in silence. Finally, there was a response from Sam.

"We see you, 27. Good to hear your voice. Send us vitals, and we'll get a crew out there in three hours. Medication?"

I cursed in my head for forgetting to report that. "Yes, painkillers and Terbutaline." I rattled off the dosages, our coordinates, and sent the vitals.

I spent the next hours waiting, with Eva pretending to cry. I had to follow up with more fake medicine and monitor the baby. Soon, the shuttle came, and I carefully maneuvered Eva inside and strapped her into the cot. I attached the vital cords to the wall unit that monitored her. Eva asked me one more thing, the thing we were warned that Vessels sometimes ask.

"What should I name the baby? It's a girl, right?"

"How about Olivia? That's my sister's name."

Eva smiled. "It'll do."

There was a loud beeping sound through everyone's earpieces.

"Ugh!" Liam said, yanking it out of his ear, then gently replacing it. "Joel, you've got to find a better way to end a drill."

Eva quickly jumped off the cot, shed the prosthetic belly, and strapped into a seat.

"Liam, do you mind if...?" I nodded toward the front seat.

"No, not at all. You did good. My gut says probably eighty-five percent, but I hope you get a ninety percent so you won't have to do it again. We don't have a lot of time left."

"Yeah, no kidding. I can't believe I forgot to report dosages!"

"You did great. Maybe they won't catch it. Otherwise—" His finger went to his ear. "Wait, what? Now? Ugh, fine."

Liam took out his earpiece and handed it to me.

"Hey there," Collin's voice said. "How was it?"

"Good, I guess. I should be asking you."

"They gave you a ninety-point-five percent. You passed…barely, but you passed. Give Sam more info, okay?"

"Right," I said, sighing with relief.

I was going to try to respond, when Eva shouted, "Oi! What was your score?"

"Ninety-point-five percent."

Their response made me want to laugh and cry at the same time. Eva opened the window, letting the cool air hit us all as she screamed out in victory, a stark contrast to the quiet forest.

Liam revved the hover-pads a few times and yelled, "Last one! Last drill of the season!" Then, changing his tone, he added, "The next one is real."

As I walked back to my Circle, the clouds lifted. The moonlight hit the stones, which made them white instead of grey.

The Hand was prepping for missions. Everyone else in Central was scrambling to get ready. They were all missing this moment: the light of the moon, my fear disappearing, my hair weightlessly blowing in the breeze. And this time, I took the chance I hadn't taken before.

This time, I looked up at the moon. I spoke in the silence to the listening heavens.

"So, I was always supposed to do this?"

There was no answer I could hear, but my heart beat faster. The breeze picked up, moving my hair around me, yet the clouds around the moon stayed eerily frozen against the rushing wind. I felt as if the whole world rushed around me, which the clouds and moon kept me still.

I whispered, "Good to know."

The next week felt frantic. I barely saw Collin, except for our stories every night, which stole more sleep than they should have. I rushed to appointments, such as getting fitted for clothes and getting told my waist was just thin enough, getting my hair cut and styled, getting pictures taken, and trying on countless outfits. The best meeting was with Patterson, Faith, and Eldridge, who had all decided, based on my proficiency in dance, that I could go as far into the Republic as 3rd Street.

I was the first Protector in forty years to dance well enough to fake it at an Elite party.

Eldridge had walked by as the meeting ended and whispered, "It's about time."

On the last morning, I read a letter my mom had mailed. Collin hugged me as I shed some tears, but no horrible rhythm came. There were kisses on the paper, my mom said, from Olivia and the boys. I placed it in the side pocket of my backpack and sewed the pocket shut. One moment to be sentimental and do something as normal as sewing. I was told I couldn't write back, but Collin promised he could get something small through. I wanted to write more, but in the end, I only wrote back one sentence.

"Still scared but taking one more step."

The rush of prep continued until the last afternoon, when I was doing crunches and listening to Collin ramble off codes, including the phone number they had assigned me. I repeated all eleven digits with each crunch or push-up.

"Perfect," he said, still sitting at my feet for push ups. "That's enough. Take a trip and get some last things from—"

"Medical. I need to get some of that poison ivy cream. I don't care what anyone says, I'll find room for it in my pack."

"Good call. Then you have—"

"Dinner, right?"

"Yes. And don't forget to look intrigued by Eldridge's speech. The cameras are on you as well as him." Collin was concentrating, going over his agenda again. He wasn't talking a lot this morning, but my guess it was just nerves. "And after that... That's it."

I nodded, but he just stared at the mat.

"You okay?" I asked.

"Yeah, I just..." He stopped to run his hand through his hair. "I spent all this time getting you ready. I didn't stop... I never asked myself if I'd be ready."

I leaned in, afraid to ask. "And you're not?"

He stared at me with tired eyes, his face looking worn but relaxed. His forehead dropped to my knee, but then he stood quickly, holding his hand out to help me up.

"You should go."

"Yeah," I whispered, taking his hand.

But he didn't let it go right away. I squeezed, feeling a sensation that if I let go, it would be painful. I moved closer- too close- breathing in the air he breathed out.

He had to repeat it. "Aislyn, go."

He released my hand quickly. I ran out of the room to Medical. A nurse was giving me some last-minute advice on how to treat poison ivy allergies in Unnecessaries, which was good because I was thinking about Collin. I scolded myself. I was supposed to be concentrating, immune to distractions.

Dinner had been a mixture of meaningful moments and pangs of jealousy. It felt like a graduation, but I had only joined the class a month ago. I wished I'd had time to talk to Eldridge again as I saw him take the stage. While I listened to his introduction and congratulations, I couldn't focus on his speech until the end.

"And finally, I'd love to end on this note, for all of you who have listened to a long speech, but are still... curious."

He paused. He looked like he was gazing at the crowd. But he was staring right at me again.

"If you trained to be a hero, you wasted your time. You don't need to be a hero to save a life. That requires that you be strong enough or smart enough or brave enough. To be a Protector, you need to be vulnerable. You need to find the weak and be with them, in danger for a moment, to convince them to be strong with you. To be a Protector, you need to jump into situations you may not be able to handle. Only then will you be smart enough to find the solution and escape. To be a Protector, you need to be afraid. You can walk into fear, to put yourself in impossible situations, and you'll find enough bravery to get out. Be alive enough to feel all the things you need to feel, and you'll save a life."

Everyone stood and applauded. I stood, but his words had paralyzed me, and I couldn't clap. Judging by the look in his eyes, he didn't need me to.

Patterson seemed a little tense when he took the mic back. He ordered us to find three to five fellow Protectors to begin our journey with into the woods for our first mission. We could leave. It felt strange that he gave us so much freedom at once.

As I entered the garden, I saw the other Protectors laughing, hugging, and congratulating each other. Megan waved at me as I felt that pang of regret for not being able to even ask to be in her group. Ivy pulled her by the arm into her group.

"Hey," Cassidy called behind me. "If you don't have a group, we are forming one with Protectors 24 through 27."

"You don't have to pick me just because we're the last four," I said, pushing away her pity. "If you want someone else, I get—"

"No. Sequentially, it would solve a lot of complications if our numbers predetermined it, but that's just my opinion. The truth is that... Aislyn, we want you in our group."

"Why?" I asked.

"Why not?" she said, looking confused now. Her brow furrowed at my shock, "You're awesome."

"No!" I almost shouted. "I'd love to be in your group. I didn't think anyone would want me. That I was... lame."

I had gone from awesome to lame in five seconds. She stared at me, confused. I spelled it out for her.

"I'm sorry," I said. "It's been a weird six weeks. I sometimes feel left out and forget that not *all* of you see me as a loser."

"So, you forget that we're not all like Tessa? That's rather frightening."

I laughed and reached forward to hug her, although she barely moved to return it.

"Sorry," she said as I pulled away. "Not a hugger. I'm not good at the whole 'friend' thing."

I smiled at the irony of her words. Eva grabbed me from behind and hugged me.

"What'd I miss?" she laughed.

"I don't have to hug anyone, do I?" Lynn asked, joining us.

"No, I promise," Eva winked. "Anyway, about halfway through dinner I was thinking... it's not fair that everyone is here to support us, and they never get recognized. So, I'm going to go give Sam and Liam and everyone down there a proper send-off!"

"Apparently, the janitor is getting cake," Lynn winked.

Cassidy and Ivy ran away to the kitchens, leaving only Eva.

"I'd invite you on our goodbye tour, but..." Eva trailed off.

"But what?"

"Aislyn, I have spent my formative years studying people the same way other kids study... well, nothing. I guess most kids play or something like that." Her voice became a focused whisper. "The truth is... I noticed something recently. I almost missed it, probably because it almost didn't happen. But I know where you need to be tonight. And I think you do, too."

She turned and went back toward the garden.

She was right. But I didn't even know where Collin was. All the trainers would be gone, maybe having a few drinks, looking over paperwork, or going on a shuttle run to check on stations. I returned to my Circle, wondering if I should message him.

But there he was, waiting.

A pang of worry hit me instantly. What if he had nothing to celebrate? What if he knew I wasn't ready? I shook my head. He believed in me too much for that. I didn't know why he was here.

Unless Eva was right. If I couldn't get him out of my mind, the chances of him getting me out of his mind were slim.

I entered the room with careful steps. Like the first time I had ever walked into the Training Circle. Just like then, his head turned, except there was no uncertainty. Only sorrow. His eyes were red, set on mine. His mouth opened to say something, but he clenched it shut after his lip shuddered, as if he couldn't talk without the words shaking. I walked to him and knelt on the mat, mirroring his position.

"You know," he said, "I keep telling myself that I'm okay. That I'm going to be okay when I'm not with you, listening to you all day, here training with you all day... but I'm not. I'm terrified. I'm..." He stopped talking and breathed unevenly. "I didn't think this would happen."

I almost didn't ask, but I couldn't go without him saying it.

"You didn't think what would happen?"

He waited a moment, then looked up at me, his jaw set as fear filled his eyes.

"Us."

I closed my eyes, for a moment, but opened then quickly to show him I wasn't afraid of his declaration.

"Collin, It's okay. I'm not afraid anymore," I lied.

"Then I must have transferred all my courage to you during training, because I'm terrified. I need you to come back."

He kept repeating it as I reached out and pulled him into a hug, his head resting on my shoulder. Over and over. I think half an hour passed, judging by how the moon rose above the wall to my Circle. I got lost listening to his voice, breathless whispers repeating the same phrase every few minutes.

"Aislyn, I need you to come back."

The shadows grew deeper, drowning in the night as it formed an unending spiral. Exhaustion finally outweighed his worry. The words became fainter and fainter. His shoulder felt heavy, and I guided his body down to the mat. His skin was almost feverish, but his breathing had slowed enough for him to rest.

"Go to sleep," I said. He nodded.

His voice was fading. "Aislyn, I need you... to come back."

I stopped breathing, wondering if I should stay to hear him say it or run away. But I stayed. I heard it. The loudest whisper I'd ever heard.

"Aislyn, I need you."

His eyes opened, staring into mine as his hand reached up to cradle my head, his fingers grasping my neck. My heart was racing, my head screaming, and every inch of my body wanted to reach out and touch him.

That doesn't mean I love him, I told myself.

Except I was sure that was exactly what it meant.

I reached out, touching his cheek as his eyes closed. I fought the great war of worry and terror with whispers of promises I didn't know I could keep. Promises that I would come back. His eyes remained closed, even as he murmured in his sleep.

I laid his hand down on the mat and backed up, sitting on my knees. I watched him drift into the oblivion of sleep like he had watched me do so many times. I stayed on the mat for a few minutes, knowing I would die to be this close to him in a week, or that I might just die anyway.

And the rhythm began.

I would never see him again.

I would never see the flowers in the garden bloom.

I would never plant seeds again.

I would never braid Olivia's hair again.

I would never play hide and seek again.

I fought off every fear, pushing each one away with sheer will, closing my eyes in concentration to reframe it.

Until I got to the last one. My breath shuddered. My eyes shot open.

I would not play hide and seek again.

But I would play hide and seek again.

And what a game it would be.

CHAPTER 17

The painting represented every challenge I hadn't foreseen in six long weeks of training.

I loved it.

I wasn't supposed to love anything here. But I loved it.

Two days into my cover, I stood on a Republic street, trying to look as disenchanted as I was supposed to be. The painting in front of me was created by people who wanted to kill me. Who thought imperfect babies should die. And who believed the lie that their happiness was the only thing that mattered.

But it was beautiful. Everything about it fascinated me—the textures, the colors. It was creativity gone wild against the stark, clean lines of their concrete buildings.

Just like the city.

All the buildings were taller than I had imagined, stark lines mixed with domes. Every block seemed orchestrated so that the buildings flowed together. Efficiency, technology and art, the movement of the shuttles hovering by, almost in rhythm to a song. There were no lights to signal traffic. The shiny metal plates along that had once held them would instead alert the drivers of directions.

The architecture was simple, bold, and graceful. There wasn't one building that contrasted with the design of another. Rather, they were individualized by the splash of color in the front center level, whether a store window or restaurant display.

Music played in every store and café, even in the pristine streets. I had made the mistake of tapping my finger to a song, quickly realizing that I had attracted a police officer's attention. I made a quick assumption and took the first gamble of my life.

"It's still one of my favorites, even though it's archaic. It's kind of embarrassing," I'd replied to the officer's inquisitive glance.

I had guessed the song must be a few years old and would be white noise to everyone else. I held my breath until he laughed, along with a few others in the line. A few minutes of small talk, and I walked out of the shop with my cover, my latte, and—more importantly—my life intact.

It was hard to remember that I was in a dangerous place. People walking, living, talking, coughing, laughing; it seemed no different from our town, but also horribly normal. I hated that sense of familiarity. I assumed I would immediately hate everything about the Republic. And I questioned myself every day when I didn't.

While the Territory was not barbaric or even as rustic as our homes in the outlying area, we didn't have unique artistry in every store window or MCUs in every person's hand. We didn't have towering buildings, covered with concrete and glass. The maps of the city showed the symmetry of all the city centers, like each of the eighteen districts had an epicenter from which streets would ripple outward. The technology and sophistication in the science center around 30th Street and the Fourteenth District enthralled me, until I reminded myself it was all a facade.

The Society Party labs had all done their job very well. Every person was beautiful. And they made beautiful things to seduce those people, stealing a piece of their soul with each cheap thrill. And while their world amazed my eyes, their words burned my ears.

I had overheard several shallow conversations filled with profanity, degrading comments about Sub-Terras, and references to their casual sex lives. It disgusted me, as I'd predicted it would.

Every crisis seemed to center on having a new outfit or item of interest, and the acquisition of that outfit at a certain location. They would grasp for more money, going further into debt with looks of desperation that only ended with the purchase of a silly status symbol. It made the piece of silk I thought was beautiful seem horrid because of what they would give up for it. Adults had the emotional range of thirteen-year-olds. They got upset if someone cut in line, if their server made a mistake, if a driver took a wrong turn. "Send them back to the lab," they'd say.

The flirting was non-stop, and the flagrant way they discussed their late-night encounters served only to impress each other with how "adventurous" they could be. What they did with someone was more important than who they did it with.

I stared at the painting one more time, overhearing someone's phone conversation. Even though everything looked beautiful, they had stolen the genuine beauty out of every moment. They shared the most intimate things freely and the most platonic sparingly.

I was still staring at the art, ignoring my now cold cup of coffee, when I heard it again.

"Did you see his hair?" the blond next to me said to her friend, who scoffed.

"Appalling! He should never have made it out of the lab!"

I'd assumed these conversations happened all the time, but I couldn't stomach it. I had to leave, pretending to get a message on my MCU. I crossed the street and stared at the window, glaring at my reflection. Suddenly, I hated my clothes, I hated the air I breathed, and I hated everyone around me because I was sharing it with them. I hated myself for looking like I belonged here, pretending to be someone who would condemn a person to death because of their hair.

I moved on to the next window, which was a dress shop.

"Don't you love it?" a squeaky voice said from behind me.

I turned to three women behind me—one who had asked me the question, and two who looked like they couldn't wait for my answer.

"I do, but I don't have the right figure."

"Yes, you do," the first woman said, invading my personal space so much I had to fight the urge to back up. They always stood much closer than we did in the Territory. I made myself drop my shoulder toward her and strained my memory for the relevant facts about this store. I had dressed like a Terra. It was the end of the month.

And then I remembered the high-priced store a block over.

"Um, I meant the right figures. I blew my allowance last week on a Chantre one block up," I nodded to the north. "I'm done for the month."

"No one could blame you there!" she laughed. "Whatever it is, it has to surpass this one!"

I stared at the piece, and then at the sidewalk, pretending to be slightly ashamed as I made a comment about my allowance and they giggled. I thought it was nothing at first. But in the small hole of the intricately curled floral sewer grate, I swore I saw the swift movement of grey, followed by another, and another.

Police. It had to be.

Either the officers were chasing someone, Joel had been wrong about the police training updates, or they had figured out who I was. I might already be dead.

"What about you?" I asked, smiling at her innocently. It might have been the hardest thing I'd ever done; smiling when every inch of my body wanted to run. While my head was spinning with getaway options, I couldn't remember what language I should use to describe the outfit. I relied on the use of non-verbal.

"Because, I mean, you..." I eyed her up, then pointed to the outfit. "And that..." I ran through Common Phrases again but came up blank. If they were chasing an Unnecessary, a child would die while I discussed a pretty dress.

I spurted out, "That dress would leave you speechless and screaming at the same time."

She stared at me, and I stopped breathing.

"Wow! You're right! That's, like, my new favorite phrase! It's a Falcien must," she said to her friend. I had forgotten about the special mid-Spring festivals and balls. It was in a week, so I likely wouldn't be attending.

Her distraction gave me a chance to breathe again. I laughed along as I spun on my heel and left them to enter the store. I looked around like I had all the time in the world, even as my blood continued to pump faster and faster. Several people in the café ignored me as they stared at their portable CUs and smaller MCUs, busy creating and working. I quickly realized the end of the block was rendering and supply for textiles, along with some labs. As a non-working-class Terra, I would be out of place. I kept wandering, glazed look plastered on my face, and stepped into the café on the edge of the street.

My mind continued to race, even as I tried to ignore the marble floors and ethereal look of the dining room. If I couldn't track them, my chances of finding them were fading by the minute. I desperately needed a way out to the alley. I moved toward the hallway in back, the bleak part of the café where only the Sub-Terra workers would go. I turned the corner to find the bathroom. What I didn't expect to find was an open door leading to the alley, right in front of a sewer grate. It was too good to be true. There was a room with two cooks off to the side, but they seemed occupied.

I had a second to decide. My pulse raced, pushing me forward through the door. I lunged, jumped down the two stairs, and reached out to the grate in the alley.

As I wrenched it out of place, I heard something behind me. Someone had opened the door to take out the trash. I froze, my hands still on the grate, desperate to think of something. An excuse. A reason. A story.

But he didn't ask questions. He stared as if evaluating me. I wondered how much he knew about what I was, or if he cared.

"Following the police, are you, Protector?"

I held my breath, waiting for him to call out an alarm.

But he shrugged. "They went down a while ago. They're after the Unnecessary down there. I see her in the trash once in a while. I don't report her. She's just trash eating trash, right? Nothing wrong with that."

I moved quickly, ignoring his comments, and continued to pull off the grate. If this was a trap, it was already set. But there was no dilation in his eyes, no unusual jaw movement, no jugular pulsing in stress. He was being truthful, as sick as that made me. I took my first step underground.

"You hear stories, but I never imagined I'd see one of you. Not in a lifetime." He spoke like I was a myth, with a little awe, but his voice sounded dissatisfied.

"Did I disappoint?" I asked.

"No, but you seem normal. More... human than I imagined."

I ignored his confused reaction and reached up to pull the grate back on. "You have no idea," I muttered.

I took off my shoes and put them in my bag before I finished climbing down the cylinder. I dreaded the smell, hoping it wouldn't make me gag, but soon realized that the tunnel below was dry. My socks were still on. Hopefully, the germ barrier would work, but I didn't want to stop to spray them again.

She was down here: whoever needed to be rescued. I stopped caring about anything else.

I reached out for the wall, grasping, unable to find it until my eyes adjusted to the dim fluorescent lights. It was concave, making me almost fall off the side.

I couldn't call out to her; the police would hear everything in a structure with so much echo. The sound of dripping water made me hesitate and look behind me a hundred times.

For thirty minutes, I wandered around with no sign of anyone. There was no way I could find her using the dim lights on the wall. I couldn't use any light from my phone, or the police might see. The word "impossible" crossed my mind.

"C'mon," I whispered. "Give me a sign." Each breath became an intense, desperate prayer.

Almost on cue, one of the dim fluorescent lights flickered down a tunnel I was about to pass. I almost didn't want to act on it, feeling it was a bit irrational. But I had nothing to lose, so I turned.

I was about halfway down the tunnel when I realized that it led to a different tunnel. It was huge, with long metal lines down the middle. I strained my memory back to my HistCulture lessons, to the forgotten transportation system, before hover shuttles. It ran on rails, underground. I heard a noise, then men's voices. I couldn't tell how far away they were, so I risked getting my phone out to shine a little light. It glinted off a piece of metal.

A door handle.

I pulled at the handle. It made a noise that sounded deafening, but because it echoed, I hoped they wouldn't know where I was. I slammed the door shut behind me, almost losing my balance as I turned to face stairs. The footsteps and voices sounded muted behind the door.

This must have been a service access route, which also explained the red paint on the door. As I went down the stairs, I noticed the lights seemed farther apart. I only saw my feet as they landed on each step.

I got out my MCU, which glowed just enough for me to see an outline of a door under the stairs. I reached for the wall right next to the door. Instead, I felt skin and a small arm shaking with a fear that had to equal my own. I stopped a scream and stepped back, literally clenching my jaw shut as a small sound escaped.

I felt her hand reach me and pull me toward the door under the stairway. I dove in, still shocked, as she shut the door. It took a moment, but I stood up from the floor, turning to face my first Unnecessary—who had just saved me.

"Hi," she whispered. "You'll be safe in here. It's okay. Are you hiding from them, too? Are you... you know?"

She stared at my stomach. She thought I was a Vessel. Collin had said that the Unnecessaries help each other out, but I hadn't imagined her willingness to help me would make me fall in love with her.

"No," I smiled. I quickly caught my breath and knelt again.

Five weeks ago, I had thought that nothing could prepare me for this. But now, I knew exactly what to say and do.

"My name is Aislyn. I'm a Protector." I smiled as her eyes became wide with wonder. "And I'm here to get you out."

Her breath quickened and her eyes darted, trying to capture every inch of me. Then she looked down, bit her lip, contemplating leaving, being rescued, or any other scenario.

Her small voice shuddered.

"No. No, you're not."

I was confused, afraid I had fallen into a trap, until I heard something. A small sound. Or rather, the sound of someone very small.

Two tiny, clenched fists stretched out from a blanket behind her. I tugged the cardboard box toward me and pulled the blanket back. The infant couldn't be more than a few months old, still stretching, eyes shut tightly.

Shocked, I turned back to the girl's resolute face. Her shining blue eyes looked at the baby, then at me.

"You're here to get him out."

CHAPTER 18

"Who is he?" I asked, still in disbelief. She wasn't just in hiding, she was hiding a baby. I pulled him up into my arms. He curled up, not ready to be woken. I cradled him, rocking him back and forth.

"He was discarded," she answered. "Some makeshift lab on Seventh Street. They perform medical tests that are still considered illegal. They want the baby for more testing. Black market, you know? They have a tub full of water in the alley, and they put the babies inside and close the lid. They all drown."

I forced myself to swallow, tasting the vomit in the back of my throat.

"I was only looking for scraps. I knew about the barrel, but I'd never seen them put a baby inside. They didn't see me. Something distracted them. But the baby cried before they closed the lid. They went back inside, and the thing is... when I pulled him out, he was breathing."

"Babies have a reflex that can keep them alive in the water," I explained. "They develop and grow in fluid, and the reflex stays, even after they're born."

"Oh. I didn't know that. Anyway, I brought him here. It's been about five months. A nice Sub-Terra from a café down the street gets me infant milk and diapers."

I desperately wanted to hug her, to reach out to her, but I remembered Collin said that signs of affection could scare an

Unnecessary, since they've been alone so long. They could even have a violent reaction to a hug. I reached out my hand, my voice was shaky as I spoke.

"I think that's the bravest thing I've ever heard."

She looked up as if she had never pondered that, and her tiny hand reached out to mine, cradling it ever so slowly as the tiny shakes of nervousness melted into the gentle strength of my fingers wrapped around them. I wanted to ask her more about where we were, but from the pipes and wires along the wall, I guessed it was an old utility closet. The wall on the one side was lined with a giant collage. Her abilities and intelligence meant she had probably attended school at one point.

"What's your name?" I asked. "Do you remember?"

"Katerina. I used to live... that I don't remember. It was beautiful."

I instantly understood what had happened. Saw the scraps of Elite clothes and jewelry among the clutter.

"You were abandoned, weren't you? Because of emotional attachment?"

"Yeah. My mother kept pushing me away, left me alone for whole weekends when I was four. I would cry forever, and my teacher noticed. My dad would cuddle with me in the evenings, when no one watched, just... singing to me. I guess it wasn't my dad, but it was whoever mom was with at the time. They only stayed for about six months at a time. I made her a card once, when she was about to leave. It got stranger after that. He desperately wanted me to stay away from her."

"He told you... what would happen?"

She nodded. "But I had a nightmare one night. Got too scared to sleep. I could tell I messed up. My dad said he would take me to the lab. I guess that was good enough for my mom. He dropped me off in an alley and said he'd tell my mom he took me to the lab or a doctor. He gave me money. I was on my own."

"How old were you?"

"Seven. It was about a year ago. I was smart, which is why they held off on judging me, I think. They must have known in nursery school. With a 160 IQ, they were hoping I'd grow out of it. But teachers always notice if you're too clingy. Someone would have called me out in a week in secondary school."

"The man who dropped you off?" I said, trying to keep my voice steady. "Do you know... is he okay?"

"No, I don't think so. Not anymore. He would leave things in the alley for me. But after only three months, he disappeared. And disappeared means dead."

I reached out to hug her, ignoring the warnings of instructors in my head. She resisted a little, out of habit or the unfamiliarity of someone touching her. But then she clung to me, squeezing out the pain, hurt, and unbearable rejection. I don't know how she found the strength to breathe, let alone take care of another Unnecessary. But it made some strange sense.

She needed someone to love.

I held her for what seemed like an hour, until she looked up at me with hopeful eyes.

"So, now that you're here, you can take him right? You can save him?"

I looked from her to the baby, who stretched as he fell back to sleep.

"You can only save one of us, right? That's what they say. 'They only rescue one at a time.' And then... I can find a new place to hide or—"

"Look, right now we don't have to worry about that. We can't move. They're still searching, so we have to wait," I said, hoping that a few more hours would buy me some time.

"Okay," she said uncertainly, pulling off her black scarf to reveal the most beautiful blond hair. Her features struck me. Compassionate eyes fell to the baby as she asked, "Do you want to feed the baby a few times? So he'll trust you?"

I nodded, trying to process her intuitive genius. She held up a bottle, went to a cooler, and filled it with a tiny container of milk. She closed the container carefully. The baby awoke to the sound of her singing, his eyes lighting up when he saw her. I looked around the room to see endless wrappers and trash. How shallow I might have been to think this wasn't the best place for a baby, or to be disgusted by my surroundings. As long as the baby was with her thoughtful movements and love, it was in heaven.

Katerina asked if she could sleep. She curled up against me. Her cuddles were comforting, but it only lasted a few minutes. I had always felt a little claustrophobic when I would pace around our little house in the woods, rocking the twins. Now, I was surrounded by darkness, locked in a dead-end room with a problem I couldn't solve. The smell of old diapers and mold made it worse. But I turned to the boy, now happy and alert. I placed him on my knees and let him play with my fingers as I held one hand on Katerina, trying to soak in the calm of her sleepy breaths.

Hours passed. I changed the baby's diaper and played with him some more, listening for sounds that might indicate he needed to be quiet. I stared at the broken and ripped pictures on the wall. One section was made entirely of sunsets. The images were small, most likely because there was a lot more advertising in the picture than the natural beauty of the sunset she had found. All the small pieces had made a more beautiful sunset than any I had ever seen. I stared at Katerina, who now seemed so much younger, trying not to think of Olivia. The disparity of their homes would drive me to tears. And tears wouldn't help.

A decision would help, but it was one I wasn't sure I could make. How would I even know what to do? To take the baby or the girl?

The rules were there for a reason: to make the story, to keep us safe, and to make missions more successful. A Protector can only save one. A Protector chooses who to save. If we start taking more, we risk getting caught. We risk retaliation. We risk everything.

It wasn't my choice. Katerina had chosen. She had saved him. She was already more of a hero than I was, she just didn't know it. As I stared at her in the dim light, her blue eyes opened. She jolted only a little when I spoke her name.

"Katerina, how would you like to be the most important person in the world?"

She looked up from the baby, her beautiful eyes full of confusion. Those eyes that saw through the lies to save the baby in my arms.

"You just have to do what you've already done," I said the words as the reality hit me. "Because you're a Protector, like me."

She started to smile, not yet trusting her joy. Even in the dim light, in the smell of the stale air, and in the dirt caked on her, she was glowing. She bit her lip.

"But that's not how the story works. You only rescue one."

"I will. And so will you. You get to be the Protector. You weren't ready for it, but it's who you are. You will protect the baby, and I'll protect you. And we'll change the story. Forever."

Her breaths quickened as I placed the baby back in her arms.

"Okay, I think I can do that," she said, as if it was a fantasy, instead of the reality her love for this baby had already written. I stared at her and touched her oily hair, then her face, dirty and grey. I drew her into me, where she curled up, shaking all her anxiety away.

We had heard nothing for hours, so we made our move while it was night. She collected some money, baby items, one clipping from her sunset mural, and some other things and packed them in her bag. I wrapped the baby up in a blanket, gave him a small dose of baby sleep, and grasped the door handle. I held my breath as it opened and shut.

The minutes were long, especially after opening the second door. I insisted we remain as quiet as possible, but I knew the worst of the danger was over. The drills should have ended hours ago. I tried to breathe slower and took my steps a little less cautiously.

Until there was a crash and murmuring behind us.

"Police," Katerina whispered. "They used the storm door. You need a key. It's got to be police."

We had two minutes to hide. Or less.

I pulled out my MCU and set it to be a black and red screen, so they would have a hard time seeing it. I scanned the map of the tunnels. None of it made sense, until I remembered I only had sewage lines saved.

"Katerina, where are we? This tunnel. What's it called?"

"I don't know. They were old trains, I think. They called them something else because they were under the ground."

"Where are the other lines?" I didn't know if she would understand it, but I let her see the map.

"Down there," she said, pointing below us, "but they're full of water. They aren't sewage anymore."

That wasn't going to work. I typed in my MCU, desperate for the word that neither of us could remember. I needed to find a way...

"Subways," I whispered. They called them subways. I pulled up the map, and within seconds, I knew where we were. With every swipe and movement, the steps got louder; we'd have to choose a direction soon.

Grabbing her arm, I pulled Katerina toward the tunnel off to the side. She shook her head and refused to move.

"We have to go down that tunnel to get out," I whispered.

"Yes, but not now. Stay."

I risked looking at my device. There was an exit on the other end of this tunnel, but if we opened a manhole, they would hear us. My heartbeat raced, making it difficult to stand still. I wanted to sprint down the tunnel, but Katerina held my hand and directed me to the wall. The buzzing light above was broken, like many others, and only sparked sporadically.

Katerina gestured downward with one hand, then pointed to the concave wall. She sank into it, and I did the same. With the light broken, we might have remained hidden for a moment, but the flashlights would give us away.

She pointed down again, at the tracks. I laid down with her beside the cold metal of the tracks. I placed the baby on the ground. He was still asleep. I must have given him the right dose.

The beam of a flashlight hit the walls above me. The shadow of the tracks hid us. The police officers stopped and shone their lights in the tunnel I had tried to drag Katerina into. If we had followed my advice, we'd be dead. I watched the fluorescent light above us, praying it wouldn't flicker on at the wrong moment. The officers moved forward, keeping the light focused on the walls. If they flashed their lights downward, just three feet away from them...

But they didn't. The light was inches away when they walked past. Before I could panic, they had gone. For a moment, I thought my heartbeat would give us away and the police would turn around and come back; it pounded in my head as loudly as a drum.

Ten minutes later, there was another clang, and someone shouted, "All clear!"

It was another five minutes before I had the courage to whisper, "Are we good?"

"I don't think they are new recruits, so there won't be a Sentry checking in after them," Katerina whispered. "Besides, they sounded eager to get to that party."

The police had been talking about going to a party that night, which I was hoping would keep them motivated to neglect their work.

I watched her for a cue to move out. Two long minutes later, she nodded. We gathered ourselves and ran down the tunnel. I could barely walk, yet I was trying to run. I couldn't believe I was out of breath from standing still. My shoulders pulled back as I craned out my neck, sure I'd heard something.

Someone yelled that the skies were clear in Zone 2. It was the second time they had checked the tunnel for the day. But before I could celebrate our success, dread hit me like the thunderous footsteps that were now hitting the ground, heading for us.

A look of horror glazed over Katerina's eyes as a light appeared around the corner, just down the tunnel.

"Sentry."

She didn't have to say anything else. We ran, no longer worried about being quiet. If a Sentry had heard us, he would be thorough. He wouldn't just pass us by if we hid against the tunnel wall. I held the infant as still as I could, afraid he would never wake up. I risked a second to check him; he still had a pulse.

We passed a ladder. I stopped, but Katerina shook her head. She pointed forward, then pivoted. I realized why as we entered the side tunnel. His light would catch us climbing the ladder. We were out of view, at least, for now.

Unless he had seen us turn down the side tunnel.

My hair stuck to the back of my head from the sweat. My breath was labored, and I tried to keep my arms as still as possible. The Sentry's footsteps seemed louder, hitting a few puddles we had passed just a minute before.

We made another turn. Before I could catch up to Katerina, she was one rung up a ladder, swinging around it, grasping the old metal, wrenching upward on the plate, and pulling herself out into the alley.

"Go," I whispered after her, then started to climb. I was halfway up the ladder when the light hit me.

"Freeze!"

I did. I don't know why. I could have kept going. I was dead anyhow.

He must have seen us cut to the left. The flashlight came closer. The person behind it kept talking, telling me not to move. I didn't listen; I didn't care. At least Katerina had gotten out. She would live. But the soul in my arms, protected by both me and her, would die. The baby stirred; his eyes barely open. His arm twitched and then fell beside him as he closed his eyes again, perfectly content and peaceful.

This baby had been fighting death his whole life, and he was about to lose.

Hopelessness drowned out my anger, feeling a desperate need to run anyway. But I had been paralyzed by the fear of the inevitable wound that would bleed the life out of me.

I grasped the cold metal rung more tightly. A couple seconds to ponder the end of my life felt like a long time. I thought of the people who would cry, who would feel responsible, who would think training me was a waste... my family, my friends, Eva, Megan, Collin.

Collin.

My heart ached. The horrible rhythm began, but it was all about him. I would never see his face again, tell him stories as he fell asleep, or tell him the truth about how I felt. I could only imagine the agony of his guilt.

Instead of attacking or fighting the Sentry, I wished he could see the world I saw. But he couldn't. He was blind to everything I saw. I summoned the intensity of everything I felt for this baby and stared him down. I wasn't afraid of him; I was afraid he'd never see the real me or this child, clinging for life, because we deserved to breathe.

He stopped walking forward, only a yard away, the flashlight steady on me. It was next to the barrel of his gun, which was pointed at my head. I clenched my teeth to stop any quivering; if I spoke, he'd know I was about to cry.

"Who are you?" he asked, finally.

"I think you know," I answered, shifting, bending down as if preparing for the shot.

But it never came.

Was he calling it in to another Sentry? Did I miss something?

His light slowly descended, along with his weapon. As it did, the light reflected off the walls, and a light from his pocket turned on. For the first time, I saw his face. His eyes were dark, deep-set, and intense, but not angry. He pondered me the same way a child looks at something new that they don't trust. His face was strong and beautifully shaped, like so many I had seen in the Republic. His dark hair was edging down, just out of his eyes, which were still fixed on mine. He had slightly broad shoulders, but more of a runner's build.

My arm cramped, and I began to shake. He was supposed to be killing me. Or arresting me. Or countless other nightmares I'd imagined. His inaction made me more anxious than firing his weapon.

I opened my mouth, afraid the fear might choke me, and took a deep breath, feeling it hit my hand in broken spurts as I exhaled. His eyes closed for a second, and his head tilted forward a bit. There was a shudder in his breath. He opened his eyes, and his arm reached up again.

This was it. Maybe he had doubted whether he could kill the baby in my hands or me. But any humanity in his stone heart had only made him hesitate. We were still dead.

But he didn't aim his weapon. Instead, he touched his ear.

"Tunnel clear."

I blinked, realizing that tears were running down my cheeks. Confusion flooded my mind. My mouth hung open.

"What... why are you... I don't—"

With power and desperation I had never heard in anyone's voice, he said, "Keep going."

My muscles were still frozen by my imminent demise. I tried to move them, but nothing happened.

"I need you to keep going," he whispered.

My body screamed instructions at my limbs, trying to remember how they moved, as if cheating death had made walking unnatural. *"Move. Move!"* One leg went first. Then the other. I only had one arm to climb, but I managed.

The Sentry turned to walk away from me.

"Drill is over. Good for you, it was clear. Pack up for the day. Departure in ten. South grate."

At the top, I met another dilemma. I was holding the baby and couldn't possibly lift both of us out onto the street. I wondered if Katerina was still there, or if she had heard his voice and made a run for it. I reached out to the grate and knocked the rhythm of a song, just like I would with Olivia. I wasn't sure why. Maybe I needed every hint of innocence I could get in this hell.

I waited for what seemed like a long time. I began to count, to convince myself it wasn't that long. I had barely counted to three when the grate shifted and Katerina's hands came into view. I placed the infant in them, then pulled myself up, keeping alert as I looked around.

"What took you so long?" Katerina asked. "Who was that? What happened? I just... I can't believe you're all right!"

I was shocked that police weren't swarming the alley. I looked at the sewer grate, worried the Sentry would change his mind and come up the ladder to kill me himself. But as each moment passed and nothing happened, Katerina's questions seemed harder to answer.

"I don't know. But then... I don't even know if I'm all right."

CHAPTER 19

Within four hours, we were past the border and in Zone 3. The rest of our escape from the Republic was uneventful. It seemed quiet, even though the streets screamed with activity and movement. The sounds were muted by the shallowness that surrounded them. We had started in the alleys Katerina had memorized. Some other people came by, but we hid against the wall or in the trash until they changed outfits, threw up, or kept walking. The baby had gotten hungry only once.

I was desperate for rest. While in survival mode, I couldn't process what had happened in the subway tunnel. I took some time to write and remember details of our exit that I would need to report in my debrief.

We found our way through the scattered trees, which collected into a full forest on the other side of the fence. I cut through the barrier with my tool kit, then reconnected it once we were across. My movements weren't clumsy and forced like in training. I remembered Collin's words: *"You're learning so that this is second nature; when it counts, you'll have it down to an art."* I hadn't believed him.

I wanted to tell him he was right about everything. I wanted to rush home, run through the night, or call for an EE.

But the instant we were in the forest, I was struck with familiar scents of pine. There was dirt beneath my feet instead of concrete. My shoes sank into the pillow of earth as the forest floor cradled them. I found a sanctuary there.

By Katerina's tired eyes, she now felt lost in a world much bigger than she had ever known.

We hiked a few miles to an R-station. I pulled the kit from the underground compartment and made camp with the camo tent.

She was asleep in minutes. I got a few hours of sleep before Katerina and the baby woke. After that, any thoughts of the Sentry were interrupted by a thousand questions about the forest as she and I made the three-day hike to the next T-station.

I was now feeling the physical effects of our panicked journey. The soreness I hadn't felt at first was catching up quickly. The last time I had been in this part of the woods, I had been with Eva, Lynn, and Cassidy. It suddenly seemed too quiet without their voices, talking Tech for hours. I couldn't understand half of what they had been saying, but I loved just listening. It reminded me of listening to Sam and Liam ramble on for hours, or Collin talk to himself through EE scenarios. I felt homesick, which meant that Central, after only two months, was already home.

As Katerina and the baby napped that afternoon, I stared at my MCU. Its blank white display stared back at me. I thought back on my discussion with Collin on the morning I'd left for the Republic.

"Write to me when you get back to the forest and it's safe," he had said, sounding more vulnerable than his usual strong-as-rock self.

"What... How do I get it to you? How will you know what I wrote?" I had asked him.

"You'll make it home." His breath had shuddered. "And I'll read everything. Every word."

So, I ignored my weary muscles and wrote, describing Katerina and everything I remembered about her little closet. I wrote about her first reactions to the creek, to fish, and to squirrel. I didn't know what to write about my escape. The

Sentry still felt like a secret I wasn't supposed to tell anyone. I wrote about the parts of the story I could tell, and an apology that I couldn't run home to him faster. I didn't want to rush Katerina; she had experienced enough stress for a lifetime.

The next day, Katerina barely spoke. I wondered when she would ask what her new home would be like. With a pang in my heart, I realized it was likely that she rarely spoke to anyone, but I hoped she knew her questions weren't bothering me. Did she even know how to ask about her home? Did she even know what home was? Did she even understand she could ask me that?

Finally, I broke the silence.

"Katerina, are you okay?"

"Yeah. Is he okay?"

"He's fine, sweetie," I said, though she already knew that.

Any concern she had voiced had been for him, which as a sister, I understood. But none of my training had prepared me to answer the questions she would inevitably have. I knew what had kept her silent all day: worry. Worry was the thief of all good moments.

"Am I going to stay with him?" she asked, her voice shaking.

That was one question I had been dreading. Maybe I should have just kept our silent parade going, instead of being stuck with the only answer I had.

"I don't know." I tried to be gentle, not wanting to crush her hope.

But she sank to the ground.

I reached out my hand. "Katerina, I really don't know. This has never happened before. But I know the Council. Their hearts are in the right place—especially our leader's. I think we'll be able to find you both the same home."

I wished I could assure her more. As an Unnecessary, she would go to the shelter for two years before being placed. However, someone could volunteer to adopt them both early, but they usually had to be financially secure enough to drive them to the shelter for therapy every day. That would be up to Hannah to make it happen, because the baby would be placed right away.

I had to ask her a long series of questions when we took our next break. We sat in the sun as I hooked up the MCU to the lie detection monitors for her final test. I had to look for any sign of deceit, which was difficult after connecting with her so intimately. She passed, so I unhooked the wires from her arm.

"So, what does that machine do? And what's in your other bag?"

I laughed and said, "Well, the monitor on your fingers and toes told me what your heart rate did when I talked to you, just to make sure you were healthy."

And that you're not lying to me, I added mentally, *but you'll find that out, eventually. Don't hate me for it.*

"And the other bag had the cell phone I bought and a few other things for when I go to the Republic," I said.

"Oh, like clothes and stuff?"

"Yes, as well as different ID cards and Republic money. It's not worth anything in the Territory."

"Oh. Well, you can have the money my father gave me," she said, digging through her bag. "I don't need it anymore."

I was about to protest but was left speechless as she pulled more money from her bag than I had ever seen at one time—or even over a lifetime.

"What? He gave me his allowance for one month. I guess it's a lot. I thought it needed to last months. If you can use it in the Republic to save someone else, you should. I want to help you."

I smiled and put the money in my bag. I fed the baby as we waited. I watched her stare at her surroundings in wonder, as awe-struck by her heart as she was by the surrounding forest.

We continued our hike, hoping to reach an R-station by nightfall. I didn't look forward to Sam's reaction to my two Unnecessaries, as he tended to think analytically first and emotionally later. Whatever happened, I tried to remind myself, we were safe now. Surrounded by a little cove of trees above us and resting on a patch of soft grass. She kept grazing the blades with her fingertips, as if they were life-giving. Perhaps they were.

I looked at my blank MCU screen, wondering what to write about the Sentry. A part of me felt ungrateful for questioning my strange blessing, but the blaring questions poked holes in any peace I wanted to feel. Every time I saw his eyes in my mind, I reeled with every possibility. Traitor? Spy? Double-agent?

But I also imagined the Council's reaction to my debrief. They would not understand how to process a Sentry defecting. Would they tell me not to trust him? To attack him when I had a chance? Would they believe me? There was so much at stake that it made me more scared to tell them than to face him again.

If I were to believe it possible for a Sentry to switch sides, then they would have to acknowledge that a Protector could be turned as well. Collin, Patterson, and everyone else had dismissed every question I had about a Protector ever defecting. Sam said that the statistical probability of a Protector turning against us was more likely as the program progressed; it was simple math.

My thoughts were interrupted by a snapping branch. The silence ended. The air felt electrified for some reason, full of urgency. The forest can play tricks on someone; I had discovered that long ago.

But this was different.

Twigs were breaking under feet, only yards away. A scream of pain shot through the night. I looked at Katerina, wishing I didn't have to ask her to be self-sufficient again. I told her to wait, to stay calm, and to take my pack.

I ran, away from the sanctuary, toward the screams that split the silence again.

And again.

And again.

It was a pattern. Contractions.

Only something wasn't right. The voice calling out was too weak, too choked. Dying...

I reached a clearing, but it was like walking into a nightmare. Only it wasn't mine. This one was Tessa's nightmare.

She was dripping in sweat, trying to move a Vessel who was nearly full-term. The Vessel's cry cut short, then she became limp by the Protector's side.

"Tessa?" I called.

Tessa saw me and called my name with a desperation I had never heard before. Every argument we'd ever had disappeared instantly. I took over chest compressions while she tried to get the oxygen mask out of her bag and onto the Vessel's face. The pulse monitor was dinging low, but not flat-lined.

Tessa was crying, talking to herself. She began to shake.

"She can't die. If she dies, I'm ruined. I've never had an incomplete mission. I've never had anyone die. She can't die." She kept repeating phrases over and over, as the woman's pulse slowly dropped.

But after two minutes of effort, the inevitable happened. The flat-line alarm went off. I looked away from Tessa, into the Vessel's dead eyes. My arms shook, and I stopped compressions.

"What are you doing?" Tessa shouted. "I can't let this happen! You can't stop! I have to save her! I have to save—"

I grabbed Tessa's shoulders, barely able to speak.

"You can't save them both."

"If I don't save them both, there's no point. It means I failed. And I can't let them know I failed. No one can know."

She cursed and threw her bag. I was getting a horrible, sinking feeling. The protocol said to extract the infant. And Tessa wasn't moving. I realized she had her own horrible rhythm.

"It's already too late," she whispered. "It's too late. No one can know I failed."

The forest faded. Her voice grew muted. My stomach lurched. She wasn't going to do the C-section. Her perfectionism must have paralyzed her. I would have to do the thing I feared the most.

We only had ninety seconds.

It had already been about fifteen seconds.

Sixteen.

Seventeen.

"Tessa, the baby!"

I needed her pack, her help. She was the one who should do this, not me. My voice felt choked, making it sound guttural, frantic, and just as scared as she looked.

"Please!"

She didn't move. I didn't know if it was fear or anxiety, but she looked frightening instead of just frightened.

Meanwhile, a timer in my brain kept going.

Twenty-one... twenty-two...

I punched the ground, collecting my resolve. I grabbed her pack. As I opened it, I felt dizzy, but I was expecting that. What I was not expecting was for her to stand up and pull the pack back from my hands.

"She's gone. Don't bother."

I stopped breathing. Was there something I didn't know? The Medical lessons I had crammed for swirled in my head, but that queasy feeling overcame them. Tessa looked eerily unhinged in the small light from the MCU, and I didn't know what thoughts were running through her head.

The head of the girl who'd only ever had perfect missions.

"The baby could still be all right!" I said.

"It doesn't matter. The Vessel is dead. It will always be an incomplete mission. I can't fail at anything!"

"Just save the baby. That's not a failure!"

"No! I can go back to the Republic and just start over. I'll find another Vessel or Unnecessary. No one will know I messed up if we leave them both here."

A horrible question formed in my mind: would Tessa risk a life for the perfect record?

But her answer was clear.

And so was mine.

I lurched forward again, this time intending to rip the bag from her. She blocked, but so did I, hitting her forearm with mine. It burned with pain as the bone met her wrist. She held up her hand, as a warning.

This time, I didn't hesitate.

Twenty-nine.

I rushed forward, blocked her hand, and got to the bag. Instead of pulling it away from her, I moved with the momentum from my leap, spinning her around and pulling her to the ground with me. Her foot struck my lower ribs as she fell. I grunted and choked for breath as my hands clenched the bag.

Thirty-one.

She was on top of me in a second. I pled with her, scared that I would be just as expendable as the infant. I forced myself just to keep hitting, even as one jab hit my stomach, even as she twisted my arm.

Thirty-four.

I thought I might die, which made me think of home.

Home. My real home.

The boys. They fought all the time. My mind reeled, trying to remember their many skirmishes. I had one chance, and she wouldn't be expecting it.

I grabbed her shoulder, squeezed my knees up, slammed my feet into her chest, and kicked her up and over. She landed hard behind me. Dazed, I turned over and looked at her. She had landed on a root; the air was forced out of her lungs. She was blinking rapidly, desperate to inhale, fingers grasping at the dirt.

Thirty-eight.

Bag. Red Canvas.

My hands shook as I willed my body not to stop moving. My fingers clasped together awkwardly to pull the first zipper. She packed her bag differently than mine.

Forty.
Forty-one.
Red canvas. Forceps. Sani-powder.
I pulled things out, one after the other, frequently getting more than I intended and letting the extra scatter around my feet.
Gasping, I couldn't hear anything but my ragged breath.
Forty-four.
My leg suddenly jerked in pain.
She had thrown herself on my ankle, twisting it, still gasping for breath. There was a jab from a stick. It tore through my skin, drawing blood, and my body tried to lurch to escape her grip. I had the kit, but if I couldn't get to the mother, only a few feet away, my struggle was useless. I pulled myself along the ground, roots and needles sinking into my skin, desperate to do the thing I always prayed I would never have to do: pull life from death.
Forty-seven.
I kicked her off, but she caught a breath and pulled again. I screamed her name, breathing in dust from the ground.
Fifty.
I was inches away, knowing that I would never finish if Tessa was still on me. I looked at the scalpel. It was sharp enough to take her out.
No. Don't take a life to save one.
She coughed again.
Surprise. The element of surprise.
I had to use my left and hope it was strong enough.
Instead of pulling away from her, I lunged toward her with one intention. She blocked my right, but I hit her neck with my left hand, then kicked her in the chest, once again rendering her breathless. Once I was free, I landed a kick to her nose. She fell back, disabled enough to let go of me.
Fifty-six.
I crawled, scrambling up onto my knees.

I squirted antibacterial liquid all over me, then set off the sani-powder bomb, which sanitized everything in an eighty-inch radius and made everything white.

My body was screaming to go faster, but I made myself stop. I had only seconds left, but any surgery would be worthless if I was shaking. And I couldn't stop.

I took a breath. I could risk two more seconds to get this right. But I couldn't waste them. I closed my eyes. What could make this right?

Destiny. How many times had Collin told me that if I feared it the most, it would happen? Because I was meant to do this. And if he believed it, when no one else did, I could do it.

I opened my eyes. My hand was perfectly still.

Sixty-five.

A voice in my head echoed Collin's directions, but my hands moved as if by reflex. I barely felt myself controlling them.

I got the last incision. The fluid seeped out as I pulled the forceps to one side. The liquid was clear, but the baby hadn't turned around. Blue feet.

I kept going, blinking to keep tears back. Blue feet are not the end. The baby might survive.

The smell wasn't what I had expected, but I pushed my nausea to the back of my mind. This messy, horrid scene of blood, dirt, sweat. Tessa beginning to cry and vomit. I thanked God this child would never see the wretchedness of its first moments of life, its cry the only thing that could redeem them.

But she wasn't crying. Because she wasn't breathing.

Her mouth was full of mucous and fluid. I dug a finger into her throat to clear it. The baby's eyes were still closed, but she was moving. Struggling.

There was a gurgling sound from the infant as I started to cry, my strength giving way, desperate to just make her organs work. I had to find the bag, but I couldn't put her down.

"Put the baby on its side. Find the bag."

The order came from a choked voice, but it came. Tessa choked again.

"Put it—"

"On its side," I said. "I got it."

Gurgle again, a half a cry.

I didn't want to put her down. She needed to be cleaned, and the cord cut, and she needed a green roll I couldn't find.

All the while, Tessa was gurgling and sobbing. "I'm sorry. I'm sorry. I don't know—"

My anger burned.

"I don't need you to be sorry right now! I need your help!" I half-cried, half-shouted.

Something in Tessa snapped. Almost as quickly as she had moved earlier, she reached for the bag. Within two seconds, her bloodied hand reached out with the tubes for the oxygen compressor. She also had the nasal aspirator. Moments later, she had the oxygen out and tubes attached.

I was suctioning with the aspirator when she yelled at me to move. As I did, she took the tube and placed it in the baby's throat. She turned the oxygen machine on, but flipped three different switches that I had never seen done before. I was about to ask, but then the fluid came up through the tube, out of the baby's lungs.

"Get the other tubes," she ordered. "I'm going to switch and give her oxygen in thirty seconds."

I nodded and wiped my forearm across my face to clear away the tears. I held my breath as if that would somehow keep every last drop of oxygen for her.

Her. I had seen it without processing it.

I didn't argue when Tessa instructed me to keep rubbing the baby's back, but was also a little scared to leave her alone with it. I went back to the bag and found the insulated carrier to wrap up the newborn.

She grabbed the other tubes, making a quick switch and finally attaching the oxygen. Everything else was automatic, a series of movements memorized over time. I had run out of tears. Tessa held up the shears to cut the cord. I almost wanted stab her with them.

But I cut the cord instead. A few seconds after, the baby coughed. A gurgle, then a cry. Strong. Clear.

I had never wanted to hear a sound so much in my entire life.

Two minutes. The baby would be fine, still in the safety zone for a first cry. Pink overtook the blue on her skin as Tessa rubbed the baby's legs with the blanket, trying to get the blood to flow new oxygen down. The baby kept crying. Tessa kept sobbing. And I was silent except for breathing, thinking this scene would haunt me forever.

The rhythm of the dread I had just felt for my life and the life of the baby sounded like a drum. I didn't know how I could find the strength to move until she asked me where my Vessel was. I jumped up, still grasping the baby. My sore muscles struggled to walk across the typical hurdles of the forest floor. I turned back to Tessa, brow furrowed.

"I'll strip the site and get her ID," she said, tired.

I ran for Katerina, the baby now crying in my arms, and found her where I had left her.

"There was screaming," she said. "There was... are you okay?"

"Well . . ."

Her eyes saw the baby, saw my tears, and her face fell.

"Aislyn? What happened?"

My jaw shook, even as I spoke. "There was a Vessel, but she didn't make it, sweetie. The baby made it, but there was a complication."

"I'm sorry. I'm so... that's so sad. But why are you all sweaty? Why is your leg bleeding? Why are you crying?"

I stared at her instead of answering, more tired than I could ever have imagined, not wanting to ruin what innocence she had left.

"Another complication."

CHAPTER 20

"Did I ever tell you this is the best part of my job?" Sam's voice rang through the MCU the next day. "I'm the first one who gets to stop holding my breath! I'm a little shocked that you're calling in so early."

"The feeling is mutual. Your shock is kind of insulting."

"No, not like that. Remember, I was betting on you, 27. But you had signaled to say you found someone, then never checked in at the R-station. You made amazing time. There's a shuttle in your area, so it should just be an hour or two. Go three miles north and stay there. Since you didn't message in, we don't know who you have. Vessel? Unnecessary? Boy? Girl? Details are nice, Aislyn."

I paused. I would have shared this in my first report to him, but I had missed my window because of the incident with Tessa's Vessel.

"I have two Unnecessaries: eight-year-old girl and an infant boy. Tessa's with me. Newborn girl. Vessel died in the journey."

There was silence.

Yeah, this is going to go over well, I thought.

"Aislyn, can you repeat that?" he asked, a little louder.

"I have two Unnecessaries, Sam." I meant for it to sound more confident, but it didn't.

"Aislyn, hang on... just wait a minute. Patterson heard you that time. I flagged him already. He looks a little irritated, by the way... Oh, sorry, sir. Okay, I need to confirm first, we have the 2nd and the 27th, passengers are one child—female, eight years—and two infants." Sam must have been talking to the shuttle driver because his voice seemed further away. "Yes, that's correct. No. It's not your job to ask why, Michael, it's not even my job! Just pick them up, darn it!"

I almost laughed at Sam as he gave orders but was too afraid to move. Within seconds, there was a squeak from my earpiece and my MCU changed modes. A label on the screen read "Locked call; secure private line. Patterson."

"Why do you have two Unnecessaries? Short version. Go."

Patterson sounded as angry as I was expecting. I choked up.

His tone changed. "Aislyn, I report to the Council in ten minutes. I need a reason why you did this that's better than their rules. You have one minute left on this line. Talk."

His urgency calmed me. He wasn't angry. He wanted to help.

"Katerina's father abandoned her a few years ago. Emotional attachment. She found the abandoned newborn. She's been taking care of him. She asked me to take the baby instead of her. But I couldn't leave her. I couldn't, sir."

There was a sigh on the other end, feeling the weight of the bureaucracy that would bury him in paperwork.

"I'm sorry, Patterson," I added.

"No, Aislyn. You're not sorry. And neither am I. Good job. Tell Tessa she did a good job too. Matheson will have your back. Leave the rest of the Council to me. I know what you want. I'll try to get them placed together. Keep your head up, feet moving."

"Copy." I detached the comm wire from the ground wire and then from the MCU, trying to ignore his comment about Tessa. It had almost made me gag.

I turned around and gave everyone the timetable and sat down. Tessa was holding Rachel, the baby named for the mother who had died to give her life. She still needed the portable incubator blanket. The oxygen filter was low on battery, but would last the three hours we had left.

I sat next to Tessa, who hadn't spoken in a few hours, and looked up at the sky. She was looking at Katerina, who was running around the small meadow next to the station.

"You should tell her she shouldn't try to catch it, Aislyn. It's just a moth, not a butterfly."

I shook my head. Something about what she had just said felt wrong. I didn't have time to think about it before she spoke again.

"So, I guess you'll be famous now. Saving the baby from the Protector who had the meltdown," she said, her voice shaking.

"Tessa, what happened to you?" I asked, trying to maintain my anger. "Is there any chance you could remember why you do this? A good reason? Because you almost murdered any reason you had left."

She looked down at the baby in her arms, her black hair hiding her face.

"I just wanted to be... a legend. I wanted the world to see me that way. To respect me. To want to be me. Now I've become something they will detest, and you... you'll be the hero they always wanted." She paused. "A part of me thinks it's so unfair that you'll get all the attention when we get back, but that is so messed up. You always knew I was messed up. I hated you for it."

I stayed silent, trying to think of some advice. But instead, I had a memory.

"You know, I didn't go to the Academy, but I'm guessing that whatever is in your head, that pressure to be perfect, started there. I'm sure someone told you something that wasn't true, and you believed it. The same thing almost happened to me."

She sighed. "What?"

I stared at Katerina again. "When I was a kid, I chased moths all the time. But one day, my mom told me that it wasn't a butterfly. It wasn't beautiful. It didn't count. But I didn't believe her. I chased them anyway. For days. For weeks. Because I believed it was beautiful. And I wanted to find beauty, not see it."

I paused. "And according to the Republic, that girl over there is a moth. So are you and I. Avery and Collin. We're all moths compared to the perfect, beautiful humans they make in those labs. They named the moth ugly, but so do you. You keep thinking that by saving someone, you make it beautiful again, so you compete against everyone and try to be the hero. But that's not how it works. You just need to see what's already there. Find the beauty in anything, and you'll start saving the moth again. It's there. See it, Tessa, and try to change the story you've been telling yourself in your head. Change the story."

Tears formed in her eyes. She remained still, opening her mouth several times to talk.

Then, she handed me Rachel.

Tessa never told me what she was thinking. She never had to say a word.

She spent the next forty minutes helping an eight-year-old catch a moth.

A few hours later, the shuttle's hover-pads revved in the distance. Katerina clutched my hand, shivering. Tessa was just as nervous.

"What are you going to tell Patterson in debrief?" she asked.

I had wondered about that since I'd cleaned the blood off my leg in the stream. I saw it in her eyes, the part that worried about what others thought. But the truth might mean her probation—or expulsion.

"The truth," I said. "I got there. You panicked, forgot what to do, and I helped." I wanted to give her a way out of her condemnation, but I wondered if she could live with that.

"What are you going to tell them?" I asked.

"I don't know. If I'm not too scared, the truth. But I'm too afraid that they'll never let me out again. I guess you'll know in about thirty minutes how brave I really am."

Ten seconds later, the shuttle came out of the brush and stopped twenty yards away. I didn't recognize anyone except Lynn's trainer, Will, who ran to Tessa. The trainer shadowing Will came out shortly after. He was the one to reach me first.

"Hey, Aislyn. My name is Michael. You did great. First time's the hardest. You're almost there, okay? You'll sit right next to the baby. I just need you to know..." His eyes searched for mine amid the noise and chaos. "I need you to know it's okay. Patterson had your back. It's already getting sorted out."

I gave him the pack and baby, but my arms felt strangely empty. Soon, both babies were in the seat-cribs and attached the monitors. I tried to calm myself as I sat in the shuttle, feeling the soft leather, a strange reminder of the place I now called home.

Within twenty seconds, we had reached full speed. A counselor from the shelter was already talking to Katerina, on her knees, eye to eye with her. She seemed so gentle. Katerina was looking at her, back to me, and to her again.

"She's okay, sweetie," I said. "She's from the shelter."

"And guess what?" the counselor added. "I already have the best news. A woman named Hannah contacted me and told me that you rescued the baby boy. I have already talked to a family who has told me they always wanted a girl and a boy. You will get to meet them at the shelter and go home with them in a few weeks. Then you'll just come back to the shelter every day for school, and we'll be talking a lot. I'll be the best of friends to you. I want to know everything about you, but not today. Today, we can just be happy. Do you want to be happy with me?"

I smiled, breathing a sigh of relief, stifling a cry with a laugh, and feeling the burn of tears, even as Katerina hugged the counselor.

Michael looked at me across the shuttle seat, putting monitors on the baby.

"I told you," he whispered.

I nodded, smiling as I turned to the counselor who had pushed away the weight that had been crushing my heart.

Silently, I mouthed, "Thank you."

She smiled and mouthed back the same message.

I got off the shuttle, and my heart felt defeated again.

"Wait," Katerina screamed, the little hand clutching mine. Blue eyes and golden hair had been revealed in water and sunlight, and the smell of pine pulled me away from reality once more.

"Aislyn, will I ever see you again?"

I steadied my voice, remembering the script they taught me.

"Maybe, but not tomorrow. Not for a while. I have to go back. You wouldn't want me to stop, would you?"

She looked in my eyes, touched my face, and said, "No, but I don't want to forget you either."

I smiled, trying to hold back tears. "Then don't."

Her last words were a whisper that caught my breath.

"They asked me the baby's name, but I never gave him one. I want you to name the baby. That name you kept saying while you were writing and while you slept. Collin. I like that name."

She smiled and walked away, holding the counselor's hand.

Michael's hand was gripping my arm, but I didn't realize it until I pulled away slightly.

"Steady, 27," he said warningly.

I wanted to run back to the woods where it was just her and me and an infant crying. My heart ached more than I thought it could, but Michael's arm squeezed mine a little harder.

"First time is always the hardest, 27. I'm supposed to keep telling you that, so you keep it together. I'm going down to Medical with the baby. Don't get girly and cry a lot. Please."

My reaction to coming back to Central must be common, so trainers must be taught to cope with it. His honesty made me smile. All the same, I needed to see a familiar face.

And then I did.

"Liam?"

"See? You're fine!" he said, as if he were trying to win an argument. "Backpacked and wearing black and back from your first mission. And you thought you wouldn't be okay."

I reached out and hugged him, far too tightly

"First time's the hardest, 27," he said in a melancholy tone. "It gets easier. I promise."

"I'm sorry," I said, finally letting him go.

He nodded. "I'm here to collect your Med report and to make sure Michael takes the infant down to Dr. Swanson."

"She's fine," the Med tech said from behind me. Liam took the clipboard from him. "Bandage to lower leg due to a 'fall or something,' as she reported. Pretty sure she lied about it."

I shot the Med tech a look, and he glared back. "Vitals are stable. I sent them to Sam and Patterson with my notes."

"Okay, so you're fine, did you hear that?" Liam said, as if we had discovered a new fact by reading a book together.

The Med tech handed the baby to Michael.

"Name?" Michael looked at me expectedly.

"Collin," I said, kissing the baby on the forehead.

Michael went down with the Med techs. I didn't move, but my breath shuddered.

"You said it gets easier," I said. "How much easier?"

Liam gave papers to someone rushing by, then moved to face me. "Not much, 27. But enough."

I nodded, blinking. "What now?"

Liam stared at his MCU. "Debrief. Follow me. Tessa's going first. She outranks you. You're in... Room 221. Water and a meal bar in there for you. You have to wait alone, sorry."

I stepped into Room 221 moments later. It was silent, with metal walls, like the ones I had seen on my first day in this building. That seemed like five years ago now. I remembered everything I thought I might experience, but also everything I could have never foreseen. Saving two Unnecessaries, fighting a Protector to save a baby, performing a C-section on a dead mother, having a Sentry let me escape, and...

Almost on cue, the door opened, and he was standing there—the one person I could never have predicted to love.

Collin looked out of breath. I was so desperate to tell him everything, but I didn't move. He had the courage to do what I could not.

He crossed the room in an instant, his arms stretched out, grabbing me and pulling me so close to him I could barely catch a breath. His arms closed around my shoulders, and I could feel them shaking a little, clutching my neck so my head rested against him. I clung to him like he would disappear if I didn't hold on hard enough.

Almost too soon, he pulled away.

"You did an amazing. Two of them?" he asked, shaking his head. "All that beating yourself up and 'I'll never be good enough' and... two of them?"

I cut off my tears with a laugh, but my debrief still loomed over me.

"What's wrong?" he asked, lifting my chin so I'd meet his gaze. "You're okay, right? I asked Medical twice already. I looked at your chart. I've been annoying. Is your leg okay?"

He had to know that would make me laugh, but then I became more serious as I tried to explain. "You will not believe... I can't... and Tessa was a nightmare..." I choked up. He looked confused, thinking we had come back together out of convenience. "Katerina, and the baby. She said on the shuttle..."

"Aislyn, Patterson was brilliant. He knew the media would love it, so he told them first—which he can technically do. The public opinion was so overwhelming that by the time he got to the Council, even after only ten minutes, most members were praising your bravery for the sake the media coverage. Cordon, Zander, and few others are mad about policy—you'll have to watch your back with them—but most people are enchanted by the beauty of the story. Hannah was on the fence, but loves political wins with the public, so she made the call. A family volunteered to take them both already. So, Katerina and... wait, what's the baby's name?"

"Collin. She liked that name. His name is Collin."

I smiled, watching his features soften and his lower lip quiver. He hugged me again. "It's a simple debrief, okay? You'll be fine."

I closed my eyes, trying to push out the stress, unsure how to tell him there would be nothing simple about this debrief.

"I'm not supposed to see you until later," Collin whispered. "You'll debrief and go to your Circle. You'll be alone for a bit. It's a good time to take a shower and just... recoup as much as you can. I have to meet with Patterson to go over the details and prepare you for the Council debrief tomorrow. I'll find out what happened, and we'll talk, I promise."

He reassured me with a smile. He hesitated, but then pulled me in and grazed a kiss on my cheek. With a vulnerable glance, he ran out the back door.

I was alone, waiting for the inevitable, still not sure of what to say. It felt cold, even though the air was comfortable. I wasn't in his arms anymore. The only part of me that burned was my cheek. I had to add Collin to the list of secrets I was keeping. I don't know how Patterson was going to take any of this news, and I thought with a tinge of regret... Patterson could see the footage of the camera that was in the room, if he wanted to review it.

But Patterson did not come in a few minutes later, which made me wonder what Tessa was saying, which made me feel more pressure. Forty long and lonely minutes later, as the silence was becoming deafening, there was a beep. The door slid open, and Patterson entered. He looked exhausted.

"All right," he started, leaning against the wall, "I know this is your first real debrief. It always annoys people when I ask a lot of questions. Deal with it. It's my job to make you relive some moments you may have hated, and for good reason. I have to ask you for details, and I'm sorry."

I took a deep breath, preparing myself.

"Tonight, however, is the exception."

I didn't realize what he meant at first, but slowly, it dawned on me. "Tessa told you everything."

"Yes. So, if you were wondering if you should lie to protect her or tell the truth but have her deny it, don't worry about it. Tessa told me every detail. I hope your leg is okay, by the way. Looks like you came back with three Unnecessaries, 27th, and few people will ever know except me. I guess this is my chance to tell you that—" He took a breath. "You have earned all the respect I could give, and I am sorry for ever doubting you. I did, by the way... just a few times. At the beginning. Don't hate me."

I laughed as he smiled through his tired eyes.

"In other good news," he continued, "Rachel is doing great, according to the medic's report. We got her in the incubator for a day. Your Unnecessaries both look healthy. Katerina told us about her father, or whoever protected her. He was a former Sub-Terra. Sam checked, but he's disappeared. We'll wait to tell her he's dead. In the meantime, she's going to be put on a special diet. She has some dangerous bacteria, no doubt from living underground. And she's low on vitamin D from lack of sunlight. Nothing a few months on meds won't fix."

He swallowed, and I could tell we were about to enter another uncomfortable discussion topic.

"I have to leave after your briefing and decide whether Tessa is under probation, expelled, or even court martialed. Eldridge doesn't need to ask for your opinion, but he did. So, should Tessa get another chance?"

"I think," I said slowly, fighting my impulse to say anything to never see Tessa again, "that she should probably have another chance, but a part of me hates she's going to get one. It feels like she's getting away with it, except... she helped with Rachel, even during her meltdown. And she... caught moths with Katerina." This didn't mean anything to Patterson, but it felt important. "She's changed. Just a little. But I think it's enough."

He sighed. "Well, I'll pray it is enough then. Probation means she can't go back out for a week. It'll give us some time to get a counselor to confirm she's ready for that. The truth is the Council loves her, so unless Eldridge argues, she'll stay. Thank you for being honest, though. While you're being so honest, are you okay? Should I be calling a counselor for you?"

"I'm good. I can't really explain it, but I'm fine."

He nodded and then said that Collin would still have to fill out a Post-Traumatic Stress Report. Then, the real debrief began. He asked questions sporadically, like what song was playing when the police officer noticed me dancing. He had what I assumed was an audio recorder running, but was still taking some notes. We got to the police, the tunnels, finding Katerina, and the escape. I mentioned the location of the café because I couldn't remember the name.

Patterson stopped the recorder, poured a glass of water, and gave it to me. "You're doing great. Just a few more—"

"Is the recorder still off?" I interrupted.

He turned to look at it, nodded and whispered "Yeah." He sat down, as if he was afraid to ask why I wanted it off. The room was silent for ten seconds before I could speak, but he waited, on the edge of the table.

"You aren't going to believe me."

"Try me," Patterson said, with a tone that made me believe him.

"I got caught. A Sentry pursued us, followed us down the last tunnel. He had a light and a weapon and I was frozen. He knew what I was. I was dead." I paused as Patterson's reaction of shock set in and his anticipation rose. "He let me go."

Patterson was still. He moved, as if to ask a question, but nothing came. I went through all the details again as he rubbed his forehead. Once he'd found his voice, he asked twenty questions about the Sentry's appearance, what alley we were in when we came up, what the names of the squad members were, and said something about wanting a normal night as he stared at the recorder, still off and still muted.

"This could be a trap," he said. "You realize that."

"I do. A way to get me to trust him again. But it seems like if they wanted to gain someone's trust, they'd choose a target with more margin for escape, hoping that maybe they'd catch me easier next time. But there was no more advantage to be gained. I was already dead, he had a weapon and a clean shot."

His fist was over his mouth in concentration. "What is your hesitancy to tell the Council? That you won't get as much credit for your escape?"

"No," I said, thinking briefly about how that was something Tessa would have considered. "No, I know they are going to have a ton of questions I can't answer, and I want a chance to find those answers first. And if I decide to trust him again, I will. I don't want to have to disobey an order that I shouldn't." I paused, now thinking clearly what I had wanted to say.

"I don't want their doubts in my head, sir."

Patterson raised his eyebrows and tilted his head to one side. I realized that he still had the power to tell the Council everything. He stared at the recorder for about five more seconds before he hit the button.

"So, 27, what did you do after climbing the ladder with Katerina?"

The rest of the debrief was over quickly. Before I knew it, I was back in my Circle. I allowed myself a long shower with a few tears. Despite Collin's claim that he would be up ten minutes after my debrief, he still hadn't arrived when I got out. It was so empty without anyone there. I hit the comm, connecting to Sam.

"Aislyn," he greeted through the speaker, "the hero of the hour. What can I do for you?"

"Hey, is Collin still in the meeting?"

"Oh, yeah, and not just with Patterson, but with Eldridge, Avery, and Hannah, too. What happened out there?"

"Nothing I can tell you about," I said jokingly, yet honestly. "Is anyone else back?"

"Um, you weren't quite the first back. Megan beat you by three days. She found a kid in the woods, up north in the abandoned warehouses. They found shelter in the derelict rooms but escaped to the woods for food. So, Megan didn't even go over the border to find someone."

"Nice," I said, breathing a little relief. "Anyone else?"

"Brie and Sarah are on their way back to the Territory now. Everyone else has checked in fine. I'll keep you posted on Eva. Earlier today, she sent word that she has a Vessel and may need an EE. Everyone's alive. Chloe hasn't checked in for three days, but neither did you and you were fine. If you want to pray for anyone, that's who we're rooting for today."

"Thanks."

He responded with a nonchalant, "No problem."

I felt a pang of awkwardness in wanting to go to see Megan. Did she know I was back? She might not care.

I sat in the middle of my Circle, unable to concentrate. So, instead of praying, I flew through every circumstance in my mind. I screamed accusations to heaven: *"Where were you? When Tessa went crazy, when Katerina's father died, when Rachel almost died? Why didn't you intervene?"*

Flashes of memory played like a movie in my mind: a Sentry had known what I was, looked me right in the eye, and didn't shoot. I had beaten Tessa. I had gotten two Unnecessaries out of the Republic. My blood pumped harder as I remembered every impossible thing that had happened until I sank into the peace I desperately needed.

Maybe prayers did work. I'd have to admit that to Collin, which annoyed me.

I heard footsteps and opened my eyes. Collin stood above me, looking like he was about to cry.

"I'm sorry. How are you... Tell me you're okay. Or how I'm supposed to not punch Tessa every time I see her?"

I opened my mouth, but despite the peace I had just felt, the wound in my leg twinged in pain and the scene became fresh in my mind again. He pulled me in and hugged me as his hands shook, his breath cut short by panicked, stinging thoughts. He asked me if I wanted to talk about it, while examining my leg.

"No," I said. "I need to let it go."

"Well, it was a long meeting. Tessa is under probation for the rest of the year, so she won't be going back out for ten days. You get to go out in three if you want."

It wasn't until I heard him say it, even nonchalantly, that it sank in. Three days. I had to go back in three days.

"That doesn't leave us a lot of time," he said, his eyes full of sorrow as he pushed a strand of hair behind my ear. "Got a story?"

I nodded and went to my room, fell on the bed. I told him all about the Republic. I talked about a butterfly I caught once, learning later that it was a moth. He responded up to the last sentence, when I looked up to see him fast asleep, leaning on the door frame.

Despite feeling tired, I couldn't sleep. I felt like I could never sleep on a bed again.

I pulled out my journal. The paper felt comforting in my hands compared to the MCU. I loved the fact that it was dirtied and inked up, compared to the sanitary world of the Republic. I opened it and read 'after the first mission' from the fourth 27th Protector:

Don't feel the guilt of coming home. If you didn't cherish anything at home, you wouldn't have the wisdom to cherish anything. To love warmth, cozy blankets, friendship, candles, and books is to know that beautiful things should be cherished; that's why you brought them back here, to discover what you cherish.

I laid down, feeling the softness of my pillow. An ordinary thing holds the most value for someone who has never experienced it.

Katerina had a pillow now, able to sleep and dream.

Every worry lifted, and I fell until sleep caught me.

CHAPTER 21

I woke up, only wanting to hide under the covers again when I saw my Council review on my agenda right after breakfast. I spent the morning reading with Collin, perusing maps of where in the Republic I had traveled. We discussed how I should have ordered my food differently as a Terra on a budget and where I could rent a cheaper room next time.

Eva returned later that morning with a Vessel who was twenty weeks along and having early contractions. Collin had rushed down for her EE, but Michael went out again. The contractions stopped within minutes of getting the right meds, and both the Vessel and the baby were soon looking better. Eva's debrief ended faster than mine and she met me in the garden.

Megan ran out of her Circle when she saw Eva and me on the garden wall. She gave me a quick hug and said she would have visited sooner, but her trainer had warned her I might be in therapy. When she asked why, I said I couldn't say, but then I blurted it all out anyway. They listened. Megan checked on my wound. Eva cursed and paced like Collin, who I had to tell to not punch Tessa. Megan told us about the kids who lived in the warehouse areas. Eva laid on the stones underneath the growing flowers as she listened.

"My Unnecessary said there were more kids around that area, living in the warehouses and foraging in the forest for food. He wanted to go find some of his friends, but since the rule is to protect one at a time—"

"Yeah, looks like someone missed that memo," Eva said, giving me a mock-judgmental glare.

"Hey, after the Council grills me for disobeying the rules, I don't know if it's going to be worth it."

Eva looked at the flowers above her as she picked some petals off. "Yeah, it will."

I turned to Megan, who seemed like she was in a trance, looking up at the growing vines on the strings. "It will always be worth it. You better never regret it, Aislyn. Any of it. Ever."

Their words gave me the confidence I needed to get to the Council room and through most of my debrief without stuttering.

Most of their questions were simple and concerned certain details in the debrief which Collin and I had prepped for. Several people, including John Naderville, commented that they were in a rush to get to the next review. There were some who asked me nearly four times, in slightly different ways, about my "motivation for breaking policy" and my "reasons for throwing away tradition." I answered the same way each time.

"I didn't rescue two. I rescued one. I allowed her to be the hero she already was. She saved him, and I saved her."

Murmurs followed. A reporter with an MCU typed furiously every time I spoke. One smiled and whispered loudly enough for me to hear: "I got tomorrow's headline." They didn't realize their headline would arrive in the room after my Council review. The rumors and conjecture about Tessa hadn't solidified into anything close to the truth.

Matheson, the leading Council member, commended me for breaking the rules to save their lives, at which Eldridge winked. When asked about Tessa, I told them what I told Patterson. I tried hard not to say anything with anger. We needed to save as many as possible; I didn't want her as an enemy if it meant she couldn't save any more lives.

After the review, everyone took a break in the hallway. Patterson dismissed the reporters. I wanted to ask him about my mystery rescuer. Instead, I ran into Eldridge, beaming with pride.

"Well... that happened."

"Do I get to ask a question?" I asked, rather playfully.

"Not before me, but I'm sure you aren't ready for mine."

His grey eyes were half-closed, almost a little suspicious. I tilted my head to the side, smiling, sure he was joking about something.

He raised his eyebrows and said, "My dear, you know my position and my rank, but you may not understand what talents would propel a career to these heights. I excel at several things, not the least of which is knowing when someone isn't telling the whole truth. And you left something out."

My smile disappeared. I felt more vulnerable than if were stuck in the Republic without an MCU. But to my surprise, he smiled.

"When you are ready to tell me, let me know. I can't wait to hear it. Until then, I'll have to trust you, which is both a thrill and an honor, curious girl."

Eldridge touched my shoulder as he walked past, already deluged by people making his hair greyer by the minute. I wondered if anyone else could tell I had lied, in a place crawling with instructors in espionage.

My thoughts evaporated when I noticed Patterson and Collin talking. I could only see Patterson's back, but their conversation seemed intense. Collin glanced at me with a look of confusion and conviction I had never seen before. Quickly, he looked at the floor, nodding as he listened to his boss. Patterson said a few more things and walked off, leaving Collin still leaning on the wall, looking straight at me.

He turned to join me as I moved down the hall. "How was the review? Patterson said you did great."

We discussed it on the way back up the stairs and through the garden. Back at my Circle, he prepped the punching bag as I wrapped my hands in tape. After a few punches, I remembered the conversation I had seen in the hallway.

"So, what did Patterson want?" I said, keeping my timing steady to show him I wasn't nervous.

"Nothing," he said, holding the bag and staring at the floor.

"Collin? The truth."

It must have been Patterson's conversation that had unnerved him. Had he told Collin about how I'd escaped? I had planned on telling Collin about the Sentry at lunch break. It wasn't clear why I was hesitating. Maybe I didn't want Collin's skepticism to destroy my chance of finding out who the Sentry was.

He chuckled slightly at that. "It was more about me than you. A warning... a career warning, if you will."

"What about?" I had to admit I was confused. Patterson had been all for the training style changing, and after my great victory, I would have thought he'd be more confident about Collin.

But my heart sank to my stomach as I remembered that Patterson knew the truth. I was closer to death than anyone realized.

"No, it was..." Collin hesitated, then looked from the floor to me. "... a reminder of a certain policy. He knew I always dreamed of this career and this life, even being Head Trainer one day. I've worked my whole life for this. I... didn't expect this to happen."

"What, me?"

His voice became low and breathless.

"Us."

I stopped punching.

So, Patterson had checked the security camera.

I wanted to punch Sam instead.

I stared at the strings holding the bag together. My breath, loud and uneven, gave me away. Biting my lip to stop it from moving, I let my eyes find his. They drew me in like a magnet, intense and swirling, a storm I couldn't understand raging behind them. A realization hit me.

The same thing that had brought us together would now rip us apart.

Collin broke the silence first. "That was two minutes. Pulse."

I placed my hand out, like I always did. His fingers rested on my wrist, feeling my blood pumping, though my heart was racing for a very different reason.

My voice was a little irregular, giving my fear away before I got to speak it. "There can't be an 'us,' can there? You can't..."

I couldn't say love. It felt so strange to be already suffering so much loss for something we hadn't even said out loud yet.

He took a breath. "Actually, there can be. Council members aren't stupid. In the early decades of the program, when all the trainers were as young as me, they predicted it would be a potential issue. And then it became a real issue, a few times. It's frowned upon, but there was, as they put it, 'no reason they shouldn't be together.' They came up with a rule, though."

His words piqued my interest. He continued to stare at the mat below us as he continued.

"The rule is, should a trainer act on an emotional attachment to a Protector beyond friendship, the trainer will resign on the day of the Protector's last mission. It allows the trainers to teach at the Academy in a few years, to serve in Central, but..."

"You'd never be able to train anyone again. You'd lose the position, the hope of being Head Trainer one day. You'd lose..."

His eyes closed, my last words hanging in the air, no conclusion needed. A part of me wanted to scream that I was more important, but I understood what this meant to him. He had been training for almost all his life. Teaching at the Academy would be his retirement gig, not his lifelong pursuit. But still...

"I get it. I do. It makes sense. And it's not like we can't be together, it... would ruin your career."

I wish I had another word for "career." It was what I had accused him of a long time ago— caring for it instead of me when he was pushing me to keep me alive, desperate enough to become something he wasn't. I wondered if he had cared for me even in the beginning.

"It's not only my career, Aislyn. It's my legacy and my whole life. I swore I would do this forever... I promised—" He cringed as if something were physically hurting him.

I had expected him to say this was hard for him because he loved me. Or that telling me how he felt would be difficult, but not impossible. I had not expected a deadpan stare at the floor.

"Right. Well." I took off my tape and gloves with one movement. "I'm sorry I ruined your life."

"Aislyn, you don't understand." He grasped my hand.

"What, isn't this what you want? I can walk away, Collin, if that will make this less complicated for you. And if not—"

I took a step toward him, only inches away now. Even as I threatened to walk away, I couldn't move. I felt him take a sharp breath and let it go, feeling it against my skin.

I backed up one step. "I know how important it is to you, Collin, but I don't know why. And you won't tell me, will you?"

"I can't. It's the only thing I'm not ready to tell you."

"Why?"

He looked at me, almost as if he were evaluating me again. "Because you're not ready to hear it."

I took my hand back and walked out of my Circle, feeling like I had far too many times before—like we were broken.

I was sweaty from the debrief and the workout, so I went to shower again. Afterward, I dreaded going back to my Circle, and even considered staying in an empty classroom beneath Central. Upon opening my locker to get dressed, I found that it had been filled with more than just my training outfits. It now had white clothes, black clothes, and two standard Republic outfits in it.

My camo suit hung in front.

I ran through the consequences, but I didn't care. It was like I was forming an escape plan in Intel class with Eric. I wanted to run away. And I could. I could make running away look brave.

Getting dressed, I grabbed my pack and camo tent and slammed the door. I ran down the long flights of stairs to the Hub, scanned to see if Collin was there, and walked into the Hand.

"Sam, is anyone going out tonight?"

He didn't look up from his screen as he answered. "Megan is. Why?"

"Does she want company?"

"Well, I don't know if... whoa!" He had looked up and seen me dressed, pack at the ready.

Joel looked up briefly. "You're not supposed to be down here, 27."

"Give it a rest, Joel," Liam shot back.

"Wait, are you reporting?" Sam asked, pulling a pen from its resting place behind his ear.

"Yes," I answered, knowing I had forgotten what I needed to do, other than report to Sam. Was there paperwork to be filled out? Was there a procedure? Collin did all of that.

"Well, she's leaving in ten minutes... comm, call Collin."

"Why are you calling him?"

"He needs to sign off, that's all. As on top of things as he is, I can't believe he hasn't yet. He signed you off medically this morning, psychologically... this morning. And... yeah, that checks out. He didn't call in the code. Comm, try Collin again."

I forced myself to put my pack down and lean on the door like this was an annoying technicality, pushing down my panic with a deep breath. I wondered if he wasn't answering his comm because of our conversation. It was terrifying to think that my plan to run away might end before it began. I imagined how embarrassing it would be for Sam to drag me back upstairs to hear a huge lecture from Patterson and see the pain of my betrayal in Collin's eyes.

Collin answered.

"Hey, bud," Sam said, putting him on speakerphone as he typed out paperwork with my name. "Give me more warning next time. Aislyn reported about two minutes ago, which means I have enough time to discharge her still, but I need a discharge authorization code from you now, then you have to report back to Patterson in an hour, and you didn't change your itinerary yet. Megan's leaving in ten minutes. Tick tock."

The silence I had feared followed.

"Collin, you there?"

"She's down there now?" Collin said. I could hear the ache in his voice.

"Yeah, all ready, backpacked and wearing black." Sam was still typing. "I need code clearance for the second mission, dude."

More silence. His voice cracked slightly.

"Four-Y. Beta. Fifty-four. Release authorization immediate."

"Thank you. Report in ten, Collin." Sam silenced the comm and looked at me. "Go upstairs, to the end of the garden. Megan will meet you up there, and you're clear to go. Good luck."

"Thanks," I blurted and ran up the stairs.

"Try to come back with one this time!" Joel yelled after me.

It took a while to get through security. As I ran up the stairs, my MCU beeped with the message I'd been dreading.

"Don't do this, Aislyn. Please."

"It's done," I wrote back. *"I'm going. Megan's leaving any minute."*

I walked out into the garden, but Megan hadn't arrived yet. Collin was in view within seconds, putting his fieldwork jacket on over his sweater. I tried to keep looking away even as he raced up to me.

"Aislyn, I don't want you to do this because of what I said," he said, sounding out of breath. "I need you to know that I care."

"But not enough, Collin. Not enough."

I would have laughed at the irony of my words if they didn't sting so badly.

His shoulders fell, and his expression turned accusatory. "You don't even know what I'm going through."

"How can I?" I said, rushed as I saw Megan coming. I risked grabbing his hand. "You can tell me."

"I can't..." He had a pained look on his face as he closed his eyes. "It's the reason I yelled at you when I didn't want to. I thought it would keep you alive. And now I'm doing this to..."

As he trailed off, placing his head in his hand, I realized there was only one other time that he had refused to tell me what bothered him. I had seen that pain before... the day I had read the journal entry quote out loud.

"I'm sorry," he said. "I'm not saying no to 'us' yet. We have time. But I need you to know this. Aislyn, it would be a lot easier if I could just ignore this, push you away... if you weren't everything you are. It would be easier if I didn't feel anything I do. But if I risk speaking the truth now, you'd know everything I felt. And if I said it, you'd still have to go. Do you want me to say it?"

My comm beeped, and Liam's voice said, "Megan and Aislyn, you ready to go? The shuttle is at the end of the yard."

I closed my eyes, trying to breathe despite what he had almost said. My childishness and the rashness of my actions stung as if someone had poured lemon juice on them.

"I'm sorry. I'm so sorry I—"

"You overreacted," he interrupted, finishing my thought with a tone of approval. "The last time you did something impulsive and overreacted... you brought two Unnecessaries to the Territory and kicked Tessa's butt. It's better to go with Megan than travel alone. If you want me to say it, come back. And if you... if you feel the same way, you can tell me."

Megan's shouts tore my eyes and soul away from him. My feet felt like air and lead at the same time. I wanted to stay with him; his eyes, his worried brow, his broad shoulders sinking a little as his arms wrapped around me. He held me in the hug almost too long. I felt the stubble on his face, grown over two weeks of worry that I was about to put him through again.

Megan's voice called out once more. The clock was ticking, and it might count down the last moments of a Vessel's life. The sewers, back alleys, and cafés called to me; they hid an Unnecessary needing to be saved.

I was holding the heart responsible for training me to save those lives, but they would die if I couldn't let him go.

"There's so much at stake. I don't know what to do."

He sighed and spoke into my ear, grazing it with his lips.

"Yes, you do. You've already done it. You are making me want to do it. Change the story."

CHAPTER 22

We left the drop-off point and walked for hours before taking a break. It was amazing that it didn't feel awkward to speak to Megan, although most of our conversations were about Central, the Republic, and the horrible taste of meal bars. She was able to give me more details about the warehouse section and where more children hid. She couldn't return for months. Patterson had instructed us to avoid a certain sector and not look too familiar, or someone might recognize us and connect the dots.

"Police are dumb, but they aren't that dumb," Megan agreed.

We were sitting by the heating unit, listening to our MCUs review Common Phrases 10. There was just one problem: I wasn't listening. I had the earphones on, but there was no file playing. Instead, I was looking through Protector profiles, searching for the quote that had made Collin so upset. I could barely remember what generation it was from—twenty years ago, maybe? The profiles from the 167th were familiar, but none of them stood out.

"Do you know what day it is?" Megan asked out of nowhere.

I stared at her across the heater, the waves rippling from it in the chilly night air. There should have been a fire in its place, with my brothers and sisters around it. It made the day of the week, or anything normal, hard to pinpoint.

"I don't remember. Is it Wednesday?"

She let out a long breath. "I don't know either. It feels like we should know. I think it's a Wednesday because there's only a month left in spring and I looked at the star charts before we left. By Wednesday, we should see Mars, right by the moon. And I think that's it. If not, we could just say it's Wednesday."

I pulled away from my MCU as the last file ended. Nothing had connected Collin's reaction to the quote, but I wasn't even sure I had chosen the right generation.

"Did you and your dad watch the stars a lot?" I asked.

"Yeah, about every night. At the clearing up on the ridge."

I sat up to lean on my elbow. "My dad used to take me there once in a while when he hunted late at night."

"When? We stayed there almost every night, an hour before midnight."

"About two o'clock. He'd sleep, wake up, then we'd go." I realized the tragedy of it and spoke more to myself. "Just enough to miss you."

We both stared up at the sky.

"I heard you like to write," she said after a moment, "and were in the art track at school. Not the most popular track compared to math or science, but I was glad your parents let you do what you wanted to do and didn't make you do math."

"I thought you were good at math?" I asked, surprised by her jealous tone.

"Being good at something and liking it are two different things. It did get me into the Academy, which is what I wanted all along, so it all worked out. But to be honest, I hate math."

I laughed. "Who told you I was in the art track at school?"

"I wondered, so I called in a favor. There's a lot of show-offs at the Academy, and Lynn looked you up for me a few years ago one night, when the teachers weren't paying attention.

I wanted to know, yet I never bothered to ask when we were both in the same school."

She paused, but I didn't want her to feel guilty.

"I didn't ask much either, did I?" I said.

We were both silent for a moment, as if to acknowledge how much time we had lost. But when she mentioned a funny story with one of our second-year teachers, I laughed, which made her laugh louder. We shared school memories for hours. I told her about Olivia, the twins, and the stories I would tell at bedtime. I told one of my favorite stories as she grew tired, one that began with, "Once upon a time" and ended with, "happily ever after."

I missed Collin with an ache, kicked myself for my recklessness, and fell asleep, praying he could fall asleep with an echo of a story. Maybe he believed in happy endings enough to know that he would see me again.

Seventy hours later, I stared at a shuttle dashboard. I had just been dropped off on a pristine street with beautiful blue jewels embedded in the sidewalk. The remaining money that Katerina had given me was stowed in my bag.

But that wasn't the reason I was so nervous. I had never been further away from the border. I was in the center of the city, surrounded by people using Elite language I only half recognized. I had to use many phrases and slang just to order food.

I continued downtown, closer to 5th Street and the extravagance I'd only read about. We had little footage of these areas. Even here, I had to stomach the same shallow comments, hearing a woman with black hair, straight but for one curly strand, complaining about their daughter wanting too much attention.

"I have a life!" she exclaimed.

Oh, the irony of that statement.

I resolved to follow her. Her poor child could be days away from being disappeared. I managed to overhear where she was going. Sector 4. It was an extravagant part of the Republic. I was thankful to be dressed as a Citizen. My heart raced as I walked out of the café. It didn't slow down for a few blocks. I kept the woman in view. We were on 4th Street when I reached the point where I was surprised that no one could hear my blood pumping. I concentrated on every detail as if I was dancing: feet low, eyes on phone, look at street, feet low, eyes on phone, look disenchanted, feet low, laugh at message, look interested in someone walking by.

I followed the woman, hoping it was a viable lead and not a dead end. I kept repeating to myself, risking what small faith I had: I was destined to save this girl.

Until I realized I was wrong.

I had almost missed it: a coffee cup from the same café near a box in an alley. As if someone else had made the same trip. I left my target and turned down the alley, hearing my feet crunch on the gravel until I got to the discarded cup. There were footprints around it.

Someone else was going to save her daughter, not me.

That person grabbed my arm and pulled me down behind a box that smelled like rotten eggs.

"What are you doing here?" Cassidy said.

"I heard the mom in the café. What are you doing here?"

"The same. But..." She nodded toward the other side of the street.

The woman with the single curl went into a high-priced house with a red light above the door.

I sighed. "Oh, no. Security?"

"The best," Cassidy said, pocketing her MCU and pulling out her phone. "I'm not sure how much longer Julie has, but her mom sounded annoyed a week ago, when I first saw her."

"Wait," I turned back to Cassidy. "A week?"

"The house is secure. They only take expensive cabs. Erin, the mom, drops Julie off at school, which is monitored. This kid is locked up or shielded everywhere she goes, except none of that effort will keep her safe."

"Okay, but... why are you still here? Following or extracting her at this point would leave you vulnerable. I thought after a week, you needed to find a new target..."

I trailed off, leaving Eric's quote from Intel unfinished. We weren't supposed to engage one target too long if it seemed like it wasn't a high possibility that the mission would be a success. Cassidy had broken the rules.

But it felt way too hypocritical to condemn anyone for that.

"I realize that," Cassidy started, then bit her lip. "It's against protocol and I shouldn't be here—"

"Don't worry about it," I said, changing my tone. "I'm the last person who should be bringing up the rules right now."

She looked at me curiously but didn't ask any questions. I continued, almost apologetically, "I don't want you to get hurt, Cassidy. Do you have a plan?"

She shrugged. "Sort of. I'm kind of hoping that something triggers a possibility for me to intervene." She stared at the house, speaking more to herself than to me. "The first day, Julie wanted a kiss before her mom left. Her mom refused. She was on the doorstep. I should have grabbed her then. But the probability was eighty percent of capture because I was dressed as a Terra. I could bypass the security system, but I'd need a distraction for that as well, and Julie and I still might get caught."

She ran through a few other strategies and probabilities.

"I need to wait it out," she finished, "until Erin is so frustrated that she's ready to let Julie go. Then, I can help Erin with her 'problem' and take Julie and head home."

"How would Erin believe you were able to intervene?"

"Well, I was thinking..." Cassidy said as she pulled out a precise replica of a Society lab worker tag. It had a very distinct, shimmering watermark and featured her picture.

"That's more than thinking. That's awesome! How did you get one?"

"It doesn't matter. It's worthless out of context. These lab workers and doctors, they're Elites. They're loaded. And they almost always have assistants or a driver or someone around them. Being seen by myself would break my cover faster than anything else. But I figured if she's desperate, maybe she won't care, and she'll hand Julie over to me to take to a lab, either to fix or kill."

I sighed, not sure what to do next.

But my guilt faded with one simple insight: I could stay.

"Cassidy, what if you had an assistant?"

"What?" she asked. "You? No, that's not how it works. One Protector, one Unnecessary."

I stepped forward, rolling my eyes. "I must have missed that class. But if one Protector can save two Unnecessaries, two Protectors can save one Unnecessary."

She looked at me, moving her head forward as her mouth gaped open slightly before jolting her head back, making her hair bounce.

"You didn't!"

I smiled at her reaction but turned back to the house, hearing her whisper behind me.

"27, I knew you were going to be fun."

It was hours before we had my outfit and a practiced cover story. We didn't see Erin go out again for days. Stuck in a waiting pattern, I had to message *"hi"* to my assigned number, letting Central know that I was okay but hadn't acquired a target. Cassidy had messaged *"PFT?"*—which was the current abbreviation for "plans for tonight?"—to let Central know that she had a target Unnecessary.

I blew some of my money on food and hotel rooms, giving us lots of time to talk. It felt almost strange, as if we maybe could forget what we were there for. Like if we weren't careful, we'd get sucked into their definition of normal. But then something—probably the mortal danger, I suppose—would pull us out. Still, it gave me time to think about, and regret, leaving Collin like I had. It gave me time to listen to music. It gave me time to tell Cassidy about Katerina and baby Collin. It gave me too much time, some days, spent staring at the glimmers of light that reflected through windows.

The best thing about this was that our cover was easy to blend in. We were on our MCUs, looking like we were busy working in several places, switching areas every couple of hours. She taught me how to make a fake ID and where to print it without getting caught. The Sub-Terra in the printing shop tried to help another Sub-Terra sneak in to get medicine from the lab. She didn't even know who she was helping.

It also gave us a lot of time to talk about Julie, as we caught glimpses of her each day.

"I didn't get it at first," I said, shifting my mug slightly. "But then I realized that a child like Julie could ruin the system. They want her mom to be independent. Not to be who she truly is, but who the Society wants her to be. She's not expected to be reliant on anything but the Society. Not even love."

"I think it works both ways," Cassidy nodded. "The Society sees killing some kids as a kind of weeding. If kids like Julie grew up, making genuine connections with people, how would she be managed or manipulated? She would be the kind of person who was crazy enough to be a Vessel—to want to hold the child growing inside her."

Cassidy gazed out the window. "No one wants to admit it, but love is their worst nightmare. The system is not built with love in mind. She could wreck the whole thing just by falling in love. Nothing could be more dangerous. She's the equivalent of a bomb."

Her words haunted me and made it impossible not to think about Collin for the rest of the morning.

We left after finishing our breakfast, setting up to pass the house when the cab usually arrived for Julie to leave for her twelve-hour school day. We were walking by as the cab pulled up. Erin came out first, followed by a pleading voice.

"Mommy, please!"

It was happening. What Cassidy had hoped for.

We stood a short distance away as Julie hugged her mother. Almost a week of waiting, talking, doing nothing—yet, now that the moment had arrived, my words escaped me.

But Cassidy knew what to say first: nothing. She stared at Erin, who was trying to unwind her daughter's arms from her legs. Erin noticed Cassidy's attire and her badge. Her face turned white like she had gotten caught at the scene of a crime.

"This... this is the first time..."

"You're lying," Cassidy responded in a monotone voice. "I was on my way to see you, considering the school's correspondence."

"No, I'm... this is the first time today," Erin said, recovering. "To be honest, I should have had her evaluated by a specialist a long time ago. Maybe she should go today."

"Excellent idea," Cassidy said, and I pulled out my MCU, as we'd practiced. "You know, we are... more than able to help you with this situation, ma'am, if you would like us to examine and decide about the girl. It's clear—"

"I don't want it on my record," Erin said, quickly, almost too low for the girl to hear.

"We understand, ma'am. This is just why you are such a vital part of the Society. You recognize what the goals are."

"Yes," she said, unsure, but then she received a message. She smiled, felt the pull of her world, and with only a few more questions, Erin placed her child in the shuttle with us.

"Don't worry, ma'am," Cassidy said. "Just think of her as free. And now, you are too. Free to be anything you choose."

The woman's eyes lit up. "Thank you."

She was on her phone by the time her confused daughter had gotten in the taxi. Her mother giggled about something as I swallowed the vomit threatening to rise in my throat.

"Let's just go," Cassidy added under her breath, "before she uses her 'freedom' to change her mind."

We sat in the taxi, where Julie's heavenly eyes looked up at Cassidy. She may have, being only two or three, believed she was going to the doctor—that nothing was wrong. We stopped in front of the doctor's office, but once Julie realized we weren't going in, it was all up to Cassidy. I kept watch, pretending to be busy on my phone while Cassidy explained, as best she could, what was going to happen.

I didn't want to hover. It wasn't my story. Cassidy held the sobbing child, caressing her hair and rubbing her back.

And after a week with Cassidy, a week praying and hoping to get Julie out, I felt an odd mixture of peace and pain as they left down the other side of the alley.

Julie got the hug she had wanted.

Cassidy would get the rest of her hugs on the way home.

But there were none for me. It felt lost and alone, with a mission to find someone even more lost and alone.

I walked aimlessly for a day, determined not to be as idle as I felt. I probably fit in perfectly around the idle rich of the Republic.

The stoic buildings of the police headquarters stared back at me, and I wondered if the Sentry who saved me was working inside. I walked from 4th Street to 1st Street, gazing at the art and fashionable bags in the windows. I suppose I played my part well.

In the afternoon, there was one piece of the beauty that did distract me from my thoughts: a dress that could've been from that story with the brave princess I had told Collin. My reflection in the window haunted me, mocking the image of the brave girl I thought I was. I looked longingly at the red dress while secretly hating the dumb expression on my face. That dress could get me into an inner-city party, but there was no way I could afford it, not even with the extra money Katerina had given me.

Go in.

I ignored it at first, but the voice became louder.

Go in.

I shook my head, confused. A call from the universe had certain expectations, the most significant being that if God were ever to break his usual silence, there would be lives at stake and there would be a vitally important mission. Being nudged to go into a store shouldn't qualify as divine intervention. Not even close. I pushed it away.

But the thought screamed again.

The thought panicked. It had a temper-tantrum in my head.

Go! In!

I gave up. Turning, I stepped through the door, remembering to be lighter on my feet than I was just now. Maybe some determination to buy a dress was typical, but better to not risk it.

The red dress had a price tag of fifteen thousand dollars, reminding me why one of our informants was a dressmaker. They made the most profit in the Republic, with lots of time on their hands and lots of resources.

I kept browsing, but stopped after a few more dresses. The salesperson hadn't approached me yet. There was no music playing, either.

Someone grunted in pain.

I took a few steps behind the front counter. The store owner gasped for breath, his back contorted.

"Sir, are you okay?" I asked, wondering if I should even ask that question, as a Citizen's apathy would disallow my concern. I added, "I haven't received any service yet, and now I see why. If you need medical attention, I can notify someone."

He looked up, cringing. "I threw out my back or something, I think. I snapped it back, but it's just..." The man was by no means young but pushing his late forties. I would've loved to jump the counter and help him, but it would blow my cover. I might as well tell him I had a baby in my pack.

"Do you want me to call a medical unit, sir?" I repeated.

"No. If they see I've hurt it again, I'm done. They may send me to retire, but with a bad back, they could probably send me somewhere else instead."

The euthanasia of the Republic wasn't as bad as I'd imagined from the pictures in school, but it did exist. While the Society Party destroyed children that might burden the economy or wreck the system, they recognized the value in coercing voting adults. Many retired far south, but they kept others in a vegetative state until it was time to vote. These people would be revitalized and kept awake for only a month, and then sedated again. This infuriated me, but Collin had reminded me we had to choose our battles. We couldn't save everyone. But looking at a man facing years in a coma or worse, I couldn't ignore my desire to help him. More importantly, I could help him without having to break my cover.

"Sir, I came into your store today, dreaming of wearing that dress in the window to my party tonight. But I'm four thousand dollars short, and I don't get my allowance until next week. But I have something else."

He looked up. I wondered if I could imitate a Citizen—distinguished, snobbish, but desperately longing for what was in the window.

"I have a drug for pain," I continued. "I've needed it for a while, so it's free for me because I'm a Citizen. It's pricey, even on the black market."

"I don't have that kind of cash here, dear, even if I take—"

"I don't want cash," I said, glancing at the dress. He got my meaning. "I have four pills. You need them. I give you these and nine thousand, you give me a dress."

"Fine, but one thing has to change," he said. I prepared to bargain with the rest of my money, but he continued, "Take the one from the window display, not the rack. I put a lot of personality into it, but the fabric is cheaper. I can make another one with the money you give me. Besides, it'll look better on you."

I made the exchange, took the dress from the window, and went to try it on in the dressing room.

I stared at the three mirrors. The rhinestones around the edges of the red satin skirt made me dizzy. I didn't recognize myself. The dress conveyed confidence that I didn't feel, driving me down in doubt. I lost feeling in my legs and dropped to the ground, scared to death I couldn't pull this off.

Could the girl from the woods honestly convince the prince she was supposed to be there? Dancing, talking, mingling. And was such a risk worth it? Everything Faith had taught me about dancing left my mind in a blur. I wondered if I even could without Collin. The marble beneath my hands felt like ice, freezing me in place.

But Collin had sent me here. Cassidy had left me here. The voice had pushed me here. All to do this.

I recovered and stood up. My back straightened. My phone vibrated; one minute till check in.

If I typed "hi," Sam would know everything was all right. If I sent "hey you," Sam would realize I had planned a mission. I looked at my reflection in the oversized mirror. Was I planning a mission right now? My finger dashed over the buttons, typing a message I might not have the courage to send. But maybe I could fake it until my courage came back.

"How's it fit?"

The store owner's voice came from outside the dressing room. His medicine must have worked.

"Perfectly," I answered as I sent the message.

"Hey you."

In the two hours that followed, I spent half of my remaining money on my hair and makeup, listened to music on my MCU without ceasing, and practiced dance moves in several public bathrooms, glad there were reflective surfaces in the stalls. I hoped no one would ask me to dance before I found an Unnecessary to save.

I went into a restaurant with my dress in my bag, claimed to have to go to the bathroom, and went right to the alley in back, where I dropped my backpack and changed. The last of my money got me a taxi from the end of the alley, so it would appear I called a shuttle for a party two blocks away.

Along 2nd Street, I watched as rare, stained-glass windows went by, each belonging to the house of an Elite. When the shuttle arrived, a Sub-Terra opened the door for me. I stared at the other Elites and Citizens entering the party, invitations waved but not examined. Most parties this exclusive required no identification, only a classy outfit. I held my breath as I passed the security guard. His glance would have been flattering if it didn't sicken me. My disgust didn't last long.

I entered the most beautiful room I had ever seen, finding it far too difficult to appear disenchanted with anything. So much splendor, light, and color filled the space, I couldn't help but be impressed. It felt like I was walking on air, but I looked down to see a thick wool rug with white, silk-spun patterns. The art in the hallway across from the mirrors made the colors bounce off the ceiling and walls. Affluent tables surrounded the room, covered with indulgent food. Part of me wanted to try some, but I figured nervous vomiting might give me away. I walked down the flight of stairs as gracefully as I could. The array against the velvet tablecloth matched the rich color of the stripes along the walls, draping down to the exquisite hardwood floor that glistened like glass.

I passed the dance floor, dreaming of rescuing someone in a kitchen, someone lower class, a child forgotten at a party, or maybe a scared Vessel. I paused by the table with the shrimp and the steak until I spotted the doors that the service staff used. Before I could move toward it, a stranger blocked me, reaching out for my hand as I steadied it on the table.

"Well, Alania-Cordia, my dear. I don't think I've seen you before. You are gorgeous."

"Cordia" was an expression that meant you were friendly on the eyes. The intent was to flatter me in the most intense way. "Alania" implied he had picked me out specifically. I forced myself to look flattered, which I almost was.

"Really? Well, coming from you, that's quite impressive," I said, thinking about strategies to get away from him.

If you flatter him, he'll be less suspicious. He'll assume he's famous because he wants to be.

He was easy on the eyes, so he was likely a player that had won the Society's game. There was a pin on his coat. He was an Elite.

"Well," he whispered, "would you care to dance, then, Alania? Or should I call you by your name?"

Another compliment, making my rejection make less sense.

"I would consider it, but unfortunately..."

"What?"

I had hoped he would lose interest the second it wasn't easy. He shouldn't be pursuing me with any passion if someone else would join him in bed with less effort on his part. The protocol was to imply it's difficult to get me, and he'd wander away.

But he wasn't wandering.

Sweat began to bead on my skin. Soon he would feel it on my hand.

"I came here with someone else."

"Ah, but they should never have left you alone for so long, so someone like me could catch you. So why not one dance, until he appears again?"

I scraped my memory for the next song's dance moves. Maybe, if I looked around, I could try to find anyone I could pretend was my date.

But I didn't need to.

My date was behind me. His arm almost made me jump, sliding on my shoulder as he spoke.

"Really, Linden? You have nothing better to do than steal my date?" The voice was familiar. I had heard it once before. In a subway tunnel, when I'd thought I was about to die.

I forced a smug smile, holding my breath as his hand slid down my arm and grasp my hand. "See? Maybe next time, Linden," I said, trying to look seductive—not that I had ever tried that before.

Whatever I did must have worked. Linden sighed through pursed lips and turned around to pursue someone else. I turned to face the wall, looking down at the hand now holding my wrist. The last time I had seen that hand, it had been holding a weapon on me.

He hadn't shot me, I reminded myself. That helped a little.

But only slightly.

CHAPTER 23

"We're going to have to dance," he breathed in my ear as the next song started. He shifted his other hand to my hip and spun me around. He was as tall as I remembered, just as striking in his presence and appearance, but his eyes seemed lighter. They were dark, but with a hint of green around the edges, like pine trees. His face was flawless, and he still looked muscular, especially compared the Elites and Citizens around him. "I hope you know how to do this."

"I wouldn't have stepped in this room if I didn't," I said. "I'm not suicidal."

"Could've fooled me."

He held out his hand to lead me. If I relaxed, I could pretend to be the girl the prince had picked out of a crowd. Only in this version, I wasn't sure if I should trust the prince.

Curiosity pushed out any fear I had left, and I took his hand.

He led me to the dance floor, ignoring the sweat making my hand clammy. His hand was rough like a soldier's, and it held mine with a strong determination as he walked with me. He moved with ease, graceful in a way that almost made him appear like an Elite, but without the arrogance.

I faked confidence, recognizing the tenth dance in the first movement. I would have to get close to him. Very close. He spun me out. It gave me just a bit of assurance as I pulled it off and turned a few heads, enough to put a smirk on my face as he pulled me in, almost right on top of him. As he led me through the next steps, he pressed hard on the small of my back until I was moving in perfect time with the music. With each step I pulled off, I breathed easier.

"Okay, so you obviously know what you are doing. In case you forgot—from wherever you learned to dance—this song lasts about seven minutes. Are your palms going to keep sweating for that long, or are you going to trust me just a little?"

"I don't know, should I?" I said, willing myself to sound more confrontational than I felt.

"Well, you aren't dead." He tilted his head to the side as he skewed his smile, then his voice changed to a heavier, more anxious tone. "But maybe you're right. Maybe I'm as evil as you've imagined."

I didn't want to aggravate someone who had already saved my life—and was currently saving my life again. I wasn't sure why he had saved it, but I didn't want to ask him yet. There was something else I wanted to know more.

"I don't even know your name."

"Alex. Well, my full name is Alexander André Sanderson. Citizen. Pre-Elite. Sentry. All reasons that you should be dead by sheer proximity to me." He spoke with an authority that frightened yet reassured me. "And you are? Don't you all have a number? Or do you get to keep your name?"

I could tell he was testing my stress limit. He said it all while pulling me in closer, though I didn't budge my expression.

"I'm a Protector of the 188th Generation." My voice softened a bit as I added, "And Aislyn. My name is Aislyn."

"That's a beautiful name. Aislyn." He repeated it as if it were sacred. He looked down for a second to regain the composure. "Well, I'm not calling any backup, and my gun doesn't go with this suit. So, you're not going to die tonight. After this dance, I'll lead you out the back. Everyone will assume what they do about two people like us leaving together, but that's your cover story, so don't get squeamish and flirt a lot. Who's your target?"

I was still getting over "what everyone else would assume," which I understood and tried not to blush. His eyes shone green whenever they caught the light. He looked calm and playful, but his shoulder tensed below my hand.

"You have a plan, right? You know what you're doing? And you... I'm going to spin you, hang on." He spun me out, along with a few others I observed doing the same thing, and pulled me back in, to which I had only the truth as he grasped my hand.

"No."

He looked like I had dropped something heavy on him. "No? Well, that's—what were you thinking? The only thing you have to walk in here with is a dress and a decent skill... where did you learn how to dance, by the way? Protectors usually can't dance worth—" He said a curse word and spun me out again.

"My trainer taught me, not that it matters," I said feeling a little defensive now, though I told myself to keep it playful so no one would hear. "Where there are Elites, there will be Sub-Terras looking for an escape route. Am I wrong?"

"No, you're not wrong. The people who threw this party have dozens of Sub-Terras running their house. But that's not the biggest issue tonight."

My eyebrows raised. I didn't need to ask for him to continue.

"The family has a secret. That's why they invited me. As a favor. To keep that secret."

"Which is?"

He looked nervous for the first time. "Look, if they know you helped me with this, they might report me."

"Are you saying you don't want my help?"

"No, I'm telling you we have to do this my way. Follow my lead. If the family finds out, they'll have my badge—or worse."

"Even though you are helping them?"

"Yes. They don't think like your people, Aislyn. They would gain a lot from turning me in and aren't afraid to cash in on it."

"So, what's the big secret?" I asked, reminding myself to move faster as the song's tempo picked up.

"There's a baby, I think. Their daughter became pregnant again and wanted to keep it. In the Elites, that's what they do. They want the connection they deny everyone else and non-docile heirs. They hide it, they pay off doctors, fake papers—"

"How do you know that?" I asked, wondering why we didn't review this in HistCulture.

"Because... it's the way I was born. My sister and me. We're Naturals. The best brand of Citizens and Elites there are."

I stared at his eyes, now seeing at least one secret about him for the first time. There was something there that felt tangible, real. Maybe he seemed more human than they were because he truly was.

"Makes sense, I guess," I said. "The Citizens and Elites would have different rules and privileges. But if the baby's already there, what are they—"

"It's a boy. She wanted a girl."

I could barely keep my fake expression on. "You're supposed to take the baby and kill it, aren't you?" I said under my breath.

He squeezed my hand and pulled my head into his chest.

"Yes. And here I thought we would at least make it past one song before you knew how much you could hate me."

I knew why he had pulled my head into his shoulder. I couldn't keep the fake smile on my face. I started shaking with rage but stopped myself, remembering where I was. Still, I had to know.

"How many times have they have asked you?"

Alex sighed. "By them, this is the second. Total, twelve."

"And I'm guessing you would have had no problem killing this child if I didn't show up?" I was feeling the vomit rise.

He stopped pressing my fingers together and leaned down to my ear to graze it. "Of course I would. I didn't kill all twelve, for your information. Nine of the babies are alive. They're Sub-Terras, but they're alive." He could probably sense my confusion because he continued to explain. "A few wanted proof. I slipped the other babies into the lab. I'd change the logs for the day to include them."

"So, you did kill some, but you saved the rest by..." I stopped because he spun me, but then he interrupted my thought as well.

"Like I said, maybe I'm as evil as you've imagined."

"Why are you doing this?"

"The long game? You don't get to know. Tonight? Because it's perfect timing. I believe you're here for a reason, if only because Palmer and the Republic would hate me for saying it. And I believe in you. I can get this kid out of here, but only if you don't die. But you have to do everything I say. Follow my lead. Can you promise me that?"

Pulling back, I stared at his tortured eyes for a moment. There were many reasons I shouldn't trust him: those three babies and countless other missions when he had done the unthinkable and killed innocent lives.

But here he was, desperate for someone to escape. He was just another victim trying to break free. And I had a chance to protect both him and the baby he had decided to save.

He asked again, pressing the lower part of my back with his hand that was now shaking. "Promise me, Aislyn."

"I promise."

He sighed in relief and pulled my head into his chest again. Maybe he knew that I could not hide my confusion anymore.

When the song finally ended, he led me down a hallway and into a room. The room's purpose was obvious. Candles and mirrors lined the walls, and soft, rhythmic music played in the background. I froze, petrified at the thought of being stuck in this room for hours.

"Don't worry," he whispered, "we just have to wait in here for ten minutes. You'll leave. I'll get the baby a few moments later. I'll meet you out there."

"Okay, so will they suspect me if I leave early?"

"I'll just say I brought you for cover, but you can't leave too early. Stay in here with me for about eight minutes, just so people think that we... you know..."

"Yeah, I got it." I turned away quickly, not wanting to hear the rest.

Eventually, my discomfort faded as fear overwhelmed it. We settled in, leaning next to each other on the wall near the door. I couldn't relax. Not only were we waiting for a baby to kill, or not kill, but we had just made this life-threatening for each of us.

I didn't know why, but I asked Alex if he wanted to take the safer option.

"Alex, if you take the baby to the lab, the child could live and you wouldn't risk getting caught with me. That was your plan when you came in here, right?"

"It was. But now... please, take him. Besides, my original plan meant the child could have a life. But with you, he can live a life. What happened to the baby after I let you go? And the girl?"

I told him about Katerina and baby Collin without getting into too much detail. I thought back to earlier that day, and the urge to go in the store earlier, feeling like some destiny had been fulfilled. But I also wondered how this child would fight the despair when he learned the truth one day: *"You were perfect, but you weren't a girl, the live baby doll your mother wanted to dress up and show around, so they gave you to a Sentry so he'd kill you and erase the evidence."*

I felt petrified and disgusted when I heard two people giggle as they walked down the hallway to another room like ours. As noble and morally conscious as Alex was trying to be, I didn't know if he had a clue how uncomfortable I was to be in this room with someone else. Especially with him.

He must have sensed what I was thinking. "This is all very different from what you know, isn't it?"

"If you're referring to sex as a casual activity, yes. You're supposed to find someone you love, really love, and be with him no matter what. Only him. Forever."

I stopped, thinking of Collin. It hurt my heart to say, "no matter what." Would Collin ever be able to love me like that?

"It sounds beautiful." Alex's voice was far off. "It sounds... like they would make fun of it... but like nothing I'll ever have."

A few seconds later, he pulled out his phone, and I was almost glad to talk about our life-threatening situation again. It was vibrating in a strange pattern. He cursed as he opened it and gestured for me to be quiet as he placed his hand up in desperation. I nodded. The conversation was short, though he said "yes, sir" about three times before saying some Elite language phrases, and then finishing the call.

"About five minutes," he said, nodding. He returned to the wall to lean beside me. He seemed to be calm, but I looked in the mirror. I noticed the hand that was not next to mine was shaking.

I hesitated, nervous to touch him. But if I died in the next moments, I would regret not acknowledging his risk. I grabbed his hand, which was rigid at first. He looked up at the mirror, seeing my eyes from across the room.

"We all need our moment to be as scared as we should be. Don't hide it from me. I'll be scared with you."

He squeezed my hand back. His other hand stopped shaking. He whispered, "Thank you."

I nodded, now concentrating again. I pulled my MCU out of my dress purse. He looked curiously, but I pointed to the wall.

"I'll be scared with you, but I don't trust you that much. Face the door."

He rolled his eyes, but did as I said. It took me two minutes to come up with a plan. I told him where I had left my pack, and he shared the fastest way to get there. I put the MCU back in my purse as he turned around to face me.

There was a knock at the door.

"Go. Keep going," he whispered urgently.

I left through the back door, out into the alley. It was just a minute, standing there in the cool night with a warm breeze. I tried not to pace too much as my shoes seemed to clack loudly against the dark, dirty brick. I waited, listening for any sign this was one massive trap.

The door finally swung open, and Alex appeared in front of me, an infant in one hand, covered with his jacket.

"He's under slight sedation."

"I get it," I said. Although sedating infants always made me nervous, it had ended up saving that baby's life the last time.

I was expecting him to hand the baby to me, but he just was staring at him. Then, in a choked tone, he said, "Take him."

The baby who squirmed a little as I took him.

"Alex, what's wrong?"

"Nothing. I'll deal with it."

"Deal with what?" I asked, holding the baby a little tighter.

"They want proof. They're one of the ones that wanted it last time. And I can't... I can't kill him if you're holding him."

He had a choice, but I could tell that he had already made it. His tortured eyes kept looking from me to the baby, his lip quivering.

"You'll be okay, right?" I asked. "Even if you can't?"

"Go," he said breathlessly.

"Maybe we can fake it. Take a picture, make the baby still. I'll use the baby sleep, and you can filter the photo—"

"Just go, Aislyn." His voice was shaky but determined.

The weight of his choice was already pushing my feet into the hard concrete. His shoulders shook a little, his hands wringing through his dark hair.

"Alex, I can't believe I'm saying this, but I can't... I can't leave you here to—"

"Die? I can assure you of one thing, Aislyn." He grabbed my shoulders and pulled me toward him. "If you knew what I've done, you would know that I deserve to die. Anyway, why do you care? You just got what you wanted."

I lost my breath for a moment, shaking my head as tears formed. "I'm a Protector, Alex, but that's not all I am. I'm not just the number. I'm still me. And I want you to live."

He looked at me, moving a piece of hair out of my eyes. He let out a shuddered breath. "You can't choose two people every time, Aislyn. This time, you have to choose one. Trust me. Choose him. About a block from here, you'll realize you made the right call." He touched my cheek. "I promise. You'll realize it, and you'll forget me."

He pulled away and nodded to the alley. I took a breath and ran. I kept running, turning around only once. He had leaned against the wall, his head in his hands as he sank to the ground. With each step, I hated myself more.

I traveled for one mile through alleys, under doorways. To my relief, my pack was still where I had left it. I took a trip down in a dumpster, carefully placing the baby on my pack, while I changed out of my dress and stuffed it into the bottom pouch. As I was about to jump out, I realized that my hand was shaking. I stared at the baby on the dumpster floor, now not even sickened by the smell or my surroundings. Saving his life might mean that Alex would die.

I unraveled my braided hair, Alex's promise unraveling with it. I was more than a block away and I hadn't forgotten him. I kept telling myself to focus on the journey ahead.

A door crashed open in the alley. I heard a half-grunt, half-scream.

And a muted gunshot.

I knelt, ordering my body to remain frozen. The next sound was a knife hitting the asphalt in the alley. There was scuffling. The knife scraped on the asphalt again. Then, a groan and a short scream, as if the knife had hit its target. I felt adrenaline take over my body.

I knew that voice.

It was Brie.

I didn't think as my feet moved to jump out of the dumpster. Someone had Brie locked in their grip, their arms wrapped around her neck. I ran up behind her attacker, grabbing the hair of the woman and pulling back. She was strong and managed to keep a grip on Brie's neck as she pulled out her gun. But Brie did something—probably bit her arm—and the woman yelled and released her. She kicked Brie forward as she did. Then she fell backward, sending me to the ground.

I was prepared, catching myself and jumping back up. But I wasn't prepared to see our attacker from the front.

She was pregnant.

I moved to block her next kick as I tried to process what had happened. She must have been trying to entrap Brie, who hadn't fallen for it. I blocked the next kick, then knocked her gun away. Brie coughed again.

A Sentry wasn't far behind. He would kill us. They might find the baby.

And if they traced the baby's DNA, Alex was dead, too.

I was fighting for four lives.

I tried a quick jab, which hit her in the neck, but she blocked my next kick. I kicked higher. That was a mistake.

She grabbed my ankle and pushed back, kicking my other leg out from under me. I hit the ground, hard, the air sucked out of my lungs. She was pulling out her knife. Brie was still on the ground, whispering her plea, "You'll be safe with us. Please."

The woman pinned me. Her knife was inches away from my face. Her knees dug into my arms. I could feel my pulse raging, wondering how much longer my blood would pound through me. She cut one side of my arm before lifting the knife up over her head. I couldn't stop staring at: the weapon that would tear through my flesh and push out my soul.

But it never fell. It only jolted. And then froze.

I felt the pressure of her knees release. I scrambled out from under her, trying to shuffle away. I heard her, losing breath on top of me, and looked away, so I didn't have to see death overtake her eyes.

I barely had time to think before trying to get out away from her, now able to see the knife in her back. Brie was on one knee, gasping for air, the arm in front of her red and soaked.

"C'mon, Brie, we have to go... you're bleeding." The gunshot must have only grazed her because she was still moving her arm. "Brie?"

She wasn't moving. While being entrapped and nearly murdered must have been horrible, I didn't think it would paralyze her. Not her. She was staring at the woman, then moved to turn her over. There was a wired comm on her, attached to what must have been a synthetic stomach.

"Was she a Sentry? Or an officer?" I asked.

Brie was frantic, taking off her backpack. She ignored me, focused on opening it.

"How did she get past you? I thought you were supposed to check her with the ultrasound... to see if she was pregnant."

Two seconds later, she pulled out her red kit, and rolled it out.

"I did," she said.

It took me a second to realize what she meant. By the time I did, she was throwing me the antibacterial powder. With a pinch of the bomb, the powder spread. I choked back vomit for many reasons other than just watching a C-section.

The woman hadn't used a decoy stomach at all. She had been pregnant and betrayed the life that was growing inside of her.

"Aislyn, we need to get out of here the second this baby is out. She could have backup. Do you have someone?"

I nodded toward the dumpster. "My Unnecessary is in there. I was changing and needed a place to lie low. He's only a few days old."

She turned to look up, pushing her braid behind her. "Go. Get him now."

I opened the dumpster and crawled in. The baby was fine but waking up. I grabbed him, climbed out, then slowly let myself down with one arm.

The second I hit the ground, Brie said, "I need your help if you can."

I got the sanitation liquid and squirted it all over me. She told me to only touch the instruments, not the baby. I silently agreed and pulled on the clamp she gave me.

"Here we go," Brie said as she pulled the baby out more quickly than I ever could. She ordered me to cut the cord as she wiped the infant off.

"She tried to kill me after I confirmed she was a Vessel. I had her at knife point after she first attacked me and asked her how this could happen. Apparently, she had gone to the hospital to find out how to 'get rid of it' and they'd recruited her. Offered her one-million dollars to lure and kill one of us. They'd take care of the baby later. She'd agreed to be live bait."

Brie was shaking but determined. I couldn't hide my panic.

"Brie, why aren't Sentries here? Or backup?" I'd assumed there would be reinforcements. Or that we'd at least hear sirens.

"Don't know. Don't care. Just move."

We walked as fast as we could. We both had infants, which made it hard, because I wanted to run but couldn't. I was glad we were together, which made us less suspicious to the few people who may have glanced down an alley to see us. Brie had to stop once to wipe the baby down again. The birth had worn the baby out, so Brie only gave her minimal sedation.

"What are you going to name her?" I asked. It hardly seemed like the right time, but I didn't know what else to talk about.

"I think Hope. It seems like she should have that name." Though she was still despondent, her shakiness was gone. Every move was smooth and calm. Her icy blue eyes were calculating everything around us.

We both ditched our surgical kits in a locked box outside of a club. From our packs, I pulled out the holds for the baby's arms and legs. I silently thanked the person who designed our bags to double as infant carriers. We crossed a dozen streets before stopping again.

"So, I'm thinking we take a break soon. Hit the border just before daybreak?" Brie grunted as she dressed her wound.

"No. We can't," I said, embarrassed that I needed to push her, but also because I'd have to explain.

"Why not?" she said. Her hand gripped my arm, forcing me to stop, then turned me around. "Let me check your baby. If it's fine, we're pushing on."

She unzipped my bag and made sure the oxygen tubes were on tight enough, and he was comfortable. As she zipped it up again, I realized I had no choice.

"I need to get my baby out. By tonight."

"Why?" she asked again. I turned to face her, she was facing the wall. I followed suit and unzipped her pack.

"I... have to get out of here. I can't get caught. I got the baby from someone who has to prove the baby is dead or they'll be killed."

"What? Who did you get the baby from?"

"A Sentry. The baby is an Elite Natural. The parents wanted to get rid of it, so they gave it to a Sentry who was supposed to dispose of it." I zippered up her bag as I said, "If they find us, he's dead. He can't die."

"A Sentry?" she said, almost scolding. She turned around, revealing all the emotions I expected to see in her face. Her eyes drilled into me, then she blinked away the anger and confusion. "Never mind. I obviously have not proven to be the best judge of character tonight and was almost murdered by an undercover Vessel turned spy. We'll go with your plan, and you'll explain later. Let's go."

We walked for another hour and reached the public shuttle in time to hit the last run of the night. I was thankful for a moment to sit down. No one was in the back part of the shuttle, which could usually hold up to forty passengers. We unzipped our packs for a moment. I tried to calm myself by feeling the baby's back rise and fall with his breaths as the shots of light from busy restaurants, parties, and sports events flew by our windows.

We got to the border by about 2 a.m., crossed it, and went another five miles to find an R-station. Then we called it.

As Brie sat down, pulling out her camo tent, I turned to look back to the Republic and stared at one of the largest buildings I could see: Police headquarters. Against the early morning skyline, it appeared so strong, tall, and even proud. Something so proud might be unaware it had failed to retain one Sentry's allegiance.

I prayed they remained in their conceited ignorance.

Otherwise, saving this baby's life would be the death of him.

CHAPTER 24

By the second day, I finally had the time and energy to tell Brie the whole story, from the beginning. Although I had trusted no one except Patterson with the secret of Alex, I was now trusting her. Hours of her silent stares wore me down. Besides, Brie had saved my life and rushed out of the Republic despite being wounded to keep Alex safe. She had earned the truth.

Brie listened without asking questions. She held the bottle, rocking Hope and humming. Her only response was to make me promise to tell Patterson. She admitted to being as confused as me. My baby curled his fingers around mine, sleeping. I named him André, remembering Alex's middle name. It seemed fitting, and I liked it, even though it sounded like such a Republic name.

We made it to a Q-station, which I had never been in before. It reminded me of a bomb shelter, only much nicer. Brie called in and reported that she was injured but healing. Joel must have known her well; he laughed when she said that she was fine. He ignored her and planned an EE on the edge of the Zone 2 border, about three days away.

We took the babies from our packs, washed them in the Med room, and gave them a full check-up and anti-viral shots. I snapped some pictures and got the footprint impressions. They reminded me of the twins. It was beautiful and felt familiar, so it hurt my heart a little. We must have stared at them for hours; a strange disparity, to feel so much joy after so much despair.

We reviewed combat moves in the evening. She insisted, and I figured she wanted to use exercise as a coping mechanism. I agreed to her request, only to get beaten ten times. I took a shower and cried. That was my coping mechanism.

By the next morning, we were out in the woods again. We had traveled quicker, stocked with supplies and having had a good meal. We had set up a sleeping schedule. One of us would sleep for six hours, the other would watch Hope and André. At 4 a.m., we switched, and one of us would sleep until 10 a.m. On day two of the journey from the Q-station, she made breakfast, woke me up, and then we moved out. We traveled for another fifteen miles.

Once again, I was perusing my MCU for the story of the Protector I had once quoted and made Collin upset. What instructor at the Academy had set Collin on his path with such passion that he couldn't abandon it? After a long day of walking and listening, I asked Brie if she knew. She said it was the 167th or the 165th Generation. She almost hesitated, looking at me nervously. I listened to the profiles as the evening wore on, rocking the babies and settling into the darkness of the woods.

I was about to give up when I got to the 19th Protector's profile and heard her most famous quote. *"All of this begins and ends with you finding something worth dying for, then living for it."*

There was nothing tragic. She had succeeded in all her missions. She had even opted to serve another year, just like Brie and Tessa. She seemed to have Lydia's compassion, Eva's quick remarks without the drama, and Brie's strength. Maybe it had nothing to do with her.

The MCU paused, like normal. I waited for the prompt to move to the next audio file, but instead, it asked, "Would you like to hear the post-career work file?"

I sat up straight. No file had ever included this option. The word "listen" blinked on my MCU, pulsating eerily, holding back whatever secret I had yet to discover and now wasn't sure I wanted to know. Had she taught at the Academy? Is that what it was about? I pushed the button.

The 19th Protector of 165th Generation had served two years with great success. During an off-season attempt to gain intelligence on a discovery she had made in the Republic, she was asked to return. The attempt failed, and a Sentry killed her for trespassing. The Tech assistant assigned to the investigation of her death was also killed in action—see file 459B. The only message Central ever received was three words: 'They are not.' There is further intelligence added to the case file, but many facts remain unknown. She was survived by her husband and child, two years old at the time of her death.

I sat close to the heater, mesmerized by the waves and the tragedy of the story. I thought of the babies sitting next to me, from mothers who had thrown them out. Instead, this poor woman had to leave a baby behind. But if she never taught at the Academy, there was no way she could have taught Collin, no way could she have known him, and...

I froze. The MCU was muted, waiting for my next request, yet the earpieces burned with the sound of my heart beating faster. There was a way she could have known Collin.

Only one way.

She was survived by her husband and two-year-old son. As I thought my MCU could not work fast enough, Collin's name appeared.

Something lurched in my stomach, and I opened my mouth to take a breath, but my lungs seized. Nothing in my body seemed to function. I wanted to scream, not caring if it revealed our location. Out of everything I'd imagined, it hadn't been this. My knee hit the ground, but I barely felt it hit the tree root under me.

And then I thought about that promise he'd said he had made—to be Head Trainer, to see this through. No wonder he couldn't give it up. Not even for me.

"Are you okay?" Brie asked.

Tears ran down my face. I was still on my knee, shaking. I didn't answer her.

She sighed. "Collin didn't tell you, did he?"

I opened my mouth to ask, but then I said, "That's right. Collin shadowed with George last year. You knew already."

"I wondered when you asked. He doesn't share it a lot. Look, let's switch shifts. You can get some sleep. I'm not tired."

"No, I can't sleep." But even after speaking the words, my body ached.

"Yes, you will. Go lay down." Brie pulled me up. I sighed and landed on the sleeping bag a few seconds later. I told her I'd changed the diapers about an hour ago and then closed my eyes. As I lay in the dark, I couldn't get Collin out of my head. My mind kept wondering why my heart was so shattered.

As much as I accused him of being unsure of his feelings, I was equally unsure. So, I did what I always did when I was confused.

I shifted one arm up, just enough to write. Brie ignored me or gave me space, but didn't order me to fall asleep again. I wrote under the blanket on my MCU for nearly ten minutes: every word I wish I could say to him and every tear I had cried for him that night.

Then I wrote the three words I shouldn't have. Seeing the words on my MCU made my fingers freeze and my breath turn ragged.

I deleted them, but not because they weren't true. I absorbed the truth, making it a part of me, weaving it all into my mind, heart, body, and soul. As I fell into the darkness, closing my eyelids, I spoke the truth out loud, in a whisper that shook every cell of my being.

"I love you."

When I awoke, it was 3 a.m. Both babies were awake, and Brie said she'd rather move to our EE location four miles away, get our ride, and sleep in our Circles. I agreed. By the time we'd hiked there, both babies had fallen asleep again. I still smiled at Sam's words: "27, you are aware that you are supposed to come back with just one person one of these times, right?"

The shuttle arrived. Saying goodbye was easier this time without Katerina clinging to me. I was eager to see how the babies were doing, particularly since André was under sedation for longer than I would have liked. The nurse said they both looked great, but she was glad we put Brie's baby in the incubator blanket. I was so relieved I could've cried, but I found my tears were spent and my worry was worn. One moment of pure joy came from André's little coo. Even Brie broke her hardened features to smile and give her baby a kiss before the Med team rushed away.

"You're going right back out, aren't you?" I asked her as we walked off the shuttle.

"Yep, as soon as my Council review is over. Ten hours. You?"

"I feel like I need a few days, that's all."

"Take it. That's what they're for. I'm up first for the debrief. I hate waiting, so this is the perk of being the 1st Protector. I'll tell Patterson you did good, 27."

After some 'good job' compliments and Liam bringing me breakfast, I was back in the waiting room. It felt too quiet again. I wondered if it would ever feel normal and when I would see Collin.

Maybe Collin was right. Maybe loving me and leaving this place came at too steep a cost. Maybe I could try to push him away. Maybe I needed to retreat, for him to be who he was meant to be.

But then all the doubt left me with one click of the door handle.

Collin lunged in and pulled me into his chest so hard I lost the breath to say his name. But I realized the truth.

If I tried to push him away, I would fail every time.

"Aislyn, are you okay?"

"Yeah," I said. Everything I wanted to say threatened to erupt out of me, but I held it in. I still had to debrief with Patterson.

"I'm sorry I said those things," he said. "I'm so sorry."

I squeezed harder, realizing my missions had left me more distracted than him. He had been left for two weeks with our discussion fresh in his mind.

"Collin, it doesn't matter."

"Yes, it does," he whispered, dropping his head right next to my ear. His strong, broad shoulders crushed with worry. "Aislyn, I never would have forgiven myself if you had gotten hurt because I was being... because I said what I said. I realized I should tell you. I need to tell you something..." He released me so our eyes could meet.

"Collin, I know. I found the profile on your mom," I said, choking out the last word as his expression changed. "I'm sorry. I know why this isn't going to be easy. I should have trusted you."

His eyes responded to a familiar pain. "I should have known you'd figure it out. You probably guessed..." He bit his lip. "I barely remember her. I do remember the day I promised to do this. And every day after, when I promised to do this for her."

"We can talk about it later—"

There was a sound outside the door. I detached and saw the look on his face, a painful wait still coming. He ran out of the room. One second later, the door opened to reveal Patterson.

"Well, 27, can I just say... You know, never mind. I don't know what to say. Have a seat."

I sat down and began my summary, starting first with meeting Cassidy. Patterson shared that Cassidy had returned safely. Julie was fine. He raised his eyebrows at the part about giving the old man the drugs, and then me taking the dress. I told him about the party, but not what I did there or where I got the baby. I got to Brie. He insisted on hearing every detail about the attack, so I had to recount the death of the spy, the birth of her baby, and our rushed journey home.

"Well," he said, "There are just a few things on which I'd like to prep you. For the debrief tomorrow. I think you can go."

And with that, the red light was off. He changed tone and sighed.

"Aislyn, please tell me you have facts for those gaping holes in your story, and please tell me I don't have to keep the recorder off for them?"

"Um... yes to the first, but..." I stuttered; his demanding gaze seemed to paralyze me.

He moved forward on his seat in anticipation. "You get a name this time?"

It was the first time I had said his name in days, and I didn't know if I was saying the name of a dead man.

"Alex. Alex Anderson."

I walked through everything that had happened at the party with great detail, including repeating everything Alex had said. Patterson took notes, listening with little emotion until the end.

He deadpanned stared at the floor, dropping his head.

Then I spoke my worst fear. "I need... the family wanted proof. Alex implied that if he couldn't provide proof..."

"That they would kill him? Yes, no doubt." Patterson rubbed his eyes and exhaled slowly. "Well, at least we know his name, hopefully not an alias. Sam can pull off a level-three hack to see if he's alive. We're going to see if a certain Sentry is still on duty, that's all. I will advise you to avoid questions from the Council. They'll have more to ask about what you and Brie experienced."

"I do have one question. Why weren't there reinforcements? Backup? There should've been someone tailing a decoy like that."

He shook his head. "It doesn't make any sense. They could have easily captured you both if she had a wire on her and they could hear anything. But Aislyn... I honestly don't know."

Only he didn't sound frustrated; he sounded hollow with fear.

I went through the motions for the next hour, took a shower, got another meal-to-go from Joel's assistant, then went back to my Circle. Collin was already reading the summary of the debriefs, sitting on the mat in the center of the Circle. He seemed nervous.

"Aislyn, there was a note from Patterson on my copy of the debrief. I don't want to make you feel defensive, but..."

I looked at the screen of Collin's MCU. There was an annotation: *"I know her story has holes. If she trusts you, she'll tell you."*

"What does that even mean?" he asked apprehensively.

I sighed. "You wouldn't believe me, Collin."

"Of course I'll believe you!" His boyish confidence in me wasn't helping my resolve to keep Alex a secret.

"You won't believe in someone," I clarified, but my fear was still the same. "I don't know if I should yet either."

"Well, I'll just have to promise to trust you first, no matter what. Please. Tell me."

I took a deep breath and told the story of the unnamed Sentry who had let me go. The story continued with a dance, the room we waited in, and the baby we rescued. It ended with the death sentence I had all but placed on Alex.

Collin processed everything without speaking. I could tell he was agonizing to find his next words.

"What if he's just like the spy who tried to entrap Brie?"

I sighed, placing my head in my lap, staring at the mat before coming up again. "I know. I thought that a million times, but... the thing is, I don't know. That spy tried to kill Brie the first moment she got a good chance, right? Alex had loads of chances. And then..."

"What?"

"I have this feeling I can't shake about the woman who attacked Brie. It's all wrong. The scenario, protocol, objective. They didn't send backup, as if they were using her as bait but never set a trap. Does that sound weird?"

Before I could hear his opinion on that theory, Liam came running through the door. Panting, he realized he had done and quickly pulled himself back out.

"You can come in, Liam!" I shouted.

He was out of breath, sporting the same look of terror I had seen when the bombs dropped. He pointed down, cursing at Collin for having his comm off-line. We ran across the garden and down the staircase, then pulled open the barred metal doors into the center of the Hand. By the time we arrived, Eva, Lynn, and their trainers were already there. Others were following us.

"What is this?" I asked.

"It's the media segment that aired on the national news in the Republic this evening," Patterson said, looking tired.

There was a shot of the head of the Committee for the Continuation of a Free Society, or the Society Party president of sorts, who ran the committee that created the policies for the Republic.

He began by giving greetings and then announced he would report on one of the gravest situations that the Society had tried to protect its people against. His voice held authority but sounded like it was selling something—most likely the lies they believed every day.

"Some people talk about Protectors from the Territory, who, as you know, we allow to live in peace, and have never once threatened in any way." There was a general shift in the room, and Eva cursed. No one reprimanded her this time. "People, even our own inhabitants, have idealized these Protectors, while some have made them into villains, and others tell stories as if they are imaginary. But it is time for you to know they are real and learn just what they are capable of, caught by surveillance cameras, for you to witness."

What were they going to show? Us saving children? There weren't enough cameras around the Republic for them to catch us, as the Society kept their mask of freedom in place by refusing to line the streets with that technology. Yet, I could have sworn a tiny smile was tucked in the Head Counselor's frowning face.

A horrible fear took hold of me. Even before I saw the first shot, I grabbed Collin's hand, and whispered, "Oh no."

The footage showed Brie and I fighting the spy.

But the Society had edited it; it was cut together as short glimpses and clips. The spy's gun couldn't be seen, even as I kicked it away. There were an entire two seconds missing. Brie's fatal attack came. There were shots of us working to save the baby. We were hardly more than silhouettes, which never showed our faces—thank God—but made the scene that much more chilling.

"As you can see, if you have ever thought these Protectors harmless or benign, you are mistaken. Remember that they do not live like you do. They cling to silly ideals and old religion that clouds their mind, making them unable to see the beauty in our refined ways. And they don't even respect the mother of the kind of life they want to protect. They killed this woman, just to harvest a child from her, because that is all they think women are good for. We have also discovered that they brainwash these Protectors to come and do this, so they are victims and our enemy."

The room was eerily still, everyone frozen except for Patterson, who was rocking back and forth. Out of shame or anger, I turned, facing the wall instead of the monitor. Collin's hand squeezed mine again as he kept watching and I kept listening. My head fell right next to his shoulder as we stood there, withstanding the lies and waiting for what we knew would inevitably come after them.

They accused the second dark figure—me—of killing another mother to get the baby I had pulled out of the dumpster. I was thankful that I had changed clothes and hair. I looked drastically different than I had at the party. That would keep Alex out of additional danger. What would Alex, and any others who might have faith in us, do now?

When Eldridge entered, I could barely look at him, humiliated. We had fallen into a trap so big that we couldn't see we were in it. He looked at me with sympathy but kept moving toward Patterson and whispered something. Brie followed him. I turned back to the screen right as the voice on the monitor called for "everyone's understanding of the enemy."

The Head Counselor's eyes were light aqua, but foreboding. The camera closed in on him as his voice boomed his last words.

"And to those Protectors who think this will be worth it in the end, I assure you of this: there is no victory you will find that is worth the cost you can endure. And make no mistake, it will cost you and you will pay."

As it ended, the room remained silent and still. Fifty people, all staring at the now-blank screen. After a few seconds, Patterson screamed orders as people on each Tech team burst into action around us. People were asking for Brie's debrief, wanting to know what had happened. Other were trying to decide the best response. I could barely even register the "sorry" or "this is not happening" comments swirling around me. But Collin and I stood still, staring at the static left on the screen. I managed enough courage to turn toward Brie, who was still behind me.

"Do you remember when I told you that nothing could ever make me hate them more?" she said.

I stood in the waves of people and shouts, staring at her icy blue eyes, full of anger and tears that didn't fall as her voice choked out three words.

"I was wrong."

CHAPTER 25

"Are you sure you don't want to talk?" Collin asked.

I had given up on sleep. Collin had asked me what I wanted to do, and I'd answered that I wanted to beat the heck out of something. He usually gave me pointers or kept me motivated while I was at the punching bag. Now he just looked concerned that I was going to snap.

"No." I jabbed the same spot on the bag, pretending it was the Head Counselor's face. "What's his name again?"

"It's Terrance Palmer. He's the Society Party's number one, head Council. Not that it matters. You don't focus on him. You don't worry about the giant with the eggs. You need to keep stealing the eggs and ignore him."

"You know," I stopped punching and tossed the sweaty hair away from my eyes, "I'm not sure that strategy is working. The giant is roaring right now, angry I took the eggs, and saying that stupid 'fi fum' thing."

He sighed. "I'm aware. But this is technically the first time he's stepped out of the castle. Maybe he'll get in a better spot to be toppled, eventually. Isn't that what we're after? In the end?"

He was right, but I ignored him and continued to imagine the punching bag was Terrance Palmer's face.

"Do you want to talk about something else?" he offered. "Anything else? I got all of your notes from your MCU downloaded, except some are corrupted for some reason."

Maybe it was an annoyance at being told something obvious or the need for truth that made me answer him. "Because I deleted some."

"Why?"

I would need to tell him the truth. I wanted to tell him the truth. The truth I had spoken into the dark that night.

"Because... they..." I stopped punching. "I wrote them to you. I wrote things I shouldn't have written. Not if I want you to be a trainer. I'm sure those words are illegal to say to you if—"

I stared at the ground, afraid of his reaction. The bag shifted as he leaned on it.

"Aislyn, look at me."

I looked up, his deep blue eyes as tortured as I expected.

"Aislyn, I have wanted to do this for as long as I could remember. But I never guessed it was going to cost so much. I made a promise to my mom. Now I met you, you—"

"Messed it all up." That sinking feeling returned, the same feeling I'd had when I saw myself on the broadcast.

"No, that's the thing. You—" he grasped my hand "—you made this happen. Eldridge was right. We didn't need a hero. We needed someone who was alive enough to see the reasons we do this. To stop Tessa's arrogance, to help Cassidy, to save two Unnecessaries, to believe a Sentry might turn against the Republic. And now I can't stop wanting to be as alive as you. I want to tell stories, sing, dance, be brave or scared, do it anyway. I think that's why I can't stop... feeling this way."

His hand grew tighter with his last words. I realized no one could see us, hiding in the shadow of the punching bag in the most hidden part of the room. But I could see our struggle more clearly than ever: frozen in worry, holding our breath and still not saying the words that would condemn us. Because at the end of this journey, he could still choose the journey over me. I could still choose to die over coming home to him.

His head was still resting on the bag, like mine, as if it was holding his weight in case he couldn't handle the answer his eyes were asking.

I leaned in. He edged forward.

His breath was warm. I took in every detail of his features and my surroundings, like I was on a mission. My mind blurred with Patterson's warning, the children still to be saved, the war still raging, Alex's life in danger. I should've been pulling back. I should have been trying to resist this. But he wasn't pulling back, and neither was I.

His head tilted to match mine and hovered. His lips almost grazed mine. The voice in his head must have been making the same protests. He spoke, his breath hitting my cheek with every word.

"I can't stop being afraid that if I tell you that I love you, everything will change."

"Maybe it will. The truth usually does. But if it's the truth, you need to tell me."

His fear faded with my words. His eyes closed as he pulled me closer. There was only a moment to breathe before his lips drew me into his, his other hand grasping my neck. I thought he might stop, pull back from the kiss too soon. I pushed my lips into his, to prove to him he didn't need to be afraid.

Every second, the kiss became more intense. I was still leaning on the bag with my shoulder. For balance or so no one would glance in and see us. At any point, this could end. And I didn't want it to.

Finally, he pulled away reluctantly. His forehead rested on mine, his hands cradling my head. My eyes stayed closed. His breath was unsteady and heavy. I'm sure mine wasn't much better. I was terrified that he would regret it, that I'd open my eyes and hear him say that this was a mistake.

But I opened my eyes despite my fear. His one hand still held my cheek, grazing it gently.

We both jumped when his watch beeped. Collin breathed out slowly and answered. "Collin here."

Liam talked on the other line. "Hey, Eva and Lynn are ready to go tomorrow night. Will she be ready?"

I bit my lip, which was still burning, fighting back the urge to say no. I looked at the boy who had lost his mother, the trainer who hesitated to answer Sam, and the man I loved who feared losing me. His jaw was shaking.

I choked out the answer he couldn't find.

"I'll head out tomorrow."

His hand squeezed mine as his head dropped.

Liam said, "Thanks!" and disconnected.

We stared at each other for moments that stretched into minutes. The air seemed electrified and made me unable to move.

"You know what I'm going to ask."

"Yeah," I whispered.

"Promise you'll come back, Aislyn."

I pulled him in, his head resting on my shoulder, my lips kissing the side of his head before grazing his ear with the whispers I had spoken into the dark.

"I love you. I don't have a choice. I have to come back."

My lower lip quivered, but only for an instant before it crashed into his again. His kiss felt more urgent this time, but it was only a second before another beep rang in my ear. He buried his face in his hands.

"Council Debrief, man, in thirty minutes. Are you two coming down?"

For the rest of the day, meetings, debriefs, and small battles pushed Collin and me apart a hundred more times. My lips still burned when I thought about him. Anytime we stood together on the elevator or in a meeting, I felt as if I reacted to his every move.

The only time I forgot about that moment was during my debrief. Thirteen people staring me down, ready to blame me for my failures, was enough to push anything else out of my mind. Everyone had very detailed questions, but most Council members felt sorry for me, even the ones who didn't like me such as Zander. They used their sympathy to make a case to retaliate, which caused an uproar. I didn't like when a few of the counselors congratulated me for killing an enemy soldier.

The day echoed of tension, but not just from Collin. The tension was everywhere, causing aches and creating hope. I felt it when I saw Tessa was out on a mission again. I felt it when I found her note, a single word: *"Sorry."* I also found a note from Cassidy, with a single word: *"Thanks."* I felt the tension as Brie, Lynn, and I watched our babies through the nursery window that night, making funny faces to hold their attention. I felt it when the doctor explained that André had a small birth defect. I held his hand through the incubator as his fingers curled around mine. Then I felt it as Abby and Sarah left that night, and they surprised me by crying as they hugged me in the garden. I felt it when I saw a picture Katerina drew of me. I felt it in every touch from Collin grazing me in elevators and hallways as we raced to meetings and answered more questions, all while trying to keep Alex a secret.

Later that night, as I headed to my room, Collin was sitting in the threshold, his legs crossed. He looked up at me as I approached and reached out for my hand. He looked at me, solemn, as he kissed it gently.

"I'm staying here, Aislyn," he said. "Only here, at the door."

I could sense a silent promise being woven between us as I stepped over his legs. I landed in bed without changing and curled up under my blanket.

I never got to tell a story that night. Instead, we tried to write one: a story that would explain why Alex had saved me. A story we were still struggling to create hours later and into the next morning. And we weren't alone.

I paced up and down the secondary Central Hub mezzanine with Sam and Patterson. But the recycled opinions with no facts left us weary.

"He's a Sentry and an Elite, or nearly there," Collin argued for the third time. "He's so entrenched in the system he has succeeded in it in every possible way! It's entrapment!"

Sam agreed, typing away at his console. Patterson was pacing on the upper level overlooking us. He had read Sam in on the situation just twenty minutes before, but Sam had moved past shock to help us solve the mystery of Alex's fate. Collin and I had stopped pacing again, and were now sitting on the level just above Sam, our legs swinging off the bottom of the mezzanine as we rested our arms on the lower railing.

"If he wanted me dead," I said, "I'd be dead. Twice."

Sam cleared his throat. "Technically, you can only die once."

"Unless he's trying to improve his chance of becoming an Elite," Patterson interjected. "Focus on the hack, Sam. Aislyn, I don't trust someone if I don't know their motive."

"I wouldn't trust him at all. He could be trying to gain your trust for intel, not just a chance to kill you," Collin said, pushing the agenda he had behind every theory the night earlier.

"That doesn't pan out. I wasn't stupid enough to let him even see my MCU screen. I made him turn around. And there's no reason to gain my trust. They've never used that strategy, and with the anti-Protector mentality, they wouldn't be starting now."

I hoped they hadn't, as I wasn't entirely sure. My HistCulture lessons did only go back six weeks.

"It's not worth it," Patterson said. "It's not worth multiple events or efforts to catch one of you. It's just not their style. They don't take prisoners, and there's nothing they could get out of anyone with torture."

"How do you mean?" I asked.

Patterson seemed strained, even more than usual. He rubbed his hand on the back of his neck. "We don't tell any of you enough to make you worth capturing for intel. We wipe your MCU clean two times after someone enters the wrong password or with your voice command. Very few of you even know the basic ins-and-outs of what we do, or even locations on all EE spots or stations. That's why we give you limited updates and switch the T, R, and Q-station schedule all the time. It's why trainers aren't allowed in the Republic. They're worth more. No, he would've killed you if he didn't have another agenda, one that isn't evil."

"I agree," I said. Collin was deep in thought, staring at his swinging feet.

"Well, Sam, what's your theory, then?" he said, looking for support.

Sam rolled his eyes. "I get to have an opinion? Look, who in the Republic would ever rebel against it? It would have to be someone who saw the Elites, the system, and its victims inside and out and could discover the truth buried in the lies. I always guessed t it would be a Citizen."

"I see you've spoken to Michael before," Patterson said. "That's always been his theory. That it would take someone close to them to hate them."

Collin had his hands on the railing, squeezing it, strangling it with the stress he felt. There was already enough unknown and uncertain. Adding more just created restless anxiety.

"No matter what you do, Aislyn," he said, "don't trust him when he might drag you into a riskier situation. So far, he's been in situations where there is a minimal risk of him getting caught or killed, and I know you might argue that. But no one was holding a gun to him. Don't put yourself in a situation where he has to choose his life or yours. You might have to pay the consequences."

Patterson nodded. "I agree. Until we find out more about his past. Maybe when his family became Citizens, he became disillusioned. We need to know where he stands on his ranking and allowance, too."

Sam smiled, pushing his hair out of his eyes again "And that's why I'm here doing a hack. Yay. A reason to exist."

Patterson gave a little impatient sigh. "Well, that's why you're supposed to be here. Though you're taking your time..."

"Almost there, oh ye of little faith." Sam hummed a song I didn't recognize. We all stayed still and silent for ten minutes when he said, "I'm in. We have one minute."

I copied Collin and slid beneath the railing to land on the floor below. We ran to the console, shaking the desk as we got to Sam's station.

"Okay, Patterson," Sam said, "here we go. He is fourth generation Citizen, paid in full. His parents were trying to gain Elite status, so they were loaded, although they never finished paying. He... gosh, he has enough to pay for Elite status now."

"And he doesn't buy his commission?" Patterson asked.

"No. There's a reason stated by his superior. The gist of it is that he loves the action of being a Sentry and wants to serve a few more years. I also found a memo from another superior: 'may retire in a few years.' Although we all know he doesn't enjoy killing, or at least killing you... he..." Sam trailed off.

Collin pushed him slightly. "What is it?"

"I got him. He's alive. He bought breakfast this morning, one mile from headquarters. Expensive menu, too. Dang!"

I breathed in relief. Alex's lie had worked.

"Um... okay, still digging," Sam said. "He turned twenty last month, big allowance, big salary, big house... whoa!"

The mansion on the screen made my mouth drop, and even Collin whistled in response.

"Twenty-eight Unnecessaries caught. Not too high, although that feels morbid to say. Protector kill count... one. Three years ago. Mary, 15th, she was Avery's Protector, I think."

My stomach sank. I thought back to his words: "*Maybe I'm as evil as you've imagined.*" That's what he meant.

"No... but the 15th of the 185th Generation? Patterson, I remember that one. Something was weird, right?" Sam asked, as he turned back to the monitor and typed furiously.

"Yeah, we did an investigation. What was it...?"

"He didn't kill her," Collin said, his hand rubbing his forehead. "I remember the case file. He had a clean shot, he took it, and it hit her, but the Sentry didn't kill her. She went sixteen more blocks until another unit caught up with her."

Patterson pointed to the screen and scrolled down the summary. "He got credited with the kill because they let her bleed out. That's what Hydech's version of mercy is. But if she had gotten to the border, she might have made it. Maybe Alex didn't mean to kill her."

The sinking feeling in my stomach lessened, but only slightly. They saved the summary. Sam had to sign off. I watched him work, but Collin and Patterson left the room, looking like they didn't want me to follow.

Sam turned to me. "His middle name is André. Same as your Unnecessary?"

"Yeah," I said, looking at the saved screenshot of Alex. I touched the screen, taking in his eyes and easy smile—the mask he wore to hide his torture.

"You know, for trained soldiers and spies, you girls can be very sentimental."

I rolled my eyes. Sam smiled and placed the drive with the downloads in his pocket. I went up the stairs and saw that Collin and Patterson were still deliberating. They had probably made their decision.

"What's my directive, sir?" I asked, trying to sound as impartial as possible.

"Trust him at your own risk," Patterson ordered. "And if your life is at stake if he changes his mind, be careful. We will assume he may be sympathetic to our cause for some reason. He might help you, but only when the cost to him is minimal. And you have a standing order from me, 27. Ask for motive. I need to know. And until we have one, don't get drawn in too far."

"Okay," I said, meaning it on all counts. It made a lot of sense, and I wanted to know his motive more than they did.

Patterson joked, "And keep pointing him to walls when you pull out your MCU. Don't give him any intel. Not where Central is or where shelters are or my name or anything. Nothing."

"Understood," I answered.

Patterson opened the door. Collin was silent, staring at me. He remained this way on the walk back to our Circle, partially because I realized he didn't like this situation, and because as we passed people, he must have felt the pressure of this secret.

When we got back to the Circle, he went straight to the HistCulture room, pulled out the room's CU, and opened the monitor on the wall.

I asked, "What are you doing?"

"Sending Sam the new codes, before I forget them."

"I get new codes?" I asked, but the answer came to me quickly. "... to message my assigned number in the Republic. To let you know if I had contact with him, or if I'm with him."

"Yes," he answered, continuing to type.

"That's brilliant!" I exclaimed and eyed him suspiciously.

"Yeah, it was my idea," he said, but only half-smiling. "It's three codes, the usual slang, which I'm assuming you recognize," he explained, and I nodded, trying to memorize them. "The first means you have had contact with him. The second means you are with him and on a mission. The third one is you are with him, but you have reason to believe you may be in danger... or that he'll betray you or kill you."

He turned away from the screen to lean back on the table and slid his hand next to me. I faced the screen with the new codes, still trying to memorize them and ignoring his gaze. But he stretched his arm in front of me now, leaning closer.

"Do you realize what this could cost and how much..." Collin couldn't finish.

"Isn't it worth it?" I asked, looking at him. "A part of you must know that this is worth the risk."

He closed his eyes, tightened his jaw, and leaned down, almost on his shoulder.

"A part of me still wants nothing to stop you from coming home. And I know... he's gotten you home twice. But it's a lot to risk when you love someone to tell them to trust someone else. I think it's one of the hardest things I've ever had to do."

I looked at his eyes, building with intensity. Our foreheads touched. I wished I could take the pain of his loss away, so he wouldn't have to be so afraid. I wished I had a moment to breathe freely with none of this hanging over us. I wished I could tell him I was here now. Safe now. The moment was ours now. But there was only one way to show him that.

I leaned up slightly, making him catch his breath, and my lips caught the edge of his.

He leaned in, and I lost myself again. The world became silent. He reached his hand behind my neck, and it made me want to kiss longer.

But then the world became loud again.

With one knock.

Not a simple, refined, strong knock. A playful knock.

A knock that could only belong to one person in Central.

We released, mirroring the look of panic.

He opened his mouth to say something, but he clenched his jaw. I turned away from the doorway to stare at the screen.

"How long have you been standing there?" Collin asked, letting go of me, his voice dropping out a bit, to face Eva.

"About ten seconds," Eva said casually, "which I think I might mentally file under, 'never tell a soul' and store a copy in, 'things that remind me that love is real.'"

I finally turned around to see her leaning on the door frame. "Eva, what are you doing here?"

"Look, you said I could come in whenever as long as I knocked. And... I knocked, so..."

"What are you doing here?" Collin said.

She deflated. "My mom's looking for me. She gave me one of her pep talks and I'm trying to hide, okay?"

Collin sighed and cursed under his breath. The tone changed, and I realized I didn't know what was going on.

Eva almost looked ready to cry, but still tried to smile. "Yeah, my thoughts exactly. It was the kind that started with inspiration to do my best, be brave, all that. But it ended with the usual demands. 'Uphold the family honor,' 'your life is only worth something if you give it to this,' and other things that marginalize my soul into a job description and prepare me for martyrdom or indentured servitude. I didn't know where else to go. I'm sorry."

Her voice choked at the end, and her casual stature broke. She looked at Collin and blinked away tears. I was absorbing what she had said when Collin nodded, as if this had happened before. I looked back at her, hiding behind the composed calm she was trying to pull off.

"I'm sorry, Eva," Collin said. "Just stay here. I'll go get you two some dinner. You can learn the codes when I get back, Aislyn." He passed her on the way out, reaching out to her shoulder and squeezing it as he went by. He said "Sorry," under his breath.

We both stood, maybe both embarrassed and more vulnerable than we wanted to be.

"Sorry," I said to her.

Without thinking, I touched my lips. I was still breathless, my cheeks, hand, and lips all feeling like they were on fire. I just wanted to be back in his arms. But I also was determined to help Eva. The only thing was that I couldn't think of what to say.

"Sorry," I repeated, and closed my eyes in embarrassment.

When I opened my eyes, she was smiling. "I wish I could say it was the first time it happened. I'm glad you aren't blaming me or my mom. Or trying to fix it. That's why I came here. Plus, the other trainers are usually on my mom's side. Collin is the only one who seems to get it." She pondered the monitor. "So, what are the new codes for?"

I reached out my arm, without moving any other part of my body. I hit the standby button twice. The screen beeped, turning black behind me.

"Nothing."

She reacted with amusement at my rigid appearance. "Okay, I guess one secret will have to do for today." She was smiling at first, but then looked more somber as she said, "And don't worry. I'll keep it. I have had to keep so many secrets for so many dumb reasons. I have two good reasons to keep yours."

"Which are?"

"Out of all of them— from missions, to codes, to the classified info I overheard on the elevator— I have never had to keep a secret so beautiful. It's kind of flattering that anyone could trust me that much."

It took me a moment, smiling at her conclusion, but I also asked, "And the second?"

"I need to believe it. In your secret." She smiled and breathlessly finished her thought. "I need to believe that love is real. That people can fall in love. That not every mother wants to use her child. If everyone knew that, I wouldn't be hiding right now. I need to believe… that love is real."

I reached out, hugging her as she let some tears fall. I caught a few, but not nearly enough.

CHAPTER 26

Less than twenty-four hours later, Collin walked me to where Eva and Lynn waited. He whispered the new codes one more time.

After Eva had left, I was worried that Collin would focus on Alex, but he didn't. The night had started with a kiss on my hand and long stories told until the break of dawn. But it seemed distant. Collin now placed a backpack on my shoulders, squeezing them assuredly as he said I was clear. I turned to see him, torn between wanting me to stay and ordering me to go.

I reached out and hugged him. He wasn't ready for that. His broad soldiers tensed under my arms, and I wondered if he might push me away because of Lynn and Eva standing so close. But he leaned into me and clenched my back.

Lynn scoffed, but Eva elbowed her ribs and said, "You didn't see that."

Lynn looked at me suspiciously. "If you say so."

As he relaxed, his hands reached out to touch my shoulders again, his shaky breaths started to even out.

"I don't know what to say," I murmured.

Hesitantly, I reached up and touched his head. His eyes were red, still drowning in pain but holding a glimmer of hope.

"It's all been said, Aislyn. And now you have to go. I couldn't even ask you to stay. It's not who you are now. So go be everything you were meant to be. Besides, nothing is going to change while you're off saving the world. It'll still be the truth, when you get back. I love you."

I nodded, and with that last pull of my hand, he let go.

And I walked away. We could both live out our destinies for a little while longer. Someone's life depended on it. The same truth that drew me to him now pulled me back to the forest.

I whispered it as I walked away. "And love is real."

A week later, I stared at the shards of sunlight through the broken walls and windows of the abandoned warehouses. I had traveled to this sector to find an Unnecessary that lived in the warehouses that Megan had mentioned. Eva and Lynn had split off four days ago, leaving me headed north through the forest.

I missed Collin. And as shallow as it made me feel to complain about something so trivial, I missed real food. The meal bars tasted gross after about two days—flavorless sustenance that didn't sustain.

I looked up to the sun, trying to gauge the time without my MCU. It was strange that I played this little game with myself, almost certain it meant that I might be delusional or lonely, but it made me satisfied with my survival skills. My answer of 4:20 was close to 4:34 which was on my MCU display. I looked out over the hills and wondered if I should go for the border now. It was too late, so I set up my heater, trying to make my meal bar warm to see if that would help.

It was almost impossible to concentrate on any potential mission, with my brain continuing to spin. I stared at the dandelions growing, until a butterfly landed at the base of a tree;

the first butterfly I had noticed all spring. It was a fascinating clash of glossy dark blue and black. The sun hit me; the warmth coming in rays through the now-full leaves. Pieces of heaven in front of the grey abandoned stone and broken glass. I wanted the beauty to cut deep enough to leave some hope behind. I told myself to hold on to that moment, because at least it was mine.

At least I thought it was. But I was not alone.

Within seconds, I heard the things that told me I had company. A whoosh. A twig snapping too quickly. A breath. The small events that left me clues as they all seemed to happen in a circle, surrounding me.

"I'm not going to hurt you," I said. It might have been just a shout into empty forest, but if I was right, I needed to talk to whoever watched me. I waited, hearing one more noise above me.

"Who are you?" a small voice asked.

"My name is Aislyn," I said, playing the part of the mythical character once again. "And you probably know what I am."

The tiny girl came out from behind the branch. She was light, airy, perched on the branch almost like a cat. Her hair was curled up; the light breeze never seemed to let it land on her shoulders. The strands of her hair hovered, disappearing in the brown tree bark as it swam in the gusts of air.

"What's your name?" I asked, silently processing a plan for our departure.

"I don't have one," she said. "I mean, it's usually just 'girl,' but I always wanted a pretty one, just for me."

My heart ached a little, especially seeing her curls dance. A little reminder of Olivia threatened to derail me.

"Do you live out here?"

"Yes. Well, I hunt and eat, anyway. I usually try to sleep in there, but in summer I don't have to. I like it because I can see the stars. I think that's what they are called. I go to the buildings when it's cold."

"What about everything else you need?"

"Someone brings me some things. A Sub-Terra. We have a drop-off point, and I give her some berries. She always wanted one of you to find me. She said once she believed it would happen. I don't have much school. Is that the right word? Believe?"

I reached out to her. "Yes, little one, it is."

She jumped down. This one was easy; I'd be back in no time. I could even message Central the abbreviation for "see you later," which would tell them I was en route home with an Unnecessary. But as I put on my pack, the girl looked hesitant to leave.

"You know," I said, lowering the straps on my back, "you can trust me. That means you can believe in me to keep you safe."

She sighed, looking out at the warehouses. "I know. She kept me safe."

She was being pulled in two directions. I could tell. I knew how it felt to be torn.

"It's just... could I tell her? Just leave a note? It's almost drop time. No one will see it, I promise. Barely anyone is out here anyway, and most people just ignore me."

Her eyes were pleading, but I almost said no. It was on the tip of my tongue, followed by a very sympathetic reason. Then, my tongue stopped, stuck to the roof of my mouth. My message would be much safer if sent within three miles of the border. Her face dropped, and I imagined what I would leave her caretaker with. Horror? Dread? Sorrow? What if she instead felt relief and a sense of accomplishment for keeping this soul safe for all these years?

"Okay," I said, the answer evolving from the refusal I had intended to give her. She smiled in response and led me down the hill to the fence. There were holes in the fence wires already, meant for the children who so often snuck through.

I spent the first mile asking her questions. She had escaped as a Sub-Terra, after being made to work illegally at age six because she had been a "lab defect" that they had let slide because the parents' debt was excessive. A coworker had helped her escape.

"I thought, at first, that I would work off the debt and be fine. I even met my parents a few times. They promised that they would stop spending money, but then they would blow it all until I was in debt again. They felt guilty. My dad died of a drug overdose—the free one they give you to handle regret. The Sub-Terra who takes care of me says that it's the Society's plan: to kill people with happiness."

I nodded, not sure what to say in response. I asked a few more questions and even had time to place the pulse monitor on her. She cleared the lie detection test without even a hint of deception.

We kept walking to her meeting point. When we arrived, she placed some rocks in the shape of a "P." She also made a heart in the gravel, which made mine beat a little faster. A few people rushed by her, but ignored her.

In their rushed pursuit of beauty, every passerby missed one of the most beautiful things in the world.

"I just hope she doesn't miss me. Or the berries," she said as we left.

I sent my message for the day to my assigned number, thankful that Collin could feel some relief. She held my hand, and we strolled back through the abandoned warehouses. I told her where we were going. After being in the woods so long, the girl knew how to navigate efficiently. She even showed me a compass which was old, and not at all like the digital ones we had. I almost envied it; my father had an antique one like it.

"You can keep it. If you're ever lost," she said, handing it to me.

I smiled and thanked her. It had been twenty minutes, traveling back, before I realized that something was buzzing.

It was my Republic phone, the one I had just used to send my message. I was worried and slightly annoyed that I had to deal with answering a message from someone. The chances were so slim that anyone in the Republic would ever answer back. I held out the device, ready to type in a response refusing to go to a party or hook up with someone.

My mind read the words, but my body froze, forgetting how to breathe, think, or even feel.

I wished it was someone boasting about a dress, a conquest or someone's dumb comment. But the message wasn't sent from anyone in the Republic. It was sent by the one person from whom I never wanted to get a message: Patterson.

"399621. You've all been compromised. Get out now. P."

The number blinked, mocking my heart, which could stop beating at any moment. The single letter "P" held all of Patterson's worst anger and urgency.

I tore the phone battery out and threw it twenty feet down the alley. The phone went into a nearby dumpster. I took off my shoes. It felt like any other reflex, thanks to hours in training. I took a breath, suddenly realizing I'd been holding it.

I turned to my Unnecessary, now wishing with all my might we had never come back into the borders. Such an innocent mistake with such a tragic outcome.

"Sweetie, I need you to go. Now. They might be following me. I don't know. They won't follow you. You need to get out of here..."

"But I'm with you now. I'm safe." She looked as if she might cry. I closed my eyes and tried to detach enough to say what I needed to say.

Which was... what? Would she die because they'd be tracking me? She couldn't survive without me.

But she could. I threw off my pack and handed her the MCU from the front pouch. I said, "Breaker," which was the code word to delete all intel files without disabling all functions.

"There is enough in here to make your way back. Read the positioning intel on the MCU. Go three miles north, three miles west, toward the Territory, and then three miles south. I'll find you there. You can map it all out on the MCU, do you see that? Meal bars are in the bag. If I'm not there in fifteen hours, go without me."

She looked frightened, but with each instruction, she nodded until she was breathing slower.

I'm glad I could at least give her some sense of peace; I wasn't feeling it at all.

I took a breath before I spoke to her again. "You know those woods, and they know you. You were meant to know what to do in the woods to help you escape. So do it." I swallowed. "You were always meant to do this."

She hugged me, awkwardly all the same, then walked down the alleyway, looking in several directions.

I ran as fast as I could in the opposite direction. My head was spinning. I needed a story, but there was no point. The character I was didn't have a chance. There was no dress to hide behind this time. They would stop every person in this area to check for ID.

The sirens rang a moment later. I jumped up an old fire escape and crunched into a ball under a tarp. I hoped my black outfit was enough to hide me temporarily.

They'd be looking for someone running to escape, and the first group would set up a perimeter. My hope was that they would pass me. I waited, which was more painful than running. Minutes later, the first squad ran down the alley without looking up. I wondered how many of them there would be, until I heard the distant shuttles.

It was the optimal time to make my move. If the unit had just gone by, they would be given directions to set up a perimeter. It would be full of holes at first, but the other unit wouldn't come back up the alley. I had to move.

I jumped down the fire escape, curling up at the last minute to roll out of the fall. I could barely believe that it worked. The sound of a shuttle got closer. I would have to bust open a door and find a better cover. There were only seconds before someone would hear me.

I ran for a worn door, made of wood or metal, something old that looked familiar—like home. It was locked. I went to the next door. Locked. The sirens became louder. I tried to kick it in. The third kick finally moved it slightly. The sirens stopped. I kicked again and fell to the ground, the gravel sending a shot of pain through my knee.

At the end of the alley, there were two blurs of white. The shuttles had flown past.

I stood up but didn't run. My whole body was shaking, but I couldn't walk a step. My lungs were burning as if I were drowning, even though I was taking heaving breaths. I stared at the corner of the alley, listening to the shuttle door open.

They should have been shouting orders. Running out and take positions. But if they had seen me... they'd be quiet.

The story. I had to rewrite the story.

If they weren't talking, it meant they were whispering. If I couldn't hear shuffling, it meant they were loading weapons silently. And if I couldn't hear them move, it meant they were hiding. And if they had seen me in the alley as they flew past, I couldn't wait anymore. Noise wouldn't give me away; they already knew I was there.

I sprinted for the next exit, down another alley, when I heard the first shots. They were fired from blocks away, but they made my legs move faster. I jolted from the left and right, randomly so I'd be a difficult target. The first bullets hit the wall next to me, then the ground two feet away, then the ground one foot away, then inches in front of my heel as it hit the ground.

I saw my exit. I had to dart to the left, out of the line of fire.

But when I turned, I would give them one clear shot. One place where they could lead the target, between where I was and the entry to the alley. One shot that could kill me.

I held my breath and turned. Two more shots came. They sounded louder than the others. One missed me.

The other didn't.

It shattered through my right arm, still pulled back from finishing my stride. The pain was instant, acute, and stole the breath I had left in my lungs. Nothing I'd felt before could have prepared me for this. I stopped, unable to move or think. It felt like they had ripped my whole arm from my body.

I could barely hear anything but my heartbeat, thankful it was still working. But I made out some shouting. They would head down the alley they shot, seven blocks away from their shuttle. I had to keep moving.

I pushed on a door. It opened. I took off my jacket and wrapped it around my injury. The pain was excruciating, and despite still walking, looking for another exit, I moaned.

There had to be a back door. I saw it moments later, making sure to leave a fake blood trail in three directions. I went out the back door, being careful to check behind me as I quietly closed it.

They trained the police and Sentries to read that building like a book. A building with an open door. A blood pool in the middle of the floor. A blood trail up to the stairs. This was the story of a panicked, wounded girl. It would be rational for them to assume I was in the building, until they couldn't find me. I'd bought myself the ten minutes it would take for them to swarm it and confirm I wasn't anywhere inside. As I walked into the next building, I realized that if I went from building to building, I would slow them down. I could travel through them faster than they could, until...

I didn't know what followed that. My arm was screaming. From the quick glance, it seemed that the bullet had gone right through, but my arm was now useless. I wrapped it in another cloth I found, checking behind me for a blood trail. I could feel the blood seeping out and tried to apply pressure by pressing it against my stomach.

I heard their steps from the window. Someone barked, "In here. The trail is upstairs."

All but one entered the building—or at least, that was what I guessed from hearing someone named Smith being told to stay behind to watch for... they cursed instead of saying Protector. I expected that.

The other shuttle left. Someone shouted to Smith that there was another one up north. I wanted to stay, but I would miss my chance if I listened to what they had to say.

I slithered across the alley to the other door. Open. Of course all these doors would be, but not the ones I had tried earlier. I entered the next building, closing the door behind me. I moved from building to building, leaving fake blood trails in many of them. It took thirty minutes for my pursuers to start shouting again. One shouted perimeter while another claimed to find another blood trail.

I was about twenty buildings away. If their leader was shouting orders, they would all be watching him. I looked down the main road and saw no one, so I ran. I could gain the most distance now without worrying about being seen. Twenty other buildings went by in under a minute. There was a defining shout; that would the captain finishing up. My time window had closed.

I ducked into the next side alley and into another building.

My eyes closed in despair. The floor was empty, with no cover. No equipment or machines. I felt a chill, like I should crumple on the floor right there.

I looked up, hoping God still wanted me to keep breathing, and noticed nothing except...

The ceiling was low, unlike some other buildings.

The building seemed just as tall as the others, but the architecture was different. I ran for the door in the corner, and behind it...

Stairs.

I ran, but not far. Each floor was only two flights up. This must have been an office, not a warehouse, although it had a pool on the penthouse floor. Desks littered the second floor. I kept climbing, watching behind me, making sure my blood wasn't giving me away. I realized that my footprints would misdirect them if they got this far. But when I looked down, there were already footprints all over the stairs. They were probably made by Unnecessaries. For once, they'd protected me.

I chose the seventh floor, mostly because I couldn't move anymore. I ignored the perfect cover—they would check it first. Instead, I picked a place closer to the door, where there was a desk and a box one foot behind it. That means I wouldn't have to move the box, revealing a dust trail. The desk, the box, and the darkness might be enough to hide me. I groaned as I unwrapped my jacket from around my arm.

I wished I hadn't looked.

I heard something in the distance—gunfire miles away. As I viewed my shattered flesh, I felt every pang of every explosion ripping through me. I was able to tear off a smaller portion of my jacket with my teeth and wrap it tighter around my wound.

My lower lip trembled as I waited for what seemed like forever. It was probably only thirty minutes. I heard them go through buildings, flinging items out of windows. The anger toward them grew with each second they pursued me. I finally thought about the other Protectors, being hunted or killed. There were four more shuttles now, but they concentrated on the buildings with the blood trails, moving back to where I had been earlier.

They knew they had me.

I knew they had me.

It made the waiting more intense. It made me jump when the door downstairs was kicked open.

There was shuffling down the floors, followed by someone yelling, "No blood trail, but give every floor a sweep anyhow." I almost didn't care if anyone came at this point. There was no great destiny to fulfill anymore.

I wondered if I had the courage to kill one if he discovered me, so I would at least take one down with me. While revenge seemed pointless, it felt unfair that only I suffered when I died.

Collin.

Collin would suffer.

The voice in my head reminded me again, as it had every minute for the last hour. The last moment of my life would devastate him. Because if I died, everything we worked for would suffer. Every bit of courage it had taken to admit that he loved me would haunt him.

I dropped my head to my knees. A few feet away, the door swung open. My ears were ringing; I only knew that there was one person per floor. I waited, breathing quietly, still as the stone under me, until the footsteps crunched the papers on the ground close by. I couldn't see his face, covered by the mask they were wearing—probably because of the dust. He moved past me, but as I opened my eyes to look, I couldn't see his light in the back of the room. I leaned up, unbending my knees slightly to get a glimpse.

A hand grasped my mouth from behind. The other arm clasped my other hand and held it against my back. Then a force pulled me out, back to the ground, on my knees.

I was done. My thoughts swirled in panic and pain.

It was a miracle that I recognized the voice.

"Aislyn, you are going to die one of these days."

His hand released me just enough for me to speak. I whispered out my reply, more to myself than to Alex.

"So I've been told."

CHAPTER 27

Alex leaned in to turn me around, carefully lifting my arm up and assessing the damage. He was out of breath. I couldn't imagine what he had done to get here. It almost proved my prayers were heard, but as he held his hand up, the tension rose again. There was rarely more than one Sentry on duty.

"What are you doing here?" I whispered.

"I got reassigned to this sector. I thought with all the kids living in these buildings, I'd be able to help some of them. Then it all became chaos tonight. There were too many of you in the Republic for any Sentry to be on standby. Yager and Hydech are both around here. We were together at first, but we split up."

He looked like he might be sick.

"Did one of them shoot me?"

Alex didn't answer. He pulled out and injected some kind of painkiller which gave me some instant relief. Still, he avoided my gaze. An idea pierced me, almost as sharp as the bullet. My voice shook.

"Did you shoot me?"

I was ready to unleash whatever energy I had left to condemn him. He pulled out another med pen. His eyes couldn't meet mine, but they stared at my wound, full of worry and regret.

"I'm sorry... I'm so..." He stopped to inject the next meds. "This should coagulate your blood, but if not, I'll have to cauterize."

"Please don't," I begged. If there was one part of field Med that scared me, it was having a flame-heated knife hitting my flesh.

"If the bleeding doesn't stop in five minutes, I'm doing it," he said, his voice unsteady but somehow resolute. "And I'm sorry. If I hadn't fired, Hydech would have taken the shot. And he doesn't miss. I told him I had you and I was locked on. If I'd missed you, he would have known I let you go. He would've killed both of us."

My anger boiled. I would have hit him if I had the use of both arms. Then again, his anguish might have stopped me. I found myself drawn into this game with him by still being alive.

I was now the piece of the game everyone was chasing. It made me wonder what move he was on and what move I should be making.

"What do they think you are doing here now?" I asked.

"Sweeping the building. I sent two of my men to the bottom floors. I have a few more minutes as a window to clear the building. Not enough time to cauterize, so keep pressure on it."

Alex looked toward the door, straining to hear. Footsteps echoed, climbing to the next floor.

His hand grasped the side of my head. He whispered, "Stay down, Aislyn. Stay down." He stood up and placed his gun on the opposite side of the room with the flashlight in his hand. Barely balanced, I lunged forward when he stood up, clinging to his leg so I didn't fall over. Alex turned as the door opened.

"Hydech, what are you doing here? I've got this floor."

"You've been up here for two minutes. If you were always this thorough, Sanderson, you would have killed your target instead of wounding her."

Alex lowered his weapon near his hip, pointed at the ground, inches away from my face. His stance was arrogant, but the hand holding the gun shook. I realized I was in the position that Collin never wanted me. Alex's life was now at risk, just as much as mine.

"You didn't do any better. At least I can hit one," Alex said playfully.

"Oh, you didn't hear? Since you were so busy on your little hunt, I got one five miles north of here about ten minutes ago."

Alex let out a scoff. "What about the 'it's not a competition speech' that the sergeant..."

Alex continued talking with Hydech. But I couldn't hear the words; the ringing in my ears grew louder. I clenched Alex's leg, hoping he wouldn't react in pain. I stared at the gun, still inches away, and a part of me wanted to wrench it out of his hands and kill Hydech where he stood. The sorrow paralyzed me, but I also couldn't risk Alex's life just to get revenge. When the ringing in my ears died down, I heard Hydech curse and Alex curse back, but jokingly wish him luck. Hydech left and continued up the stairs.

I looked up at Alex, now heaving breaths, his shoulders bent down in defeat. His expression looked pained. His eyes closed. I released his leg and he melted down to the floor.

"I'm so sorry, Aislyn. I was hoping he wouldn't get there in time. I even tried to divert him. I'm so sorry."

I listened for something insincere in his apology, but didn't find it. He reached for my hand, pulling it up to look at my arm.

"It looks like the bleeding is slowing, and considering how fast your blood was just pumping, I think you'll be okay to get home. I only have one minute, so any questions will have to wait until I get back. You should know..." He pulled my head up to see one glint of hope. "We saw your Unnecessary get to the fence. They didn't pursue because of the higher targets in the area. She's okay."

I breathed some relief as he moved some boxes around me. He pulled a vial from his pocket. I didn't recognize it.

"This isn't for sleep, is it?" I asked.

"No. This serum will cool your body temperature and slow your heartbeat. It changes your bodily functions, just enough to register as non-human on a drone's thermal scanners. The drones only identify anything with a temp 98.1 or higher to expedite searches. You'll be cold and miserable, but alive. It'll wear off in five hours. In eight hours, I'll sweep the buildings again, because we will have moved all the units off to other areas. I will come back for you. I promise I'm doing everything I can to keep you alive."

"Like shoot me?" I asked.

But I couldn't hide my fear. My lower lip quivered. Worry stretched over his face, contorting his striking features. He hesitated, but held out his hand. There were a hundred reasons why I shouldn't grasp it, but seeing him risk his life still made a strong case against them.

"You can trust me," he spoke in an urgent whisper. "But take this vial now, or we don't have a chance."

I stared in his eyes. Intensity and concern swirled there, both of which I had never expected to find.

I needed to know why he was helping me.

If I didn't take the vial, I'd never know. Once again, curiosity pushed me forward.

I took the vial and downed it, swallowing hard against the cold and harsh tasting substance. He held out a water canteen for me. There were gunshots in the distance as I drank. I panicked, but found it impossible to react, as if the meds had paralyzed me. If he betrayed me now, I was helpless. Maybe he recognized my fears. He laid me on the floor, as gently as he could.

"I've got you. Don't worry, Aislyn. I've got you. I'm not giving up on you now. I'll be back. I promise."

My teeth chattered. Something muffled my hearing. The cold overtook my body faster than I thought possible.

I stared at dirty cardboard, inked with a handwritten message. I couldn't think of how to read it or make any sense out of it.

A part of me screamed something in my mind, to remember it, that it was important. But I didn't. I fell into the power of drug-induced sleep, thinking of my promise to Collin.

That I would come back.

And Alex's promise was the only hope of me keeping my promise alive.

I woke up, weary, confused, and freezing. I remembered not to move. I tried not to think about what I couldn't afford to think about: a friend dead, my little girl in the woods waiting for me, Collin. They made my heart hurt far more than my arm, which was throbbing. Collin must have thought that I had died.

I wasn't sure how long I needed to stay here. There was no context for how long I had been asleep. Then I heard something outside, hovering. The drone. I froze again, remembering Alex's words. It flew away seconds later.

I closed my eyes, falling into a more restful sleep. It was shorter because the pain kept returning. But with the pain came my ability to process what had happened, and the many questions I had lined up for Alex to answer.

I looked back up at the words on the box, which didn't make any sense. They may have been in a different language. I thought back to the noise above me hours earlier, realizing I must have passed the drone test. My relieved sigh caused me to breathe in the dust from the ground. I lifted myself up slowly, only to hear a bang down the stairs that made me freeze again. I gripped the bare ground and began slow, soft breathing.

The door opened, and the footsteps ran right for me.

Alex pulled me up with one motion. My legs were numb, and it was hard to stand, but he steadied me. He glanced down at my wound and cursed.

"What is it?" I asked, wincing. My arm was still in excruciating pain, but it wasn't feeling as strange as my legs.

"Might be infected," he said, "but I'm not sure. It's not supposed to look like that. We've got to get you out of here. Aislyn, your legs lost some oxygen so they might feel a little weird, even painful..."

I shouted, but he covered my mouth. Invisible pins and needles hit my legs. My mouth opened wide in pain even as he begged me to stay quiet. It was as if my feet had gotten numb from kneeling so long, only the pains shooting up my legs were much more intense.

"Yeah. I can tell," I said. I leaned on him as the feeling started to come back.

"You've got to be quiet," he whispered. "Squeeze my hand."

I nodded, but then whimpered. I wanted to be braver than this, I told myself.

"It's hard," he said, moving his head closer to whisper in my ear. "Breathe. Just breathe."

"Has anyone else...?" I started to ask, but had to clench my mouth shut from the pain. He tried to shush me again.

"Don't worry about anything now. Hydech moved further north and shot some poor kids who were hiding up there. Someone tried to help them. He missed this time. She fell two stories to escape and still made it to the fence. We can't cross the fence, according to our regulations. She had reddish-blond hair, really curly. That's all I can tell you right now."

So, Cassidy was okay.

"Alex, you can tell me more."

"No, I can't. I need you to make it. I've risked both our lives for it. Get home. Mourn them then."

He penetrated my fears with his. He had almost died for me twice today, and I owed it to him to keep going.

The shards of pain intensified, but it felt better to be moving. He had to hold my hand down most of the stairs, and I had to stop and lean on him a few times. I was afraid my weakness would frustrate him, but he waited with me, told me to squeeze his hand, and said, "It's okay, you're doing great," over and over again. By the time we were on the ground level, I could walk. My arm didn't bleed again. Alex said it was about half a mile to the fence. We jogged to the border.

"So," I said, instantly regretting the agreement to run, "you are still alive. The last time I saw you in the alley... I thought the family would ask for proof that the baby was dead."

"They did," he said, sounding a little disgusted, "but I told them I had an emergency and couldn't deal with it. The sirens a few blocks away made that believable. And I bribed them, saying if they called me out on anything, anything, I would reveal the pictures of the first boy I killed. They backed off, and two days later, I got a raise, to make sure there were no hard feelings."

"What, a raise ensures that?"

"Most people know—I'm sure even you may know by now—how close I am to the Elite mark. No matter how much money I spend on things, I'm still close. I'm guessing the baby is okay?"

I smiled. "Yeah, André is fine."

He stopped right at the end of the last building. "You named him André?"

"Yeah, you saved him. I thought it fit."

He shook his head. "You shouldn't have. You forget what I've done, who I am—"

"For the record," I interrupted, "I come from the Territory, not the wilderness. I've only told three other people about you, but that was enough to do a simple hack. We reviewed your record. We also know you didn't kill the Protector in cold blood. You are close to Elite status, but you keep blowing your money to stay a Citizen. You've helped me. You've shot me. But I don't know why."

His head fell forward. I wondered if I could ask a simpler question.

"For one thing, why don't you become an Elite?"

"I couldn't fight back against the Republic," he said as he surveyed around us. "They give Elites the money and power to either impress or oppress anyone, but they are monitored and expected to waste time at parties and political events. Helping a Protector or Unnecessaries would be out of my reach. The only way I can help anyone is by being close enough to kill them."

We were within yards of the fence. He stopped and turned around again. I glanced back and then entered the small hole made by my Unnecessary much earlier. He said we should go out of the border by about a mile. Then he would leave me and cover my trail on the way back.

"How is no one else out here with you?" I asked as he moved brush away.

He sighed. "Protocol is that the search was over. There was the infrared a few hours ago, and it showed nothing. They assumed they must have missed you or you went underground and swam in the sewage out to another sector. I kind of played the part of the obsessed Sentry who let my target get away, a little desperate, and said I'd search again, but everyone else left to—" He stopped short.

"Let me guess," I asked, disgusted. "Celebrate? The deaths of the horrible Protectors? Did Palmer give an address?"

"Yes. For the record, there are plenty of people who didn't believe that footage from earlier this month, though. About the Protectors harvesting the baby from a Vessel? They thought the whole thing was staged since they couldn't see the faces. I might have started a rumor it was paid actors. That spread around town quick. That was you, right? In the footage?"

"Yes," I said. "What was the deal with that?"

He shook his head, snapping some branches ahead of him. "They hired her to entrap one of you. She got half a million for agreeing. They wired her so they could hear everything. Her handler heard her talking with the Protector and alerted the Sentries. When the Sentries heard the fight begin, they formed a more insidious strategy. They had an opportunity for an incredible propaganda piece. But because of the lighting in the alley, it didn't turn out as well as they'd hoped. Half of the people still bought it, but everyone is aware of what the Society Party is gearing up for."

"Jubilee Day," I said, trying to save my breath for our fast hike. Something acidic churned in my stomach.

"Don't think about it," he said. "Try to push it out of your mind. I shouldn't have said anything, sorry. Keep moving."

But I stopped. We were almost a mile from the fence, and I knew my window for questions was closing.

"You still haven't answered my question. Why?"

He sighed as he paused, looking down at the ground.

"You're a Sentry. You should want me dead," I said. It wasn't a question. I wanted him to argue, hoping it would motivate him to give up some truth more than asking a question had.

"It's a long story," he said, looking ashamed suddenly. We walked again, but only a few steps before he broke the silence. "Aislyn, I have a reason, but I can't tell you. It would only make you hate me more. After what happened... I didn't want to kill a Protector. Not anymore." He kept his pace fast, forcing me to follow behind.

We walked in silence again, but my mind raced. I had told myself I could never imagine a reason that would make a Citizen change enough to want to help me. But as I tried to imagine now, after seeing the shame like sorrow in his eyes, I wrote the story in one breath.

I stopped walking, feeling the truth weigh on me as the words left my mouth as I turned around to face him.

"Who was she?"

He stopped. The leaves under his foot crunched as he dug his foot into the ground. His mouth fell open, but then he clenched his jaw just as quickly. He stood eerily still for almost a minute. I waited as the air thickened like it does when secrets are told, spoken out loud for the first time.

"My sister. She was, as you call it, a Vessel. I didn't help her when her boyfriend wanted her to get rid of the baby, but she wanted to keep it. I pushed her away. I told her to deal with it, or we'd lose everything. We'd worked to be an Elite family for so long. It brought us closer than most brothers and sisters in the Republic. Our reputation. Our money. And when she asked for help again and then she went missing, I reported her."

I remained silent, trying to hear more details so that maybe if a Protector had gotten her out, I could ask her questions.

But then I remembered the sorrow.

"Did she make it out?"

"No," he said. "She tried. They found her body ten miles from the border. The coroner told me her heart had been too weak to deliver the baby. They never told me if the baby made it, but I snuck a look at the report. It didn't. The baby died. I wanted to blame it on her, on the baby, but then I read they found tears and blood that weren't hers—probably DNA from a Protector. Someone had loved her enough to cry for her and her baby. More than I did. And after that, I stopped blaming her and the baby, and I blamed myself."

He was still turned away from me as he spilled his secrets to the forest, as if only the darkness could draw the truth out of him—or maybe only the darkness could keep it hidden.

"I'm sorry." I lost control of my voice, wondering if it was worth it to try to blink back the tears.

He released a weary sigh, then turned around to look at me. "I should have helped her when she asked. I should have refused to kill anyone. I should've given you my gun so you could kill me. But I can only keep helping you if I don't die. I can only help Unnecessaries if I don't die. I can only fight them if we don't die."

He walked again, and I struggled to keep up his pace. The ambient light of the moon hit his dark hair and reflected off his eyes just enough to see the glint of green. He kept looking at my wounded arm with concern. I supposed it was safe now he had stopped and looked at his device. He was trying to gauge distance. I had one more chance to know everything.

I took it.

"One more question. Why me?"

He hesitated, and then looked at me, as vulnerable and honest as I had ever seen him.

"Two reasons. One, you saw me. I've seen other Protectors. Seen them barely escape. Seen them not escape. Your eyes didn't accuse me, they were desperate; desperate to do something you didn't know you could do and you were scared you would fail. You thought I had a choice whether to kill you, like I was human. You looked in my eyes, not hating me, but loving the baby. Your eyes made me see the baby like you did. I didn't know anyone could have that kind of passion. It's like a fire. It burned my pain away. There was no way I could touch that fire, let alone kill it."

I didn't know what to say to his response—how someone from a society so out of tune with emotions had pegged mine to the last detail.

"And the second reason?"

He smirked. "You don't want to know. Trust me. This is a safe distance for you. I'll cover up the trail back to the building. I just reported that I went out but couldn't see a trace of you."

My need to thank him was enough to make me grasp his arm as he turned. I didn't know what to say, so I just squeezed his arm. "I can't thank you enough. Just be careful. Please. I wouldn't want you to get caught."

"Yeah, that would be tragic—the guy who shot you, dying." He said it nonchalantly, almost willing it to happen. I gripped on, as the seconds slid by, ruining both of our chances for escape.

"Alex, please," I begged in one more effort, not to get the intel for Patterson but because I needed to know. "The second reason?"

He stopped, and instead of pulling away from me, drew a little closer, his brow creased. Something in his dark eyes softened so the green glinted and drove his heart into mine. The power and concentration on his face left me speechless while he remained uncertain to speak.

"You saw me, but I also saw you. Just you. Only you. I didn't see my failure or the Unnecessaries or Vessels or the endless dark tunnels or death or tired nights alone. That same fire, it was mesmerizing. All I saw was you. And now, you are all I see."

The wind rustled, but softer than the pounding in my head, which was getting louder. My face must have revealed the shock I was trying to hide. Unsure if I should pull away, I stayed in place. The air felt too tense to pull away, as if something might break if I did. He looked at me, expecting me to be disgusted. But I didn't move, so he leaned in, making the air less breathable.

He reached out his hand, placing his fingers gently on my cheek, right underneath my eyes. The warmth from his hands burned while the words he had spoken became an unbelievable reality. He reached in, and pressed his lips to my forehead, just below my hair, causing it to stand on end as he held me. He released.

"Go, Aislyn. And when you feel like you can't, keep going."

There was a small fear that these could be the last words he ever spoke. He left, almost pushing me away as he withdrew his hand, releasing his breath, leaving me wondering why my forehead now burned.

He couldn't mean what I thought he meant.

Only it might be exactly what he meant.

CHAPTER 28

I stared at Alex until I couldn't see him anymore, frozen by his words and the fear he wouldn't make it back alive. But then I sprinted in the opposite direction. Urgency pushed my fear for him away. I pulled out the old compass, hoping it could lead me to the Unnecessary who had placed it in my hands. I ran for her, almost a mile, before slowing down. Only then, because I had no sign of my Unnecessary, did the memory of Alex's eyes send my mind reeling again. If his sister had died, he had a reason to betray the Society. But if he was lying...

With a lurch that killed my arm, I fell over a branch. I looked at the stars again, thinking of my game earlier. In a few hours, we had to get to the EE point, especially if we were all compromised. I got up and kept running. The painkillers still numbed the pain, the glue held, but my arm was swelling.

I dreaded having to search for her and worry, but as I ran up a hill, I could hear a crunch of leaves. I took another four steps before I heard my name.

"Aislyn, I'm sorry. I think I got lost."

She startled me, making me jump despite seeking her so intensely.

"Hey, sweetie, you can jump down. We're okay."

She jumped from branch to branch carefully, but almost too fast to seem natural.

"I couldn't see a lot from up there, although I was trying. I saw you, at one point, but the wind started, and I was too high up. How did you get out? Who was that who helped you?"

"Honestly...?" I trailed off as I reached up to my forehead, where he'd kissed me. "A person who should want me dead."

She looked curious. Thinking I said too much, I added, "They all want us dead, right?"

"So, he was like the Sub-Terra who kept me safe? He was different?"

"Yes," I nodded. That was an understatement.

She stared down at the ground and then turned around back to the border. "I'm really sad, thinking about if she is safe. No one is there to save her, now. They'll be okay, right?"

The wind hit her hair, making it float again in the still night. I spoke, not knowing if he was lying or telling the truth.

"Yes, they will."

My arm throbbed. I told her since we were only seven miles to an EE point in Zone 2, we needed to keep going until we got there. I didn't tell her we had to worry about drones if we didn't get there in time. The pines kept the ground relatively clear for a path in most spots. No wonder Megan had made it back in record time. I prayed she'd made it back alive this time.

We kept a nice thirty-minutes-per-mile pace for a while. The pressure from my swollen arm hurt more than the bullet wound. Walking became trudging. She had my pack and had proudly told me she could carry it. I distracted myself by listing off nearly every name I knew. She had never been named, and so we talked for hours about what she wanted to be called. But the pain got worse. Soon I couldn't feel the beauty in the moments.

As we came up on the EE point, everything seemed louder, awaiting the early dawn. The sound of the animals and insects grow louder than our footsteps. I looked at the MCU again. The pain made it hard to breathe. I felt dizzy, but we were only half a mile out. We reached the small, hundred-yard clearing right before the woods that concealed the station. I turned around, realizing she had stopped. I looked back at scared eyes, like the eyes I'd first seen—only there was no desperation or wanting, just fear and sorrow I couldn't understand.

"Sweetie, what is it?" I asked, falling to a knee.

"I avoid the open spaces," she said, her voice sounding distant—so far away, traveling through the miles of nightmares I couldn't see or imagine. All my nightmares seemed small. I held out my hand, fighting the weight of the fear, hers and mine.

"Not anymore."

I felt the world slow down again. Or was that my pulse? My arm shook, but I ignored it. I resolved to remember this moment.

At least one nightmare would end tonight.

"Come on, sweetie. Don't anymore. Don't hide from the unknown. There is far too much of it. If you hide, you'll miss out on everything you were meant to find. Trust me." I closed my eyes, releasing one tear I was trying to hide. "Take the next step that makes you scared."

Her eyes stared at me instead of the vast clearing as she reached for my hand. She moved forward with me as I walked backward, feeling exposed. But I didn't want to miss a moment of her eyes in awe, her mouth dropping as she looked up. I knew what she would see, far away from the lights of the Republic.

The reflections of the stars stayed in her eyes as she held her breath. It was as if she had discovered the world all over again. She released her breath slowly, her anxiety silently falling away.

"I never saw so many stars. Are they different out here?"

I looked up for a second, comforted by the sight I had loved for a lifetime. My arm screamed in pain again, but I could hardly care.

"No, they aren't different. You saw many of them where you were. But you didn't see the others until now. You just... have never seen all of them. Until now."

She looked up at what her step of courage had brought her into, and said breathlessly, "But everything changes when you see it all."

I stared at the tiny girl, for a moment wiser than me, and pulled her away from the beauty.

We trudged through the forest. I reached out for nearly every tree to catch my balance. By the time we were a hundred yards from the EE point, I could hear voices. I told her to get down. I hadn't called for an extraction yet, so there was no reason for anyone to be there.

But then I remembered that we all had received the same message about being compromised. The rule, if I remembered, was that they would wait for us.

I worried I might have gotten confused, but I recognized Liam's voice about fifty yards away. Adrenaline made me sturdy on my feet for a moment, but it almost choked back my voice.

"Liam!"

There was silence. I yelled Liam's name out again.

"Aislyn? Aislyn, I need you to call again!"

I shouted again. Someone cursed in shock, someone else said "Thank God," and a third person shouted to call Central. I recognized George's voice giving orders, which meant Brie was safe at Central. Or was she dead, and he had nothing better to do than to search the woods for other Protectors? They were using the comms and not MCUs.

Liam ran to me, along with what looked like a medic. I called again, despite the fact they could see me. I ran, even though I was closer than ever to home.

George sped up behind Liam, but he went for the girl, quickly calling for another medic. Liam hugged me so fast and hard that I thought he'd knock me over. He pulled away and spoke into his watch.

"She's okay for now, that leaves our count at fifteen. Sending the private shuttle back in two minutes. Tell Patterson we're here. ETA five."

I tried to process what I just heard as I saw the shuttle was already at the EE point. There was no way...

"Liam? What do you mean, fifteenth?" My voice shook as I spoke. Liam didn't look at me. The medic spoke next.

"27, I need to know if you have sustained injuries, and—" The medic stopped as I lifted my arm slightly. He held it and cursed. "I need the C90 kit ready in the shuttle," he called behind him. He quickly put a blood pressure monitor on me.

"Liam?" I pulled him away to look at eyes that were far too tired, far too weary. They were grey, like the void, against the sharp lights shining in the night, trying to fight it.

He kept an arm on me, and I felt the horrible weight of it hit me. "Five confirmed dead is the current count now. Only fifteen accounted for."

The world around me faded, the outline of the trees evaporating into the darkness to create nothing but black.

"Aislyn?" It was George.

Maybe he was worried by my blank expression. Maybe he knew I was losing it, even as the medic kept saying, "Breathe, 27!"

The air seemed to thin, like it didn't fill my lungs anymore. The pain intensified. George let me lean on his arm. I heard him arguing with the medic.

"Brie? George, where is Brie?"

"She's fine. In Central. Don't talk."

Then George had to stop and help my little girl, who was crying. She was probably scared and not used to so many people.

"Forager," I called, hoping George had it covered. Liam let me lean on his arm instead as the medic injected something into me.

George got down on her level, four feet away from her.

I was staring at them when another shuttle pulled in front of it. Patterson ran out before it had completely stopped.

"Is she injured?" Patterson yelled.

"Arm wound. Looks like the gunshot we reported. Bled out. Her BP is a mess. George thinks it's compart—"

Everyone became muted. I turned around to try to see George, but almost blacked out.

Patterson yelled something, and before I knew it, he had moved behind me and lifted me.

"Don't pick me up..." I argued. "I'm almost there. I—"

"I'm not going to lose you, 27, just because you can't remember what a BP of seventy over fifty means."

I searched my brain and somehow remembered how low that number was. "I don't... Where is she? What if she—?"

"Aislyn, this isn't under debate," Patterson answered, his worry seeping through his usually steady voice. He laid me down on the shuttle floor. "You don't want her to see field med, do you?"

George came over to the shuttle, holding the girl. Michael was with him.

"Aislyn, we've got her. I'm taking her back, and we're okay," Michael said, pretending to be playful. George was faking calm. "We will name every star before we get back, right? We can name them whatever you want."

I owed George and Michael. She was scared, but not crying. She grinned as I forced a smile on my face. The last thing I heard was Michael singing as her face faded away.

"All right, I'm infusing you," the medic said, pushing my head down. "Lay back and..."

"Patterson!?" Liam yelled. I strained to stay conscious, watching the medic insert my IV.

"Patterson, we've got 14. She's safe. She's got a Vessel who's got some hypertension, but other than that..."

"Megan? She's..."

"She's fine. You just heard." Patterson pushed my head back down and kept his hand firmly on my forehead. "I need you to calm down. I know it's hard, but you can't help them right now. I need you to—"

The medic pulled Patterson away to whisper something to him, reminding him he couldn't stay in Zone 2 long. My arm still burned, despite the painkillers. A needle slid into the artery in the middle of my arm.

"Her BP is settling," the medic said, "but this stress isn't helping. We need to do an incision. Quickly."

"What incision? Patterson?" I called out, more scared than I ever wanted him to see me.

Someone climbed into the shuttle seat next to me, talking to the medic. Patterson moved his hand to hold mine.

"We think you have compartment syndrome," he said.

"That's impossible," Liam said. "She was shot less than twenty-four hours ago."

Even as Liam argued, a sinking feeling told me the medic was right. The fluid filling up my arm was a telltale sign, and the pressure had gotten unbearable.

"It wasn't bad a few hours—" I started, but Patterson interrupted.

"You used more oxygen in your muscles when you ran tonight. Now your muscles are running out of oxygen and breaking down, and you've lost blood, too."

I knew what was at risk. Permanent muscle damage. "Why aren't you cutting?"

"The medic is giving you some local anesth—"

"Do it!" I didn't care how much it hurt now. If we didn't do something, I wouldn't be able to ever lift a baby again.

"Okay," he said, a little scared by my urgency. "I don't want you to look. You still might go into shock or pass out. That's fine. But you need to concentrate on something."

"I can't." I needed to be strong. It felt like I was sinking into everything, the confusion and chaos pulling me deeper. The illusion that we were Protectors and not soldiers was fading; this felt like war and I wasn't ready for it. The tears I had held back finally came out in sobs. "I'm sorry. I can't..."

Patterson looked at me sympathetically, and any hard edge in his voice disappeared. "Yes. Yes, you can." He reached down and touched his watch. "Comm, call Collin."

My eyes snapped open, and I stared at his wrist until I heard the familiar voice.

"Patterson, tell me she's alive!"

"Collin?" I cried out.

"Sam, make it a secure line," Patterson barked. "Collin, find a private place, now. I need you to keep talking to her. She has compartment syndrome. Ischemia has set in. We did a local, and the medic is cutting an incision to release the pressure. Only the local anesthetic, but we can't wait any longer. I'm giving her the comm and doing the incision."

Patterson took off his watch laid it on my chest. The words "Secure Link" blinked at me as I stared at the display and Patterson put an earpiece in my ear.

I could hear Collin, as if he was inches away.

"Aislyn, stay with me, please. You've just got to listen to my voice, and we will get through this. I promise you'll be okay. I'll tell you a story. It'll be fine."

"Which one?"

"You've never heard it. I wrote it... while you were gone."

In the next breaths, I listened. I groaned but fought the desire to close my eyes. Patterson held my hand. I felt my skin ripping, tearing, and heard the fluid draining. The sensation was sickening. When they cut in the area to which the anesthetic hadn't yet spread, I screamed so loud that it was amazing Patterson could stand so close. He stayed only inches away, ordering me to breathe. I was determined to stay awake just to hear Collin's voice say the last few words—which had never felt more misplaced.

"... and they lived happily ever after."

CHAPTER 29

Thirty minutes later, someone rushed me to the Medical floor underneath Central on a stretcher. Though I was on anesthesia, it angered me to be rolled there. Then I looked at my arm and instantly wished I hadn't.

No wonder I was being carried around.

As my bed passed a hallway, Collin stepped out, putting on field gear.

"Where are you...?" I tried asking but lost my voice halfway through.

"You're safe. You're here," he said, running alongside the stretcher and helping the doctors lift me onto a rolling bed. "That means I can go out. Anyone who has Protectors safely back was asked to do the next shift. Patterson can't be out in Zone 2 or 3 with drones. George has been out for ten hours. But you're here. And I need to go."

"Collin, if there's drones... I don't want to be alone. I don't..." I didn't want to sound selfish, but I also didn't know if I could bear to be without him.

"Don't worry," he squeezed my hand. "You won't be alone."

"Collin?!" Eva's voice yelled down the hall.

"Take her," he yelled. "I've got to go help George."

"Go," Eva ordered him. He squeezed my hand, and his eyes shut for an instant as he mouthed "I love you," then let go.

Two seconds later, I sighed in relief and stifled a sob as Eva's skewed smile came in view.

"Hi," she said, her eyes more bloodshot than Collin's.

I should have said more. I wanted to say more. I could barely remember what I needed to keep a secret and needed to tell everyone. An alarm went off. The same alarm as the day they dropped the bombs.

There was a drone in Zone 2.

"They've been going off for an hour. Don't –"

"Collin," I interrupted. "Collin will be out there. Collin—"

"Will be fine," she reassured me, though her voice was choked. "We'll all be fine."

She lied, and I knew it. Everything around me lost color and turned grey.

Eva shouted my name, but from a mile away.

The alarm got louder as the light faded.

And there was dark.

I woke up in a room I recognized. Recovery. I had an IV, but it was on a low drip. Another next to it was empty. The orange fluid IV, used for rapid healing, was also half empty. I must have been out for at least twenty hours. It was quiet, except for the sound of someone eating next to me.

"Eva?"

"I don't know why everyone is always dissing hospital food. This food rocks compared to what we get in the cafeteria."

I laughed, but then stifled it. It had been a long time since I'd smiled or seen something as fresh and white as the hospital wing. But it was unnerving to be clean, not in pain, or laughing. It was too unnatural, considering everything that had happened. It made me want out of my bed.

"What happened?"

"You passed out. I held your hand. You woke up a few times. They finished draining your arm, put some oxygen patches on. I got to try one—they are incredible. Your BP went up, you're on remarkable pain killers, and it looks like"—she craned her neck out, then wrote a check mark on the chart—"your vitals have been back to normal for five hours. They moved you to recovery then."

"No, Eva. What happened?"

"You know, I am a Protector," she responded. "I do actually go on missions. I might not know what happened here while you were all gone and might not have the detailed description you need."

"So, you weren't in Central?"

"No, I was, I just... I wish I wasn't." Her voice got distant. "So I didn't have to feel the terror in real time."

"Why did everyone think I was dead?" I asked, figuring that it was a good place to start. But then I realized I wanted to start earlier. "And how were we compromised? And how did Patterson message all of us without compromising us all?"

"Whoa! Okay, first, the Hand is almost certain that the Society somehow cracked the time code on our messages. That means they tracked down everyone who texted a generic message at the allotted time. They pulled everyone over who messaged in that minute, Citizens included. If the carrier of the phone was not a Protector, they let them go. If they were suspicious, they shot first and asked questions later. At least a hundred innocent people in the Republic died. They happened to send a message at the same time we did, and that was enough to kill them in cold blood. Sam caught the chatter and the updates. Then, video images confirmed Tory was shot and killed. Patterson didn't wait. Protocol is to send all Protectors a message, but he knew better."

"What do you mean? I got the message."

"You and about four thousand other people. Patterson wanted to mask it so the police couldn't do a trace on all of you, but they had a good idea where you were, Aislyn, because you were close to the border. Still, it was genius. Probably one of the few reasons that some of us made it."

"How did the Republic know what time? That's not something you can hack."

"I know, but they said that there wasn't a leak. A Protector would have had to tell the time, but that can't happen."

I noticed her tone change with her last statement. They had unyielding faith in Protector's allegiance. I felt more suspicious. If the Republic had a traitor, then we could have one too.

"They declared you dead when we heard shots fired," Eva continued. "But someone shouted, 'It's a miss.' They caught it on all police field cameras and sent it on to Command to ensure that the Sentry got credit for the shot. Bad shot by the way. You're the second Protector he hit but didn't kill. It seemed to jolt Patterson and Collin. I couldn't read their reaction. And then Collin insisted on knowing if it was a clear shot, and they watched the video over and over, and kept whispering about Hydech, but he didn't take it. Patterson kept pacing. Worried that the 'chosen one' had died, I guess, but they were obsessed with tracking the Sentry, too."

I raised my eyebrows slightly to fake surprise, and it seemed to be convincing enough. I had to imagine Patterson's shock at seeing Alex's name.

"We had to stop the hack as you headed into the warehouses. People were already analyzing what you did wrong. Some Council members wanted to declare you dead. Some Council members asked for a prayer hour just in case you weren't. Brie and I—"

"She was there too?"

"Yeah, she had gotten back before it happened. Her Vessel was only five months along, and Brie being Brie, she didn't require any praise or spectacle. She couldn't debrief. She looked more worried than I'd ever seen her, but she didn't cry. I still thought she'd never cry."

"Sometimes she does," I whispered, though I didn't think Eva heard me.

"She came in, talked to Eldridge, and then waited like the rest of us. Within two minutes, another Vessel was killed fifty miles away. I think that was Katherine's. And Talia was missing. They reported her captured. They were suspicious and taking her in when she made a run for it. When they caught up to her, they shot her."

There was a change in her voice. She sounded detached. I almost felt guilty for making her recount it.

"It was quiet. Sam was... I don't know how he kept moving, calling out info. He and Liam were both working until they sent the shuttles out to the EE spots. George, Carla, Michael, and... I don't know who else went. But there was only so much we could do."

She looked away for a second, then up at my vitals.

"And... Lynn was the one who tried to hack into the Police Substation to erase the intel they were using to track us. She must have made another EMP. She set it off. That's what all the men were screaming over their comms as they tried to make sense of it. They were searching a building for you when it happened. They lost contact with the station, so they took forever to decide what to do next. She saved the rest of you, frying the original intel. That's what they're saying. She's a hero, but she was right at the police station. Shots fired. There's no way..."

She didn't want to say it, and I felt this void in my stomach as I spoke it out loud.

"Lynn's dead, isn't she?"

The sorrow on her face was enough to answer my question. Her eyes fell, and she lowered her head to the blanket. I reached out my hand to touch her for a minute, stroking her hair until her tears slowed.

"After that, we waited. There wasn't chatter about you for hours."

"Collin?" I asked.

"In Central, he kept it together," she nodded. "He kept pacing. No one could blame him. Patterson only wanted the trainers who weren't distracted out in the field when he decided on the massive evac from all stations in Zone 2, so Collin had to stay. After you were shot—and still missing, two hours later—he said he was going back up to the Circle. I followed up about ten minutes after that, when Allison and her Vessel were gunned down a few miles north of where you were. I felt trapped in the room, like I might murder someone just by hearing about their death. Terror by association or whatever. Pretty lame. I was one step up when they reported that Sarah had been shot too. I ran up the stairs faster than I had ever run them before, but it took forever to get to the top."

Even though I knew how many had died, their names bore into me like another bullet. Even in that warehouse, I don't know if it would have hurt this bad. Maybe that's why Alex didn't tell me. But I was here, in this place, the only place in which I had known them. The last place they were known and loved before they died.

"I threw up in the trashcan before I made it to my Circle," Eva continued. "Brie held my hair, her eyes just looking blankly ahead. I started to think she felt nothing. I wanted to hit her. She only cried one tear, but she didn't even wipe it away. Her eyes... it looked worse than throwing up. They hadn't found you yet. I figure we owed Collin some hope."

"Was he still in the Circle?" I asked.

Eva scrunched her forehead. "He had rolled the punching bag out of the room and into the center of the Circle. He was beating the living crud out of it, until he fell to his knees. I had no clue what to say. I was going to help him up. Brie said to let him go—that he wasn't going to be okay until he knew you were alive. So, we figured we should wait outside." As she spoke, she held her hands over her feet, her knees drawn up under her chin.

"You don't have to keep going if you don't want to," I said.

"No, it's all good. It's like free therapy or something like that. We took turns standing outside your Circle. Brie left to get Collin a glass of water. She made him drink it. I checked for updates once in a while and tried not to think about Lynn. I got a shower, had a good freak-out like Collin, only where no one could see me. When I came back, Cassidy and Crystal had checked in. Shuttles were bringing them back, and their trainers went out to help. You were in limbo, along with Lydia, Chloe, and Emma. A few others had been declared dead. Collin stayed curled up, on his knees, grasping for intel. Brie would redirect someone if she saw them coming. She got up and hugged Tessa when she got to the garden. She was in shambles because of Sarah. Brie held her hair back, too. And here I thought I was special."

Her voice was starting to quiver as she tried to add the laugh, so she stopped it short.

"Then, there was some good news. Ivy checked in, was on her way back on a shuttle with a Vessel who was going into early labor. Eldridge came up, checked on us, saw Collin, and told us to keep an eye on him. After he had gone, Collin called me. He must have thought Eldridge had told us you were dead, but I told him there wasn't an update. He just closed his eyes; I got him to drink some water. I turned on my comm. I rewired it to hear the shuttle comms, and we listened. The Vessel had the baby en route. We got to hear the baby's first cry. Then..."

"Then what?" I asked.

"And then we heard another one."

"What?"

"Twins. The first natural twins since your mom, and a century before that. And from the Republic. Something so happy, but it felt so strange to be happy about it. More waiting. More crying. I went to see the twins cling to each other in the same incubator. In the waiting room, I cuddled an Unnecessary who was crying. Two more Protectors dead, and then..." She trailed off again. She kept doing that.

"What?" I asked tensely.

"I think we were all on your Circle's floor by then. Cassidy was there, meditating. The rest of us were laying on the mat under a blanket, trying to sleep when the message came in. Someone yelled, 'We've got 27. She's injured. Med is on site.' I just..."

Her tears fell again, though I didn't understand why.

"Someone confirmed you were alive. Liam, I think. We all ran down. Collin kept asking what was wrong. We heard compartment syndrome." Her tone changed. "Which must have been horrible for field Med. I can't believe they only used local anesthetic and you didn't pass out. Patterson cut four inches."

I smiled. She sighed.

"Megan was okay. All the rest of us seemed to pour in. They asked Collin to get ready to go out, so he headed back up for a shower and his pack. He saw you, I met you in the hallway... and you passed out. I've been here since then. Collin came back once, with Amanda, then headed back out."

I stared at the walls, which were too white and sterile. They didn't match the tone of these tragic rooms and the stories they held.

"Final count?" I asked.

"Eight dead. You're the 27th Protector of nineteen Protectors now."

I swallowed. "Was anyone other than Amanda injured?"

"Nope. Not seriously. Cassidy had a lot of scratches, but you got the only scar we can see. Bethany was dehydrated and will need help." Eva looked at the bandage on my arm.

"Is Collin back?"

"They're on their way back now. They have Bethany. Like I said, she was dehydrated and passed out. She was wandering around when Collin and Michael found her. She'll be fine with a few hours down here."

"Speaking of down here, can I leave yet?"

"Actually, they might let you out soon." She hit a button on the comm. "They might give you one of those recharges we stole from the Republic. Not a level 5, but maybe a level 2."

It may have seemed insensitive for her to sound okay again after talking about all that, but she had to cope some way. There was a little question in the corner of her eye where the twinkle usually hid.

"What?"

"You know, trainers don't normally react like that."

"I guess not. Did you spill?"

"No," she said, as if convicted. "And Cassidy and Brie promised they'd keep your secret, too, as best they can."

I nodded, trying to match her tone. "Because love is real?"

"I guess so. It wouldn't hurt so much if it wasn't, would it?"

She popped up from the bed and smiled. Tears still drying from her eyes, she walked away, never looking back for my reaction. I sighed, echoing off the cavern that sorrow had created.

"No, it wouldn't."

CHAPTER 30

Collin was at the threshold when I woke up. He hadn't wanted to wake me. I wished he had; my nightmares might not have been as long or terrible.

He told me to continue to lie down and that I had to stay in bed for a day. My mind wanted to argue, but my body seemed glued to the bed in exhaustion. Collin grabbed a pillow and stayed at the threshold all day, unless my monitor beeped. They kept the IV in since I was still dehydrated. He came into my room a few times, kissed my hand, and walked out. It was the only thing that woke either of us from an almost fourteen-hour sleep.

When I woke up, Brie was there, asking to come in. I told her she could. She sat with me, but didn't mention Collin at all. Apparently, George had spoken to my parents and told them I was safe. Brie told me that she'd come up from Central to let me know Amanda was still here.

"Amanda?" I asked, curiously. Even though she'd always been nice, I'd never connected with her as a Protector.

Brie breathed a laugh. "Not that one. Someone called out that Protector-Amanda was alive and Collin was coming back with her. Your Unnecessary liked the name—said it was beautiful. So, now it's her name too. I've been hanging out with her since she trusted George so much. She's playing a game with George and Lydia, then coming to see you. They will put

[352]

her with a family who lives near a forest, on the outskirts, so she'll be more comfortable. I overheard it was... the Walters?"

I smiled. "They would love her." I thought briefly of my mother's comments, realizing how far away she felt. "They have a boy, but my mom always said they wanted a girl. I think she's had three miscarriages. I always felt so bad for—" I cut myself off, remembering who I was talking to.

"It's okay, Aislyn. Pain is pain. I don't believe that mine is any worse than hers. Don't place more tragedy on me today. I can barely stand it anymore. I'm sad she lost so much and happy for her today…That's how I feel for you, too."

Then there was nothing to talk about, a million words to say but no way to say them.

"What day is it?" I asked.

"I woke up thinking it's a Sunday," Brie sighed, "but it's Tuesday. The memorial is tomorrow. Last day of spring."

"It's Rosemary Day tomorrow?"

"I'll call Liam when you feel better to order your flowers. They take care of all of that for us, you know. I had to get like a hundred white carnations, and they got a ton for the ceremony and... white roses for the parents, you know?"

She lost herself in the middle distance, then smiled. Amanda came in to my Circle, looking around in awe.

I smiled, faking joy for a moment. George and Lydia waited with what I guessed was a counselor. Amanda ran into my arms, light as a feather, it seemed. Her brown hair had turned a little golden, probably from being washed. She thanked me a hundred times, each one making it harder not to cry.

I did anyway. She pulled out of the hug, catching a tear on her finger.

"Sorry," I said. "I'm so happy for you. We all are."

"But that's not why everyone's crying, is it?" Her innocent gaze fell on my tears, wiping another one away. She felt connected, sorrowful, and from the gloom in her eye, guilty.

"They died, didn't they?" she asked. "The ones that aren't in the Circles. They won't tell me, because they're afraid."

I tried to spare what innocence was left. "Yes, they died. They had a choice. They took it. They'd always choose you. And so would I."

She looked at me tentatively. "But none of us are worth that."

I closed my eyes. When I opened them, I'd summoned the confidence I needed.

"Amanda, you didn't ask us to do this. We protect who we love, and we choose to love you."

She hugged me, and I could feel her shoulders rise, the burden lifting. She told me she heard about Rosemary Day, but didn't know what flowers to get everyone.

"Well, if you've lost a parent or a child, you get a white rose. If you have lost a cousin, a sprig of rosemary. If you lost a sister—"

"Which flowers are you getting? I want to get you a flower for losing a friend. What flower do I get you for that?"

I stared at her eyes, brown and beautiful, and a thought entered my mind that wouldn't give way. I whispered in her ear and sent her on.

Brie stayed behind, and I gave her my list for flowers. She looked confused, even as she called it in. She hugged me, which she had never done before, and walked out.

Collin came back into the Circle only a moment later. It took ten seconds for his arms to find me, but my tears had dried out. So had his. Our foreheads touched.

"You know," I said, "I didn't know what would happen that night. Or what will happen next week. I never will. But before I almost die again, or before one more minute goes by, I need to say it. I love you."

His eyes closed, his expression peaceful, and he pulled my head back into his shoulder. He held it there, saying those words back to me, over and over.

I pulled away. "And I don't know where that leaves us, Collin. I mean, the last few days... what if you were meant to do this? I don't want to pull you away. This is too important."

He shook his head, and his eyes met mine. "If the last few days have shown me anything, it was that I was meant to train you. And if that's all I ever do, so be it. But not now. Today is just today, and you need to go pick up a ton of carnations for the service."

His look of sympathy faded into one of confusion as he watched my face fall.

"Aislyn... what don't I know?"

"I'm going to pick up lavender, Collin. I ordered lavender."

"But... lavender is what you give someone who has lost a sister."

My lip trembled, but my voice was steady. "Exactly."

This was love and war, the horrible mixture that left nineteen girls wearing white, standing in fields, with sorrow crushing their bare feet into the earth.

Hours earlier, I had seen the first of the flowers at my door: three carnations, with little tags showing who they were from. Along with them were twenty-four sprigs of lavender for my eight sisters. They filled the air with their essence and my soul with hope. I guess my idea had spread. As I bent over to pick them up, I saw a pair of feet walking toward me.

"Guess you had one good idea, hero girl," Tessa said.

I rolled my eyes. "I don't want to be the hero."

"But you are. Accidentally, I guess. Your whole being is an accident. It's annoying."

"Well, I'm here. So you'll just have to be annoyed."

She raised her eyebrows. "I'm getting that vibe. Anyway..."

She placed a bundle of eight lavender sprigs wrapped in a ribbon into my arms and walked away. I didn't want to waste any more thoughts on her, except one: I was still glad she was alive, and I couldn't hate her anymore. I couldn't spend the energy it took to hate her when I could love someone else.

As the day went on, the lavender continued. I had to go to Medical twice. Patterson and I debriefed. He didn't record any of it; the whole thing was off the record except for the notes he took for Collin. I told him that Alex had mentioned his sister, but let him believe the conversation had ended there. Patterson was satisfied with that as a motive.

"Collin will read this, then delete it," he said, nodding toward the door. "We'll check on Alex as soon as I can."

"Okay," I said, standing.

"How does it feel, 27? Five Unnecessaries in three missions?"

"I don't have five," I corrected.

"Yes, you do. That'll be the secret I wish I could tell. Tessa will know, but it's not the same. I wish I could tell the world you found your bravery after all." He smiled sadly and left the room.

I touched the table, grazing it with my hand, so that every time I saw it, I'd remember those words. My eyes took in the walls, still sterile but not cold. This room, where words of missions were spoken and my secrets spilled, had so much meaning now. I left the room to return to my Circle, both of which now felt more like home than I had ever thought possible.

At dusk, Collin stepping into my Circle, now littered with lavender. He left only a small path to where I stood, awaiting the saddest moment of my life.

"The procession is in twenty minutes. It's dark, but the moon's out. You'll have the torches. And I have to carry the box for Lynn. It's empty. You'll be alone. We put..." He stopped, almost choking on his words. "You and your ideas. They put lavender around every one of them. Every last one."

Anguish pierced me like an arrow, but a horrible one, deformed and evil like those who hunted us. I looked up at the stars, but found no comfort in their beauty. It felt like my body was the sky, riddled with holes of despair, nothingness seeping in instead of light. But I walked, one step at a time, and made it to the field outside the Academy where heroes lay and were honored by all of us, even Sam and Liam. And we sang.

Carrying the torch was the only thing that kept me from toppling over; giving light to the mourning gave me a purpose.

They set the nameplates in the ground. Just as Collin had said, sprigs of lavender surrounded them.

These were sisters that didn't know it, yet understood it completely, more than many people do; because it wasn't just love or friendship, it was both, mixed with courage.

What an odd gift they gave me in the end: courage. I would always have it because of them. For the first time, death couldn't frighten me. Heaven could have me. There was only one reason to resent heaven, for taking them and leaving us. Nothing but dying would make it right.

I didn't wish for death. They gave me the courage to fight the battle they left behind. I knew there would never be a day that I would regret seeing them again.

I would always be jealous of heaven.

The trainers finished taking the parents back, then had a short meeting to talk about a timeline to get us back inside the Republic. The Council wanted to over-complicate that process and keep us for three weeks, but I tried to ignore the chatter and rumors. I walked, watching the moon light the way, until I got into the garden around midnight.

And noticed Eldridge's eyes studying me.

"Well, time for a question." His voice was playful, but he wasn't smiling.

"I guess it's your turn," I said, feeling a surrender without defeat. "You want to know how I got out."

"As long as you're offering," he said nonchalantly, "yes. I would love to know."

"Okay. I was in a building, hiding. They were sweeping the building, but there was a Sentry assigned to it. He's let me live. Three times. This time, he grabbed me, shoved me in a hiding spot, then disobeyed his direct standing orders to kill me by telling me when and where to get out. He caught up with me eight hours later, got me out of the Republic and then..."

I stopped. Alex's words still silenced me with disbelief. My left cheek burned where he had touched it. What he had said might be hard for me to believe, but his acts of rebellion screamed louder than any of his words.

"And he helped me get to the border. He got me out."

I was pulled out of my introspection to see Eldridge's reaction. It was not that far from what I'd imagined. He looked at me first in the simplest shock, like that of a child, but there was panic in his deep-set eyes. His face was filled with wonder, dread, fear, and hope—the strangest things to be felt simultaneously. Eldridge took in a breath and paused, his tongue not leaving the roof of his mouth.

Finally, he asked, "Did he tell you why?"

My forehead burned again.

"He said something," I muttered. "But to be honest, I can't make any sense of it."

There was silence again. This time, I was the one who broke it. He wasn't reacting with any answers that would have made this revelation worthwhile to him.

"They said this couldn't happen, right? A Sentry would never turn. A Citizen would never turn. It would never happen."

Eldridge stood and smirked. "And a writer could never be a Protector. Could never save two Unnecessaries in a mission. Could never fall in love." He paused, giving me the same look as the day we'd first met. "If I've learned anything, Aislyn, it's this: Everything happens eventually."

He started to walk away. This man, or a voice in his head, had chosen me. So maybe he was entitled to a warning.

"Sir... this mess, the breach, Alex, Tessa, the drones, Collin... which you've obviously noticed... It might cause trouble."

He stopped, turned back to me, and smiled.

"My dear, don't you remember? I'm looking forward to it."

Eldridge left, holding a white rose and a red rose. My sorrow was too deep to ask about them. I remembered that Collin would be back from his meeting and went to my Circle.

He was standing in the center, waiting for me. He was always waiting for me.

"What do we do now?" I asked.

"Status quo," he said, his eyes sure and still. "We train to fight another day. We have Dance 5."

The music started. I wandered over, and he pulled me in closer than I thought possible. He was trembling a little instead of leading me, but it slowly became steadier and stronger.

"I almost don't want to ask. I was so happy you were back... but I read the report. Even before I did, I knew the only way you could have ever gotten out was—"

"Alex," I nodded. "He... he came so close to getting caught, you wouldn't believe it. And I know you're probably furious that he shot me, but he said Hydech was going to do it if he didn't."

"I know," Collin sighed. "Hydech wouldn't have missed. In the part of my mind that's a soldier, I can see where he made that call. But I still don't trust Alex. At least I don't want to. But I read what he said about his sister. Sam is going to do a hack tomorrow and check the details. If it's true, it leaves me at least one more reason I shouldn't doubt him. Did he say anything else?"

I found myself recalling more details than in my debrief, but I still didn't tell him Alex's last confession. The light kiss that had brushed my forehead remained a secret.

"No, he didn't." I took a breath. "You know, I feel so tired. I wonder if this will ever end, and then I realize it's just beginning. And that's when I get scared."

Collin sighed and leaned into me. Our foreheads touched, then he leaned in to kiss me, gently, briefly. He lingered for a second, breathing in the air just over my lips, making each moment more intense.

"Then don't think about the beginning and the end," he whispered. "Think about now. Amanda on her way to the shelter. The twins in the incubator. Eva and Brie's Vessels. Andre getting adopted today. You and me. Dancing. I prayed so much for you to just be alive. Just be alive, with me, for one more dance."

Courage is strange. I needed it when I least expected it.

But it worked. I let every fear leave me. And I danced.

There was a world to save, a Council in debate, a child praying that I would find them, a Vessel crying in a bathroom, but we could steal one moment from the war. It would still be raging in the morning, and I would still be there to fight it.

Eldridge's words echoed as I clung to him. I made those words my strongest hope.

Everything happens eventually.

Epilogue

When grief is heavy, things are missed. When seen through tears, details slip by.

The last transmission received on the last minute of the last day of spring was seen by Tyler, Joel's assistant,. It was instantly stored in archived messages. He was emotionally spent, and had seen the poem shared many times that day.

There is always something that no one knows,
In the darkest shadows, a light can grow.
And light can make the hardest hearts
Melt and bleed as hit by darts.
For sorrow may not be the end,
If it teaches us to feel again.
And feel it must, to rise above
a world of darkness, to find love.

What he missed was that the message was sent by a phone during the outdated scheduled messaging time. That phone had already been assigned to the 3rd Protector of the 188th Generation, presumed dead, which is maybe why she sent the 2nd message:

Find me. L.

The 188th Generation

High Counselor	Richard Eldridge
Secretary of the Council	Andrew Matheson
Undersecretary of the Council	Margaret Zander
Head Trainer	Luke Patterson
Supervisor Technical	Hannah McKinney
Central Technical Hand	Joel Conrad, David Stow, Matthew Boyles, Archer Landry, Samuel Crane

Protectors and Trainers

1. Brianna Coulson — George McAvoy
2. Tessa Franklin — Avery Harper
3. Lillian Hoover — William Jensen
4. Abigail Parkinson — Clara Riley
5. Sarah Macy — Sharron Whitaker
6. Maya Turner — Charles Davenport
7. Adrienne Yates — Conley Bridges
8. Emmy Coriander — Maria Lucas
9. Chloe Karpa — John Wilkins
10. Erica Stuart — Owen Parker
11. Lydia Mayberry — Sara Dodson
12. Talia Kemper — Peyton Booth
13. Kayla Yerger — Dylan Newman
14. Megan Crawford — Cameron Marks
15. Katherine Reed — Emily Banning
16. Crystal Peyton — Katie Douglas
17. Emma Myers — Amy Gallaher
18. Ivy Wells — Theresa Duran
19. Azaria Marksen — Richard Pierson
20. Alice Harrison — Mark Barrett
21. Maria Stone — Sadie Robeson
22. Allison Boyd — Amelia Hopkins
23. Amanda Warren — Craig Rhodes
24. Tara Daniels — Stephanie Adams
25. Cassidy Johnston — Naomi Page
26. Evangeline McKinney — Eric Banks
27. Aislyn Williams — Collin Pennington

Go to www.laurajcampbell.com for book updates and exclusive content, character profiles, art, quotes, and more!

Acknowledgements

This story almost wasn't written. It was like a war no one else could see, just to get words on paper to match the story in my head. But despite everything, this book exists. These are the reasons why:

Because Jesus loves me. That simple truth changes eveyrthing.

Because Dan told me to keep writing, even while bills loomed.

Because my girls reminded me there is beauty in small things.

Because Gretchen edited this book before it was good.

Because Alex edited the book when it was good, but not great.

Because Juliana agreed to be on the cover of the first book.

Because a bunch of bored college seniors waiting on campus before graduation agreed to be the characters for the wedbsite.

Because Bo is an amazing photographer.

Because Kelly and Kieri kept reading.

Because Michael, Super Dan, Jennifer, Bonnie, Melody, Steve, Odette, Shelly, and Sarah gave to a crowdfunding campaign.

Because some people did not care that I authored a book or assumed it would be bad, and it made me want to prove them wrong.

Because people are Protectors everyday, and no one sees them.

Because love is real.